I0661363

DARKNESS

Book II

Katarzyna Szewiola-Nagel

DARKNESS

BOOK II

BY KATARZYNA SZEWIOLA-NAGEL

***

ALL MATERIAL CONTAINED HEREIN IS COPYRIGHT

COPYRIGHT © KATARZYNA SZEWIOŁA-NAGEL 2020

***

TRANSLATED AND PUBLISHED IN ENGLISH WITH PERMISSION.

***

PAPERBACK ISBN: 978-1-7353456-9-7

EPUB ISBN: 978-1-3934190-0-6

***

WRITTEN BY KATARZYNA SZEWIOŁA-NAGEL

PUBLISHED BY ROYAL HAWAIIAN PRESS

COVER ART BY TYRONE ROSHANTHA

TRANSLATED BY SZYMON NOWAK

PUBLISHING ASSISTANCE BY DOROTA RESZKE

***

FOR MORE WORKS BY THIS AUTHOR, PLEASE VISIT:

WWW.ROYALHAWAIIANPRESS.COM

***

All rights reserved. No part of this book may be reproduced or transmitted in any form or by any means, electronic or mechanical, including photocopying, recording, or any information storage and retrieval system without prior written permission of the Author. Your support of Author's rights is appreciated.

The following is a work of fiction. Any resemblance to persons living or dead is purely coincidental or used in the form of parody.

From the Author

I am giving to the Readers another volume was released from my hands. This time I present a piece of the world quite different from the one in which the main character moved. Now the city will appear before your eyes. Dirty and foul-smelling, extending its disgusting hands just to catch. But don't be afraid. I will light you the way thanks to the second leading protagonist, which is Lilian. This cheerful and feisty mage has the gift of winning over people in such an extraordinary way that even the toughest killer succumbs to the glow of her eyes. I will let you immerse yourself in the sticky and heavy atmosphere of the Schools of Magic. You will learn the magic etiquette, and those who like sweets will go down with King Aaron to the palace kitchen, enjoy delicious fruit cakes. You will learn the name of the Alchemist of the Baroness and savor at least a bit of his gloomy mood. You will hear the clink of broken glass, merry singing over a calyx. You get a book slightly thicker than the previous one, in which I included a full year. The action takes place exactly at the same time as Leto hits the village. Archal is visible from afar against the sky, majestic and proud. It attracts merchants and small thugs. And among the mob, those who are called the Shadows lurk. I even ventured to place a love thread. The female part of the Readers should be satisfied after I caused want of it in the story of the assassin elf. At the request of one of the authors, I put Leto at the very end of the text. In this way, closing it, I open the door to the third part. I develop characters such as Baroness Alvena and King Aaron.

I had fun writing. I managed to soak up and taste the atmosphere of the world I created. To be honest, I liked these people and although not every one of them will last until the end, they will play a huge role in the life of the main character. I still learning and developing. It is thanks to you - the readers - I have that chance, for which I thank you. I write because I like it because it makes me happy in the gray Polish reality. If I can color it for a moment, I'll be the happiest author in the world. After all, it's for you, reader. I would like to provide entertainment for a few evenings, maybe afternoons. And remember. You get light, easy, and pleasant literature. My goal is to evoke positive or negative emotions. I'm honest with you. So if you are looking for something really sophisticated, my "Darkness" is not like that. I create in the fantasy canon. A world was full of magic, rapid action, and waves of the excitement of the characters. I greet everyone and wish you a pleasant experience while reading the second volume of the "Darkness" trilogy.

CHAPTER I

Darius was in no hurry. He went downstairs to the kitchen. Baroness with her unexpected intrusion made him anxious again. He should have gotten used to it a long time ago, but every time, outraged and full of anger she called him, something was cracking in him and he was getting nervous like a schoolboy. In the kitchen, there was uproar typical of that time of day. The commis chefs bustled here and there, urged by a loud baritone of the old cook. He always smiled when he saw her. She might have been frightening, noisy, with the appearance of an old, wrinkled toad, but every time he appeared on the doorstep of her kingdom, she gladly gave him a demijohn of wine or mead, drinks imported from the lowlands.

"My sweetheart," he heard the deep voice as soon as she noticed him.

His lips twisted into a flirtatious smile that he liked to charm village maids and alewives with so much.

"My favorite hostess!" He reached out to embrace her warmly.

The woman accepted the gesture, closing her eyes with satisfaction. He reminded her of the son she lost years ago in a mindless rural scuffle.

"What does my master want? One of the girls will serve you soon."

"No, my dear, I don't need food, I dreamed of a decent pint of something stronger. Our favorite lady is storming and sulking again, spoiling the mood. So I thought that the drink would clear my mind, and some companies would also be useful. Then I will think what to do next."

She patted his shoulder with a large, rough hand.

"Yes, sweetie, I have a great wine straight from the royal vineyards, young and light. It will quickly put you on your feet. I will make sure that our angry lady cools out after a delicious and decent meal. Today she will get a raspberry cake for dessert. It always works. Dear, take the bottle and run along, because you are distracting my ladies with this shapely body."

Darius smiled. He gratefully accepted alcohol. The woman kissed his cheek with fleshy, warm lips.

Tramping with the heels on the polished floor, he quickly found himself in the chambers. He closed the door with a snap. After a while, he snuggled down in an old chair. Next to it, on a wooden table, was a bowl filled with fruit. When he had left, it had been almost empty. There was one wrinkled apple at the bottom that he hadn't wanted. Now it strutted, full of juicy grapes. He leered. His stomach hissed and bubbled at the sight of fresh morsels. He plucked a few fruits and looked at them carefully. There was no indication that anyone had dipped his fingers into the food. All he saw were drops of water. In truth, he trusted the servants, but after the last rotation he hadn't yet given new employees a vetting, and this could have planted anxiety in the heart of the killer. Fortunately, he managed to immunize against most poisons, taking them in small doses, so standard methods of inexperienced poisoners could only cause a hangover, vomiting, or gut pain. He settled himself in the chair more comfortable and enjoyed the sweetness. The bottle was tempting. He stood up and uncorked it with the bone corkscrew. He didn't bother taking out the goblet from the cupboard, he took a solid sip straight from the bottle. A somewhat tart fluid filled the viscera with a pleasant warmth. Now a good whore and I can work, he thought and put the wine down on the table.

The thought of the mage suddenly appeared. He began to wander around the room. He intensively devised to develop a capture strategy. Hunting apostates was one of his favorite pastimes, he called them "hunting". He had never let Alvena down, so she respected him and allowed him to live in the castle. After all, he was born as a nobleman - the son of one of the lords, and although his father's status declined after unsuccessful business with dwarves, the Baroness apparently decided that it had nothing to do with the ambitious son she took under her roof. The youngster had aspirations, bettered his parent, and thanks to his persistence he quickly got to the castle guard. Connections probably helped, but he believed that it was thanks to the talent and innate charm that he was able to achieve goals that others can only dream of. Gaining trust turned out to be a breeze. A trifle that made him proud. Always diligent and punctual, in addition to a seductive glint in his eye, he gained confidence among the entourage of this cool and inaccessible woman. The rest came along. After some time, fame began to overtake him. The Baroness, tired of the inept hunters and the eternal defeats of the bodyguard, finally started to pay attention to him when he once again brought a fugitive from the School of Mages. Later, she watched from the windows as he happily devoted to torturing prisoners. Inflicting pain made him excited, he enjoyed it. The blows came only from passion. He knew it flattered her.

He looked out the window at the square. A sunny day warmed up huddled figures, walking slowly along with it. Maids walked in the cloisters clad in colorful dresses. There was a garden nearby, full of flowers and hidden gazebos, which were suitable for a tryst in the evening. He took another sip and left the chamber to visit the Baroness' library again. He wanted a portrait of a certain Lilian.

He found her with her back to the door. The superior stared at the green garden. She stood with arms folded, straight as a string, absent. She didn't hear him coming in, he had to clear his throat. She thought back to the library, turning her head slightly to indicate that she knew he was right behind her.

"Madam," he began calmly. "I would like to see the portrait of the wanted one. Is it..."

"Yes," she waved her hand. "It's on the table."

She turned away, ignoring him completely.

Darius dug up a pile of notes. He didn't like to do it. He always had the impression that he would move something he wasn't allowed to, and the Baroness would notice it and, enraged, would burst into his chambers at night in her underwear, raucous and furious. The superior's fervor worried. Sometimes he wanted to hit her in the face.

He found a portrait drawn by the skillful hand of the cartoonist Evans. He could depicture every face, he didn't leave out even the smallest, characteristic details. Before his eyes, he holds the image of a woman with a mass of hair surrounding a small freckled face. The artist strongly outlined the eyes, as if the energy he put into this work had focused on them. The wanted's look peeking out from the sheet of paper. He looked at the arched eyebrows, reminiscent of gull wings. He didn't know why these birds came to his mind. She appeared to be a harmless maiden who could be inveigled and seduced. He liked to destroy innocence so much...

This time it was the Baroness who roused him from his meditations, moving behind him. He didn't notice when she got away from the window. The soft boots dulled her footsteps.

"Have you found what you were looking for?"

"Yes, madam," he replied, showing the portrait in his hand.

His heart pounded in fear. He didn't hide that he was slightly afraid. She looked at the image and tilted her head slightly. A strand of hair fell on the face, making the gloomy visage more delicate and feminine.

"He is a really good cartoonist, she looks lifelike." She took the sheet.

She went to the window again and stood sideways to it. The man could look at her in silence now.

He didn't deny it.

She studied the drawing for a while. Darius didn't move. He was used to her always sending him back whenever she wished. He waited patiently for an answer. She was staring at the portrait of the wanted with great attention as if she had wanted to remember every detail of the sketch. He had no idea what she was thinking. He had a strange feeling that she recognized someone in him. She was gazing at it, every now and then stopping and analyzing it carefully. Her face didn't express anything, but the small muscle on her forehead, corresponding to the twitching of her eyebrows, showed her emotions well. Finally, she turned and walked over. She stuck the drawn image in her fingers.

"Here you are, don't louse it up," she said. "She's important, more important than that damn Evans and damned magicians locked behind the School walls. I want her alive and bound. You have to hunt her down with the Alchemists and bring her here. I want to look into those eyes and then watch her die. You understand?!"

"Yes, madam. As you wish." He bowed low.

"Wonderful. Get to work, I await results."

Having been said goodbye with a sweeping gesture of a white hand, he left the office. He didn't like working with the Alchemists, he preferred to act alone - in secret. He worked discreetly, gained trust. Then he hit a raw nerve. And not necessarily wounding. He supposed that the Baroness would assign him the worst of his minions: Lonan, a ruthless and merciless individual. He didn't like the character. After all, this was a serious task, requiring radical steps, so he knew that it must have been HIM.

***

The Baroness strolled around the chambers, checking order. Maids scurried at her sight like startled hinds. Called, they lined up and waited for the assessment of the work done. That day Alvena was kinder than usual. She didn't scream even once, but only showed with her bony finger what she didn't like. The girls quickly carried out her silent orders. When they were accepted, they bowed and disappeared into the gray of the corridor.

It was mealtime. The woman went down to the dining room decorated with portraits of the most eminent figures in the history of the kingdom, placed in elegant golden frames, carved by the skillful hands of local artists, and showing hunting or lions among lush vegetation. Others had vines and rosebuds for which the land had been known for centuries.

It was dim in the room. The windows were covered with heavy, velvet curtains that didn't let in too many rays. She preferred candlelight to the sunshine. Its warmth irritated her. Once she had liked hanging out in the garden with her former friend Katlyn. Things went wrong and the governor's wife, affected by magic, was banished with her family from the kingdom. At least she thought so. To this day, she felt nausea at the mere thought of it. She couldn't forgive herself for not seeing a magical possession, as she used to say about people holding a gift. She had no mercy. She reported the matter to her cousin. She remembered it as if it had happened this afternoon when Aaron was in despair and was writing the letter with the banishment order. After all, her friend's husband, Anders, was one of the best advisers and held the office of his right hand. That day she was full of pride. She only missed roses. Katlyn had a beautiful garden full of these flowers. Only there, they grew luxuriantly and climbed high on the walls of the property, surrounding the shutters with vines. The friend created floral arbors, and the interior of the property always smelled of them, regardless of the season, for she was able to obtain essences from the most delicate petals.

A hostess roused her from her meditations, carrying a tray with a platter.

"Hello, madam." She smiled brightly.

She replied with a cold look.

"Hello," she said curtly.

"Today I have a raspberry pie for you for dessert," she said, placing the tray on the table.

"Thank you," she said.

The woman prepared dinner. She pushed back the stool, put a pillow on it. She stood behind it. She waited for the aristocrat to sit down so that she could help her move it closer.

The Baroness followed rituals. Among other things, they included a lonely meal.

"Would you like a dessert now or bring it to your office later?"

Alvena took the silverware in her hands.

"You can deliver it to the library, I have to work." She thought of an urgent message to the representatives of the Alchemists' Guild, but she didn't want to pass it on to the cook. What for provoke gossip?

"Of course, I will commission it to one of the girls." She bowed and left the room.

The Baroness thoroughly chewed on every bite with undisguised celebration, as if forgetting the world around her. The culinarian did the cooking perfectly, constantly brought new dishes under the nose, created based on original recipes, enticing the nostrils with an unusual aroma. As a result, the kitchen became dangerously exotic, and at the same time temptingly fragrant, full of herbs and spices unusual in the kingdom. The aristocrat respected her work, the landlady was the only woman in the castle she didn't raise her voice at.

After the meal, she rinsed her mouth with wine and left. There was a pleasant, velvet atmosphere in the library, in the air hung the smell of parchment and dust, which glistened in the light of the setting sun, creating pleasing streaks. She glanced at the desk stocked with papers as it had been during Darius' visit. She didn't like the order on it. This time, however, she sorted the paperwork by dates and addressees, and then put it in the drawers on both sides of the desk. She sat down comfortably and started to write a message to the Alchemists Guild, of which she was the founder. It was a separate School of Magicians, to which belonged students chosen by means of a strict selection, who after receiving a proper education, joined the guild bringing together the hardest and most experienced killers, and all it under the watchful eye of the Baroness. Their task was to bind magicians or to execute on the order of the patron. The organization also had a list of executioners. However, they remained anonymous. They appeared on call, like shadows emerging from nothingness. Rumors said that they could be recognized by the tattoo on his hand, but no one had any idea what it looked like.

She leaned over the desk and began to write a message to Lonan.

Dear Lonan,

I got a letter from Evans from the capital's School of Magicians with the news that another magician had fled. This time, however, I have something better for you than just chasing a novice. The game is worth the effort. Find a certain Lilian Vaal and you'll get a lifetime post of the Guild high priest. There is only one condition: the girl is to be bound and brought to me ALIVE! I attach the latest decree signed by me and a copy of the portrait. Look at it carefully, because the woman in it will become a pass to the highest position. I will send spies in the morning. You will follow them with your chosen guild minions. Darius will leave tomorrow. Wait for news from him.

Sincerely,

Baroness Alvena

She leaned back in her chair and stuck the tip of her pen in her mouth. She wondered if she should have added something else. However, after reading it twice, she concluded that this was enough. She put the writing instrument down to the inkwell. Then a knock on the door sounded.

"Come in!" She ordered.

An elven maid entered the room with a tray on which lay a raspberry cake and a pot of hot tea.

"Wonderful." she said. "I was about to send someone." She smiled. The girl was surprised by the lady's behavior. She returned the grimace.

"May I help you with anything else?"

"Yes, put it here." She pointed at the desk. "Take this and bring it to the gate, let the messenger deliver it to the Guild." She handed her the sealed letter.

"Yes, madam." The elf bowed, picked up the parcel and quickly disappeared behind the door.

Alvena sank her teeth into a fluffy cake and relished the sweet and sour essence of raspberries. The favorite delicacy melted slightly in the mouth, exquisitely irritating taste buds. Outside, it was darkling. She glanced at the first stars. She took a few sips of mint tea and went down to Darius' room.

He was sitting by the window with a bottle in his hand, while in the other he was holding a portrait of the fugitive, staring intently at it. From his meditations, he was roused by his superior, who entered the bower without knocking. The locks on his door had needed oiling for some time, so they gave a moan with a stronger push. On the baroness' face appeared disgust:

"Damn it, order to oil this trash!" She said angrily.

"Yes, madam." He jumped up and spilled wine on himself.

"Alright. Tomorrow you go to Archal. I will await the reports, at least one weekly." She folded her arms.

"Madam, so soon?" He tried to protest, surprised by the unexpected turn of the matter.

"Yes, Darius. You leave tomorrow at dawn. Lonan will join you after a while. Find a cozy place there, because it is most likely that you will be wintering. I will also inform the local Municipal Police about the activities."

He grimaced at the very word "wintering". He didn't like to leave for such a long period. After all, the palace life made him a comfort-loving dog. He liked the sophisticated cuisine and good drinks.

"As you say." He bowed.

From his expression, she concluded that she would be reluctant to carry out the order.

"Great, I will await the news." She left without closing the door. He slammed it shut. The wine stain had already soaked into his shirt. He ripped off his stained clothes and threw them to the corner. He was thrashing for a few moments. However, anger gave nothing. He looked for leather bags and packed the most necessary things. There was a richly decorated bow in the corner, he looked at it tenderly. "The only gift from my father that was useful," he thought. He threw the saddlebags on his back, took the weapon with arrows proudly protruding from the quiver and went down to the stable. The stable man greeted him with a low bow. Darius wandered around the box stalls for a moment, then finally chose a mount. On the gate to the pen he hung a sack and the rest of the equipment.

"It is to be ready in the morning," he ordered.

"Yes, sir," said the man.

He left the stable as soon as he appeared in it. Along the way, he entered the kitchen, had a solid portion of raspberry cake and disappeared into the darkness of the cool castle corridors. That night he wanted to party for the last time and knew which door to knock on.

***

Lonan turned the sealed letter in thin, gray fingers. The seal was carefully made, as always. Everyone, even the tiniest symbol could be seen. He liked this accuracy and attention to the smallest detail. He put the small silver coin in the messenger's hand and chased him away with a grunt. The courier left the room, terrified rather than pleased with the visit. Nobody liked Alchemists, especially the high-ranking ones. The public said that it is better not to frown on them, because they are ready to cut your throat for just raising your eyebrows. He broke the seals, leaned against the bookshelf and delved into the words Alvena had outlined. She had a beautiful, slightly slanted script, and each sentence began with a decorative letter. He read the message several times and then threw the parchment on the ground. He saved the portrait of the wanted girl for last. He looked at it closely.

"Alright," he said, "let's hunt."

CHAPTER II

Night came. The wind was whistling in the branches of trees, knocking the last leaves that fall. It was cold and humid, and the underbrush smell was in the air. The path hadn't been trampled for long, so it became overgrown with dense clumps of grass, now yellow and protruding, as if someone had combed them. It rustled under feet and didn't let move unnoticed. It annoyed. She tried to steer clear of the cursed vegetation, but the more she tried, the more unbearably she made noise. She brushed a strand away from her forehead. Fatigue and hunger took its toll. It would have been nice to find a place to sleep, because one more night like this and she wouldn't be able to travel further. The only support was the extremely beautiful rod, which she acquired not according to the rules of the kingdom. Namely, she stole it from one of the basement cells that meandered under the buildings of the School of Magicians. She didn't regret it. The stick reciprocated handsomely. Now as an extension of the hand. It was crowned with boughs splitting upwards, arranged in the shape of a flame. An irregular white crystal was trapped inside the wreath. It seemed as if it had been embedded in wood. She tried not to let the magic wake up too often, so she tirelessly fought with a somewhat impetuous character. She tried not to abuse power when she didn't need it at all. It was hard to do because, like every young girl, she liked to boast about her skills and scare the villagers and strangers. She had known for a long time that she could do much more than her novice friends, but she didn't care. It didn't matter now.

The best masters took care of her at school. She was teached healing, because it was her talent. She thought, however, that it was insufficient. Endless want pushed her to the knowledge they had forbidden her. In the evenings after class, when most of the students disappeared behind the door of the dormitories, she slipped away. She used barriers that allowed her to become invisible. She directed her steps to the library, where she lucubrated with her nose stuck to books about martial arts or fire magic. Nobody found out about it, and the unperceptiveness of peers and Masters turned out to be a silent ally. During one event, she was irritated and gave a surprising display of skills, which ended with a talk with the Archmage, who couldn't believe that the adventurous intrant knows the spells "from the air." Cornered Lilian finally confessed to escapades and rummaging through the forbidden book collections. As a result, the library locks were sealed at night so that, despite strenuous attempts, she couldn't break them.

On the path, nobody paid attention to her. She became another traveler seen in these areas. A woman dressed in old, ruffled rags. She wandered slowly, didn't disturb anyone. She was distinguished only by a stick and red strands released from under the wide hood shading the pale, freckled face. People in those areas, which she encountered rarely, were soft in the heads. The peasants' only interests were farms, crops and fat wives giving birth too many children. However, sometimes they allowed her to stay in barns, but not for free, but for small favors - a help in a pen or during harvest. So again and again she cleaned the barns and looked after the flock.

In the city from which her roots originated, she was considered a threat, freak or, according to all rumors - witch. Born as a peasant woman's daughter, that was what at least she thought. The parent never talked about the past. Sometimes she had the impression that she was hiding something. And it was certainly true. Once she was looking for a dress, and she came across a bundle hidden at the bottom of the trunk. Before she could unravel it and find out what it was hiding under the gray canvas, his mother pulled it out of her arms and chased her away from the cottage. After a while, she tried to find the mysterious bundle, but unfortunately she didn't find it in the underwear box anymore. The parent didn't revert to the event as if it had to have disappeared from memory. She didn't know her father. Similarly, he was an enigma that she couldn't talk about with the sick woman. Attempts to talk about the issue ended in evasive answers and moving the conversation to other tracks, which for the girl eager to have the knowledge, turned out to be extremely frustrating. She envied other minions. They had families, grandparents and aunts, several siblings with whom they could play and misbehave, and only she, probably the only one who lived in Undercity, grew up lonely with the dried woman. The mother was sick, so food appeared irregularly at home, forcing women to starve. The plot, which stretched narrowly next to the cottage, maybe well cared for, became barren with time. Raised in poverty, she learned to take advantage of the opportunity, although in the eyes of others she appeared as a common thief. As a child, she stole half-live rodents from cats, treated them and released. It seemed funny then. For some time, she considered herself unique, but she knew that in the world she lived in, magic wasn't something that would put her on a pedestal. Magicians were feared, despised, locked up in places that eventually became mythical. She kept the gift to herself. Nothing would change if it wasn't for one of the neighbor's sons who noticed her excitement. When he came closer, Lilian, who was eight years old at the time, seemed to be playing with a rodent who lived despite the belly torn by a cat. He made noise, which despite silencing attracted a crowd of onlookers. As fate would have it, the young magician stood out so much that the common people outdid each other in coming up with guesses about her origin. As a result, it wasn't easy for her to be in a world dominated by rumors. Even worse, now materialized into human fears.

After a while, a Royal Guard appeared on the threshold of the dilapidated hut and ordered to take her to the master's houses to check if she dealt with magic or it was only slander. At Baroness Alvena's order, anyone suspected of talent had to be examined. For the child, this incident turned out to be such a huge injustice that the wounded heart remained traumatized forever. After all, what she did was only innocent fun. She was unaware of the consequences. She wanted to do well. She hated the damage that hurt as much as the blows she had received to her back when the owner of the robbed stall somehow managed to capture her and administer due to justice. She was whipped from her mother's arms on a cold and rainy morning. She didn't forget the leaden sky, raindrops on her cheeks and the crunching of weapons attached to the soldiers' belts, who had to delegate the prisoner to the place known only to them. She cherished a feeling of hatred and the belief that nobody should be treated like this. Schools turned out not to be as bad as people talked about them. They gave her what her mother wouldn't give. Shelter, food, warm bed and clean clothes. In return, she and others had to participate in classes, educate herself and practice under the watchful eye of trained and strict mentors. She knew what they did with those who didn't submit to the control. They were judged and killed. Some were locked in the dungeons of Schools, subjected to torture, most often to psychological ones. Lonely and emaciated, they finally committed suicide. They also had other ways to neutralize the disobedient, but this wasn't discussed in novice classes. She spent fifteen years at Schools. Because of that she became someone completely different. After a while she grew up, transformed into a young woman with an intriguing face and an unenviable character. The school wiped out rowdiness and ignorance, turned them into self-control and accuracy, but didn't destroy the spirit. Although somewhere at the bottom of her heart, she was still living with cracks that prevented her from sleeping soundly. Secrets and injustice marked her like a seal so much that she matured, making a plan for the future and it wasn't the future associated with the School. She had to know the truth. She felt that she was obliged to find out where she came from, delve into the past to understand who she was.

The goal had remained the same for years - a family home. Then she could be locked for eternity in the cold and damp walls. Then it wouldn't matter to her.

She managed to escape less than a year ago. She lurked in the shadows, often changed her whereabouts. She traveled along impassable, overgrown paths only to reach her destination. She was aware that sooner or later someone who read the arrest warrants that the guards had left in the taverns would pay attention to a woman so unlike others. She hid the hair under a scarf or a hood. It depended on what she carried on her back and the season of the year. It was worse when it comes to her eyes. She got used to talking with lowered eyelids. She pretended to hate sunlight. Usually, little inquisitive people didn't ask questions. They accepted her version. On the little face with a tiny nose and full, sensual, but pale lips, there were large, yellow like a cat's, eyes framed in extremely long eyelash bushes. The eyebrows curved subtly resembled the wings of seagulls floating in the wind, and the skin was decorated with millions of tiny freckles that covered the face, arms and breasts. In the midst of grayness and commonness, she bloomed like a rose on a compost heap. She wore gray or brown clothing, and she also hunched over to become less visible. Her stature wasn't beautiful. She was thin and not attractive to others. Fate maybe endowed Lilian with typically feminine shapes, but clothing perfectly masked the virtues. Thanks to this, she avoided harassment. None of the peasants tried to pick her up. They saw the shapeless and ugly mass. Thanks to magic, she spread around the aura of inaccessibility and coldness, and this sufficiently deterred fans of free fun.

It was dawn. The night before, sleepiness had overwhelmed her so much that she almost fell asleep standing. With drowsy eyes, sandy by fatigue, she looked around the area. There was no doubt - she had to take a break. Right now. She would think about food later. Tired muscles inexorably reminded her of the route they had to cover recently. They were outlined with narrow bands under bruised skin, strained and malnourished all the time. Somehow, she didn't care too much that her stomach hadn't been getting enough food for some time. The goal was what counted, not the quality. She always found something in the woods. It was full of the underbrush fruit or bird's eggs. Not much, however, it was enough not to die in a roadside ditch. She thought about her mother. The memory of a stooped figure, nibbling at the weeds just below the windows of the hut, made her sleepless. How much regret she had to bear, how much sadness nestled under the thatch of eternally tousled gray hair. She never wondered what she looked like when she was young. For Lilian, she was always the same. Quiet, wrinkled and sick. Thoroughly steeped in loneliness. She hadn't received a message from her for so many years. She desired so much the heat of hands cracked from work. A rough touch that stroked the windblown red strands, a kiss of the mother's lips on the freckled forehead ... Return to the nest. So long and arduous. As risky as the reckless use of magic. Now she didn't see the retreat, she didn't even consider it. She wanted to touch the ordinariness again. Ask a lot of questions. The closer to the desired goal, the longer were the days which turned into the endless hours of painful march. "I'm almost there," she repeated. "I will flash covered by night. I'll sneak in. Nobody will notice. It's a good plan." The only one she had.

The grass turned out to be pleasantly soft and smelled sweet with moisture. She put her head confidently, sleep stuck to her eyelashes intrusively. Here today she would rest, sheltered by thick branches of a furcate shrub. Not far away winded a narrow path, a branch of the path along which she tirelessly walked. They must have been trampled by animals or other travelers. It doesn't matter now. Now it's time to rest. From the lead clouds, unbearable drizzle started to seep, which stubbornly settled on the clothing with a fine mist. She wrapped her arms around herself and pulled her knees to her chest. She fell asleep immediately, soothed by the sound of drops. Overnight, the clothes soaked through and heavily overwhelmed and adhered to the girl tired due to the journey. She was awakened by the sun and warmth, which began to wander on the cheeks with glares. She didn't know if she was rested or still unconscious because of exhaustion. She only guessed that the sky was stretching with a blue ribbon devoid of gray clouds.

Time didn't matter. The crackle of branches somewhere in the woods awoke her completely. Frightened by the unexpected sound, she gathered what she had with her and hid in the denser thickets. Oh, thanks to the Creator that clothing blends with the surroundings - she sighed and nervously tucked the ruffled strands under the scarf. She strained her sleepy eyes. She sought looming shapes and after a moment saw two figures. A dozen steps from her. Individuals moved quite quickly, gesticulated and shouted constantly. She narrowed her eyelids. The sight sharpened enough to easily identify the gender. Men. In addition, they wore characteristic sheets on the backs of the brotherhood. "Magicians! But why are they here?" She wondered.

"You're crazy! How could you do such a thing?!" Shouted one apparently of more serious age than his companion.

"What was I supposed to do? They should have killed us?" The shorter of them curled up.

"Fool, why did you use magic? You should have dealt with it in other way. Now the Baroness will find out for sure. Soldiers can't be treated like that! By Creators! Why you always start something?"

"She won't find out."

"She will, she has some great Guardsmen. They are familiar with magical damage." The older of them got mad, and the younger man was rolling his eyes as if his companion had been annoying him.

"Well, there will be trouble, but I think we will get out of it somehow? By Redeemers, we have to! Let's go, or somebody will see us," he urged. "We have to get to the isthmus before winter closes it. There they will be waiting for us. Don't stop."

"Magicians ... hmm ..." she sighed. "So the city is close, and if there are bodies, there are also spoils. I have to check it, though it's risky," she said. She looked around nervously, as if expecting a sudden attack. However, only she was sitting hidden behind the branches of the prickly perennial plant.

With a fast, cat's movement she moved in the opposite direction in which her predecessors went. She didn't get far when she saw two startled horses tied to a tree by tethers and a tiny bonfire guttering out. Why didn't I see it at night? She wondered. She lurked again and skimmed over what was before her. When she didn't notice anything suspicious, she came closer, still carefully scanning the surroundings. Two corpses. Soldiers spread out on the grass. The faces of the dead were partially charred.

"Fire mages," she said to herself.

"Yes, the armor are scorched and the fingers are twisted in a characteristic way, they probably used curses, clever guys."

"I think I'm freaking out, I'm talking to myself," she shook her head disapprovingly.

She strained her hearing. When she made sure that no one would come anymore, she straightened up and leaned on the staff, then calmly started examining the battlefield. In the pockets of horse saddles she found small coins, and at one of the killed, only a wad of irrelevant love letters from a horny maiden, probably some noblewoman.

"Ugh, shameless!" She snorted after reading the notes made with a decorative script.

To the great disappointment, she didn't see any food near the corpses or the fire. The abdomen rumbled significantly when information about digestion ran through her mind. She untied the horses and drove them away with strong slaps on the rumps. They would find a way, they weren't stupid. She didn't want to drag the animals with her. It would have been too noticeable. In addition, the mounts belonged to the guardsmen, so she would have been immediately captured and convicted. Rush was not recommended here. The city wouldn't run away. Since her legs had brought her so far, sooner or later she would see its high walls in the distance.

She disappeared from the scene. She dissolved like a ghost in the morning mists. She aimed steps at one of the largest settlements in the kingdom. Divided into several smaller districts embedded in the interior of the megacity - Archal. In the center was a school of magicians, separated by several streets from the square leading to the headquarters of the mayor. Under the walls lived peasants, elves and the typical urban poor. The richest part of the fortress was the dwarven quarter - strangely always open to newcomers. Dwarves carried in their blood hospitality and limited trust. They willingly hosted a man tired from his journey and give him a great beer made of lichen. However, over the years of exploitation and injustice that fell upon this people, they became harsh and inaccessible. Rarely did anyone try to mess with their merchants or the nobility, because it usually ended in bruising, or "disappearance" of a too "clever" delinquent.

She didn't know the districts hidden behind thick gray walls. She drew knowledge from the stories of her mother and those who shared a dog's fate staying in the suburbs, and they were inhabited by a group of elves and people, so mixed marriages were common. The children from these relationships were called Jerms because they inherited the traits from both parents. So much that anyone who wouldn't have known the origin of this creature would have said that it is perfectly beautiful, but not every child from the human-elven relationship was born a Jerm. Often, these mixtures were characterized by pointed auricles and unusual eye color. As is well known, of this blood was one of the four Redeemers. The most spiritual and pious. According to beliefs, he suppressed the irrepressible wrath of every creature. The stories say that thanks to his song, the aggression was bound in the shackles of ice and hidden at the bottom of the heart so deeply that even the darkest magic is not able to bring it out. Of course, for Lilian, the story was a perfect addition to the prate that she liked so much. She had never seen as much evil and violence as there. Young Jerms, gentle and devoted to nature, hated violence, which is why they were victims of the humiliation from the children of the mob. Despite this, they grew into strong nature magicians or petty rogues. Those who didn't engage in any of these professions became farmers. They never shed blood, usually the disputes ended in a sharp exchange of opinions. They were therefore considered harmless, tormenting and blaming them and causing them problems. Naive community members often paid for the offenses of others. Often the highest price.

After a short walk, she realized that the luxuriant forest on both sides of the road began to thin slightly. To the woman's ears were coming muffled by the rustling of foliage, screams and the tumult typical of a waking settlement. She knew she was "at home". The smell of air filled with cow manure brought back memories of early childhood. She wanted to speed up the pace, but the sore legs definitely reminded her of their condition. So she slowed down reluctantly, and plodding, she basked a clearer and clearer view of the destination.

She walked a few more steps. Before her eyes appeared the beautiful gray city, set on white rocks. Surrounded by a high stony wall, at the foot of which were small stone houses. This is Archal - home. Lilian's heart was filled with fear. In her head swirled a mass of thoughts, which circled like crows over smelly scraps of meat. She was afraid of being recognized again, captured and that history would repeat itself. On the other hand, she greedily sniffed the air and let herself go back to the source in her dreams. A few more steps and she would come out on top and the journey would end. A soothing sense of security filled her chest. A moment later, a picture of the mother running out to the road appeared before her eyes, when she was dragged to the magicians' house. She remembered her scream. She remembered the chill rushing behind her collar and the Guardsmen's words to say goodbye to the past. Never! Now she would make up to her mother for those lost years.

Absence and emptiness. She would be the best daughter under the sky vault, she would never be hurt again!

The road widened, here and there she saw branches that headed towards houses, small farms or plots. The huts were built in even rows so that the inhabitants didn't disturb each other. Each house had a stone, low fence like a border separating it from others, and a wooden, squeaky gate with rusted nails protruding from it. At least that was what it had used to be. Slowly, with her heart fluttering in her chest, she was approaching her former home. People were bustling around their mini-possessions and were looking after small farm animals. They ignored the ragamuffin lurking like a thief. The early air smelled and vibrated from the sounds she missed so much.

She fixed her eyes on the designated target. The cottage was set right by the city walls. Tucked in a cluster of wild apple trees. In the summer there was a pleasant coolness. From a distance, the house seemed well-kept. It had clean windows and a new wicket. A little surprised by this view, she came closer. Something was wrong. The mother couldn't buy a new wicket, because she had no money. She also wouldn't have been able to care about the yard so meticulously. At the mercy of her daughter or neighbors. That's the way it is in poverty - you support me, I will help you.

With a shaking hand, she pushed the gate and came quietly closer. She crouched near the window. Inside she saw the figure, but she didn't know if it was a man or a woman. She was hiding in the twilight. Even though she strained her eyes as much as she could, the mysterious figure didn't reveal its identity.

She heard foot shuffling behind her. She tightened her muscles in readiness.

"Hello," the newcomer said.

"Hello," she said to him without changing her position.

"If you're going to rob us, you better do it at night."

"Ha, very funny," she muttered.

"Who are you and why are you looking through my windows?"

She straightened up, resmoothed the folds of her clothes and looked at the stranger.

"Your windows? I thought mine." She bit her tongue.

"Yours?" He laughed out loud. "Nobody lived in this hut for about ten years." He laughed further.

"How is that?" she was alarmed.

She felt the blood drain from her face. "That's true that I haven't heard from my mother for a long time. But? No, no…"

"The previous owner died and the plot was free, but why do you need to know that?"

Slowly, she rolled back the scarf overshadowing her face, leaned on her cane and stared at the young man with her cat's eyes.

"By redeemers! Witch!"

Before she knew it, he flashed beside her with a leap and jumped into the hut.

"Father! Lilian is back!"

"He knows me," she thought, then quietly entered through the open door.

At the table, with his back to the entrance and the window, an old man was sitting and turning the wooden spoon in his fingers.

"Yes," he whispered in a flat voice. "I knew you would come back. Magician schools are not for you."

She approached him. She looked into his face.

"Orian!" She shouted cheerfully.

"Well, I didn't expect that."

The old neighbor always helped them. But why is he...?

"Why do you live with Adam here? By the way," she turned her face toward the youngster: "You've grown up so much. I knew there's something familiar in your face."

"Don't look at me, witch!" Adam waved his hand in front of her, as if he had been chasing away a fly.

"You're still funny." She laughed.

The upset boy left the room to return in a moment and hide in a corner, he was muttering a litany under his breath, as if spells that were to scare away evil spirits.

"I think it's because of your last clash." Orian nodded in the direction his son went.

"Come on!" She shrugged. "I was eight years old."

"Yes, you was, and he was nine and was fascinated by you, and you ..." He laughed. "You raised a dead mouse before his eyes."

"Oh, so it was about it. I didn't know it would change him like that. I remember him running away crying, and shouting: "Witch! Witch!"

"Oh yes, I remember that too. You must be curious why we are here. Sit down." She rested beside. "Our house has collapsed. Your mother is dead, so the cottage was empty. I wrote to the mayor and after a long time we received a letter. He agreed that we would move from the old headquarters to this place."

"What about mother? Where's her grave?"

"I don't know. I just remember that the gravediggers carried her body. They probably buried her in a mass grave on the other side of the city, or burned just like any poor man. Now they do so more and more often, it's less work. And that damn plague, shit pestilence, half the people died."

She squinted at him with tears in her eyes.

"Don't look at me like this."

"Forgive me." She recovered. "I just feel ... sorry."

"I know what you mean, but I don't think you remember her well."

"I remember only good things and poverty. Do you know what she died from?"

"Probably a bloody cough, here every second person dies from it. Damn plague. Marwa was also led to good redeemers. I hope she found there peace and relief from her aching body."

"I'm sorry," she moaned.

The old man bowed his head towards her. The memory of a not-so-good wife loomed in his tired due to age mind. It faded after a while. As if it had been supposed to happen. As if the flashbacks had been to go into oblivion, giving way to good, soothing and safe ones.

Lili felt guilty. The tension became unbearable to such an extent that the hair began to sparkle at the ends.

Orian glanced unmoved.

"Don't burn the hut."

She stroked the rebellious strands.

"Don't worry. The phenomenon has disappeared. I'm better now."

"Do you want bread? It's in the oven, still warm, take it."

No one had to encourage her to have food. She found a knife and cut the loaf.

"There's milk and cheese." He nodded towards the pantry.

She knew where she was. Orian's kindness flattered her. In the pantry was sitting Adam and was gnawing the curd.

"You eat fear?" She brought her face closer to him.

"Leave me alone!"

"No, I like to tease you and now I have the opportunity," she giggled.

The glaze of yellow eyes flashed in the dim light.

"What a man," she sighed amused. "I will toy with you sometime, I promise."

She put things on the table and ate a little. The old man was looking at her in silence. He finally said:

"Are you going to stay here?"

"I don't know, maybe I'll move on. There's nothing for me here. Even the questions that tormented me for so many years, and which I put together during my journey, suddenly disappeared. As if they had never existed." She bit a piece of cheese. "I don't have a home and mother. I only have some clothes, a few coins and legs."

He frowned.

"You ran away, right?"

She stopped chewing suddenly.

"Yes."

"They'll look for you."

"I know."

"Is it worth running away? If they catch you, they'll kill you."

"I don't care." She shrugged. "I don't have a family anymore."

"You have memories," he said.

"They are worthless," she sniffed.

"It's sometimes worth learning more than mortifying and crying."

"What do you mean?" She bit a piece.

"Since you ran away, maybe you'll even find your mother's grave? I can ask the scribe to write a letter to the gravedigger. Maybe the records were saved, but in fact ..." he rested his chin on his hand. "I don't know. It's been a long time."

"Over ten years," she interrupted him. "Ten long years." She swallowed food.

"You would have a destination, you would end your journey or maybe even escape?"

She looked at him. He was kinder than she could have expected. She didn't think that way. The reasoning was overtaken by the old man who probably forgot what he had eaten for supper the day earlier.

She spent the whole day in one place, she didn't feel like anything. Even matters as important as physiology have fallen into the background. The worst thing about a magician is that when he falls into melancholy, he may lose control of the power that, freed from the chains of the mind, can harm not only the bearer, but also the environment that can't bear the escalation. She was well aware of this, but the flood of thoughts overwhelmed her so much that reality just faded. She was suspended between the past and the present, which had nothing to do with what she had planned.

***

Morien was awakened by a magical glow that settled heavily on her chest. The blow of power took his breath away for a moment. He took a few greedy gulps of air, threw back the quilt, and sat on the bed. He felt sweat drops bead up on his forehead pale with fear. He wiped it with a shaking hand. He took a deep breath again. This time, so deep that he felt the force of the expanding lungs hidden in the rib cage. It couldn't happen. No one was able to emanate the power of magic so much that it would have disrupted the strong barriers surrounding the school. He stood up on soft legs and went to the window. He opened it slightly. The morning air burst into the room and refreshed the magician. Small hair growing on the body rose with a slight shiver. A strange impression didn't leave him. He strengthened his willpower. He combed the smallest fragment of the walls surrounding him. He found nothing but particles slightly hovering beyond the reach of thought. He focused harder. Blood in his veins boiled, fueled by growing emotions. It had to be someone special. Much stronger than the masters of this place. However, something bothered him. As if the shakes that were destroying the perfect picture of what appeared before him. As if this person still couldn't had fully controlled the gift. Or maybe that man had no idea what miracle he or she bore? He debated with himself for a long time. White long hair was moved by light gusts entering through the window vent. He almost choked on the power of magic ... not his own. Is that her? The one Evans mentioned? No! It is impossible!

"Impossible ..." he sighed deeply.

He stopped fighting something that overwhelmed even him. The day at the School of magic had just begun. Although he expected another wake-up call, he believed that it would bring him more solutions.

***

"How is the capital?" she heard shy Adam's voice behind her. The boy was getting used to Lilian's presence, though inside he was torn by irrational fear that was difficult to control.

"Big, dirty," she sighed. "There's nothing to rave about."

"But how is it there? Well, you know."

"I don't know." She turned her head toward him.

"Well, you know, elves ... dwarves ... people ... interesting life."

She pierced the boy with semi-conscious pupils. She thought she overheard, but she didn't. The youth's words bounced off the inside of her ears.

"Interesting life? Are you kidding me? Say you are kidding."

"No." He shook his head firmly.

"I'll tell you how it is." She turned to him with her whole body and crossed her arms over her chest. "The poor everywhere, the wealthy districts are separated from the rest by a wide wall. Only the gates lead to them, at which guards stand day and night. Shall I continue?"

"Yes."

"Alright. The castle towers over the city. From a distance, it appears as a soaring structure carved out of white stone. However, if you get close enough, you will see that the walls are gray and mossy. Only one road leads to it, the rest is separated by a wall. It is in case the enemy dares to attack. Before it reaches the center, some soldiers will be shot. The towers are manned by seasoned archers. Under the wall of the king's seat is the wealthy quarter and the School of Mages, which is also surrounded and has one entrance, at least that's what I can say. This place has several larger and smaller houses and buildings in which classes take place. Masters and Archmasters rule there. They say that everything was built by willpower, that no worker laid a stone. Anyway, these universities are like internal states. They have superiors and the main Archmage who reports to the king. In addition, the Baroness, fearing for security, called the City Guard to maintain relative order. We know how it is. I don't have to explain much here. Let's think further. Below this rich mob are two districts. The dwarven one, where it's a lot of fun." She laughed. "Dwarves are crafty, but they have business acumen. You have to be able to bargain with them, otherwise they will bleed you of the last denier. Instead, they make fine vodka, and their beers are famous throughout the kingdom. On warmer days in the air you can feel a delicate note of malt, which with a light cloud settles on the world-weary inhabitants. There is also a district of richer and poorer nobility, but wealthy enough to have servants. The workers are mostly peasants who have received a job or elven women. And since nobody respects elves, you can imagine the situation in these residences. They work hard. They are paid, yes, but not always worthily. And now the best. The district of the mob and the poor stretches with a wide stripe around the whole ideal construction of the city. It is full of dirt, hookers, cheap pubs and suspicious characters. There are also barracks that no one can enter, unless he miraculously obtains an order. They are stuck in a rock like in a safe shelter. The guard likes cheap entertainment." She laughed again. "Regularly during leave, they visit the home of joy and waste their money and health. Then the healers have to deal with the grunge because some idiot dropped anchor in the suspicious harbor. I think you know what I mean." She winked at Adam. "Strangely, there is no typical elven district in the capital, even though there are plenty of elves. They didn't put down roots, as if they had been afraid of something. And behind the walls, like here, farmers live. They plow, raise animals, look after orchards and vineyards. They are like a machine driving the mob. If it wasn't for them, people would starve, and there's a lot to be done. Fields stretch to the horizon." She took a deep breath, tired of the monologue, but continued until the exhaustion of the thoughts.

"On the one side, one can see scattered tiny vineyards. The coastal climate is conducive to viticulture, but these plantations are really far away, which doesn't change the fact that they are also part of the agglomeration. And also trade is booming. On the path you can always meet caravans with materials and spices."

"It must be great." He was dreaming.

"Fool," she bridled. "You wouldn't survive there even a week. They would cut off your head for a handful of small change."

"Stop it," he interrupted her. "What future is for me here? Just look around: poverty and nothing more, I would like to get out of here."

"Fool," she repeated more strongly, almost hissing. "I had the opportunity to be here and there. Healers dragged me around the homes of the rich, aristocracy and merchants. I could see how dissolutely the gentry live. We treated shameful diseases, injuries in fights. Skulls and bones were shattered because the young masters wanted to have fun and ventured into Undercity at night. We aborted illegitimate babies. You don't know what life is like in places as big as the Capital. They are just waiting there to take advantage of you. Enjoy being here. This city may not offer great opportunities, but it is calm. Besides, the Baroness probably keeps the local school of magicians under her thumb."

"I don't know, my father is probably more with it." He looked at her warmer. That look made Lili sick.

"Why are you looking at me like that?"

"It has just happened to me that we are no longer children and although we have always had our differences, now this wall is even bigger. You experienced world life, you didn't starve, and we here fought for every bite of bread."

She laughed resonantly.

"My poor Adam, School of Mages is not morning oatmeal." She stroked his rough cheek. "This is a place where the disappearance of people and death for any offense is something normal. Less than half the intrants survive. Most kill themselves with their own magic because they can't control it. Yes, maybe there is a bowl of warm food and a nice sleeping place, but it is a cage they let you out of after many years, but only if they are sure that you won't kill yourself. The leaves are once every six months for twelve hours, sometimes twenty-four, and except that you see nothing but the mossy wall around you. Do you think it's so wonderful there that we're sitting and learning spells? Nonsense, my Adam, we fight for every day there ..."

Words got stuck in his throat in anger. The tightened larynx didn't allow a single sound. Anger and bitterness boiled beneath the skin, but that didn't change the fact that he dreamed of a great capital, though the mage outlined it in such an unfavorable way. It was good that no one could read his mind. Because he cursed the redhead by all Redeemers. He wanted her to be captured and put back in that damn prison for magicians.

She turned her back and stared at the fire. Bored, he left the girl alone and disappeared deep into the house. Outside, it was darkling, and only the crackle of burning wood disturbed the silence. After some time the household members went to bed. Lilian stayed in the room, slowly absorbed by the thickening darkness. She was constantly thinking about her situation. Confusion in her head didn't allow a constructive assessment of the situation. She tortured and blamed herself. "Too late, not fast enough, hopelessly slow," she scolded herself. She achieved her goal. And what's next? Where to go? After a while, she began to consider whether escape was so important. She became a savage, additionally a fugitive, apostate pursued by the king's guard. She had fantasized about it for so many years. Why did no one send a letter, notification of mother's death, anything? Of course, the suburban peasantry wasn't literate, but someone could go to the scribe and ask him to write a few words. She didn't get it. Loneliness sat heavily on Lilian's weak shoulders. She sobbed quietly, surreptitiously wiping tears at the dirty sleeve of her dress. She loved her mother. The image of the parent had existed as the only consolation in difficult times. When she was leaving, she shouted to her not to worry, that she would come back before she knew it, and the situation would return to normal. It is a pity that the magician's life is not like it was before the school admission. Mostly those who completed training were conscripted into the army, guard or placed in Healers' Homes, where they helped the doctors. They rarely returned to their homeland. The greater the truth, the mob was afraid of magicians. Gossip took on a terrifying form over time. Maybe fear had a legitimate source, after all the unknown is the most terrifying form of fear. It was the imagination and news passed from mouth to mouth that made the School intrants appear like demons dragged from the throat of the original evil. Because of her multi-faceted talent, she belonged to the worst type of magicians. A healer, and yet something more, hidden under the guise of inaccessible talents. A battle mage who mastered the terrifying art of pyromancy. She was constantly struggling with the impetuous nature that, unleashed, was wreaking unimaginable havoc. Hiding in the basement, she was able to resurrect the dead, killing bears by force of will, not to mention people. It was useful on the trail. The game worth a candle, now not worth a hoot.

She decided to disappear. Fly away imperceptibly. She didn't want to be in a place that brought back waves of memories. She felt the walls tighten around her. She felt as if she had been choking, as if invisible hands had been wrapping around her in an iron grip.

The only salvation was to go out and slam the door behind, and let the cool wind sit on your burning cheeks. Quietly like a mouse, she took things. She stuffed the bundle with some food, and in exchange for refreshments, left a handful of small change on the table, then slipped out into the dark, cold night.

The wind was nipping in the face with the first frost, so she wrapped herself more tightly and slowly delved into the depths of the city's evening life. If I'm to risk, then it all, she thought, having crossed the city gate. Two guards leered at her. The crunch of armor caused by the impatient movements of frozen people metallically burst into the woman's ears. Only clouds of steam were rising from their mouths. She flashed. She pulled the scarf tighter over her face. She was still aware that she must have disappeared, blended into the crowd. Start doing something ordinary that doesn't arouse suspicion. Winter was hard on her heels. It's that bad omen that drives towards places that will allow to survive, even if it means vegetation. As long as nothing drips on the head and the fire buzzes within reach of ossified fingers.

The city had a specific smell. It is no longer crisp air, in which one can see cobwebs carried by gusts or whirling leaves. It's stinking slush, contaminated with what no one needs anymore. The stench of dishwater, vomit and feces, mixed with human sweat and digested alcohol, exhaled from toothless mouths. All-encompassing gray, merging every element into the drab solid of reality, enlivened only by colorful costumes and children who with innocent brought pale sparks of hope that also in this depressing world, there is room for happiness. She didn't feel defenseless. She had a weapon. Inviolability.

She didn't remember the layout of the streets, so she blindly followed the alleys. Streets, houses and alleys seemed as if smaller, dwarfed under the influence of time that had passed. Gray buildings with blue windows and doors repelled with peeling paint. Stumps of withered plants hung sadly from ceramic pots arranged on window sills. She wanted to wake them up, touch them, to feel the rough structure of withered leaves. In a flash she realized that it would be stupid. It is not known how many pairs of eyes were now staring at her. A few drunken elves passed Lilian. Around the next bend, despite the cold, undisputed whores were waiting, proudly displaying their round breasts. Near by, the dwarves were singing in a loud voice, a tale about an underground, ancient kingdom.

"Hey, you," She heard a low male voice behind her. "Give me money for a pint of Styg, madam."

She turned slowly, her yellow eyes glowed in the dark.

"Do I look like somebody who gives money for Styg?"

"Yes, you do."

She took a closer look at him. The sponge with a face destroyed by drinking was sitting on the threshold. Something creaked over their heads. Above her, moved by the wind, a shabby sign was swaying. She was staring at the piece of wood for a moment, as if analyzing its constantly changing position.

"I will drink and sleep here tonight," she sighed.

"What are you whispering, madam? Will you give me money for a pint?"

She leaned low.

"I already said no," she croaked.

She felt the sharp smell of vomit, urine and cheap beer. She stepped back abruptly and stopped the disgust.

"Bathe, old man," she said and put her hand on the cold door handle, but before she pressed it, she heard:

"You are a magician," he hissed. "Only eyes of this filth are glittering."

She responded. She grabbed his collar and yanked it. The sobering up came a moment later when she felt fire irritating the tissues of her fingers.

"One more word! Do you hear? I will shorten your lousy life if you wag your chin like that."

Resigned, he breathed a sigh of relief.

"I don't care about my lousy life"

She let go of his collar. He leaned his elbow back on the step and closed his eyelids. She knew that there was no hope for him. Probably the gravediggers would take care of his body this winter.

The pub was called *Under Ram's Head*. When the door was opened, the typical closeness and stench of the cheap taproom hit her. Inside, however, there was a fairly friendly atmosphere, slightly too loud. The man behind the counter was lazily polishing chipped cups and glasses. At the sound of the gate opening and closing, the residents' eyes hung on the new guest as if by order. However, they quickly returned to interrupted conversations and as if nothing had happened, they indulged in interrupted activities. On slightly bent legs, she walked to the counter. She sat comfortably on one of the free chairs and beckoned the innkeeper with a nod. He glanced several times from under the swollen eyelids. She had to wait before he graciously finished the work and started to handle the service. She asked for wine. Without a word, he disappeared in the shadow of the back room, and after a while he returned with a bottle. He poured her a sweet drink and pointed to a free table.

The girl swallowed a few sips and, when warmed up with alcohol, got her face covered with significant blushes. The man noticed pink cheeks. She removed the headscarf from her forehead so that she didn't reveal her face too much. She didn't want to heat up even more, discretion above all.

"Do you have vacancies?" She blurted out, sipping alcohol again.

"Can you afford it?" He asked.

"And if I say that I can?" She put the glass down on the counter.

"Then there is one upstairs ... But occupied," he grunted and raised a corner of his mouth as if trying to smile, but the crooked grimace only exasperated the girl.

"Ha, very funny." She rolled her eyes.

"You can sleep in the kitchen if you pay double," he cleared his throat. "Near the furnace it's supposedly quite nice."

The drink delightedly spoiled the body. After a moment, nervousness, as if at a touch of power, faded away lightly and almost imperceptibly. She felt more confident. Maybe it was because the innkeeper seemed quite a nice man, or it was just her? Probably it was the fault of the drink she didn't know. She slowly removed the cover that protected her from prying eyes. She knew that the man who had returned to polishing the cups was staring at her, but his eyes showed nothing suspicious, but only uncontrollable curiosity.

"How much for this kitchen?"

"Silver piece, madam."

"Alright." She drank up.

"Pour me more, then I will go to sleep."

He twisted his mouth in a grimace, which probably meant: have it your way and he filled up the glass.

She threw several copper coins and a silver one onto the counter and drained the dish. The host pointed to the same place where he had gone when she had asked for a drink. It turned out that around the corner of the bar was a narrow corridor, in the depth of which were hidden small rooms, including, probably one, located on the floor. The one that the innkeeper just mentioned. Narrow stairs led to it. She quickly realized where the kitchen was. The smell of herbs and cooked meat was leading her. In addition, a dim light was coming from under the door, as if someone had left a lamp inside to illuminate the room. She pressed the door handle. The door yielded invitingly, and the hinges smoothly opened the leaf. It was pleasant dusk inside. Indeed, a tallow lamp was placed on the table. The logs were glowing in the furnace. It seemed as if a resourceful woman had run the place. On the wooden shelves, in the jars there were probably spice mixtures. Near the furnace, there was a bucket half filled with liquid. And in the corner there was a washtub packed with dishes. It is not known whether dirty or not. The fact was that it had a specific place there. At the window, near the furnace was placed a small bunk. She couldn't determine what this archaic pallet was, because it couldn't be called a royal bed. Fortunately, somebody had left several thick skins on it, a cushion filled with rags, and next to it, by the carve leg, was an aged potty of unknown color. Clear, fortunately. She undressed quickly, fearing an unexpected guest who right away would come in with a bang for something specific. Fortunately, intimacy wasn't uncovered. So she buried herself in the safe harbor of the temporary bed and covered herself with the skins up to her nose. Alcohol played nicely under her skin. She didn't know when the dream stuck to her eyelids. It had to be a moment.

The night passed way too fast. The rays of the sun coming through the small window awakened her. She yawned slowly and put her hands on her face. The brightness of the morning was trying too hard to enter under the eyelids. Luckily, she hadn't drunk much, so she didn't feel nasty hangover, but only the bitter aftertaste in her mouth that stuck to her tongue. An elderly woman entered the kitchen. The night thoughts were true. She knew that no man, even the most well-organized, would ever run a kitchen as well as the skillful hand of a seasoned female cook. The comely lady stopped midstride, noticing the mage observing her in hiding. She swore ugly under her breath and put her wide hands on the plump hips.

"Damn it, Mark took pity on someone again."

Lilian yawned and ran her fingers through her tousled hair.

"Yeah." The girl rose on her elbows and glanced at the arrived with scared rather than sleepy eyes.

"I hope you paid because I'm never well-informed."

"I paid," she repeated after her.

"That's alright then." The woman nodded and didn't wait for the conversation to continue.

She began vigorously bustling around the room, while doing an unbelievable tumult. She stopped after a moment, stared at the washtub full of dishes and snorted:

"Rogues, they'll never clean after themselves, old Erica must do everything."

She would keep banging about if it wasn't for the guest sitting on the bed which quietly asked:

"May I help you? I don't have anything interesting to do so far."

The woman wiped her hands on a gray rag and came closer just to look at her more closely. She reached out and grabbed Lilian's chin.

"You're pretty. You could ask this quad, Mark, if he would hire you. Probably customers would like the new maiden carrying beer."

Lilian pushed her hand away.

"Yes, I could ask."

"Talk to him when he arrives. And now, when you are so eager to work, light a fire, because this fool again forgot to add wood. The stove has gone out and now how am I supposed to cook this damn goulash?" She threw a rag over her shoulder, heading towards the door hidden in the corner, which Lilian hadn't noticed in the evening.

She opened it wide and disappeared in the dim light. After a while she came back with a bowl in which there was meat scraps. She threw it on the table and, having reached for a large knife, started cutting. The girl realized that it was probably a cool pantry full of good stuff. Her stomach rumbled.

She pulled herself together. She calmly made the bed, adjusted her clothes and went to the hearth. It contained only ash and the remains of almost completely charred logs. She pulled them out carefully and put fresh ones in it. She looked around carefully. She was looking for something to light them from. Unfortunately, the lamp on the table had long gone out, and Erica, absorbed in cutting, didn't pay attention to her. The cook was singing a lively melody unknown to Lilian. The mage thought that for the cook, who had her back turned to her, wouldn't matter how the fire would appear in the furnace. Blue flame danced on the tips of her pale fingers, which she transferred to wood. Moistened, it hissed knowingly, but didn't take fire, toying with the impatient magician. She tried again, this time concentrating harder. The color of the phenomenon caused by the spell took the color of bloody red, which immediately hungrily embraced the hearth. A smile of satisfaction marked her freckled face. The girl brushed off the remains of sparks and turned around.

"Done. Something else?" she asked.

Erica, glancing at her and then at the furnace boiling from the heat, almost choked on air delightedly.

"Already? Great. It takes me a lot of time, especially now when the wood is wet. Nice. Now go to the main hall and see if he has already come. It is not known if he drank or wised up yesterday, although the latter is unlikely." She pointed at the door.

"Alright."

A moment later she was walking down the corridor, which despite the day was still dark.

The main room of the inn, which was now deserted and quiet, seemed to the girl a completely different place. Were it not for the man who had served her wine standing in the doorway, she would have guessed that she had miraculously moved to a completely different place.

"Hello," he said dryly and tossed the wool coat over the counter. "What are you still doing here? You shouldn't be here anymore!"

"I should."

"You paid for the night, get out now." He sniffed and, passing the girl, moved toward the tables, which he began to set, restoring order only known to him.

"Erica says I'd be good to help," she said, hoping he wouldn't drive her off like a mongrel.

"Erica says so?" He scratched his head. "An old toad, doesn't she have any more strength?"

"I don't know that, but I can see that you "love" each other." She bit her tongue. Excessive fraternising has never worked out for anyone. And with that, unfortunately, as well as with sharpness, she always had a problem. No matter how hard she tried, the rebellious nature prevailed over reason. Fortunately, the innkeeper didn't find it offensive. On the contrary, he giggled under his breath, warily putting his hand on his face. As if he had wanted her not to find him a fool.

"Oh, yes," he said, and his stomach started twitching with suppressed laughter."We've known each other for so many years.

For so long that I could have sworn that hundreds of springs have passed, not just twenty. With her bad, without her even worse," he sighed, calming a bit. "The skilled pair of hands will be useful if you have nothing more interesting to do." I hope you learn quickly because I don't need another girl who has bunches of carrots instead of fingers.

"Don't worry," she said. "I can promise you won't regret it."

"Alright. Let it be, just be careful. Sometimes some people forget themselves. You know what I mean?" He gave her a knowing look.

"I will try," she hissed.

"Oh yes, a girl like you is needed here. Maybe you can teach mores some of them. Oh, and one more thing. Don't take the bait. I don't like quarrels."

She nodded.

Little time passed when two female helpers appeared at "Ram's Head", who animatedly took care of the premises. Later, in the afternoon, when the sun was shining high in the sky, a strange gentleman stood in the doorway. He exchanged a few words with Mark and disappeared into the corridor of the back, to emerge from it a moment later, wielding a few nails and a hammer. Lilian followed him with bored and slightly sleepy eyes. Erica still had nothing for her, so she deployed herself in silence. This man undoubtedly amused her. He had an extremely specific way of moving, as if his joints had been slightly stiff. It seemed quite familiar, but for the world she couldn't remember where she had seen something similar.

"Don't stare like that." The female cook whispered in her ear, who, like a phantom, stood next to her sprinkled with flour. "They say he's an old magician and that if you upset him, he'll curse you or something like that. I don't believe in such stories, but you know

... they talk. When they talk, you have to listen. But you also have to listen to your own mind."

Lilian looked at her first in disbelief, and then with growing amusement. At last, she couldn't stand it and she laughed so loudly that almost all eyes focused on her. When she came to herself, she straightened up and having swallowed a few sips of air, she finally said:

"Oh, forgive me, but I haven't heard such a bilge in a long time. Curse." She continued smiling.

"Calm down," the cook scolded her, then angrily told her to scrub the tables.

So you made me curious. I have an eye on you, she thought and took on errands.

He had been in the corner of the room for some time, turning the knob of an old lamp. Every now and then he glanced toward the new worker. He was a slim man with a long face and sparse blond hair, dressed in a thin braid at the back of his head. His lips were narrow and constantly tight, and his bony hands were skilful. Lili seemed a child to him. He couldn't resist the impression that the girl with the mass of flaming red hair would rock the boat in this peaceful place. That "Ram's Head" would no longer be the same as it had used to be.

Lilian slowly learned the customs and specifics of her activities. She knew that it wouldn't be easy at first, but she also knew that she would get used to it over time. In the afternoon she came across Mark and the conversation dragged on too much. When asked about the past, she presented the current state of affairs in a chaotic way, as if it had done anything good. She quickly came up with a neat story that she was a lonely traveler raised by herbalists, who deviated from the path and visited houses to relieve the distressed and in need of support.

The host didn't look like he believed in this poppycock, but she touched him with ingenuity and alleged helpfulness. He had already seen a lot in his life, many also came to these thresholds with all sorts of stories that were far from the truth, though were catchy. He had the gift of a good listener, he let those who needed it spoke out. Maybe because there wasn't much going on in his life. Well, unless there was a fight spiced up with the intervention of the City Guard, when the topics for conversation formed intrinsically, and people willingly shared with him guesses and speculations. But this also quieted down over time, and the bored innkeeper returned to the order of the day, which consisted of always the same errands. So he agreed that the red-haired vagrant would stay near the furnace. He thought that probably her usefulness would be mediocre and after a short time she would walk away like most people. And Lili, thanks to this, found the job and crash pad. In addition, food almost under her nose and as much wine as she could pour into the throat. Of course, with reason, because no one liked when abused were goods that weren't shared willingly.

It never crossed her mind that she would become a common beer maiden. Although there was no going back. Winter was coming, hard and cold. She wouldn't survive on the path. She had to bite the bullet and do her job. In addition, stabilization for a while would do her a power of good. She would calm down and rest, although it might have been apparent. No magician would stay long in one place, not with such temperament. She decided to try. By the time the situation got complicated and she bolted again, to disappear somewhere in the tangled streets.

Mark ordered one of the maids to bring for the new worker clothes in which she would appear in the room without shame.

What she wore on her back was more like a rag than a girl's outfit. It wasn't without snorting and moping about. Fortunately, a silver coin placated the huffed girl. In this way, Lilian was enriched by two confections, which to undisguised misfortune flowed too loosely around the worn out silhouette. She consoled herself with the thought that it would be enough to surfeit and the body would gain some soft curves that now remained in the sphere of misty memories. Erica help her giving her an apron, which she put on, let's say, a new dress. It hid loose pieces of clothing and the young magician now looked much more impressive than the day before, when her leg had crossed the threshold of "Ram's Head" for the first time.

Regulars dined during the day. They washed down landlady's stew with the good quality dwarven beer, and on the threshold appeared travelers, tired from the journey. Usually, in a sea of foreign faces, she saw buyers dressed in fanciful, colorful mantles. All clients, as one man, loved the stew of Erica, who usually stood leaning against the corner of the counter and followed with small eyes what was happening around her at the same time threatening that if someone didn't like it, then get out! Nobody denied these words, which made the woman content and she willingly topped glasses up.

"Ah, these customs." The girl was smiling to herself. In no time she realized that no matter how dangerous she thought she was, the woman in a checkered skirt, despite the rustic character and sometimes the unbearable surliness, was the rabble's favorite.

The mysterious "magician" disappeared around noon, having fixed the defects from the previous day. Dressed maids held court between benches and tables, distributing liquors. They sat on revelers' laps, kissed their foreheads and made the atmosphere slightly frivolous. Mark was observing, ready to react when one too willingly reached out for something that wasn't his. The new helper warily hung back. She watched the pleasant uproar carefully. Once in a while, she emerged from the dim corridor and timidly served the ordered food. Her hands trembled. Often, the sauce dripped from the dishes, dirtying the freshly starched apron and marking the boards of the inn with greasy stains. Every now and then she heard murmurs of dissatisfaction, which like the worst scolding reached her straight from the innkeeper's throat. She didn't hide her embarrassment and focused on her duties as much as she could. However, she preferred to flee into the dark and safe back of the kitchen, where she felt more secure, hidden behind the closed kitchen door.

"It's the beginning," she thought. "I have to get used to it," she sighed. She was just taking advantage of moment of peace when people were leaving to do their tasks after sumptuous dinner. Therefore, the inn, maybe not completely deserted, because it still hosted people imbibing various drinks, quietened slightly. There was more room and each member of the staff could sit down for a while. Late afternoon was approaching, so they were preparing for another wave of tired and thirsty clients.

Lili felt bad at one point. A strange numbness settled on her shoulders, as if it had wanted to suppress her and eventually lead her to the edge of fainting. She fought. She put her knuckles against the edge of the kitchen table. Thoughts revolved around a bizarre weakness, inexplicable and incomprehensible at the same time. She caught a single gulps of air like a fish emerging from water. She was recalled to reality by her boss' voice, which pierced through the hazy mind and made her sobered up slightly:

"Here you are, take it to a man sitting in the north corner, under the window," he ordered, pushing the mug towards her. "I don't keep this beer in the room, it's too expensive for the common people. Come on, on the double!"

"But me?" She said, pale and shaky.

Mark didn't notice the state she was in, busy thinking in counting the takings, which on that day extremely generously enriched the bag.

"Come on. Don't let him wait. Beer hasn't killed anyone yet."

"I would argue," she muttered under her breath, but immediately felt a thunderous look. "I'm coming, I'm coming."

Fearfully, weak-kneed she slowly approached the gentleman. She put a drink before him and asked in a shaky tone:

"Do you wish anything else, lord?"

The man in black robes looked up from the note.

"I don't for now."

She felt the piercing pain caused by his gaze. It turned out so penetrating that her guts were burning. Having bowed, she hurried back into the back room and when she closed the door behind her, she leaned against it. She was sweating and shivering like an autumn leaf, trying to piece together what had just happened.

The innkeeper nodded at one of the maids to follow and ask her. She did it reluctantly. When she tried to enter the room Lilian was in, she couldn't open the door. The girl blocked access to the kitchen with her body. So she moved closer to the wooden structure and quietly tried to get through to the new worker:

"What happened?"

"Who is he?" Rasped out Lilian.

"Who?"

"The one you gave him the drink?"

"Yes."

"This is Morien, Lord Master, mage from the School of Mages. He likes dwarven beer. He visits the bar on Fridays after class. In fact, we are the only ones who have it outside the dwarves' quarter. Mark could get his foot in the door. These creatures rarely share with alewives."

Lilian didn't hear the follow-up. Under the skull vault only knocked: "Lord Master, mage from the School of Mages" Unbearably voiced and dangerously true. She could have guessed. Power surges cause such weakness. Stupid! How could you not notice it?

"Master," she moaned, covering her mouth with her hand.

Peas of tears welled up in her eyes and rolled down the icy out of fear freckled cheeks with a hot cascade.

"You don't like magicians? You know they are useful. Right?" She asked singingly. "I once caught an ugly illness and such a healer cured me in a moment. Isn't that great?" The girl's voice was floating in the air like a swarm of nagging mosquitoes.

Lilian didn't want to listen, she wanted her to leave her alone. However, she fought against reluctance and bypassed the subject of the said magician, then said more calmly:

"Ugly illness, you say?"

"Yes. I sometimes I go with clients. You know, when they pay well. At home, any silver coin will be useful, and the mother doesn't need to know," she calmed down.

"Useful. Oh girl," she sighed and put her hand on the door handle.

She pressed it lightly and let the door open a little bit. In the gap she saw the chubby face of the young blonde who was looking at her narrowly. After a moment, the maid shrugged and, hearing nothing more than the redhead, returned to her tasks when Mark gestured for her.

"What happened there?"

"I don't know, but I don't think she likes magicians," she whispered.

"Then she will have to like them," he replied and ordered to return to serving the guests.

Lili was sitting by the fireplace, crumpling her apron hem with her skinny fingers. She was constantly trying to calm down the troubled heart, which didn't want to cooperate for anything. She hoped that she wasn't recognized, that a certain Master is a simple, insignificant common pawn. A simple swell at somebody's service.

"Nobody worth attention," she comforted herself.

"Everything will be fine. It must be! And now it's time to forget, drink a few sips of wine and let it work. An alcohol is the perfect thing for this time." She stood up and reached for the demijohn which was on the table. After a few snorts the blush and spirit returned, which she needed so much.

After the unfortunate meeting, the evening gained momentum. When she returned to her duties, she no longer found the magician in the room. He dissolved in the air. He didn't leave a single bit of power that could have made her cry. The last regulars, encouraged to leave the tavern by the tired innkeeper, walked slowly towards the gates, which, when opened, could remind them together with gusts of cold, saturated in autumn air, that reality greedily stretched out the mitts toward them, that they must have returned to their wives, children, duties and hated errands. The alewives, having cleared the tables, disappeared from Mark's sight eagerly. Lili lumbered to "her kitchen". She dreamed of washing herself and swallowing a few bites before going to bed. She was exhausted.

She'd been running from corner to corner all day, trying to understand tavern customs. Thanks to the head of the inn, she met regulars. He discreetly described each of them, marked what one liked and what to avoid. He respected privacy, but also knew how to please, not necessarily with food and wine. She tried to remember. A huge amount of information after some time merged into one block. She would probably slip out something or wouldn't be good at something trivial. She was also afraid. She didn't suppose that on the first day she would face the past, which would materialize in the form of the Master from the School. After all, this type of individuals sat in their own dormitories and drank in loneliness. Hardly anyone of them belonged to those sociable. They were people who liked loneliness and peace. The bustle and mob disgusted them. Well, at least that was what happened in the capital ... but well, she was wrong.

***

Morien put his hands deeper into the sleeves of his robe. He smiled when a light breeze caressed his cheek flushed from excitement. He found her. He could almost touch her, although he did nothing at all. She appeared as he had imagined her. Small and strong at the same time. She hid deafening and dangerous power under her mediocre posture. The red-haired creature with the eyes of a cat emerging from the darkness. So innocent, shy ... lonely. He saddened. He knew she was afraid, and yet she came up with her forehead raised. He knew magic was suppressing her. He felt her fight with weakness, cringing in the corner like a wounded chick. He didn't want to hurt her, he wanted to have her next, so he directed Mark's thoughts so that he forced her to bring beer. He had to look her in the face. Find enough courage to meet her gaze.

Now he was going up the lane and thinking about the fugitive. What was it about her that he didn't want to betray her? To go straight to the Archmage and inform that the fugitive is right here. Within reach. Maybe he was lonely, lost and wanted, like her, to find a quiet haven and settle in it for a moment and find his peace. No one could enjoy it in this world, not even those exalted. Entangled in a network of intrigue, surrounded by false allies, alienating with time. Locked in four walls of intentionality. He understood the young woman, or maybe it just seemed? He sobered up when one of the guards standing at the main gate of the School chattered his cold teeth:

"Good evening, Lord. Did the trip to Ram's Head go well?"

***

Some good days passed. During this time, she tried not to bother about what had unhinged her. She became more and more experienced and self-confident both in the kitchen and in the main hall of the inn. She clearly stood out. She had a cheerful disposition, or at least she tried to seem so. She charmed with eloquence and dexterity, which seemed to magically appear after she had gotten used to the new situation. She had just needed time. Guests loved the new alewife, which managed to keep her distance, but also to sock it when it was needed. So she quickly gained respect and none of them tried to pat her on the butt, and even less they didn't stretch out their lusty hands to touch the maiden's small breasts. Mark watched her like a hawk. He cleared his throat significantly when a "stranger" wanted to try the cheap entertainment. Lilian used to argue with the regulars, she showed remarkable brilliance in this matter. No one was able to get any private information about her origin from her, though the mob was full of wild curiosity. She infected others with a never-ending sense of humor. She joked and subtly seduced. She knew that jealous female friends looked at her. The purse buzzed encouragingly, every day it was filled with copper and silver coins, which as a tip fell generously to it. The maids probably thought that she would soon bump them from the job, which resulted in digs and aversion that grew day by day.

The gloomy evening was approaching and the cold was squeezing through the leaky door. She thought about giving the "magician" the idea of sealing the unfortunate gap. It didn't bode cosiness, but freezing on winter nights. Although, on the other hand, a fresh breeze would have swept away the stench of unwashed bodies and the fumes of digested alcohol. About other aspects she didn't want to debate because they seemed too disgusting. She would mention this also to Mark, wondering what he would say. Very few clients were hosted, so the company rested or floated about. That day she was the boss and she was responsible for filling the mugs with good wine that the innkeeper kept in the back room, and counting the takings. So she was sitting behind the bar, dangling her legs and wiping a mug with a cloth. Mark went home earlier, Erica also took advantage of the privilege and, just like her superior left the inn, content that the day ended so quickly for her. Only one maiden stayed, who was flirting with one of the clients at the other end of the room. And Lilian, who was scouring glasses so fiercely that one could swear that she wanted to see her own reflection in porous clay cups. The door slammed open. The uninvited chill broke into the warm room of Ram's Head with redoubled force. The girl felt not only the blow of cold, but also the power that enfolded her like a shroud. She closed her eyes and tried to control her pounding heart. By force of will, she surrounded herself with an invisible barrier that, despite her strength, couldn't sufficiently protect her against the magic of the man who stepped inside.

"He's the last person I want to meet," she snorted to herself.

It would have been a shame to be compromised. Especially that none of the residents until now had figured out who she was. A blue vein appeared on her neck from the tension, and her eyes narrowed into slits, suspiciously staring at the newcomer. The gentleman closed the door with impetus and placed in the same place as before. He glanced, waiting. She felt a thrill that ran across her back.

Morien could see perfectly well what she was doing. In order to get a free afternoon, he had to fawn on his superior, despite the fact that as a high-ranking magician he could leave the school area often, which didn't change the fact that he also lived under pressure from imposed procedures. Fortunately, he never gave anyone reason to speculate about him. He galloped through the circuit of the dormitories and looked into the greenhouse to make sure that young intrants didn't plant between the crops of herbs something that could harm not only them, but also the reputation of the facility. Nothing aroused his suspicions, so happy, having thrown his coat over his back, he went along the cobblestone wet from rain that led straight in front of the door of his favorite afternoon spot. But this time it wasn't a drink that was attracting him, but the maiden. He constantly was feeling the pulsing of her power. He felt it hit him, penetrate the tissues and engrave in the brain canyons of constant fear. He craved the air she breathed. He drove mad the tormented, lonely soul. Shivering with excitement, he settled comfortably where he had used to rest and made eye contact with her. In the colorless air, he noticed how she formed a subtle and translucent barrier around like a glass bubble hiding a water spider from prying eyes of fish.

She took a deep breath. She knew that he didn't have to raise his hand to make a gesture signaling that he needed service. Here, every maiden was at his service on eyeblink. They almost fainted at the sight of the white-haired magician, who, thanks to his reticence, became not only a mysterious, but also a desirable individual. Somewhere deep down she wanted to look at him, but rather out of curiosity. Gossip does its job, fuels desires, causes the wish to capture reality, which in a way can only be fiction.

She adjusted the crumpled clothing and walked tall to him. She didn't want to think what would happen. She would simply face the fear that paralyzed her from the inside.

"Hello. What would you like to order, lord?"

In the candlelight and tallow lights, she saw a pale face and a pair of honey eyes. He seemed to be a phenomenon that didn't suit the living place at all. As if taken out of a sophisticated picture, unreal and dreamlike. The hot flash pinked Lilian's pale cheeks. At this sight, he slowly removed his coat hood and laid his lips slightly to smile. He said almost in a whisper:

"The usual, my dear."

The race of thoughts began in Lilian's head. She couldn't remember for anything what drink he had had lately. Maybe beer. Yes! Beer.

"By Creators, but what beer?" She was thrashing.

She decided to ask, though she knew it was stupid. After all, she could have nodded and move to the back room where her colleague had just disappeared, and have asked round. She must have had a clue. Something, however, kept her in place, not letting her walk even a little. At last, the mouth opened, releasing the voice trapped in the larynx. She didn't realize that the words were shivering like young leaves in the spring wind, and she was alternately creamy-white and purple. In addition, holding the barrier, as if, by Redeemers, it had been supposed to do any good, was exhausting her strength!

"Please forgive me, but as I don't work here too long, I don't remember the name of the drink you have recently had, lord."

She was trembling inside. She felt that the floor would right away disappear from under her feet, and she would fall into the abyss of non-consciousness.

"That's true. I see you, madam, only for the second time."

Morien leaned against the wall. He scrutinized the alewife's bewildered face. Then he entwined his fingers and continued:

"A pint of dwarven beer, please. Here's the payment." He reached into the pouch and pulled out a silver coin. She took it and felt the soft touch of a velvet, warm hand on her skin. He smiled and looked away, setting his sights on the fire roaring merrily in the fireplace.

She almost ran to the back room where the barrel was. She was afraid that the drink would spill along the way. The same kind of fears as the first time. She quickly moved with a drink. He took the pint, giving her glow of his honey eyes again. He thanked her and she scurried behind the bar, deluding herself that he wouldn't ask for a refill. She looked around anxiously. She was seeking something to occupy her shaking hands with. Unfortunately, everything in the room worked like in a perfectly oiled mechanism. After a while she came to the conclusion that the kitchen probably needs her now, so she didn't wait even a minute and shouted:

"Ilia, come here for a moment." The girl, though reluctantly stop the conversation, came over.

"Why are you doing this to me? Haven't you seen that I'm busy? It is not so easy for me to get silver coins into the bag as it is in your case. What do you want, slouch?" She hissed.

"Stand up. I have to go to the kitchen."

"What for?" The maiden rolled her eyes as if looking for the cause of Lilian's sudden escape. "Nobody wants food. Why are you going there?" She snorted like a mad cat.

"I have to. You wouldn't understand. One day I will tell you, but now, please sit here until he leaves." She pointed to the master with a nod. "I will give you two silver pieces."

At the sound of the word "silver", the alewife's pupils widened.

"Alright, let it be, but I warn you this is the first and last time. Fix it, no one will do your work for you."

She let her know that she understood and she moved two coins towards the maiden, after which the backroom closed the curtain of twilight behind her. It wasn't until the kitchen closed that she breathed a sigh of relief and slumped onto the straw mattress. The pulsing in the temples didn't weaken. The same as the recurring stupefying weakness from which she felt groggy. She stood up and reached for a pitcher of water, which always was on the table along with a glass. She took a few sips of no longer cool water. It didn't taste good. She looked sadly through the window, counted the stars dotted in the navy blue sky. She longed for freedom, coldness touching hot cheeks and wind softly combing her hair...

The bliss of loneliness didn't last long, for her ears reached a steady tramp of heels struck on wooden boards. She turned toward the entrance, where Ilia appeared dejected:

"Your gentleman wants a beer."

"What gentleman?" She snorted.

"The mage, and who if not him? But he doesn't want beer from me, but from you. Go, because Mark will decapitate us when he finds out what we did during his absence!"

"Like what?"

"Go, by Redeemers, I don't want trouble."

She spat something else and walked away. Lilian buried her face in her hands and tried to calm her breath. It didn't help. She had no choice. It was time to come back.

The magician smiled gently. He ran his finger along the edge of an empty beer mug.

"Would you like something else?" She said.

The slightly tilted head suggested that she was interested in what he expected of her.

"Oh, you've come. One more beer, please." He handed her the empty dish.

She reached out to take it when Master's hand clenched on her wrist. She stiffened. Countless painful bites swept through the delicate skin, giving the impression that she would begin to bleed with every pore of the skin. She wanted to give up. The spots danced on the pupil rims. The man leaned toward her and whispered:

"You are special, you have the gift."

After which, as if nothing had happened, he loosened his grip and looked at the dwarves crowding by the fire. Redbeard gentlemen were just beginning to carry the song with their low, but melodious voices, and the courage was given to them by alcohol joyfully filling the bloodstream.

Lili lost her breath for a moment. It happened so suddenly that she couldn't notice it, still focused on the suffering that had just been carving in the tissue. Before her eyes swirled drab strands, which began to obscure the field of view so quickly that the image darkened at an alarming rate and only the black warp reached her. She blinked in vain. Weakness was completed by the state of velvet bliss. The girl's body fell to the ground. From a painful impact on the boards, saved her a slender hand, which cut through the air like an arrow. Passed-out, she landed in the arms of the magician, who was looking at her with such tenderness that those gathered in the inn, not knowing the relations between the two, could swear that the man loved the unconscious with love bottomless and almost sick.

She slumped behind the mortcloth of boundless darkness. Despite this, consciousness still remained unshakable and only thanks to it she could get out of this terrifying state. After a while, the brown spots turned into flickering strands emerging from behind the curtain of eyelashes. They took on clear forms, shaped into familiar and safe images. Something blocked her breath, as if the glow that had sat on the chest, so heavy that it couldn't have been removed.

Ilia took away the curious. In her spirit she cursed the red trollop. It was a few hours to close and Mark certainly wouldn't be glad to hear that his favorite, for the first time holding the position of "boss", simply messed up. Nay! She measured her length on the boards. To make matters worse, this damned Master must have looked at it. What would she, by Redeemers, report tomorrow? That Lilian theatrically fell into his arms? She couldn't expect that he would take her side. She leered at the magician who stroked the girl's chalk-white skin. She pursed her lips in dissatisfaction and crouched on the stool. Bored, she waited for the situation to develop.

Morien looked at the maiden, who having folded her arms, was contemptuously observing in silence. He read her mind like an open book, which made him disgusted with her. After a while he talked to her. He tried to look calm:

"Please bring a cloth soaked in cold water."

Ilia nodded and left the room. At that moment, Lilian opened her eyelids. A slight blush crept over freckled cheeks, but it didn't mean a quick return to relative well-being. She clicked several times. A nagging dryness in the mouth stuck the tongue to the palate. The magician reached for the mug with some liquor, which was on the table next to him and put it to her lips.

"Drink. It should help you."

She reached out for the dish with trembling fingers. He didn't even wonder why he was helping her so willingly, he just did it. He enjoyed the fleeting moment spent by the redhead's side. At that moment the alewife brought what he had asked for. The damp rag rested on the half-faint's forehead. He sent the intruder away. She spat something under her breath and left them. Lili opened her eyes wider and saw the ugly ceiling above her. She sat up and rubbed her face with her hands. She had no idea where she was. Her ears were buzzing, and under her eyelids shapeless forms were still flickering.

"Do you feel better?" She heard a friendly tone.

"I think so."

The Master smiled with one corner of his mouth. He saw how quickly she came to herself. He leaned closer to her, a strand of white hair fell on the gentle forehead with a soft curl. The girl glanced at him briefly, then stared at him with terrified eyes:

"What? Mr. ... Mr. ... I ..." she moaned.

"Don't worry, you fainted. I think it's from fatigue."

"Ekhem," she grunted.

"Morien."

She stiffened.

"My name is Morien," he repeated.

"Lilian." She swallowed hard.

The general weakness went away into nothingness, but it was replaced by paralyzing terror. Now she was certain that she had exposed herself, although she fantasized that nothing had happened, and the magician leaning over her was so dull that the magic that emanates from her was perceived by him as a slight aura disorder.

"Beautiful name, I haven't heard it in a long time," she realized. "So romantic."

"Thank you." She moved her lips slightly, she didn't know if the words came out of them.

"You're welcome. I see that you are much better now. Well, I have to give up the second mug, but I think we'll make it up."

He gave her his hand. She hesitated only a moment, but she allowed him to help her, for what would he have thought if she had rejected the friendly gesture? Her hands were trembling. He didn't pull his fingers back for a breath. The strange bliss in this short moment settled in her shaky heart, as if the Master had poured her much-needed encouragement with his soft touch.

"These are not alewife's hands," he said. "I need to go. See you soon."

He didn't give her time to answer, dusted off the dirty fragment of the robe and left. A few scraps of dirt danced right at the threshold, settling on the protruding fragments of boards.

Lili stood between the shards. It took a long time before she gathered her wits and uncertainly started collecting the broken mug. Nothing happened, but on the other hand it happened too much. Undoubtedly, something was pulling her towards Morien. An invisible force that whispered that there was nothing to fear, even though reason said something different. She struggled between contradictions, simultaneously trying to find the golden mean. In vain. The situation seemed so irrational, almost unreal, as if whispering, that this time she wouldn't weasel out and pay for what she had done. And yet the silhouette of the Master exuded such calmness, bliss and solace that she could have been absorbed in them completely. Then she wouldn't have had to fear anything, after all he would have stood next to her, protecting her with magic like a bird protects its chick...

"That's stupid," she said to herself, clenching her fist.

"What?" Ilia heard the words thrown into space.

The companion returned from the back room, carrying a broom.

"No, no, nothing. I think aloud. Don't trouble yourself," she countered.

Without a word, she set about tidying up what the guests had left and completely ignored Ilia, who after a short while ostentatiously spat and, having collected the lumber, left the place. The young magician breathed a sigh of relief. Now she needed silence the most, not eternal binding. Work left boded cleaning up until late, but it was good for her because instead of sweating guesswork, she focused on the activities performed. When the mugs and glasses finally were placed in the washtub of water, and the stools on the tabletops, she put out the oil lamps and, after taking a look at the main hall, calm, she sat down in the kitchen, in which she finalized her duties. When she was going to bed, the moon and the starry sky were looking from above. She slipped tiredly under an itchy blanket and counted for a while the sparkling dots in the navy blue sky. Sleep quickly put the mitts on her pupils. Just a few moments passed and she put herself without murmuring into its soothing embrace.

She was awakened by Mark, who sat down on the bed. And maybe if he had done it gently, she probably wouldn't have woken up so quickly, but he, with finesse only known to him put the bony rump hard on the bed frame, setting the weakened from age structure in dangerous vibrations. It moaned miserably so loudly that the girl huddled on it and buried in bedding to the tips of freckled ears suddenly jumped up, staring at the newcomer with her eyes the size of plates. The host's face showed peace, but something lurked in his bright eyes, something that looked like concern.

"Are you alright?" The employer spoke after a moment, when he made sure that Lili was awake enough to talk to him normally, and not mumble flummery.

She propped herself up on her elbows and stared at him with her dream-blurred irides. She yawned and muttered under her breath:

"No, nothing. I'm better now."

"I know what happened in the evening. Morien burst into my house like a hurricane and told me to give you time off because you are getting tired. You believe? Such a man under my roof and burbling about a vacation for a lowly kitchenmaid. It's ridiculous. By Redeemers, what did you do here when I was absent, girl?!"

She sat up in surprise, staring at him as if he had been talking poppycock.

"Excuse me?"

"You've heard. And, by Redeemers, don't do that anymore."

After that, as if nothing had happened, he got up and left. Lilian fluttered her eyelashes, still being shocked. She quickly looked over at Erica. The cook was pretending to hear and see nothing, and was whistling off-key, cutting meat. Lilian was sitting on a bed with a mass of disheveled hair, through which the weak, almost already winter rays of the sun were piercing, creating a funny halo around the head.

"A day off," she thought. "Eh, after less than two weeks of work I begin to be given a head start. Now the girls will reproach me. I can already feel their revenge in my bones," she mumbled in her head, very dissatisfied with this fact.

The inn was covered in velvet twilight. Mark examined the place carefully and reached for handles to open the windows at least for a moment. Sometimes he ventilated the room, especially when the cold began. The cold air effectively chased away the stench that the regulars left. The door opened slightly and a man's head appeared in the gap, decorated with a fancy hat with a tassel. The innkeeper immediately recognized the messenger. After making sure that no one would chase him away with a stick, the little man slipped inside, carefully closing the door behind. He bowed politely and reached into a small purse dangling at his waist, retrieving a sealed letter from it. The owner gave him a look with his right eyebrow up. For the first time in his life, a deliverer at the magicians' service visited the inn, worse yet, he looked like a swell up close. He held back a goofy smile, his face was impassive and gloomy. He hoped that the gentleman wouldn't realize that he was bursting with amusement inside.

"I have a message, sir." He bowed politely.

"And who is it for?" Mark wondered.

"For Miss Lilian, sir." The delivery man handed him a roll of paper sealed with the House of Masters stamp.

Mark accepted the roll and looked at it with great interest.

"And that's probably from Master Morien?" He said quietly, deciphering the signs stamped on the wax seal.

"Yes, sir."

He went behind the counter and pulled out a drawer in which he used to keep the takings. The money lay in compartments in ascending order. He pulled out a copper coin and put it in the hand of the glad delivery man. He bowed low, bid farewell to the benefactor and left the inn, again taking care not to slam the door. Mark only shook his head. He still couldn't understand what the hell was going on. He decided to share the message with the cook, otherwise he would burst with impatience. Fortunately, he didn't have to go to the back, because the petticoat emerged from the shadow of the corridor:

"Look here, Erica." He showed the letter.

"What is it?" the woman grunted under her breath and wiped her hands on the apron.

"A letter from the Master himself. Guess for who?" He twisted his head playfully, making a silly face.

"I don't know. Our girls like him, maybe he liked one of them ..." She thought about it for a while. "No, I don't think he likes any of them. You know, sometimes I see him wincing at the sight of Ilia. And this maiden has been with us for several good springs and no one has ever complained about her."

"And yet, he does." He smiled sneeringly. "Lili!" He screamed.

The cook opened her mouth.

"For her?"

"Yeah. She put on quite a show yesterday," he lowered his voice as he heard footsteps. "And she's not ugly either ..." he paused, because the small figure of the recipient of the scream emerged from the back room.

"Yes?" She yawned. "You don't have to scream like that. I had to get up earlier than usual."

"Here you are." He stretched out his hand with the envelope. "I hope you can read."

"I can," she bridled, as if reading skills had been something natural.

She took the letter from the boss and stared at the seal in amazement. She brought the paper closer to the candle to recognize the signs. Her pupils immediately narrowed to the size of the heads of the pins. Mark and Erica leered at the girl.

"Oh no!" She shouted in her thoughts. "Do I have to run again? Is this a warning, or maybe an order to voluntarily surrender to the enforcers?"

With trembling hands, she broke the seal.

"Read, read!" She urged Erica.

"We want to know what you had done." Mark seemed to be eaten up by curiosity.

"I haven't done anything wrong." Bloody blushes appeared on her face.

She crumpled the message and fled to the kitchen. She slammed the door, leaving the puzzled people alone with guesses.

The letter was written in a neat, almost decorative handwriting. She watched the neat quirkiness for a moment, admired the curves and evenness of the letters, as if the message itself had been a small work of art. Even the seal was carefully stamped, unhurriedly, allowing the lacker to freeze sufficiently so that the marks would remain shapely and intact when the stamp was peeled off.

The Master wrote:

Dear Lilian,

My guess is that now as you read this you are as surprised as I am when I write this message. So don't ask why I do it because I don't know it. Your poor health worried me. I hope you feel much better today. I asked Mark for a day off for you. I hope you are not angry and it won't cause you problems. I know that the innkeeper is a good man and he will grant my request.

I would also like to invite you today for a cup of hot tea or, if you prefer, a pint of dwarven beer. I hope you will accept the invitation.

Sincerely your friend
Lord Master Morien from Aventus' house

Lilian crumpled the paper in her hand. She felt the blood drain from her face and the sweat bead up on her forehead. Many solutions flew through the brain like daggers that tore the tissue of thoughts into pieces. After all, if she used the invitation, she would have entered the lion's mouth, which she would have probably never freed herself from. Nay! She would have paid with being captured and imprisoned in the dungeons of the School in the Capital. After all, she can' mask the power that flows from the body so well. Each magician leaves behind a glow of sparkles of an aura that another magician can sense when he is a few steps away. This is ridiculous and mindless. On the other hand, if Morien wanted her to be captured, if he knew who she was, most likely the Illusionists would have appeared in the doorway of Ram's Head. There is nothing worse than these magicians - cold and selfish, who instead of hearts, have cold lumps. Maybe he thinks she is just a pretty girl, nothing more? He is looking for cheap entertainment, keeping a semblance of good manners? She sighed heavily and bent down for her coat, which lay casually on a stool next to the straw mattress. She didn't look around, threw the woolen cover on her back, shaded her face with a voluminous hood and tucked the letter into her pocket. She left the inn without a word, and walking she even hit Erica which immediately got out of her way, more anxious than irritated by the behavior of the maiden.

The morning greeted Lilian with a sharp frost, which wounded the skin with tiny blades of glaciated particles. The sun was shining, lazily scattering the moist fumes of Undercity. She walked, scared like never before. She was afraid of being exposed, she was also afraid of death. On the other hand, she had no purpose in life. Now her family was accidental people that she wouldn't have found good before, because what are beer maids or alewives ripping guests off? Nothing but black, scavenging birds. However, time verified the immature perception of those she had known only from stories. It also showed that looking through the prism of stereotypes is childish and completely off base. Now she wanted to stay in the warm rooms of "Ram's Head", surrounded by not always friendly faces, but mostly sincere and amiable.

She thought too much again. She tormented herself. A tangle of shreds of information boiled over in her head and aroused anxiety.

"If only the hair didn't start sparking," she repeated to herself and plucked with the frozen fingertips at the strands sticking out from under the headscarf.

She felt magic begin to fill the arteries dangerously. Sparks of power swirled in the tissues, pinched and jostled, making them swollen and painful at the same time. She wrapped herself more tightly, trying to disguise otherness. She was hiding in the alleys, she passed Undercity almost avoiding people. She knew that she had to do something, otherwise the blisters would cover the body, and the tongues of fire would burn her clothing, making her not only naked, but also vulnerable and defenseless.

She no longer looked in which direction the feet were carrying her. Anywhere, as long as it was behind the walls, just ahead. She stopped suddenly. She didn't stand before the gate that led to the backwood, but before the one that opened the School of Mages. She swallowed and stared at the sentries.

"How is that?" She moaned inwardly.

When the breaths escaped inexorably, and standing a few steps in front of the guards she didn't even take a step, they began to look at her expectantly. They saw that the girl was holding the letter in her hand. She wanted to say something, her mouth opened and moved silently, but they didn't hear the words. In truth, they probably saw in her only a townwoman, or perhaps a visitor, who probably saw the entrance to the School for the first time and who was simply speechless, probably delighted. However, Lilian struggled with herself, arranged the particles as if the future life had depended on it...

"Should I?" She said to herself almost silently. "Can I? And maybe it's a trap? Maybe Morien lures me with his will to capture me and insidiously hand over to the authorities? They know well how to take care of a fugitive."

She could see the inside of the dungeons through the eyes of her imagination, and then the prison wagon, which cradled on the route, sinking into muddy ruts. She felt the smell of the interior mixed with her own, as if indispensable stench of fear and doubt.

"No," she whispered and, having started up, rushed down towards the walls, and then straight onto the highroad.

Cold air was bursting into her lungs. Soon, smell of smoldering hair reached his nostrils. She knew it was starting to burn. Slightly and almost unnoticeably, but so significantly that a moment of inattention could reveal a magically disturbed state of mind. She was bathing in emotions. She had to immediately find a sheltered place and vent what was swirling inside. She knew well that one must not succumb to such states that she could easily harm herself. The masters warned her against strong raptures. She concentrated too many sparks, felt too much and couldn't deal with anger. Talent, especially hers, had a price she could carry and try to tame or give to the Illusionists and agree to be bound. And she couldn't agree to it. She loved magic too much, she loved healing and having the eye pleased by the effects of touch. She also loved fire and its destructive power. Fire control provided unlimited power, and pyromancy and the formation of matter in the shape of thoughts allowed to create or destroy. But she knew ... she felt that they were hard on her heels and wouldn't rest until they got what they wanted - her!

The road slipped away from under the feet. Like in the kaleidoscope, images changed, they seemed to fuse into one, shapeless lump. She was getting close, she could already see the line of trees behind which she would hide and rest. The muddy road, tired from the rain that was constantly falling slightly, slowed her down. She was panting, as if hounds had been hot on her heels. The first bushes, old oaks and the dusk of a dense forest enveloped her with safe arms of lush vegetation. The smell of autumn and rotting litter soothed the troubled limbs. She ran a trembling hand over her head. The remains of the headscarf slid off the head, beyond recovery, charred and gray.

"Damn it!" She cursed.

Returning, she would have to be careful that no one recognized her.

"Cursed, by Redeemers, red hair," she hissed and yanked at the curls. "I look like Jerm, damn colorful Jerm. I could swear that my father is some stupid elf!" She shouted so loudly that the birds on the trees took wing with a loud whir. "Mother! How many secrets have you hidden from me?" The power was increasing with greater intensity, was flowing from each piece of skin. Fire burning gut was blasting tissue. She reached out, a few small discharges leaped from finger to finger. Gently and almost imperceptible blue flames danced on the top of the hand. She was thinking that she was controlling her acts, but her brain was bursting with anger, fear and doubt in everything that surrounded her. She understood nothing. She seemed to be stuck in inexplicable stagnation, the world froze for a few breaths, stopped in conjunction of stars that were flickering somewhere, blinded by day. A red ball rippled over her hands. Regular and pulsating with red-orange glow. Mesmerizing and beautiful. It grew stronger, its diameter got bigger with each heartbeat, with every contraction of semi-conscious Lilian's arteries. A few more breaths, and the discharge would end ... a few more blinks of the eyelid, and there would be a final bathed in sadness. A white beam of light tore open the air, followed by a red fire in space, devouring what was in its range. A nearby tree was burning, the original heat was shining inside the trunk.

Lilian coughed. A long paroxysm of chills and bloody vomiting tugged at her body. She fell to her knees, with her face in wet grass. She didn't know how much time she spent, trembling and catching her breaths, as if they had been the last. Over time, however, the tension burning tissues flew off, disappeared, as did the rain and vegetation, which, treated with an escalation of power, turned into a sad mud. Relief sat on her shoulders, but it slowly allowed to take the place something more mundane - a tension-free present. She collected herself.

She got soaked. Now she resembled a tramp who, having encountered bandits, got dirty in a roadside ditch, trying to hide from the sword and robbery. She rubbed her face. She encountered a brook and washed herself. It didn't improve the overall appearance, but her cheeks were clean. On leaving, she looked at the reflection in the spring. The same red-haired woman was looking at her in the water table. Pale and absent in spirit. She pulled the coat's collar, and cuddling up into it, she plodded ahead. She felt hunger in her stomach. She quickly had ceased to be used to undereating.

"It's time to eat something," she sighed. "There's probably goulash in the tavern. But out of what did Eric make it this time?" She smiled to herself.

Before he knew it, the heels of the shoes knocked on the stone road winding in front of her. The city was thundering and living. The market was roaring with people hanging around and haggling with each other. The bustle filled Lilian with soothing calmness. She wanted to roam the streets, learn their meanders and dark alleys, but the desire for a warm meal won out over curiosity. She quickly found the trail to the inn.

"Where have you been?" Mark eyed her up from top to bottom.

He grimaced at the sight of her muddy clothing.

"I went for a round." She waved her hand and disappeared into the back room.

She saw that the man rolled his eyes. A few guests followed their favorite alewife with their eyes.

The kitchen smelled of stewed meat and cooked vegetables. Lilian threw off her cover and sat down at the table. She had to catch her breath because the strenuous march made her breathless. Fortunately, she quickly cooled down, got up and having washed her hands, she put a large portion of the meal into the bowl. She filled up the cup and returned to her seat. Full, she leaned against the back, yawned and stretched sluggishly. Venting the powers relaxed the muscles tense like a halter, she no more had an impression that the power would tear the temples, and the hair would show a different state. Now she could curl up and fall asleep.

The cook came into the room and, joining the girl, she folded her fingers on the counter.

"Did it taste good?" She asked.

"Yes," Lili said.

"That's good because I have to tell you something." She gave her a look from under thinning eyelashes.

"What?" She put her chin on her fists.

"It came to me that the girls don't like that you have so much ease," she sighed. "You know what I'm talking about, don't you? I think they'll start figuring out how to get rid of you."

"What?" She was surprised.

"Let me put it this way: none has been off for months, and you measured your length and right away ... Influential people put in a good word for you. Do you, by Creators, know who he is?" Erica leaned forward, staring at her so intensely that Lilian wanted to run away.

"Are you talking about Master?"

"And about who, if not about him?"

"I don't know. Master from School of Mages? Teacher? Mentor?"

"He's one of the most important magicians in the country, stupid!"

She was so dizzy at the news that she had to hold on to the table. Blood drained from her face. It left behind a chalk-white mask.

"What are you talking about?! Then why does he drink in such a despicable place as 'Ram's Head'?"

"Because only we in the city have a dwarven beer that he likes so much. And since the dwarves don't like magicians, he visits us."

"And this is the only reason?" She couldn't believe it.

"That's right."

Erica went out.

She left Lilian alone so she could think about what she had told her. Partly, she was worried about the new worker, she genuinely liked her company. Sometimes jealous maidens liked to make lives miserable, gossip usually destroyed delinquents, and when it turned out to be ineffective, they found other, equally interesting ways. Including poisoning, adding to drinks substances that cause stomach disorders and other unpleasant things. In her heart she knew that Lili would handle them. Something whispered to her that the redhead would usurp half the company more efficiently and faster than they would have her shapely ass.

Lilian buried her face in her hands. She sobbed softly. It was too much for one day. Huge, salty tears rolled down her cheeks. Now she had no way back, she had to use the invitation. It didn't matter that she would fall into the trap. It was better that they would capture her behind the walls of the School than make a spectacle, coming here. She managed to stop crying. She stood up and opened the window. A few cool whiffs of afternoon air came into the kitchen and in a crack mixed with the closeness. Relief didn't come. She stood for a moment, staring at the bag in which she had stuffed the second dress she had received from Mark. At least it was clean, unlike the one she wore. She was also more challenging. A considerable neckline revealed too much for her taste. And the broad sleeves were more like a robe than a kitchenmaid's uniform. And the color ... so bold. She felt strange in burgundy. It emphasized the lightness of the skin and made the hair appear redder than it actually was. Unfortunately, she didn't have another one. She had to wear this one. Slowly and reluctantly, she prepared to leave. Surprisingly, the frippery wasn't very slack. At the waist, she banded it with a wide, heavily worn leather belt, which hid the ugly creases of the material. Her hair was high up. For this she used pins, which she once had gotten from a peasant who she helped bring the little bull into the world. The gift of gratitude held for the first time the unruly thatch of eternally tousled curls. She checked the overall appearance in a bowl of water, which served as a mirror. In a blink of an eye she changed from a modest young lady into a neat and stylish one. A smile of satisfaction brightened the concerned face. Only the clean coat was missing to complete the whole. If she came out as she was, she would have frozen unavoidably. Perhaps the old cook had something to use. She walked quickly through the back room to find the woman. She was standing at the counter as usual and was watching the regulars.

"Erica," she said shyly. "Do you have a coat? Such for special occasions? You know ..." she sighed. "My coat today ..."

She didn't manage to finish, because Mark got into the conversation, all too eagerly.

"There are things left by guests. In the trunk, in the storage compartment. Check it, maybe you'll find something. There is not much of it, because here everyone watches his junk."

"Thank you, host." She bowed theatrically, which made Mark very confused.

Erica chuckled, covering her mouth with her hand.

The magician took the first thing on the top, too embarrassed that she had to dig in someone else's lumber. She took out a too big capot that she could have wrapped around herself twice. It had a large, face shadowing hood and pretty embroidery winding on the edges of the fabric. She grabbed the letter and stuffed it into the cavernous pocket. Now she was ready to face what fate would bring. She tenderly glanced at the cane, which was hidden in the corner of the room and had been unused for a long time. She wanted to take it, but quickly got the idea out of her head. After all, she didn't go to the Master as an intrant, but as an alewife. Maybe he really didn't recognize anything and thinks she is a simple girl? She wanted so much to cherish illusions.

Before she left the tavern, Mark looked at her with a dreamy gaze. And it was a rather lusty sight. He hadn't seen her like this yet. She seemed perfectly beautiful, none of the girls caused such emotions in him. He swallowed and pretended that she was indifferent to him, but under his skin he felt his blood boil.

"I'm leaving," she said. "I got an invitation for tea from Lord Master. After all, such a person shouldn't be denied, let alone keep him waiting."

At the sight of her, one of the maids stumbled over the edge of the bench, breaking glasses.

"Yes, Lili, go," Mark whispered. "You can't refuse him."

He followed her with his eyes, walking her to the door. The sight of glass shards on the floor cooled him down.

"Pick it up, stupid," he hissed.

He hurried into the back room to talk to the cook.

"Did you know the master invited her to a meeting?"

The woman glared at him like at a beaten dog.

"What's so strange about that? She's pretty. Probably he is looking for the opportunity."

"No, Erica! Something is going on here and I don't know what the hell it is!"

"You're sensitive, that's all."

"No," he screamed. "He was in my house at night, woman! The most important mage in the country came to my damn house to ask for free time for her!"

"There must be something about her that interested him."

"Maybe she's a savage mage?" He whispered conspiratorially.

"You're raving now." She laughed in his face. "If she were a magician, she wouldn't worked in a shack like this. You're nuts, man."

"Maybe you're right," he breathed a sigh of relief. "May you are!"

Lili stood on the threshold of the inn and took a deep breath. Cool air swirled in her throat, and a cloud of frozen steam escaped from her mouth.

Well, let's do it, let's go straight to the lion's mouth, let's get ourselves killed," she sighed and walked slowly down the steps.

She slowly moved towards the gate. There were very few people on the streets. In the late afternoon, hardly anyone left home, especially when it was getting colder. The first ice on the frozen puddles crunched beneath her feet. The echo of her footsteps was reflecting rhythmically from the walls of the houses lined up tightly one next to the other. All the way she wondered what to say when she stood at the gate: Hello, I'm a fugitive mage. Come hang me. Or: Hey boys, who wants to have his mustache burning? A mean smile came to her face. She remembered the jokes of older students when they charred each other's down that they proudly called facial hair. Then they walked for a week with a green burn ointment, with which the medical women saved the damaged skin. This picture put Lilian in a good mood. She relaxed a little, though not enough to feel confident. The narrow street widened over time, leading walkers to the square. Then she went a little up the street and she was there. Before her, rose the great gate of the School of Magicians. Lili looked at it carefully, because the first time she hadn't noticed the intricate work of the local blacksmith. It was captivating. It was decorated with a school coat of arms, surrounded by beautiful bunches of vines flowing down in cascades of fruit. The guard grunted warningly.

"Get lost, girl! You have nothing to do here! Now! Get out!" He waved his hand as if he had been chasing away a stalker.

She frowned and gave him an angry look.

The man paled when he saw the flash in her cat eyes that he hated. The angry mage never boded anything good.

She reached out and handed the letter signed with the seal of the School.

"I have an appointment with Lord Master Morien, he is expecting me."

The sentry glanced at the stamp, then the signature. He didn't even bother to take the note. He wanted to get rid of it as soon as possible. He whistled and disappeared into the wicket gate. The girl closed her eyes.

"Come what may, there is no turning back," she said thoughtfully.

The waiting time dragged on mercilessly. When the guard reappeared, he announced that she still had to wait, because the master's assistant was required to deliver something to the scriptorium. She nodded and didn't show that she was starting to get impatient and already slightly freezing to the ground. She kicked her heels and, pressing her hands deeper into her pockets, rolled her eyes and gasped, bored. The man pretended not to notice it. His attention was caught by a group of drunks who, having staggered around the bend, loudly sang a slightly raunchy song. Lilian turned toward them, and they, having noticed the woman, bowed clumsily and plodded in the opposite direction. The sentry sighed with relief.

After a while, a swarthy woman appeared in the wicked gate, wrapped in a thick wool cover, slightly breathless and confused, as if someone had forced her to suddenly detach from the assigned activities. The woman's nose was marked with tiny, glistening drops of sweat. Her eyes were large and significantly protruding. Lili smiled friendly.

"Miss Lilian, right?"

"Yes, madam." She bowed politely.

She returned the gesture, putting her lips in a kindly grimace.

"Follow me, please." The woman pointed to the square behind the gate, then stepped back a little and made room for the guest to cross the school thresholds.

When the girl bypassed her slightly, she closed the door, turning the key.

Lili followed the maid. She could feel her heart pounding and blood pressure buzzing in her ears. Intense power vibrations bounced off her like off a mirror. A familiar experience filled the skull, surprisingly very subtly. She expected a deafening roar of magic, and received only voiced sparks that irritated the skin. She stared at the ground. She followed the invisible footprints the maid left. In silence, she chased the fluttering robes of the guide. She knew that Schools were built according to the same scheme as universities, apartment houses, masters' houses, classrooms, utility rooms, canteens, latrines and everything needed for life. It was a city in a city. Self-sufficient, carved in gray stone, made by willpower. So precisely that you can't press a pin into the gaps between the stones. Only dwarves can construct like that, and magicians, of course.

They passed through the square, bypassing a flowerbed surrounded by a low hedge, inside of which benches stood in a circle, and in the middle grew a large branchy tree - probably an oak. The woman led to the largest building in the school. University - Lilian paled. Oh, great, now I'm like the cook's stew - right on a plate! Before they could be absorbed by the squat walls, the guest managed to sweat, and the coldness increased by the humidity of the skin bitten even more painfully. However, she didn't show that the cold was paralyzing her senses, and she obediently headed to her destination. The swarthy lady used a lot of force to open the large wooden door, which creaked ominously.

"Ah, those hinges," she said under her breath. "For a week, I have asked to lubricate them. This sound irritates me terribly."

The young magician felt a favorable look on herself.

"Come. Lord Master doesn't like to wait."

She led her deeper into the corridor lit by tallow candles. The room smelled of medicines, herbs and other peculiarities used by healers and poison brewers. She knew the smell well. She even dared to say that she missed this fragrance a little.

"Wait a second." The servant pointed to a stool next to a large, effuse pot flower.

Lili nodded and took the indicated seat. The Redeemers knew how much time she would spend waiting for an audience with the Master. The maid disappeared into the room, closing gently door. After a while, a large group of novices dressed in colorful robes left the room. Everyone turned their eyes to the woman they didn't know. She felt strange, she felt that they knew. That they see what she hid so carefully, surrounding herself with an impermeable bubble of power. One of the female intrants bowed to her and joined the others. Lili returned the greeting, trembling like a young leaf in the air vibrating from the heat.

"Come in," said the maid who silently appeared next to her. "Lord Master will receive you."

Lilian came to oneself in a moment and jumped up. The servant pointed to the room, bowed and, with no regard for the guest, she walked into the corridor.

Lili took off her coat, adjusted the dress and slightly ruffled hair. She rolled the thick cover and hugged it, hiding behind the large fold of material. Such safety, of course, was an illusion, but she wanted to trust and believe that it would protect her against the worst. She sighed to encourage herself and crossed the threshold of the lecture hall. Between the bottles of crafted animals, plants and a pile of books was sitting an almost completely obscured man, frantically flipping through a manuscript. He mumbled something to himself incoherently. She noticed small discharges that jumped from one jar to another, hissing and falling apart into small particles that were absorbed by the dim light. She walked quietly to the desk. She didn't want to disturb, but since he invited her ... Feeling the fearful soul sit on her shoulder, she opened her pale lips and tried to sound as true as possible:

"Good morning."

He looked up. The magic escalations disappeared, and the interior was filled with cavernous silence, broken only by the hissing of oil in lamps.

"Welcome my dear." He beamed.

He looked completely different than in the inn. His loose hair fell softly on his shoulders and stood out against a black robe as intense as a crow's wings. On the man's chest rested a medallion with the coat of arms of the brotherhood. His face was calm and full of dignity. She tried to estimate his age. She was thrashing between thirty and forty, though in spirit, she tilted to the first number. She liked the master's hair - white, almost silver in some places, glistening with reflections whose color was enhanced by the lights burning around. She knew that the shade was reserved only for a few. Sometimes the explosion of magic causes the dye to burn, and the magician is then marked by majestic gray hair. Usually he wears it with pride, although some terrified with otherness shave their heads and don't part with the scarves that bind on the temples, hiding a disgusting ailment. Morien must have had unusual abilities, since at such a young age he held the Archmaster's post. In general, for this honorable position were nominated noble and serious old people. This thought didn't give her peace, it dug tunnels, asked a lot of questions, but common sense whispered that she shouldn't have been nosy, that it wasn't her business.

He was also surrounded by strange magnetism. She had noticed it before, and not only her, because the maids in the inn chattered about his "values" many times. She could see it clearly now - he belonged to the type of men to whom the rabble carried the torch, and he stubbornly remains unmarried, as if not noticing all those fainting and praying for his favor. She didn't hide that on closer acquaintance, she could have lost herself in the arms of the handsome magician, but ... she preferred not to think about it, besides, it was Lord - Magician. He could have easily combed her thoughts, shelling out what she would have liked to hide. So she decided not to clutter her head with unnecessary and potentially damaging stupid things. What mattered was now, that was counting down every second of freedom.

"I hope you feel good already? From the blush, I see that I'm right." He gave the newcomer gentle curving of his lips, as if trying to smile, but the grimace came off rather shyly and not very neatly.

"Yes, Lord. I'm much better now." She looked at the floor.

"Come on, let's leave this place. You must be frightened by these creatures in jars."

She glanced briefly at the desk. She wasn't afraid, she was used to such views. She could even swear that they fascinated her a little, hidden behind glass, surrounded by yellowish liquid. Dead and silent. Letting discover their insides to those who were hungry for knowledge.

"A little," she lied.

"Put on your coat, we'll leave."

He reached for his, already well-known to her, then for a cane, which turned out to be similar to the one she had. She took a deep breath with worry and started choking.

"Are you alright?" He put a hand on her shoulder. She was confused.

"Yes. I have an itchy throat."

"Alright, let's go. I invite you for something hot. Today we won't make up that dwarven beer, you are too cold. I don't want Mark to fire you because over me you are sick.

He held the heavy door in front of her and let her leave. She felt uncomfortable, but this kindness took her nervous heart.

"Can you read?"

She looked at him in surprise.

"If I couldn't, I wouldn't be here," she thought.

"Yes," she said.

"Oh, great." He was pleased. "Then I must lend you something interesting. Do you like to read?"

"Yes."

"What?"

"History."

He stopped. The light brown eyes in the color of honey pierced her through.

"I should have lied and said romance novels," she scolded herself. "Uh! Stupid! Stupid! Stupid!"

She wanted to roll her eyes, but she came to her senses in time. After all, it was not appropriate for a young and well-behaved woman. So she lowered her eyes and stared at the tips of her shoes. She hoped that he wouldn't continue the strand. But he did. The words came out of his larynx and hit the ears of the cringing girl.

"Really? It seems to me that I'm dealing with someone special, because you know the art of reading," he continued. "It is an art that many people do not have in this city, unless we are dealing with nobility or merchants. Oh yes. They are familiar not only with letters, but also with numbers." He laughed.

She returned the grimace. She also sensed that he was making sentences so that she could understand what he was saying to her. Magicians had keywords that meant nothing to the mob. In addition, all the time she was surrounded by an invisible and impermeable bubble of power. After a while, fatigue began to bite. Sparkling drab spots was spinning before her eyes. The same as the pupils were marked by before the unfortunate fainting. She struggled with growing weakness, tried to direct her thoughts to a different path. Unfortunately, the efforts proved futile, and she weakened at the knees with each passing moment.

As they left the university building, a few magicians passed by and greeted Morien with a cordial bow. Her presence did not escape their attention, they pierced her with power like with daggers. Dryness in mouth bit her tongue and gums. However, she straightened up and pretended that she didn't care what they had done. She walked quietly behind the magician. He led her through the courtyard to a small house. He stopped at the door.

"I hope you won't feel uncomfortable if I invite you to my house? We can't experience intimacy in the school canteen."

Her eyes widened. She must have looked like a squirrel now, which can't get over how big a nut it found. She realized that he was probably inviting her for known reasons, because what for sane individual leads a stranger to quarters, if not for the obvious. She bit the bullet. She wanted to gasp: Who do you think I am? She was silent, however, although inside she was bursting with anger penetrating her veins.

"No, I won't feel embarrassed," she said, heeding the tone of her voice. "I spend a lot of time with men, I'm used to ..." She bit her tongue. "Oh, I should watch what I say," she sighed inwardly.

Again she saw the row of snow-white teeth emphasizing the charming smile.

"I like your honesty."

He opened the door with a large copper key.

"Don't worry. I will abuse you, and then decide what to do with you," he joked.

"I take your word for it," she sighed.

After a while, she let herself be absorbed by the twilight of the hall, smelling of wood paste with a light note of rose oils.

"What am I doing, by Redeemers?" She whispered to herself. "What am I doing?"

There was a pleasant, velvety state of blissful lightness. She was surrounded by wooden objects immersed in gray, shining with the smoothness of polished edges. Her heels clattered on the floor. She looked at it, puzzled. The fabulous mosaic winded under the shoes. She wished that the pall wasn't enveloping it. She was interested in color and texture, because she could feel bulges under the thin soles of her shoes.

Morien saw this interest. Despite the twilight surrounding them, he surreptitiously watched glittering from excitement eyes that scrutinized surroundings hungry and excited at the sime time. He raised his hand and whispering several spells, he illuminated the hall with dozens of flames. They trembled in time of words and gained power. They shot up, gilding what was clinging to the dark.

"Oh, I can't do that." She thought.

The fears that had been boring the bones just a moment ago, now miraculously drifted away. She felt frisky and safe. She didn't understand the texture of the air that rippled around saturated with balsamic fragrances and oil lamp smoke. As if they had been filled with the hitherto unknown essence of magic. She didn't know if she was to fear this suspension between fear and bliss, but she knew that she couldn't succumb to delusions and had to be constantly alert. After all, hallucination was a favorite activity of magicians.

"Give me the coat." He held out his hands.

She didn't let him wait, she freed herself from too wide sleeves and handed him the outer clothing hurriedly.

He seized the capot and pierced the guest with a reflex of honey irises. She wanted to run, but there was nowhere to go. At the time the heavy door to the mage's residence was closed, she become somewhat imprisoned. Behind this gate, in a world that dangerously stimulated the senses. Which on the other hand seemed exciting.

"Forgive me, can I say that you look beautiful?"

"Thank you." She blushed and mechanically smoothed the folds of her dress.

Shy women often behaved this way in his presence, completely unaware of their own charms. And he knew the fair sex well. He enjoyed it. He bit into it as into juicy apples. But Lilian wasn't one of those he wanted to possess bodily. Something else was at stake here, something spiritual ... something that didn't allow him to breathe freely if only her name was spoken in her mind. She had the magic that seduced. She also had the beautiful face that confused.

In the glow of the lights, Lilian could see the interior of the house. She stood in the middle of a small staircase, which was crowned with an oak, carved staircase. A polished floor shone beneath her feet, depicting a starry sky with marked celestial bodies drowning in deep indigo. There was a bench and clothes rack under one of the wall. At the foot of the stairs, a storeroom was hidden discreetly, probably for brooms and other small items. On the right, there was only one door, so most of the rooms had to be upstairs or were camouflaged behind those large double leaves. Everywhere there was brown mixed with navy, purple and gold. It wasn't until a moment later, when the pupils got used to the light, when she noticed the entrance pressed into the room, still wrapped in darkness, probably leading to the kitchen or the service rooms.

"Come, I'll show you the house," he said.

"Alright," she yielded.

Vigilance, however, pulsed significantly. Made her sensitive to the slightest rustling and even the friction of the material against the material caused reactions. On the other hand, she trusted that apart from bringing her to the dungeons, nothing concrete should have disturbed the meeting harmony. She decided to focus on what the magician had to convey, to be led to the places he wanted to show, and then, if possible, to run away, pretending that it was by accident.

On the ground floor, several rooms were created, which were characterized by a mixture of sublime simplicity and elegance. Small everyday objects were in the right place, and only the thick, leather-bound books seemed to be stuck where they shouldn't be. Sometimes open, sometimes arranged on window sills, a few pieces on each. They piled up and disturbed the order, but it wasn't what disturbed, but the severity enclosed in the walls, as if the splendor of the decorations had evaporated against the white walls.

He led her to the library.

"Here you are, it's yours."

The girl opened her eyes wide and was about to say something, but he stole thunder, continuing the strand:

Pick what you want. I'll make tea. Oh yes, I would forget. Do you probably wonder why there is no service? They have free time, I give it them quite often, besides, I like loneliness and this buzzing silence that envelops the house. It is easier then to prepare a lecture or to read. You probably understand me."

He left. Lili was alone, surrounded by hundreds of volumes evenly arranged on thick shelves. The room was built on an oval plan, and its heart was a huge desk, located against the backdrop of an even larger window half-obscured by a purple curtain. Colorful little panes decorated the edges of the glass monster, arranged in a similar pattern as she had seen in the lobby. She stared for a while at the scraps connected by metal joints. They seemed black, dotted with brighter spots imitating stars. She felt a strange tingling in her neck. Horror looked into the redhead's pupils. She couldn't resist the feel making her skin numb. She approached it slowly and, stretching her neck, glanced outside. The view was captivating. Trees, a flower bed and a gate embedded in ordinariness. There were few people wandering outside. Some of them were hurrying with their books pushed under their armpits or strapped to their belts on a special harness. Some of them wielded canes, simple, completely unlike the one she and Morien had. Steel or wooden sticks rhythmically tapped on the pavement. Their owners were voraciously absorbed by the evening darkness, and the sound of steel hitting the ground faded with footsteps. Everything worked like a well-oiled mechanism.

She heard the movement in the lobby. She quickly moved away from the window and stared expectantly at the place where she had last seen the Master.

Morien entered the library backward, with his elbow pressing the door handle. His hands were occupied. He carried a tray on which she saw a silver teapot and two cups, and next to it a sugar bowl of the same color. Nearby were teaspoons with fancy handles, probably made of bronze. She quickly took a look at what he brought. She had been always fascinated by the objects that the magicians used. Usually they were surrounded by a kind of mysticism. She explained herself that most of the magicians had been leaving the headquarters in great haste. Probably then they had been grabbing the first thing they had found within reach. None of the soldiers at the Baroness' service had ever paid attention to a child clutching a curved spoon to its chest. Intrants also deeply loved beautiful objects. They loved to surround themselves with gold and expensive materials, which somehow emphasized the status they achieved over time. Morien didn't look like a man who liked collecting. Here, everything struck the guest with simplicity, interwoven with subtle elegance. She didn't see the excess, but only the most necessary things. Although she could be wrong. She didn't know him at all. And what was outside could only be a palisade.

"Here you are," he said, placing the tray on the desk.

He carefully took the kettle and filled both cups. The hot drink was evaporating, the interior of the library was slowly getting saturated by the aroma of the infusion. He reached for one and handed it to the girl who took the cup, wrapping it in cool hands. Pleasant drink warmed up the frozen pads. He took a sip.

"Yes, I like this view too. I often stand in the same place and look at these poor people."

"Why poor?" She dipped her lips in the hot drink.

"Because you see." He put the cup back on the tray. "Everyone carries a story on their shoulders, some nicer ones, others not. Some want to stay here, others repeatedly try to escape. You know what I mean?"

She blushed.

"Yes."

"Oh, tea is probably too hot." He noticed her red cheeks.

"No, no, it's good. Thank you."

"Let me finish. You see, I'm not a supporter of Schools, but I'm neither a fan of wild or feral people who after education begin to practice black magic."

She choked. She set the cup on the desk, pretending it was over tea.

"I'm sorry," she cleared her throat. "I feel better, I'm sorry." The blush still marked her freckled cheeks.

"It's nothing," he continued. "I just hope you understand what I'm talking about?"

"Yes." She nodded.

"It's great. I hope you don't hold a grudge against me. Oh, by Creators! I don't know why, but I sense that I can freely express opinions with you. I naively trust that I can afford a bit of being myself, it's very strange." He shook his head, setting his thick, snow-white hair in motion, then stood up and began strolling through the library.

"You can trust me, Lord, I'm not one of those who commit indiscretion."

"Oh, that's not what I meant." He made a nervous gesture with his hands. "Schools are prisons. This is the Baroness' fault. They could be quite useful institutions were it not for the yoke. I wonder when stifled and forced to stay behind the walls, they will gather, and without considering the consequences, will start a revolt."

"Revolt ..." she repeated in a whisper, looking into the inscrutable eyes of the magician.

"Yes. You see, we have turbulent times. How to put it ..." he sighed longly. "That's one of the reasons I called you."

Lilian felt an icy sweat run down her back, freezing the spinal cord. She wanted to move but couldn't. Fear pierced her.

"I'm lost," she moaned in thought, but she kept a stiff upper lip and spoke almost inaudibly:

"Why?"

"Because ... because ... I don't want anything to happen to you because of it." He walked a few small steps and stopped almost in the center of the room.

The pale glow of the oil lamp lit part of his sad face. Was this a game or honest intentions? She didn't hide that the care gaping from him gave her the collywobbles. She sensed the trick. She decided not to step out of character and pretend to be the proverbial "stupid girl".

"I don't understand." She turned her head archly. "Why can an influential person like you care about someone like me?" She folded her arms. "I'm poor, I keep bad company, in addition I work in the inn. I serve cheap beer, entertain guests, but that's not all ... I'm homeless. Mark took me from the street like a stray dog. Is that amusing you? It's such a game, right? I will now be incensed with nice words that will soften rowdiness, and when I succumb, you will squeeze a silver coin into my hand, saying goodbye on leaving?"

His eyes became even more somber. She could see him softening and breaking down.

"Probably I should have bitten my tongue," she wondered. "Maybe I'm really too rough, too crude."

He approached her softly. And the closer he was, the stronger her heart was beating. It behaved like a bird trapped in a cage, which wants to free itself at all costs. She controlled fear dangerously connected with curiosity. He came so close that she could almost feel his breath on her face.

"I know who you are," he whispered and grabbed her arms.

She shivered. The blood left her blushing cheeks and drained into her body.

"You are Lilian, a fugitive from the magician school in Raghion." It sounded in her ears like the worst sentence.

It paralyzed her.

"I'm lost!" She felt such dryness in her throat, as if she hadn't drunk all day hot. She wanted to say a stream of swear words, isolate herself from words that surrounded her like a rope. She only stuttered out: "You must have mistaken me for someone."

She straightened up, and her hands slowly began to tighten around the folds of the dress. In a moment she crumpled the material, and under her fingertips she felt painful tension as the fabric mercilessly dug hollows into thin skin.

"Do you trust me?" He whispered.

"It's over," she muttered in her thoughts. "It's all over ... He deceived me, deluded ..."

"Do you trust me?" He repeated.

She didn't even flinched. She was staring at the man standing just two steps away from her. The man who had her in the palm of his hand. Defenseless and lured into a trap. Naive!

The failing light that lay on half of Morien's face gave him an alienated and distant look. She couldn't guess what was on his mind. The man's mysteriousness drove her crazy. The muscles of his face looked unmoved, as if he had put on a mask that shields from prying eyes, and the emotions he just wore, came out of him, as if they had never been there.

The stillness lasted only a few breaths, and the magician felt as if she had stuck in a whirlwind of time that hung at the moment for dispassionate eternity.

The master braced himself and approached the woman. Her chest wavered with nervous breaths. He could swear that he could hear the heartbeat of her worried heart. A moving aura rippled around. He was scared. Magic bitten on every side, burst under the robe, and irritated the coverings with painful jerks. He wanted to pull her close, but all he could do was surround her small face with his cool fingers. She didn't run away. She flinched, as if she had wanted to push him away with that slight movement.

"But, but ..." she said, and her eyes seemed to pierce through.

"Stop it now, please," he told her off gently. He wanted to put peace on her, but she didn't allow him. The harmony that accompanied him, effervesced and rippled, every now and then irritated by the magic discharges of the woman. "I know it, you don't have to pretend to me. I have known it for a long time." The voice shook dangerously.

He knew that he must have been on his guard and he didn't hide that he was terrified of the thought of death that she could have had for him.

"No ... No ... Eh," she sighed. "I am not who you think I am ..." She tried at all costs to handle the situation, but at the moment everything was doomed and sealed.

She couldn't just tell more lies she wanted to feed him.

"I won't hand you over," he said firmly.

"No?" she was surprised and blinked as energetically as if with fluttering eyelashes, she wanted to sweep away what she had just heard.

"I won't," he repeated and hugged his cheek to her cheek.

The air trembled with emotion.

"Why? Why do you let me live?" She groaned.

She didn't want to fight. Her eyes got vitreous and flooded the face with streams of hot tears. She was still shivering, but this time she didn't feel the painful tension that strained her muscles, but relief. She also mastered the barrier. She stabilized it so that it slowly became thinner and thinner. After a while, the magical envelope dissolved into the air. Lilian was naked, at the magician's mercy.

Morien wanted that moment to be endless. Sparks of power surrounded their bodies and mixed with each other. They didn't prick anymore. He had the impression that they were dancing in harmony only known to them, safe and calm. He opened his mouth, allowing honesty that painfully irritated consciousness. Not only was the girl losing her spirit. He had a feeling that he was more afraid.

"I don't know a magician as gifted as you. I don't know and haven't heard of such a person for years, despite the fact that it is written in the books that those in history walked on this vale," he sighed. "Do you know why they want to capture you? Because you are precious. Yes, they would like to lock you up and watch you thrash and swear. They would like to make you submissive so that you become an instrument in their hands. From the moment you appeared within reach of the walls, I sensed your presence, each time more. It bounced off me like off a mirror. I remained anxious because I know that I wasn't the only one who focused on searching. I predicted you would return to your hometown, though most denied it, thinking it was stupid. But I knew otherwise. I know how strong love for a family can be. I felt you are afraid, I felt energy so powerful that it choked. You wanted to hide, but you are betrayed by sparks of power, or rather their waves, which fill the surroundings. It is true that only the most powerful are able to face your abilities. We are few, but we are favorable, believe me. I couldn't believe ... you're so ... delicate. How can there be so much strength in such a fragile creature? Then I just followed the paths you walk on. I watched you haggle, deliver liquors, talk to people and, above all, fight with handicaps. Forgive me, please." The Master's eyes got vitreous as much as Lilian's eyes just a moment ago. "But I can't let you be hurt. You are so beautiful, so special ..."

He breathed a sigh of relief. Now he could do anything. Although the limbs were still paralyzed by fear. He wanted to have her so much, to wrap his arms around her and let himself be carried away by a momentary oblivion that she would most likely have rejected. He was an enemy, though he would have liked to be a lover. Yes, he knew now that she was the woman she desired, lusted after with animal passion. He took his cheek away from her face and looked at her eyes.

"The consequences, damn them," he growled.

He pulled the girl closer and stuck her lips in hers. Not gently, but strongly, feeling the salty taste of tears on them and his and her fear.

She wanted to run away, break free from the hoops of his arms, but in an inexplicable way something dissuaded her, she let him seduce her. Just like that. The kiss didn't look like the brush of longing lips of lovers. It was associated with passion. She succumbed. She tilted her head back. Her hands timidly moved toward the man. At last, she also embraced him tightly. The caress eased but didn't end. Morien's soft lips led her to the gates of previously unknown sensations. Pleasant warmth replaced the chill of anxiety. She lost herself. She taught. She absorbed intimacy like a moth light. She also stopped crying. Tenderness dried out her tears, bringing healthy blushes to her cheeks. For a long time she hadn't been surrounded by such a veil of peace, like a fog that quietly falls on everything that seemed scary just a moment ago.

"Don't hand me over." She stepped back, dipping her fingers into the man's white hair. "I don't want to die, I don't want to hurt anyone, I just wanted to see my mother ..." Drops seeped into the corners of the eyes. "She didn't write ... She didn't speak for so long ..."

"Shhh ..." he whispered. "Don't say anything. Come, I'll walk you to the gate, we've been here too long. I don't want us to go too far, not now."

"Alright."

"I also have a request," he continued, sliding his thumb along the girl's jawline.

"Yes?"

"I would like ... how to call it ..." he thought for a while.

The simple construction of the sentence suddenly came with great difficulty, as if facing another demon nestling in a lonely mind. "I wish I could see you again. On the other hand, I'm afraid that this may seem suspicious. I would not like to spoil your opinion. You know, it's very brittle matter. Once soiled ..."

"Yes, that's a great idea," she said, not letting him to finish. "I would love to ... but ..." she sighed, hanging her forehead.

"So let's keep up appearances. Bows, greetings, kind conversations about nothing. Sometimes a glass of beer, sometimes a smile ..." He brushed a strand away from her forehead. "It's safest, though I don't know, how I can handle it. A week will seem like an eternity. Can I at least write? I will attach a blank card to my letter so that you can reply. What do you think?"

"Well." She kissed his eyebrow.

In the hall he helped her to dress up and, keeping the right distance, led her towards the main gate. At her destination, Lili bowed low. Her eyes were glistening, moist and beautiful. Yellow reflections harmonized with the glare of the lanterns hung here and there.

"Thank you, Lord Master, for your informative visit."

He nodded discreetly, nestling his hands into his broad sleeves.

"I was pleased to host you. I hope that I didn't tire you out with the history of the School? It would be a shame if you considered me a bore." Then he pointed to the side door.

She denied the magician's words, shaking her head. He answered with a slightly raised corner of the mouth.

The guards jumped to the gate and opened it on command.

"See you later, Miss Lilian," he said on parting.

"Goodbye."

She went out into the empty street. Out of the corner of her eye, she saw that he stood still for a moment and watched her walk away toward the tavern. Her heels were rhythmically clicking on slippery cobblestone. She didn't feel confident. The smooth soles of her shoes made her keep her arms wide apart to prevent falling, and yet she felt lightly like a bird that had been released from the cage. On the other hand, she was afraid of what awaited her in the near future. And if he wants to get involved? Then what? What exactly is the relationship? She never went out with anybody. She had no experience. Her friends from the School used to date older students or kiss around, but she wasn't a girl the boys look favorably at. She was flat for a long time, reminiscent of a freckled whippersnapper. The only thing that distinguished her from the "male" group was the female tunic. It wasn't until one summer that femininity broke out with redoubled force. Her colleagues looked incredulously at the sudden change. At her hips, the breasts flowering like rose buds, as well as changing facial features. She seemed different every day. Even her eyes, so characteristic of her, underwent a metamorphosis, became brighter and shinier. She turned from a child into a beautiful lady. She emphasized the new look with narrow robes, tight at the waist with a wide leather belt with the school coat of arms similar to what she had seen in Lord Master's house. She noticed the greedy looks of her colleagues and jealous friends. At that time, she treated adoring as fun, but she didn't let anyone get too close. She preferred peace and loneliness. She didn't even kiss because what for? To check what it is like? No! There are more important things in the world than exchanging fluids. In the blink of an eye she realized that she had done it for the first time in the Master's library. What's worse... although... she liked it and wanted more.

"Oh, yes," she sighed to herself.

All the novices could have dreamed of such a first kiss.

She arrived at the inn. The crowded hall boomed with joyful sounds, the guests laughed and sang along with the local bard who played the lute at the far end of the room. Mark, as always, stood behind the bar and also had a great mood, as evidenced by, among others, rows of polished cups and a smile that lit up his slightly surly face. He also stamped to some off-key tones. He jiggled around lightly, completely unhindered by the bizarre dance.

"Hello," he said. He put the glass down on the counter and flipped the cloth over his shoulder. "How was your meeting?"

"Thank you, nice. He is an extremely wise man," she added right away.

"Will you be able to help today, or rather you will take advantage of the last moments of leisure?" he changed the subject.

"I will help. I have already forgotten about nighttime weakness. I feel great."

"Great. Dress up and help. We have a lot of clients today, and we need to prepare a room upstairs. He have a guest willing to stay overnight."

"Okay, although I would rather throw off my coat and girdle my apron. I have to wash the dress, but after closing. Perhaps when I hang it by the stove, it will dry up by the morning. I'm coming," she said and nodded.

Along the way to the back she passed one of the helping girls who didn't hesitate to snort at her, showing how he despised Lilian.

"Don't look at me like that, or I'll turn you into a toad," she thought and scurried around the corner.

She dropped her coat on the bed and looked around for the apron. It hung, as always, on a nail near the washtub. Erica liked clothing to have specific places. She let her hair down, the cascade of curls freely flowed over her shoulders and back. She grabbed it on one side and put a part of it behind her ear. She went to the cupboard. She gathered up everything needed to provide order in the upstairs room, and climbed the steep stairs to make it useful. The small, stuffy room was lit only by one candle, which the innkeeper probably left a short while ago, and frost entered the room through a small, ajar window. She closed it, she was cold enough today. She removed ash from the hearth and replaced it with fresh wood. She made a single, though quite wide bed, and left on the table next to it, a pitcher of water as well as a bowl, in which the person who had bought the accommodation could wash himself. She left a potty in the corner behind the screen. She also opened a small wooden closet to check if it was empty. Sometimes distracted guests liked to leave souvenirs, such as the coat that today had saved her from a total disaster. She left everything as it should have been: simple and neat. After all, the inn is not a palace, there sublime elegance was hard to found.

The evening was passing. She was talking and bearing rough jokes. She was serving drinks to the not too happy dwarves and stuffing money for the liquors in the pouch. Mark left them quite late, he didn't even say goodbye. From the far end of the room, she saw him disappear behind the door. She knew that fatigue unceremoniously pulled him to bed. She also dreamed of burying herself in bedding and closing her eyelids. Her eyes pricked from smoke, and in her head she felt roaring and rumbling. She was left alone with two helpers who, rather predictably, were reluctant to work. So she had to struggle alone and chase away those who had far too much alcohol in blood. Fortunately, they gave in and left the inn without unnecessary ceremonies, eagerly informing that they would arrive in the morning, after all, it's not proper to miss long.

Before closing the inn, the door opened with a bang and a drunk young man rolled inside. Lilian immediately recognized Orian's son. Adam stood in the middle and looked around the room.

"Wine!" He screamed.

Lili, seeing how dangerously she was staggering, quickly came out from behind the counter and at the last moment took his arm. He looked up at her with his drunken eyes. She was really fed up with the day and now she also had to deal with him.

"Look at you" he mumbled. "And I thought with father that you had left the city."

Girls in the deeper part of the room looked at her eloquently.

"No, I didn't leave. Come, sit down because you are going to knock everything over here."

"I don't want to sit down!" He broke free.

"Stop yelling," she hissed into his ear.

"But why?" He mumbled. "Don't they know who you are, witch?"

"Enough," she snapped.

She grabbed him by the collar. Without looking at anyone, she dragged him outside.

"I won't let the stray ruin my life," she snapped. - If you come here again, you will feel the hard way how mean a bitch I can be!

He turned to her, wanting to say something, but froze momentarily. The magician's eyes were burning with fire, and her hands were glowing pale blue in the dark. She was pointing her finger at him.

"I'm going to stay here all winter, understand? And if you don't calm down, one of us will not survive this time! And it certainly won't be me!" She hissed.

"Alright. Why are you in a pother over it? I'm leaving now." He stepped back in horror, suddenly sobering up.

Lilian put out the internal flame and went back inside, and Adam wandered wobbly home.

"You're good." One of the guests who was just approaching the exit laughed. "Mark is lucky to hire you. You manage it like no other." He patted the girl's shoulder and left the inn.

The rest also quickly went home. The alewives bustled around the room, collecting glass and other trash left by regulars. In the dim light she noticed a newcomer who was still sitting comfortably in the corner. She came over, locking eyes with him. The fair-haired handsome man was just drinking the rest of the beer. "He is probably the one who will grace me with his presence, fortunately in separate rooms." He handed her a mug. She grabbed it, saying confidently:

"It's probably you who will overnight here?"

"Yes, my dear."

"I will lead you upstairs. The room is ready," she said brusquely after she heard 'my dear'.

"Alright."

She put the dish back on the counter and pointed to the back room. Keeping the lamp, she led the guest to the quarters. Then she handed it to the visitor. She didn't need it, the stairs didn't sink in the dark, but the attic did.

"Good night. If you need anything, lord, please call, I'm staying here. Oh, and there's wood in the fireplace. Would you like me to make a fire?"

"No. I can handle it. Thank you."

She closed the door behind herself.

The maidens were just getting ready to leave when she appeared downstairs. She frowned slightly at the sight of them, she hoped they were gone.

"Hey, newbie," one said. "I don't know who you are, but you won't work here long," she said and pointed her finger at her.

"You think so?" Lilian snapped.

"I'm sure about it."

She didn't feel like coarse discussions with the confident maiden who almost every night offered intimate services to different men. She probably also earned a few pieces of silver today, playing around in the back room or in an alley behind the pub. But Lilian didn't care. It wouldn't be her who would get sick.

"Good night." She waved her hand at them.

Finally she freed herself from the company and ensconced in the safe kitchen. She cleaned herself up carefully and pulled out the Master's letter. She lay down comfortably and read it several times. She studied every letter, flourish, space. What's happening to me? She didn't understand the state she was in. She balanced between pleasant euphoria and extreme fear, as if it had created an inconceivable mixture of strange sensations. Sleep didn't want to stick to her eyelids, even though the moon was high on the firmament. Fortunately, with time, the eyes stood up for themselves and she dozed off, carried by intoxicating dream.

***

The fair-haired man looked at the roll of paper. He walked for a moment around the quarters, then sat on the edge of the bed and in the pale glow of the tallow lamp checked the notes, neatly made with beautiful handwriting. He rumpled yellow and stained paper, heavily excited. The eyes gleamed with excitement, and the lips formed a sly smile. He found what he was looking for, or rather who he was looking for. This someone was almost at his fingertips, the only thing left was to wait for the companion, close the case and quickly return to the castle of his mistress, pleased and willing to share gold. After all, as usual, he would give her what she wanted. He glanced toward the fireplace. A chill ran down his back, cold and unpredictable. He wanted to light the fire but he gave up. Tiredness ordered to curled up in bed sheets and finally rest a little. He folded the letter into a messy cube and put it in the pocket of a leather vest. An elaborate bow and arrow quiver rested in the corner of the room.

CHAPTER III

Morien watched Lily walk away. The further she went, the more she seemed smaller, defenseless and fragile. He controlled his emotions like one controls horses. He rebuked the slightest twitching of the muscle under the skin. He couldn't show that something was going on inside, that he was burning with an internal fever that consumed the last shreds of common sense.

He exchanged kind gazes with the guards and moved towards the mansion. He didn't like the emptiness inside it. Familiarity with anyone for people like him became uncomfortable, something that wasn't said out loud. Yes, as a young man he held a high position, but he paid the highest price for it. He hated loneliness. He was surrounded by those who either feared or worshiped him. He couldn't find a niche in this order, in which he could place himself without risk, find agreement know that he was safe. Maybe he was Lord Master, but also a man, despite the fact that due to office he was deprived of the right to love.

He knew the story of Lilian perfectly. On the desk there were piles of documents, which were sent less than a year earlier from Raghion, and which accurately described not only the girl's skills, but also an analysis of the character, behavior and amount of knowledge she had gained. He was glad that she didn't see them that she wasn't curious and in his absence she didn't poke around the library, looking for money or cheap sensation. Leaving her freedom confirmed his belief that she could be trusted. What could she have thought? Certainly nothing good, nothing that would put him in a good light. However, the more he got to know the magician thanks to the notes and relationships of the people she studied with and influenced, the more he respected her decision to escape from the School. He knew that he was seen as a sinful being, that she only deserved death or submission to those who would like to claim her. Nothing but fears, irrational everywhere, fueled by slanders and guesses. He didn't hide, she impressed him. He remembered the reports perfectly well, the accounts of the peasants written by the hands of scribes, so unusual that it is hard to believe. A man with such talent, not Jerm, was rare. Although also Jerms were weak in comparison to the redhead. She possessed power several times more powerful than his, and milder use came only from ignorance. He knew control was the hardest thing for her. The still unstable aura didn't bode well. After all, the magician accumulating affect is a living force capable of destruction. Magicians were often unaware of the energy that was in them ... for some time. He trembled at what she could have done. Her appearance evoked apparent relief for the eyes and a storm for the senses. His longing senses.

He slammed the door, walked to the library, and with relief, sank into a comfortable chair. He put his hand under his chin and began to stare at the flames merrily popping in the fireplace. It was probably the longest evening he spent alone. He was surrounded by heavy sadness, as if he had been feeding on the emotions that he couldn't release. He pondered the fate that he had to carry, although fighting with thoughts and permanent suspension between the desire to become part of the girl's life and common sense isolation, only aggravated his position. On the one hand he was happy, on the other he hated, and probably the most for this kiss.

"Lilian," he whispered. "What will happen to us ...? Do we even have a chance to occur?"

The sound of heels on the wooden floor made him awake. He recognized the maid by her light and rhythmic gait. The woman opened the door and stuck her head out through the crack.

The lady of the house was looking for the owner of the property, and when she saw him, she stepped inside without closing the door.

"Good evening," she said singingly.

The vision of red hair dissipated instantly. Morien made an incomprehensible gesture, as if to say something, but his lips only managed to bring out a muffled whisper.

"Did you say something?" She dumbfounded.

She was sure it was her fault that she didn't make out.

"Ah ... Hello. Sorry, I was just thinking." This time he spoke as always, clearly and loudly enough that even people standing at the other end of the room knew what he was saying to him.

"Do you need anything?"

He thought for a moment. "Make me some tea before you go to sleep. I will turn in later, I have a few things to do. Yes, a few things..."

"Alright, but please don't stay up too late, you have early lectures in the morning." She bowed respectfully, then left the room.

He followed with his eyes the woman who had been the support of this house for years. Always elegant and polite, enduring the

114

instability of the master, she put a plug in and served hot tea whenever the frost whitened the skin on the knuckles.

"Lectures, lectures, nothing but lectures," he growled under his breath.

Calm mixed with inconceivable sadness was overtaken by an uncontrollable desire to do something unexpected, as if new energy had entered the limbs, fueled by the fact that, in addition to loneliness, he could experience something more exciting in life. He stood up. He looked around, wanting to find the outer garment, but couldn't find it. He couldn't remember where he had left his coat. He never knew that. It's probably the only messy habit that incensed him every time he had to do something immediately. Usually it ended in a rally around the rooms, which resembled a treasure hunt. With the exception that the gold chest turned out to be a gray capot. He went down the stairs. He fastened his eyes on the handrail where the loss was found. The capot dropped carelessly hung and waited for a better time. He reached for the cover and almost ran out of the property. The maid heard the door slam shut. She put down the boiling water, looking out the window. The long shadow that followed the magician informed her that he probably didn't want a hot drink. She knew him well. Tea is tea. She never picked up a tray on which was a cup which still contained some drink. She filled the teapot, set it on the edge of the stove so that the brew didn't cool down. She would carry it in a moment, this time she would take care of more urgent things, after all, even a short absence from home brought a layering of duties.

Morien walked quickly across the square, then caught his breath and approached the gates. His cheeks were decorated by a healthy blush. Fortunately, for his state, he could blame a frost which bit like a mad hound. Sentinels detached from the monotonicity glanced at the newcomer and without a word opened the side gate.

They knew the Archmaster well enough to know that he shouldn't have been disturbed by questions about the purpose of leaving the walls of the School. Not him. He thanked with a nod as the metal gate closed behind him with a quiet moan.

The magician walked a few steps, then stopped and took a deep breath, filling his lungs with a dose of not very fragrant air. After a while he adjusted his coat and, without knowing the purpose of the walk, went forward. His head was filled with a tangle of thoughts completely unclassified and not marked for any direction.

"I suffocate," he said. "I suffocate in this damn small closed world. I need to breathe, something should be done about it. They keep us like cattle, and then we are crazy from this crampedness, we kill each other!" He hissed.

If someone heard him, he would have probably been mistaken for another deranged person due to the amount of power that burst the veins and led to loss of sense. Morien was bursting with anger. He fought the battle, and no matter what the consequences would be, he certainly wouldn't belong to the defeated. Not now!

That evening he was walking around Undercity. He was moving along the walls. The watchful eyes of the City Guards followed his every move, and his fingers ossified from the cold nervously tightened on the hilt of short swords. Morien knew they were waiting for even one wrong move, a spark that would jump from one piece of fabric to another. For the glow of the pupils, which would have been betrayed by the smallest moon glow or darkness thick like goose-blood soup. Time passed quickly. Chill climbed him like a furcate bough. He pressed his hands deeper into his pockets, but he didn't feel the warmth he needed, waves of shivering marked the body. He didn't see too many people in the streets. So no one paid any attention to the man in the cloak with the embroidered school emblem who wandered aimlessly, as if the paths he was following hadn't been exactly the ones he wanted to take.

At one point he stopped. The glow of one of the windows caught the magician's attention. He felt suddenly safe, as if a candle in the window had been whispering that there was nothing to be afraid of. To be able to look deeper into the house, he stood on a stone wall. The wind increased at night didn't give up, it lashed his face with whips twisted from his own hair. He pulled it away and tucked deeper behind the collar. A quaking light in an incomprehensible way allowed him to rest. The memories of his childhood came back, the woman bustling about the room resembled her mother, tender and delicate. Every evening she had tucked him. He had drunk from her mouth the legend of brave wars who killed dragons, and strong dwarves fighting bears. Years had gone by, and he had never had enough, though he had known every story by heart. He flinched as another wave of chills ran through the chilled bones. And he could had gotten on something warmer...

Street lanterns flashed nervously, shaded by the branches of trees moved by the late autumn wind. Ram's Head door was closed.

"Why am I doing this? Why have I come here?" He was asking.

He came instinctively, as if he had been looking for company or awareness of his existence. He walked around the building and was at the back. A small light was on in the kitchen window.

"Lili probably isn't sleeping yet," he mused.

He came closer, finding safety in the dark.

"What am I doing, by Redeemers?"

He stood on tiptoes and discreetly looked inside. The girl was lying on the bed, reading the letter, his letter, which showed signs of burning on the edges. He smiled. She had a calm face, slightly pensive, her eyebrows tightened as if she had been thinking intensely. She looked alternately at the message and into empty space. Then she turned sideways, tucked the wad under the pillow and closed her eyes. She didn't strangle the flame of the lamp. He waited a moment until she slept soundly. By force of will he extinguished the lamp. It was probably the time to go back to the walls of the School, to the home where there is warmth and no guesswork.

There was a teapot on the floor next to the fireplace. He took a cup, filled it and took a good sip, then sat at the desk. The bitter drink moistened his throat pleasantly. With trembling hands, he sought out empty vellum and feather. He sucked his tip for a few moments. So many words started to come to his mind that instead of specifics, there was a buzz consisting of different, mismatched words.

"The easiest way," he whispered to himself. "The easiest way means the best."

Dearest!

There are so many things I'd like to tell you. So much to show and even more. Yesterday's parting caused so much pain that the only solution that came to my mind was to let myself be absorbed by an icy night. I wandered around the city. I have never experienced such loneliness in my life. As if I were touching something completely foreign and fascinating for the first time. My feet carried me to "Ram's Head". I didn't plan it, but I want you to know it. I watched over the dream that lay on your eyelids. I envied it so much. By Redeemers - forgive me. This is stronger. Stronger than the bonds with which I hogtie myself. I'm looking forward to Friday to be able to talk with you, and even if it goes wrong, I just want to see you. I don't want to have egg on my face, but I crave your person above all.

Once again I'm begging you for forgiveness...

Your humble servant,
Morien.

PS. I put out the oil lamp. You have to be careful with fire. Such lamps are so unstable...

He looked at the words he wrote. He was afraid of what was on the gray paper, but he couldn't express it otherwise. He had never composed letters to a woman, at least not the letters that were written in such a tone. Everything seemed new and unexplored. He had the impression that he was a novice and was just starting his education. His relations with wenches usually took on a character of a bodily nature. He never put any emotions in it - it was just sex. He was taught a lot by the School of Mages, or rather mages of the opposite sex and whores. He experienced the sweetness of physical love for the first time many years earlier. When his career began to flourish, he already enjoyed other pleasures, more luxurious and expensive. The courtesans provided ecstasies known only to the rich and influential, but for over a year he was interested only in her. Earlier, Lilian was mentioned in letters. The Baroness wrote that a talented and dangerous sorceress was behind the walls of the School. Evans once said that she would be the future High Priestess of Healers, but Morien didn't take this seriously until the news of the escape was sent. Now his thoughts revolved around the redhead.

He sealed the letter, imprinted the stamp and went to rest in the hope that sleep would end his agony.

The morning burst with the bright sun through the open window. He stood up, quickly put on his clothes, and ran downstairs to see if the maid was bustling around the house.

The girl didn't hide her surprise about his mobilization.

"Here you are, take it to the gate, let the messenger deliver it," he said, pressing the sealed letter in her hand.

She looked at him, bowed and disappeared into the cold darkness of the corridor.

He calmed down a bit. Now he could get onto his duties. He took the apple from the fruit bowl and walked towards the University building.

***

Lili suddenly jumped up. The cook's screams tore the air apart, and at the same time sobered her up so much that she stood dead next to the pallet.

"What's going on?" She yawned slowly and rubbed her eyes with her fists. She tried to wipe away the remnants of the night that settled in the corners. "Look what you've done." She scolded the woman. "You could have left it. I would light it up faster. You should have woken me up."

"Come on... sss, ouch." Erica put her hand in the cold water pot. "You slept so well that I didn't have the heart."

"Since when do you have the heart? I don't believe what you are saying now!" She smiled at the woman who stared at her with the eyes widened in astonishment.

After a while, they both giggled vividly. Pain that just a moment ago had been hollowing the tissues, now was somewhat eased from the coldness of the liquid. Lilian saw a slight expression of relief that was painted on the cook's face. She didn't wait for another exchange, she came over and stretched out her hands. She wanted to see the damaged place.

"Show me."

"Come on. It's not a big deal, just a few bubbles."

"Show me." Lilian grabbed the cook by the elbow.

Erica didn't want to torment Lili with trifles, although she was really suffering. However, she knew the kitchenmaid and knew that if she insisted, even the Redeemers weren't able to argue with her. She gave in and reluctantly put her hand out of the pot.

"Woman, you burned half your palm, how is it possible?" The magician didn't hide her surprise.

The blue vein began to pulsate on the freckled forehead.

"Oh, you know, I poured some oil. The wood is moist, it's hard to light a fire. I helped myself. I always do that." She twisted her lips in a faint grimace that most likely meant discomfort not only physical one.

"Can I trust you?" Lilian leaned so hard towards her that she felt the warmth of her breath on the wrinkled cheek.

"What is this secret?" Erica got very lively, she liked gossip, but that one wasn't it ... although...

"I will ease the pain, but I don't want anyone to know about it ... Are you able to keep the secret? You know, if not, I can always kill you." She winked at her.

Erica sensed something was wrong. Besides, how would have the maiden alleviated this state of thing, a nasty thing that would probably give a hard time for weeks to come? Because it wouldn't scar quickly.

"What are you going to do?" She asked fearfully, still not taking her eyes off the red-haired girl.

"Can I trust you?" The girl repeated, this time emphasizing harder the word 'trust'.

"I think so. Yes ... but what are you going to do? Are you a medic taken out of the Baroness' favor? Wait ..." she thought. "Wait, are you ...?"

"Enough," Lilian interrupted. "Enough, or I won't do anything. And here one have to act. Alright, I will explain." She took a deep breath. She saw that Erica wanted to hear the explanation. "If we left it as it is and only used the ointment, it would start suppurating after some time. It's a nasty burn. There will be the scars that I can't fix. I'm sorry."

The woman was looking with her mouth wide open. She was silent because the words that formed the sentences seemed to scream. In the end she succumbed to the pressure of thoughts and let them flow out of her throat:

"Now I know why Morien comes to us so eagerly after your appearance ..." She replied so quietly that if it wasn't for Lili being so close she would only see the rhythmic movement of her lips.

"Are you ready? I don't want questions." She shut her out.

"You are a magician!"

"Am I to help you or leave and watch you lose your hand slowly? You promised to be silent. I do it because you are good to me. I want to repay you, but only when nothing gets out of these walls."

"I didn't say that I promise. But alright, I won't say anything," she sighed.

She knew it would be hard. One usually want to shout such things. After all, magic is something special and should serve others, and not be hiden under the guise of great unknowns.

"Remember, I will know. You can't hide it."

She had little time. She knew that soon Mark would unceremoniously enter the kitchen, announcing that it was necessary to do this or that. Errands, shopping lists, counting bottles and embracing the pantry were something that always caught his attention, even if the day before the women had cleared up.

She looked carefully at the damage, the jagged and burned fragments protruded at different angles, and the swelling and blisters oddly contorted the knuckles. She was aware that if she failed, the woman would be a cripple. In fact, she was surprised that she endured it extremely calmly. She would have probably wriggled like an eel, while wailing like a wounded deer.

Lilian focused. A cleansing aura flowed over her in a blue mist. Nice coolness gently enveloped the skin warmed-up by the room hotness. She grabbed the cook's hand and placed the other hand on it so that it didn't touch the wound directly, but was above it. Erica parted her lips. The girl looked like an apparition, delicate and at the same time strong, completely unlike the one she had talked to before the few breaths. She didn't have to wait long for healing effects. The room seemed to tremble and swirl, and from among the knuckles of the magician, began to emerge thin ribbons of flickering light, which tightened on the painful places, touched them lightly, and then entered them. The throbbing pain eased, and a pleasant tingling combined with unbearable itching irritated the affected skin continuity. Instinctively, she reached out to scratch herself, but she revived in time and gave up her desire. She felt better with every beat of her heart, and fatigue caused by weakness went away. It only lasted a few moments, though time seemed to drag on endlessly. When the girl finished the process, she moved away and wiped her sweaty forehead with relief. The short act of healing was weakened the vitality to such an extent that she fell on a stool and rested her head on her fists.

"Done," she panted. "We've gotten the worst over."

Rhythmic steps broke the silence that hung between the women. The host entered the room. He opened the door with such force that if it wasn't for the solid hinges, the door would probably be left in his hands. Both women first looked at each other, and then at the newcomer, who showed an extremely strong excitement.

"Here's the letter." He handed Lilian the scroll. "What's going on here? Open the window. One can die from this closeness."

They exchanged mouth twisting.

"It's from the fire," they said almost together.

The innkeeper raised an eyebrow.

"Alright, I will open it." Erica swayed her hips and walked over to the window to struggle with the door handle.

"Good. Lili, read and reply quickly, the messenger is waiting. He said he wouldn't leave until he got the letter. Then immediately to work. And you woman, why are you fooling around and keeping your hand so strangely? Come on, look alive! Start on preparing meat. Oh, I almost forgot. Have you seen our guest?"

"No, not yet today." She shook her head vigorously. "I led him upstairs and went to sleep. He probably hasn't woken up yet. He looked tired."

"Yes, probably yes. Alright, get to work. Then one of you must go to the market." He waved his hand as he left.

"Remember, you promised." She turned to Erica.

The woman was just looking at the healed hand. She stood in a shaft of bright light shining through the dirty window. The hand looked good even though there was pink tissue resembling transparent jelly at the site of injury. After a while she looked up and said under her breath:

"Thank you. I won't tell anyone. I couldn't."

Lili raised her mouth corners in a half smile. She was recovering slowly after an exhausting activity.

"You're welcome," she muttered.

She ran her finger across the spine of the letter. The structure of the paper seemed so perfect, smooth. She didn't feel any lumps or bumps under her pad. She changed the place, moved to a more comfortable bed, cradled her legs and settled down. She knew who the letter was from. Morien wrote tenderly. Nobody had called her "dearest" yet, she smiled. She saw the care he had been making a message with.

"He was worried about the fire ..." She thought. "Oh, and I forgive you," she whispered.

She folded the news and left the room. Mark kept the ink under the counter. She didn't ask for permission. She found the inkwell and pen, and the innkeeper didn't object. He arranged the bottles in an even row, while counting them. Lili returned to the kitchen and sat down at the table. Unfolded clean parchment and reached for stationery. The cook looked puzzled or rather surprised.

"You can write, read, you are a magician. What else will surprise me with, little Lili?" She asked.

"With nothing, I'm ordinary."

"I'm afraid you're not." She came closer. "You know," she continued. "Morien has been coming to us for several years, but he never paid attention to any maiden," They walked around him, talked, tempted, and he didn't care. He is a damn handsome man. I wish I wasn't so old," she giggled. "But that's not the point. You appeared and suddenly as if by magic, this man sees someone, smiles, asks for a second beer, comes the next day. He never did that." She sat next to her. "You must be unique. I don't know whether to be afraid of you or not, but what I saw a moment ago scared me more than made me happy."

"You're a peach and thank you for telling me, but I don't like watching someone suffer. I have a gift, so I will help." She put her hand on Erica's cheek. "You must know that I'm not here for no reason, but I don't want to talk about it." How to put it? It's too personal. I didn't want to come forward before anyone, but Morien got my number. It was thanks to the power and strength of his aura that I lost consciousness. If it wasn't for that, no one would have found out, but I would never have known him. Well, I'm glad, because on the other hand, he raises warm feelings that are so foreign to me."

"That's good, but remember. He is an influential man. If you have a guilty conscience, he can help you erase them, although I admit that sometimes he seems to be a little crazy." She twisted her lips in smile. "No more talk. You write and I'm going to deal with goulash."

The girl began to correspond.

Dearest!

At the beginning I'm begging you not to ask for forgiveness. It makes me feel even more awkward. You are fascinating. I can't wait for the next conversation. I would like to learn so much from you and ask so many things that I don't know where to start. You awakened in me emotions I had never experienced before. I'm afraid of this influx of tenderness. Whenever I close my eyes and imagine your face. Make me stop or I'll go crazy.

Your humble servant,
Lilian

She put down the pen.

"I hope I won't scare him with this exuberance," she sighed and went towards the main hall of the inn, where the same messenger as before sat at the counter and sipped a cup of unknown drink.

"Here you are." She handed him the sealed letter.

He drank up, bowed and disappeared behind the door.

Mark shook his head and chased away the image of the festively dressed Lilian. Ever since he saw her like this, he couldn't stop thinking about her, she was in his head the whole time. He kept repeating her name in his mind, which made him unwise and he broke some clay mugs. The alewives scowled at him. He was rarely in such a state, if he ever was.

The night guest finally came down and asked for breakfast. He turned out to be the only one at this time, so the girls were fighting for his interest for a reason. Not only did he look wealthy, but also his face seemed temptingly delightful, as if there had been no muscles and bones under the skin, but smooth marble. Perfectly sculpted chin, strong jaw and unscarred cheeks. In addition, the locks of light hair, softly falling on strong arms. It was hard to resist what was so rare.

It was Lili who had to go to the marketplace. She was glad because sitting with women who constantly lavished digs and stupid lines wasn't pleasant. And, although she was resilient, she preferred to avoid it even at the price of freezing her nose. She wrapped herself in a coat, took a large wicker basket, a handful of silver, a shopping note, and disappeared behind the door.

The morning greeted her with biting frost. The ground was shining with ice crystals, it turned out to be hard and slippery. The girl treaded cautiously, but was glad that she wouldn't get her shoes dirty. The market resonated with hundreds of noises, whistles and calls from traders. Everywhere was a blaze of colorful goods, materials and spices. Their pungent smell mixed with the not very pleasant smell of fish and meat.

"It is cold, thanks to the Redeemers," she thought. "Otherwise, the stench would have even knocked me out."

Shopping went smoothly. Here and there she had to haggle for better prices. The use of personal charm had always worked best on men, women were unlikely to give in, but mostly she got what she wanted. "Mark will be glad that I haven't spent the whole sum. Hm, maybe he will even give me a silver coin? Some new shoes would be useful," she sighed in her mind.

The day passed surprisingly quickly. Her duties absorbed her and made time fly like a flash of lightning. The morning guest disappeared from the inn, and in the late afternoon the hall was filled with thirsty and hungry regulars. Kindness paid off, small tips buzzed in the pouch. She was beginning to become a favorite of the steaming mob.

***

Morien, tired from the lack of sleep and boring classes, was turning the sealed letter from Lila with his fingers. Alchemy and lectures in this field were very difficult for the acolytes. Although he tried to explain as simply as possible each time, they were as if in cahoots and didn't understand anything. This made the patient man so frustrated that he often wanted to slam the door and leave. He didn't have a scientific mind, but he gave in to the pleas, especially of the novices, to give additional classes on this subject. Of course, he seemed to like it, but in spirit he cursed the youngsters.

He crumpled paper. Why he didn't open, he didn't know. There were several other messages on the desk, including from the Baroness, but he didn't look in that direction. Alvena wrote about the same things. Probably her cousin, the king, didn't like continuous nitpicking as well. He frowned as a maid slipped into the library.

"Would you like to eat something, lord? You didn't eat much today," she said melodiously and stared at the magician who was traveling somewhere else in his mind.

Sobered up by the melody of her voice, he glanced at the woman. She stood with her arms folded on her stomach, with that kind-hearted expression on her face. She had worked for him a couple of years, she sweetened with motherly care, although she was a relatively young person.

"My dear," he began. "I have no appetite."

"Lord, you have to. If you have any problems, talk to the Archmage."

"Where did this idea come from?"

"For the last several days, please forgive me, lord, you are so absent." She lowered her eyes. "You don't eat much, you sleep restlessly and wander around the house."

"My dear Greta, I'm fine, don't worry. I get to know an aspect of life I have never known. I just have to get used to it and believe me, it's a really pleasant state."

"You fell in love." The maid's eyes glowed in the dim light.

He felt her sticking that words into his heart like a needle. He didn't think it would hurt so much. He also didn't think that the feeling was painted on his face.

"Oh. It's not like that ... It's alright," he sighed longly. "Bring garlic bread and good sweet wine." Then he sent her away with a gesture of his hand.

She bowed and left the library.

He opened the letter with one jerk, the paper rustled. Lilian wrote in a small, delicate handwriting, and each letter was neat. She had to practice a lot. Such a character testifies well to man. Accuracy betrayed strength and methodology. He knew that knowing mages by the way they hold the pens and how strongly they create individual letters is somewhat crucial. Carelessness equals floppy, and this cannot be tolerated, not if she has a gift that rampages.

He leaned back and delved into reading. Delightful words, no accusations or anger, just calmness. He could have do that endlessly. He felt a great desire for dwarven beer. Just like that. Saliva in the mouth took on a dense form, let him know that it was worth gargle with something and it didn't necessarily have to be a sweet, homemade drink. He looked up from the message. He stared at the window view.

Greta appeared with a meal placed on a silver, richly decorated tray, on which stood a plate with bread and a mug of drink. She found the master again in a romantic mood.

"I see you are in a good mood," she said, seeing a smile.

At the same time, she put food on the table.

"Yes, my dear, I am."

"That woman is lucky." She curtsied and was about to leave when he stopped her.

"Wait a second!" He called out.

"Anything else, lord?" she became interested.

"Come over."

She did what he wanted, though she was slightly surprised.

"Please, don't tell anybody what's going on, okay?"

"Lord. I wouldn't dare ... Everyone has the right to ..."

He interrupted her:

"Not everyone, Greta! It's such a code, we are not allowed to do different things. You know it well, so I will be glad if you keep it secret. It's for the best. The less they know, the healthier they are."

"Lord," she whispered so softly that he could barely hear the voice. "I know the code, I learned it, but I don't agree with it. Your private affairs are safe."

"Thank you my dear. You can leave."

He ate. He didn't know if it tasted. For some time, everything that he took to his mouth had the same note ... or insipidness. Without expressiveness, without those stimuli that accompany tasting favorite dishes. He couldn't sit still again. He began to stroll here and there. The library seemed too cramped, the corridor too narrow. The legs asked for a walk themselves.

"If it goes on like this, I'll end up as a drunkard mage," he thought as he felt desire for a drink again. "Eh, why can women affect men so much?"

He went downstairs quietly. The corridor was illuminated by one lamp, the rest was turned off. The half-light of the house protected him well. He reached for his coat and left the residence without putting it on. It was only when he was outside that he threw the capot over his back and let a damp chill wrap him. After a few steps from the threshold, he remembered that he hadn't done something. He stopped, raised his head, and for a moment he watched the stars shimmering in the navy blue sky. Letters. It was they which bothered him. "Yes, they are probably urgent. I will read them when I come back. They can wait. Why should I worry about the worthless messages? Tomorrow. Today I have to cool my anxiety."

"By Redeemers, may the Archmage not blame me for the frequent leaving the headquarters. Recently, I have not asked for permission to leave the school more often," he worried in advance.

He could feel something in his bones and under his skull that niggled him. Foreign vibrations, which certainly didn't belong either to the discharges of his power or to the ones that constantly enveloped this place. Thick and unidentified, they irritated like malicious insects.

The sentries didn't ask questions, they opened the side gate. He thanked and slid the hood over his face. The cold night pinched the cheeks, the slippery cobblestone slowed down the march a bit, but he wasn't in a hurry, although the inner voice whispered something different. The time that would pass before he put his hand on the door handle of the "Ram's Head" would be a time of sweet waiting for that was was good. So he cooled his thoughts. He focused on what was most important.

There was a nice, lively atmosphere in the pub. People laughed, dwarven workers sang, and the maidens sat on clients' laps and poured drinks from large pitchers. He didn't see Lili. Mark bowed low. From the innkeeper's expression, he knew that he expected much today, but certainly not his. Of course, the place he usually occupied was empty. He respected this loyalty, although sometimes it seemed to him a bit absurd, especially since he really didn't care about a particular seat. He would have drunk beer even at the counter, but the host insisted on keeping a privileged corner for him. So that piece of the world belonged only to the magician.

One of the maidens immediately saw him and ran to say hello. They already knew that they could only dream about being his girlfriend, but they liked to be in the company of someone who didn't puke or farted, laughing at the stench of farts.

"Hello, Lord Master. This is not Friday. You probably missed our company?"

"Yes," he replied. "I haven't dreamed of anything else today." He was searching Lili with his eyes.

"Do you want me to serve what you always ordered?"

"Yes," he sighed, unhappy that he didn't see his favorite.

Anetha attending Morien was glad that he didn't asked for that little ginger trollop. Maybe she would have received a piece of gold, or at least a copper coin, it was always another coin in the purse. And above all, she was happy that she could do something for him.

She didn't hide that she had long followed the white-haired guy with her eyes. Which, however, went unnoticed by him.

Mark left the main room and went to the kitchen.

Lilian sat squatting in front of the stove and tried to control the fire.

"What's wrong with this stove?" He asked.

"I don't know. It smokes and goes out. Either the chimney is blocked or I'm not sure anymore, because the wood is dry."

"You have a guest. Anetha has already taken care of the service, but I think he would be happier if you went there."

She opened her mouth in surprise.

"But it's not Friday today."

"Did he missed dwarven beer?"

"I don't know." She shrugged, trying to hide her agitation.

She was glad that she would see again the face nice to her heart. Much time hadn't passed since the last meeting, but enough to miss.

"Go now," he chased her out of the kitchen.

Sad, he sat down by the hearth, fumbled with a poker in a glowing oven.

Lili burst into the room, nervously neatening the hair. Immediately she felt a burst of power, and due to the multitude of sparks she felt dizzy. She had to hold on to the door frame so she wouldn't fall. She was late, Anetha was just handing him beer and was grinning like a squirrel. He thanked, but when he saw Lili, his eyes lit up.

"Hello, my dear."

The alewife snorted. However, she gave way to the girl and returned to her duties, but every now and then she glanced over her shoulder, checking if the guest had everything needed.

"Hello." She crossed her arms over her stomach. "I didn't expect…"

"I couldn't sit at home, I wanted to drink…"

There was silence. They looked at each other, drooled over, and if it wasn't for restraint, it would probably end in something indecent.

The innkeeper just returned from the back room and, having noticed what was happening, approached them imperceptibly. He broke the silence that was lost between two lovers. "Ah, those youngsters." He nudged Lilian's hand conveniently unintentionally.

A good trick to control the situation. A gesture that called the feverish emotions to order.

"I see you have already been served?" she asked.

"Yes, thank you. Sit down please." He put his hand on the bench beside. "You wanted to talk. I'm at your service."

Lili reddened, her cheeks stinged, but she complied with his request and settled down comfortably.

"I don't know where to start."

"Well then maybe." He put a hand to his chin. "From the beginning?"

"Very funny." She rolled her eyes.

"Yeah, funny."

She knew that several jealous pairs of eyes followed her every move. She was balancing on the brink of betrayal and behaving like an embarrassed maiden.

"Well, maybe ... from that. How long have you been a master?" She muttered.

"Excellent question. Let me think. For about ten years I have held the position of Lord Master. It happened unfortunately because I was an exceptionally clever student. Apparently, I went to school when I was five years old. I graduated with honors. When about twenty-seven springs passed, my hair began to change color and I'm such now. For a year I was a teacher and taught the kids how to brew simple mixtures. Then one of the Lords died and I was chosen. There's nothing special about it. I was just lucky."

She smiled with the corner of her mouth.

"That's a nice story."

"No, sweetheart." He moved his lips to her ear. She flinched. "It's a sad story that deprives the magician of what makes people have a purpose in life." He straightened up.

He turned his face away from her and took a long sip of beer.

She was confused. He clearly made free with her, strived for physical contact, and didn't care what others would say. The problem is that if his superiors had found out about such a thing, he could have been in real trouble, but he obviously didn't care.

"Now is my turn?" She whispered.

He confirmed without taking his mouth from the mug. When he sated his thirst, he put it back on the table, leaned back more comfortably and said:

"Where were you born, specifically in what part of this nasty place?"

"I lived with my mother by the walls, in the agricultural part. We had a small field that didn't give a large harvest. As a small child, I treated animals for fun until someone noticed and reported it to the relevant services. They came a few sunrises later and locked me: first at the House of Magicians, then at the School of Magicians in the capital. I stayed here for a short time, maybe a week, but I don't remember anything about it. They directed me there, because apparently my magic exceeded the competence of the local masters," she whispered.

There were doubts swirled in her head. She didn't know if she was doing good to mention the past bluntly. On the other hand, she wanted to tell it someone. To let on in faint hope that the heaviness, which was constantly boiling over at the height of the young heart, would let go and then she would feel something that she would successfully call relief.

"Why did you escape?"

She wanted to scold him lightly. In the conversation he wandered into the areas that stung her soul with a painful thorn. She still hadn't reconciled herself to the loss of her parent. Just thinking about it made her suffer.

"Trust me." He unceremoniously hid her hand in his. "If I wanted to betray you, I would have done it a long time ago."

"For mother," she moaned, not in terror, but in pain she felt when Morien's touch burned the skin.

"That was the only reason?"

She nodded becoming purple.

"Unusual," he sighed.

A dense atmosphere hung between them. The magician suddenly seemed absent, scanning the surroundings with eyes with strongly reacting pupils. She didn't get it. After a while he got tense, and the touch became stronger, almost crushing knuckles.

"Let's go from here. Immediately!" he shouted.

"But Mark ..."

"Come!"

She jumped up and followed the visitor. She had mixed feelings about her behavior. After a moment she stopped and said over her shoulder so that only Mark could hear.

"I owe you."

"Go now." He frowned in a grimace hard to guess.

Outside, the chill had increased since he left the residence. Morien felt this clearly, so he wrapped himself close, looking at the person standing next to him, who had no outer clothing. He didn't hesitate, he took off his coat and threw it over Lilian's shoulders. He knew that he would probably pay for it with a bad cold, but he didn't care.

"What happened?" She asked and looked around. "What do you want to tell me?"

"Come on," he urged.

"No." She chattered her teeth. "I won't let you get sick."

"It's not important now." He kicked his heels.

"You're talking nonsense." She threw off the cover and shoved it in his hand. "I'll be right back. But don't go anywhere."

"How could I dare?" He smiled heartily.

Lilian disappeared back into the Ram's Head. After a while she stood next to him, wrapped not only in a thick coat, but also in a shawl at which she fumbled frantically. She tried to tame the folds and bundle them so that they didn't hurt or disturb.

He pulled her lightly with him. She quickly realized that the direction he was taking didn't lead to the School, but to the city walls. She followed the magician's footsteps. She wanted to say something, but the meaningful silence wasn't good for idle chats, so she kept her mouth closed.

When they reached the watchtowers, Morien stopped, then pushed the door leading to the dark interior. He nervously checked his surroundings again. After a fraction of breath, he grabbed the girl by the bosom, pulled deeper and slammed the door, which creaked at hinges from rust accumulated over the years. They were surrounded by a damp curtain of darkness, immediately lit by a blue spark dancing on the top of the magician's hand. Now she could see the disgust of this place in all its glory. The moldy and blackened with mycelium walls glistened lightly with freezing water. Lilian's pupils narrowed and was now reminiscent of the cat's troubled eyes. She waited in silence for what he was to communicate. She didn't hide that the silence surrounding them disturbed so much that the skin on her forearms took the form of bump structures. She trembled not only at the thought of hairy creatures lurking in hiding, but also at the vision of what Morien was busily suppressing.

"There are spies in the city," he said unexpectedly. "They are probably the Baroness' people. I hear their thoughts all the time. I got a letter today, foolish of me. I haven't read it!"

She got scared, her heart pounded and she gasped for breath. She wanted to scream and at the same time escape from the claustrophobic narrow tower. To disappear somewhere in the depths of the forest that surrounded this damn city just to never return.

"And if they heard me?! By Creators! I gave myself away!" She groaned.

"They didn't hear, don't worry. I limit access to you. You are a careless person, you constantly spread with the ribbon what is your greatest asset. Sparks of magic dance with your every step like silver bells, but it's alright. I have already learned to neutralize these escalations. By the way ..." He took a deep breath. "Have you had an unusual guest recently in a tavern? Someone you saw for the first time? Looking at the confusion in the 'Ram's Head'?"

"A well-dressed man bought the accommodation yesterday. I don't know how long he will stay here, Mark didn't mention anything. I only prepared the apartment."

"What did he look like?"

"Normal, in fact he was a little better dressed than others. I didn't see him in the morning, but I know he left things because the key didn't hang on the nail at the counter. He has it with him.

"Did you talk with him?"

"Only formally. I cleaned the room, then led him to it, that's all."

She was shivering, but not from cold. This terror set the delicate body in motion.

"Alright," he sighed. He pulled her close and put his arm around her. The blue glow blurred when he stopped controlling its creation. "You have to block your thoughts." He put his lips to her ear. "You can, right? Why am I asking? You can."

"Yes."

"Act normally. We have to be careful. I will stop writing. I don't want interception, even though I know the messengers are fast and quite clever. Years of experience mean that also they learn some tricks. But I didn't want to talk about it. I will start to visit the "Ram's Head" more often, I will inform Mark about it. I hope he will understand. It is a matter of state importance, we cannot reveal it, although ..." He thought about it. "Drinking too much beer may seem suspicious to some people. I can always lie that I drown my sorrows, after all, the fate of Lord Master is hard to bear, isn't it?" He smiled broadly.

He felt her piercing him with crystal gaze.

He hugged his cheek to her cheek, chill irritated smoothly shaved skin. Lilian felt Morien tremble. Was he afraid or was he trembling with excitement or sexual arousal? She pulled out a hand warmed with wool and put it on his face. He received the caress with a deep sigh.

"You're so good."

"I'm not."

"I'm not afraid for myself, but for you. During these few days I got more than from those women I met in my life."

She frowned at these words.

"You cause that I can't sleep, eat and think about anything else. I don't know what you did, what this damn magic is, but you possessed me."

"Don't say that," she suppressed a moan.

"But I want to say that! By Creators!" He almost choked on his words. "I must not feel such things, now I understand why."

He kissed her as if what he had just done had been supposed to be the last thing he would do in this life. She moaned slightly, succumbing to the pressure of the force he put into the act of body fusion. He kissed hard and fervently, not only focused on the lips swollen with excitement, but also the eyelids, neck and cheeks. A hail of brushes obscured her perception. She zoned out for a moment, carried by the heat that flowed down with a sudden attack of tenderness. She got weak at the knees, and a pleasant tingling appeared at the height of the small of his back. She could succumb here and now. Allow lifting of the skirts of her dress and indulge in passion in this hole separated from the world.

"Enough," he said desperately, pushing her away.

He knew that if he didn't stop now, it could end in a well-known and intoxicating way.

"Not yet," he whispered in his mind. "Not yet."

"Wonderful, I want more," she sighed and put her head on his chest.

The magician's vibrating heart was pounding as hard as hers.

"My little witch." He hugged his face to her red hair. "We have to consider what we do. There is so much fire in me that I can't control. You don't make it so easy for me."

"Shhh, dearest," she said. "Everything will be fine you'll see."

"You better be right. Now let's go, the damp and musty stuff makes me sick.

Winter was coming. The first snowflakes danced in the air. They looked at them and then at each other. They knew that this heralded a long rest time that would spread its fingers on the inhabitants of the city, but this peace wasn't for them. They had to survive the season, and when a frost decreased, say goodbye and let put down what was in their hearts. This relationship had no right to exist.

"It will be a long winter," he said, when he saw the wobbling sign of "Ram's Head" in the distance.

"Yes, sweetheart, our longest."

He watched the gates close for a moment. They parted, but fortunately not forever, but for a moment, which like eternity stretched and made clock beats so flexible that if he was able, he would have cut them with scissors, cursing endless time spent without her.

He burst into the residence, breathless and sweaty.

Tumult and vigorous strokes of heels woke the servants, who, however, didn't poke their noses outside the quarters. They guessed what had suddenly touched their employer. Strange behavior seemed suspicious, but in his presence they kept their tongues between their teeth, keeping up appearances.

Darkness enveloped the library. He softened it, lighting a few lamps that were close to the desk. He dug through the paperwork piled up on the counter. It must have been here somewhere. It had to! He probably misplaced it in this uncontrolled chaos he had recently made, unable to order documents. It's not him. It is a completely different, strange, stupid man who has taken over this generally orderly and pedantic self. He felt the rough envelope with a perfectly stamped seal. In the dim light it looked as if the Baroness had burned a sign in a bloody puddle. He shuddered. As always, she wrote in very small and compact handwriting. The oblong letters merged into a gloomy whole.

Dear Lord Master,

Thank you for actively participating in the quest to track down the magician: Lilian Vaal. I allowed myself to take certain steps to track down the fugitive faster. For too much time has passed since this event, and this causes tension in the Magician Schools to rise. The authorities seem to be powerless, and the tribe takes advantage of it, which, I must admit, doesn't fill with optimism, but to the point. I have sent spies to each of the kingdom's largest cities, which will stop at strategic locations. They will stay in constant contact with both the Municipal Police and the Archmage of the School. You will get all the information from your supervisor. So, as you guessed, I do you out of further investigation, because for several weeks I haven't received any report, and I don't intend to tolerate it. Of course, any news about the runaway will be taken into account.

Regards,

Baroness Alvena.

He threw the message furiously on the floor. The letter flew a few meters, then gently sat on the oak floor. He wanted to step on it, set it on fire, and trample it again so that there was no dust left. Now he had to concentrate, find spies, confuse them, maybe cut their thin throats. And if that didn't help, show them the road that would make them astray - to the mountains, where lurked not only wild beasts, but also bands detached from society, preying on travelers. Feeding not only on fear but also on the content of purses. And yet he never acted against the code. Without a murmur he bent his neck and implemented the outlined laws. He knew something was going on. The anxiety at school thickened the atmosphere, people whispered in dormitories, during meals, in the university yard. He knew he had to fight for his own. But how to do it?

Winter surrounded them with frosty beauty. Iced the river and made faces flushed. The snow was falling with thick flakes, wrapping with white stinging in eyes, which was graying quickly anyway, trampled by hundreds of feet. Apart from the weather, not much had changed. The city was buzzing like a beehive but somehow more drowsy, slowed down with icy sidewalks, and earlier dusk. The stalls were opened only for a moment, necessities were transported in carts from district to district, and only dwarves didn't leave their district, enjoying dried meat and thick beer whitened with goat milk and honey. Apparently, this drink was rich in everything needed to survive in the worst period. It warmed up and provided the most necessary ingredients. Bearded sponges treated cold as time to celebrate and in addition to stuff already large bellies. People who cautiously filled pantries didn't starve, while those who were poverty-stricken existed on the edge of the megacity, counted the days as if they had been to materialize into bread.

Lili lost herself in the imposed duties, and on her back she felt the eyes of colleagues as well as of Mark, who had observed her for some time with a face hard to understand. Morien, although he had promised to visit, didn't show up often. With time, he returned to the Friday routine, which frightened more than the coldness that was coming from him at that time. He drank a pint, then walked out, leaving behind only the scent of musky water.

She wanted to talk to him, bring him outside the tavern and cuddle her cheek into his itchy coat. She wasn't sure anymore whether the words in the tower were still true or if he just had wanted to deceive her. A lot of doubt poured into the brain, and the young magician fought with them and constantly confirmed her belief that it was true and she had to survive the period of silence. She was furious when the knowledge of the Whisper Speech became an insurmountable threshold for her, and she should had understood it, assimilated and let it absorb her a long time ago. It would have been simpler then. Unfortunately, she needed a teacher, and the only one who came to her mind was just drinking his favorite drink with a stony face and a dull, colorless gaze hidden behind a curtain of white eyelashes.

She fought. Distraction made her small hands tremble, whereby she was unable to count the number of broken dishes. Mark stared at her clumsiness, without a word put a slightly bruised mug under the counter. She understood that it was to be used to collect fees for damage caused. So often she reached into her pocket for copper coins. Tips melted away. Whenever the opportunity arose, she caught the cane that, activated by touch, trembled under her fingertips. She threw the spacious coat over her back and indulged in the pleasure of long walks. Most often she went out of the city, where she could rest without fear of the scolding eyes of her co-workers. Morien's melancholy didn't work well for her. She had the impression that the sadness of her beloved fooled her and deprived of rational perception. She was bogged down in it like in a swamp and desperately fought for every breath. She came back from walks, tormented and cold. Then she sit a long time by the fire to warm up the stiff body. She languished. Dark rims around the eyes and unhealthy pallor spoiled the once joyful face.

The old cook looked at her with concern.

"Dear," she said one evening, when her duties were long done and she could go home safely. "What's wrong?" She crumpled a rag in her hands twisted from old age. "I can't look at you in such a state ..."

"Nothing, Erica, don't worry about me." The girl brushed a sadly falling lock of red hair from her cheek.

"He gave you the brush off, right?" She sat next to the hearth and took her hands. "I used to love too, it was so long ago."

"No!" Moaned Lilian. "It's not like that ... I ... I don't know what I feel anymore, I only know that I'm scared and Morien too. Lately he said there were spies in the city. Apparently we even hosted one. Did you know that?"

"Spies? And why would they be here?" The woman was clearly surprised.

"You're so clueless!"

"Is this about you?" She raised her eyebrows questioningly.

"Yes, Erica." She was angry. "About me. You know who I am. The Baroness is afraid of me, so she sent these worms to scent the clues. I just have no idea if there are more spies."

The cook looked at her in disbelief. She didn't reveal the secret, although it was really painful.

"Are you saying the double guards around the school and these, as you called them, "spies" are your fault?"

"Well, kind of."

"By Redeemers," she whispered. "What did you do to them, girl?! Except that you escaped?"

"I'm one of those "magicians". I hope you understand."

"No, I don't understand or I'm too old to understand."

"Erica." Lili looked at her wrinkled face. "I carry more secrets than you can comprehend.You can believe that if someone wants to try to capture me, I will unleash hell. I haven't used magic for a long time. Alright, now I lied. Sometimes to light the hearth, but mum's the word." She put a finger to her lips and smiled wryly. "I don't know what will happen, I'm afraid for myself, because accumulated power is as dangerous for my opponents as it is for me."

Erica slowly began to understand the seriousness of the words.

"I don't have anyone to confide in. It's hard for me," she sobbed. "The only person who could help me is Morien, but he is silent. He comes here with his indifference, and I bleed inside, as if someone plowed my soul countless times."

"Don't worry, baby, I won't give you up for sure." Erica hugged her and stroked her head.

Mark entered the kitchen, with his face pink from drinking wine. He leered with the watery eyes at two women curled up by the fire.

"What are you doing here? Erica, go home! Lili to the room! And stop, fools, stare at me like that, or I will spur you with the broom."

"Screw you, lout," the cook gasped.

He just rolled his eyes and staggered out.

Sad silence surrounded the women. Neither one nor the other wanted to delve into the topic anymore. What they meant was said when the innkeeper burst into the kitchen. Erica in the last gesture grabbed Lilian's chin and kissed her on the forehead, then heavily got up, groaned and returned to what was still waiting for her. And these were only cups that she had to put back so that those maidens that would come first in the morning could take them under the counter. Lili, having put her hands on the knees, was sitting by the fire for a long time. Red tongues were jumping cheerfully from one piece of wood to another. She was staring at the dance of flames, and for the first time in a while blushes crawled onto her cheeks. It is not known whether from the heat that was hitting her or relief, which thanks to the conversation with Erica slightly warmed the stony heart. She rose slowly, adjusted her dress and straightened up. She inhaled the smell of the kitchen. She put a smile on her face, returned to the room, and pretended that everything was fine.

A man appeared in the tavern door. She knew his face, she had to have seen him, but when? However, her gaze hung on what he had on his back. Subject quite characteristic. It struck the observer with intricacy and attention to the smallest detail - a reflex bow made of bent and richly decorated wood. Few could afford such a thing. She realized that this was the same gentleman she had once prepared a room for, in which he had stayed a good few days. He had eaten and drunk with virgins, often succumbing to their games. He couldn't belong to the poor, probably his purse was full of gold, so the alewives made a point of nipping off something for themselves. Inwardly she admitted to herself that his face, not sunburnt and not damaged by drunkenness, could be find attractive despite the harshness and coldness that came from his constantly narrowed eyelids.

Darius looked around. He spent a lot of time outside, his legs and knuckles ached, and he felt he had a cold. He knew many ways to deal with it and one of them was smiling broadly at him. One doesn't reject an opportunity if it pushes itself before others. He nodded at the dark-haired girl, which ran up with eyes glittering with excitement. He leaned towards her slightly and said a few words to her ear. She nodded obediently. They were whispering something to each other, then she disappeared into the back room.

Mark watched the scene in silence, but recognized the visitor and indicated an empty seat. In response, he received twisting of his mouth, which probably meant approval.

The archer settled down comfortably, pulled the weapon off his back, and put it down carefully so as to be able to see not only his property, but also those who, according to him, were too close.

A maiden emerged from the back room, carrying a bottle of wine and a glass. Lilian breathed a sigh of relief, though she felt the stranger look at her with growing interest. Or maybe it was just her imagination? Mark called her.

"Will you take care of the guests? I'm going home, I think I drank too much wine today." He leaned toward the girl who felt the acid fumes of alcohol. She put a finger on the superior's forehead and pushed him away flirtatiously.

"Oh yes, my good lord. You have had enough."

"I have never had enough of you," he croaked. He probably wanted to show in this way how skillful lover he was. He sobered up right away, however, because he realized how he behaved and what he said. He stiffened and waved his hand as if it had meant nothing. "I'm coming. And this there, this man." He leered at the newcomer. "He'll probably want to spend the night again." See if the room is in good order. I can't trust these new cleaning women, they do everything sloppily, and they want to be paid for it," he grumbled. "He recently praised the service and accommodation, and he left a lot of gold. Take care of him. Come on," he hiccupped.

He passed the employee and staggering, disappeared into the back of the inn. Before she knew, he was coming back, grappling with the thick capot. He waved goodbye and left the tavern in Lilian's hands.

She nodded at the girl, put her behind the bar, and went upstairs. Not oiled hinges creaked as she entered. She saw a small room fully prepared, probably one of the employees cleaned it earlier, she thought. She had nothing to do but find oil for the locks. This creak caused goosebumps. "Why didn't our "magician" do this? I will ask him tomorrow morning. He must repair faults."

Finding oil wasn't an easy task, the cupboard with tools was locked, and she couldn't find the key anywhere. So she used lard.

"It will be enough till tomorrow," she sighed.

The evening passed peacefully. As Mark had predicted, the newcomer expressed a desire to stay overnight. She watched him carefully. He gestured too smoothly. There was something disturbing about it, the softness of the movements resembled a balanced dance. She knew that this is how mercenaries and the Shadows behave, who, thanks to many hours of training, mastered the art of noiseless moving. Contrary to appearances, he didn't arouse fear, but only curiosity. The uninitiated saw in him only a wealthy traveler, who, exhausted by the road, sat down for a moment to, next day, get carried away by another trip. She sensed the trick. Information about the Baroness' spies drilled channels in her brain that, fueled by fear, now became canyons burning with uncertainty.

When she handed him the room key, she smiled slightly. The fair-haired man thanked, stared at her, and then walked away. Frozen, she stood for a long time, but when the door slammed cut the air with the groan of weakly oiled hinges, she came to her senses, as if someone had poured a bucket of ice water on her head. She had to bring herself to heel. She had to stop thinking too much. She had to act, mechanically - as in a reliable mechanism.

Otherwise, she would inadvertently get into trouble. She filled her lungs with air, held it for a moment then let it out slowly. The bustle happily summoned her to the inn's main room.

It was hard to chase the rest of the guests away. They were moving slowly, staggering and cursing at the tables, which were maliciously blocking the way. Several guests were stubbornly sitting by the fireplace. The combination of strong drink and fire gave an effect all too relaxing. Soon, along with the rest of the alewives, she would be forced to kick them off at the dark winter night. Relief rested on the tired shoulders when the last dwarf who was going out into the darkness, put a silver coin into her hand and having waved with his wide hand, was disappeared into the depths of the night vibrated with street lamps. She covered herself in the bedding with joy. She fell asleep immediately.

She couldn't rest. Every night, the same nightmare jolted her awake, which then long couldn't be shaken from under her eyelids. She missed, but this state was displaced by uncertainty. She wanted to believe that time would sort the threads into one, specific whole. In Morien's case, the torment was waiting for any sign. So she was stuck in apathy, which paralyzed every time a familiar shadow crossed the road just to dissipate like smoke from a hearth.

Erica turned up in the kitchen much earlier than usual. She couldn't sleep. She blamed it on the moon, which was breaking through the windows with silver polish. Mark, tormented by terrible hangover, grunted at everyone so loudly that he could be heard in the room, which, either way, was located quite distant from the main hall. Several times the women looked at each other knowingly. They knew that today he would not let them work lightly. Lilian didn't want to get out of the bed. He poked her nose from under the cover in the hope that what was postponed would not magically fall on her heavy head. The swollen eyelids didn't add charm to the woman, she looked like crumpled matter that someone carried for too long.

Mark noticed the door opening. Quite unexpectedly, the messenger entered the tavern. The same as always. The short guy leering at the people who would have the audacity to mention something stupid. He looked around nervously, kicked his heels, then grunted and reached behind his bosom, bringing the news out. The publican grabbed the letter with his fingers shaking with impotence. However, when he wanted to give a coin to the man, he was just disappearing behind the door as if the demon had been chasing him. The hungover innkeeper didn't have to make too much effort to figure out to whom the letter was. It had been a long time since the last message from the House of Magicians. He admitted in spirit that he was happy with the scroll. Most likely, thanks to him, Lili would finally smile, but genuinely, not under duress. So he shouted:

"Lili, damn it! Move finally and come here!"

She shuffled with disheveled hair and sleep remnants on her eyelids. He looked at the woman and felt an irrepressible surge of tenderness.

"You look cute, eh," he sighed.

She yawned and looked at him, rubbing her eye.

"Really? Great. I'm happy. I go back to sleep."

"Here you are." He showed her the scroll. "Lock yourself somewhere, read it and burn. I don't want unexplained situations here."

She felt as if someone had pinched her strongly in the ass. Immediately the sleep fell into ruin. She chose the utility room, which was really a brush store.

"I'm glad I'm a magician," she thought.

She formed a little fireball in her hand, lighting up the cupboard.

Morien wrote:

Sweetheart!

Tonight at school. Let no one see you. Take the letter.

I miss you,

Morien.

She rubbed her eyes and read it two more times. She extinguished the flame and discretely looked outside. She was checking to make sure that nobody was around. Fortunately only the dim light curled the corridor. She closed the door and ran to the innkeeper. He scowled, and she gave him the sweetest smile she could afford.

"Let me go, please."

"Where do you want to roam at night?" He asked, with the tone of concerned daddy.

In response, he got twisting of her mouth.

"Go, but be careful. Strange things are starting to happen here."

She wanted to throw himself on his neck, but she was stopped by the decency and scolding look of one of the maids who having emerged from the corridor, put the cups on the counter. Mark stepped back in horror as the painful sound bored into his skull.

"She went to hell," he gasped and rubbed his temple.

Lili curtsied and returned to the kitchen. She kept smiling.

The day dragged on mercilessly. She felt the eyes of a guy who, by a strange twist of fate, today stuck to the bench exceptionally, and it didn't occur to him to go outside the tavern. He sipped light wines and ate bread and stew. Every now and then she came over and asked if she needed something or wanted company. She thought he wouldn't deny bodily pleasures, of course, for a small fee. However, he thanked her and sent her back.

The evening cradled with the warm of fire crackling in the fireplace. Guests were huddling around it and smacking. Regulars were soaking the mustaches in beers, and the dwarves were singing about the hardships of everyday life. As an exiled nation, they were talking ballads about how they had used to live well. No one denied it, but the gathered knew that they couldn't have lived better than now. Nay! They often existed at a much better level than the first inhabitants of these lands.

Lili struggled between the kitchen and guests. At one point, she sought wistfully the gaze of the boss, who saw the worried face of her favorite. He also nodded towards her. She caught the signal and before he blinked, she stood beside him, ready for what he had to convey.

"Go, but be careful," he whispered.

Lilian's cheeks instantly got colored with a healthy blush, and the eyes glistened with excitement. Thrilled, she rushed to the back room, attired herself appropriately, or rather in what was least worn, tied her hair up and put the hood over her head. She knew it was cold outside, it had been snowing for several days. Streets were ice-bound, besides fresh snow brightened the alleys and caused that the dark blue night and fear hidden in it ceased to seem so terrifying. Before she let herself be absorbed by the frosty air, she summoned Mark to watch over the new guest. Strange premonitions whispered that he had to be careful. He nodded. People constantly told stories about spies, missing magicians, fugitives and doubling of the Guard. Honestly speaking, he was so tired of information that he simply stopped listening to rumors, even though he should have, because what is an innkeeper who doesn't have the latest news? Exactly. He was also certain that Lili and Morien simply had an affair, and this type of misalliance wasn't welcome in some circles. So as their "friend" he decided to "help" them.

When she left, Mark approached the newcomer and talked about the weather. Darius jumped up, seeing that the person he was watching was discreetly escaping from the inn. The innkeeper didn't wait for the development of events and called one of the maids, who sat down unpretentiously on the lap of the guest and wheedled shamelessly. Resigned, he gave up and only smiled wryly. He took a few solid sips from the goblet. Wine tasted more when the obliging host offered a bottle at the expense of "Ram's Head".

Lili was in no hurry. She was climbing slowly towards the School. Thick layer of snow covered streets which remained icy underneath. At this time, no one poked his nose out of the door, unless it was those who went to the taverns. Few traces spoiled a single-colored carpet, which gave easily under the feet. The march turned out to be strenuous, and tired Lilian stopped for a moment. From a distance, she could see the familiar outline of the huge, intricately decorated gate, and before it was happening exactly what people had told in secret. The same thing Erica had mentioned. The guards were doubled, and the sentries wore armor completely unknown to her. She stood too far to be able to look more closely, but she strained her eyes to decipher the emblems that glistened in the light of a street lamp. She was straining her eyes in vain, the image was blurred, destroyed by a curtain of whirling snow crumbs. She flinched when she felt a heavy hand on her shoulder. She was about to burn this person's face when a familiar figure loomed in the dim light.

"Come."

She was confused, but the relief settled lightly on her chest. He took her hand and pulled her behind himself.

"What's happening?" She whispered, catching her breath.

"I'll tell you on the spot." He led her toward a dense from dark, unlit alley.

After a few turns into the dark streets, they arrived at an abandoned house. She knew this place, but in the evenings she preferred not to go here. These areas were inhabited by a mixture that even to the bravest could give goose bumps. By word of mouth was spread the fact that the walls of houses were nested by all sorts of mercenaries, mentally ill people or, worse yet, magicians at the service of the elites, which she couldn't believe. And maybe during the day the passage could take place without problems, but at night an accident was more likely to happen, especially since the lit lanterns were early extinguished. Only in the few windows could be seen the faint candlelight or streaks of glare breaking through the perforated curtains. They didn't go long. Tramp bounced off the silent stone. Before them was a shanty whose shutters bowed sadly to the ground, old and decayed, now covered with snow and a layer of frozen water.

Without looking around, Morien pulled a long key from under his coat skirts, put it in the lock, and turned it. The ratchets creaked and the handle yielded under heavy pressure of the male fingers. They found themselves inside. They were greeted by the musty smell of mold and damp walls. Lilian flinched in disgust. This scent resembled the smell of basement chambers, which she had searched so carefully when she had been escaping from the Magician School about a year earlier. Obsessive thoughts bit into the tissue of memories that she wanted to erase. She wanted to run away. Return to Ram's Head, but she probably found herself too far to retreat now. Fortunately, a cloud of uncertainty was quickly dispelled by the voice of the beloved, who softly sounded right next to her ear.

"Come on, it's warm downstairs. I took care of it," he assured.

They walked through a narrow corridor and reached a small room, also locked. In one of the walls she noticed a breach resembling a doorframe. Indeed, a low entrance was located deep inside. On the walls, she saw stained furniture marks, as if the room had once served as a storeroom. The hole was blocked by something that camouflaged it well. Now she was confidently led down the rough-hewn stairs. She took Morien's hand and slowly went down step by step, watching the unevenness. The room seemed hewn in solid rock. It was small and claustrophobic. Shelves were carved in the walls, on which oil lamps and candles were lined up. She felt safe, though her heart was still fluttering, too irritated by a portion of excitement. At the wall, she noticed a small bed, or rather a pallet made of several boards, covered with a faded spread. Next to it was something similar to a lame cupboard that, tilted to one side, served as a table rather than anything to store. The man did his best to make the cubicle look neat, even if at first glance it puts off.

"Here we are," he sighed. "There is not much here, but there is incense." He nodded at the piece of furniture next to the straw mattress. "I didn't lit it. I don't know if styrax won't torment you? Under the bed, I hid wine and only one cup, unfortunately. I also have an interesting book. It's a hermitage."

"What is this place?" She said exhaling.

"It's a long story."

"So maybe you can tell it," she said and kicked her heels while embracing her arms.

"Alright. This house once belonged to my family, it has been empty for many years, or at least the residents of this district think so. Sometimes local drunkards venture here. On the first floor, in the stairwell, children sit in the afternoons, eager to hide from adults. Most often they play knucklebones or argue about stupidity.

I come here too. This is my shelter. In addition, there is a passage to it directly from the School of Magicians." He pointed at the hatch in the floor. "You see? Many years ago my father was worried that contact with me would be very limited. As you know, annual pass lasts only one day, therefore he decided to do everything to see his son a little more often. He hired the most talented dwarves in the city. He had to pay the guild dearly for silence, but it paid off. Those sawn-off creatures." He gnashed his teeth. "I don't like dwarves. They broke through the solid rock and reached School casemates. In this way they connected the house and the university with a narrow corridor. It didn't take them much time, because as it turned out, the old soldier, Ulvar Thickbeard, had copies of the plans of the University basements. He belonged to a brigade commissioned to carve in sandstone. Mages took care of the upper part, and the rest was done by the dwarves. And since daddy always looked kindly on this nation, he showed the workers details, wanting in return only ... Now listen up, because it will be funny." He put a hand to his lips. "This fool demanded an annual portion of special red lichen that only a botany magician can sustain and grow. Apparently it's a delicacy that they add to the vat when brewing their famous beer. Thickbeard was given the assurance, and my father could enjoy my company until his death. Not often, but it was something. That's the story."

Lilian blinked, just as shocked by what she heard as by the fact that the piece of board she had taken as part of the pallet was nothing but the hatch connecting the world isolated from that which is open and full of temptation.

"And how will they know you're not home?" She said, and casually brushed away a strand that being released from under the hood, fell on the forehead.

"Don't worry about that, my maid is very good at dealing with the curious. She is great not only as a chef, besides I have always escaped to this place." He smiled. "I guess I'm lucky that no one has figured it out. In fact, I sit at home and work or sleep or other 'or'." He winked at her.

"Why did you bring me here?" She was impatient.

"Sit down."

She complied, and Morien sat down so gently that if she hadn't been aware of his presence, she probably wouldn't have felt it.

"You see ... you probably noticed long time ago that the situation has gotten worse. It happens from week to week. The Baroness stubbornly perceives the usurper and riot leader in each of the mages. And you know that the harder she pushes someone, the more clearly he starts to rebel. It started with your escape. The tribe became convinced that there is a gap in this ideal system, that you can escape the Guard and the army, as well as the Alchemists. For some time have been taking place meetings, whispers in cloisters, dormitories, and even a secret internal mail has been created, which is to provide the latest reports to interested parties. Of course, the higher-up, or Archmages, don't know about it and don't care about anything. You must also take into account the fact that there are those within the School walls who favor the madwoman, so restraint and the haze of secrecy are always advisable. Someone could report and the whole intricate plan would go astray."

She nodded at the words that flowed down to her soul like a balm. She didn't think that her act would cause an avalanche, which probably couldn't be controlled as quickly as it was supposed.

"She sent the Alchemists?" She said, when she realized that things were going quite dynamically.

"Yes, I saw one on the highroad recently. I know," he anticipated Lilian's reaction. "You are getting scared."

"Yes. Do you know what they do? Sure you know!" Her face empurpled.

"I know and I'm afraid of that. I don't know what I would do if they bound you and took you away."

"I'm careful." She swallowed a large dose of air, but the emotions played in her like a badly tuned jumble of secondary musicians.

"I believe it's true. Did you notice that you have a spy in the tavern?" He stared at her with the honey irides.

"I noticed a new visitor. He has been here for a while now and he doesn't take his eyes off me. He was here once, then disappeared and returned again. He doesn't behave like a lowly ranger that visits the tavern. There is something disturbing about him that makes my hands go numb. The maidens noticed that he's not a poor man, he often gives money, especially dwarven silver coins. Today Mark turned out to be a really good boss. I hope Marena will seduce him." She laughed, but it was more a nervous giggle than something honest.

"Heh, it would probably be a beautiful sight. Seduced spy stripped of documents, weapons and gold," the magician laughed.

"No, it probably won't happen, but I'll put him to sleep and search the room if you want."

"Yes, that's a great idea. Maybe you will find something that will prove helpful."

"Alright, so I'll do it." She took a deep breath.

"Don't worry." He hugged her and stroked her hair. "I'm watching over you all the time."

"I don't feel it," she said. "I feel like I'm alone. I miss you all the time. I thrash, drown in emotions. They flood me with waves that don't bring happiness, but only worry and bitterness. I miss you, Morien. I can't stand indifference and a dull look. I can't stand the shadows that follow me as I walk the market square. I hate whispers and unclear premises that you feed me. You are cruel! You have no idea how much you hurt me! She hit the man's chest with both fists, shedding tears."

She was trembling like a whirlwind plant, which resists the storm with the remains of still not pulled roots.

"You think it's easy for me? I struggle not to give myself away. I adore you in my mind every time I see you." He grabbed her shoulders.

She nestled her head in the male chest she had just attacked. Tears slowly stopped flowing.

"Mark probably suspects us of romance, nothing more. How convenient it is," she said, sniffing discreetly.

"May he suspect only of it," he whispered. "Do you know what would happen if he found out who you are? Do you know the reward for your head?!"

"So there is a reward?" She was surprised.

"Of course."

"I hope it's big?" She said sarcastically.

"With this money one could be well situated for the rest of his life. So please be careful."

He took her face with trembling hands and stroked her eyebrows that formed neat arches. His eyes were glassy and beautiful.

"I missed you so much." He touched his wet lips with his thumb.

The environment as if by magic changed into something dense, ethereal, saturated with increasing desire. She looked into his eyes deeply, then immediately brushed his lips with the cool lips. She did it as if it had been to happen, without thinking, instinctively and confidently.

Morien didn't hesitate. She smelled fresh and sweet. She tasted of wine, slightly tart and fruity. Her curling hair pleasantly touched his cheek. He knew that this moment would be unlike any other. He also knew that he would never want anyone else, that this night would merge them into one. Between her fear he would find the peace he had been seeking for so long. He was looking closely at the yellow, cat's eyes and drowning in the bottomless abyss of her sharp pupils. He was touching the smooth texture of the skin. He felt calm mixed with indescribable certainty.

Not many breaths passed before he kissed her passionately, savoring the moment, the taste he remembered so well and the closeness he had missed. She tilted her head slightly as he ran his fingers over her cheek, neck and décolletage. Their crazy breaths mixed up. She let him do more and more. His hands were followed by his lips, which brought him waves of burning trance. He tugged at the straps of the dress, and when they yielded, he carefully pulled aside a piece of fabric and sought her breast with the mouth. She moaned softly and pinched her fingers into his white hair. She was so wonderful, so inexperienced and submissive. She resembled a material that he could have formed in the shape of sick fantasies. However, fear warned him of harming her. He wanted something else, not just satisfying the loin fire. He fought, but he couldn't control himself anymore.

He pulled her closer, locked her in an embrace and laid her on the bed. She stared at him with burning eyes. He murmured something, touched her still parted lips and covered her with his body. She moaned again. She felt her muscles tense in anticipation.

"Don't stop," she said, grabbing his wrist as he slid his hand from her breast.

Morien moved his breath to the woman's ear lobe.

"Are you sure you want this? I know it's your..."

She turned her face towards him, ran her fingertips over his cheek, and kept them on his lips wet from kisses.

"I want ..." She breathed heavily. "Maybe we will never have the chance to be together like now."

"Are you afraid?" He asked.

"A little."

"Unnecessarily. Trust me."

"I trust."

He asked no more questions. He let thirst take control, and his hands wander on Lilian's body. She was returning every gesture and touch. She was learning. She was absorbing the experience. They quickly got rid of the clothes separating them. Nudity was sparkling in the light of the candles. The clothes were rustling under them, but they didn't notice the inconvenience, filling the room with deep sighs. Morien was slim, almost thin with nearly white, slightly transparent skin. Lilian could perfectly see the network of blue vessels that marked his forearms and stomach. The man's chest was cut by a longitudinal scar, starting at his right shoulder and ending at the left side of the ribs. She ran her fingers over it. She guessed he had worn it for some time. It got white and hard. With a soft sigh, he kissed the hollow of her neck.

"Have you had it long?" She asked, sliding her fingertips over the scar, starting from her shoulder.

"For a long time," he whispered. "A reminder of the Alchemists and paid killers." He covered her skin with thousands of brushes. "But let's not talk about it ... Not now ..."

She fell silent and gave in to the caress so subtle she never dreamed of. Morien moved his hand along her ribs, lifted her hips slightly upwards, and tucked his other hand into her hair. Every cell of his body demanded fulfillment.

The girl moaned as he pressed himself against her. Passion pulsed with the force of the element. He took her first gently. She felt slight stiffness, but with each successive push it was replaced by something quite different - excitement. He moved slowly and smoothly, lost in pleasure. Lost in her. Irreversibly. Lilian's mouth, eager for Morien's touch, feverishly wandered over the parts of his body. It almost made him crazy. He sunk his teeth in her body. He kissed and bit it with passion. He accelerated even more. Droplets of sweat danced on the bodies entwined in an embrace. She moaned again. He felt chills tearing her inside, and goose bumps forming on her skin. He soon joined the apogee. He felt that the moment, which is liquid matter, now stopped in the race, hanging over them. The candles went out, the storm filled the air, and Lilian's face lit up. All small objects shattered, destroyed by a wave of energy of the connected bodies. Blue sparks enveloped the girl like a shroud. For a moment, he saw them clearly, but with each calming breath, they faded, permeating to the mattress. They fell to the pallet. They had to take a breath, so they were lying, hugged for a long time. Without words. Now they belonged only to each other.

However, the time had come to come back to reality. Unhurriedly, but still. He helped her with clothing. Her hands trembled, and the girl blushed just as much as when he kissed her for the first time.

They left the quiet haven rather reluctantly, cursing in their minds a time that was inexorably chasing them outside. They didn't meet anyone, even stray mongrels didn't wander at their feet, begging for scraps. Silence, extraordinary, sparkling with snow silence. Soft like an eiderdown. And in the sky, hundreds of stars shone, and the night enveloped them in velvet black. Morien protected his beloved with his arm. He asked the Redeemers that these moments wouldn't pass so quickly that he could fortified himself with them a little longer.

The sign of "Ram's Head" was wobbling in the frosty wind. Morien stopped, pressed his cheek to her face and without saying goodbye, let himself be absorbed by a silent alley.

Lili went back to the tavern. The rooms were almost empty, and only a fair-haired intruder and two dwarves sat at the table discussing business. The stranger looked her up and down, as if he had wanted to quickly notice on the woman's face at least a shadow of confusion or embarrassment. She, however, smiled and narrowed her eyes. He turned to the fire and masked his dissatisfaction with a slight twisting of his lips. He thought it would bring emotions painted on her slightly chubby cheeks, meanwhile she seemed as secretive as ever. She kept secrets too deeply for the spy's watchful eye to bring them out.

She saw Mark bustling behind the bar. He set the polished glasses on the counter, checked their amount with his eyes, and analyzed their overall number in his mind. Each day brought small losses, so the stock had to be systematically replenished. Fortunately, a talented craftsman lived in the city, which once in a while delivered what was destroyed. Only one of the alewives remained, but she neither paid attention to the newcomer. Like the host, she did her chores. She watched the long-bearded creatures, which clinked their beer mugs every now and then, raising toasts.

Lilian brushed the snow off the hair. A nice warmth stroked her skin and although in the tavern she felt at home, so burgeoning longing for Morien pinched her heart.

"Oh, you are still here? I thought you would go earlier," she said to Mark and put her hands on her hips.

"You have such blushes as if someone had burned your butt with cast iron." The innkeeper didn't take up the subject, rubbing the itchy nose with the back of his hand.

He was in a good mood, despite the late time had chased feasters away.

"Pour me something good." She pointed at the demijohn.

"What are we celebrating?" He grabbed the vessel and refilled one of the cups.

"Do I have to celebrate something?" She shrugged and clambered onto one of the lame stools.

"Well, usually. I will ply you with, for example, Agrag. Is it alright?"

"Oh yes. I hope you haven't adulterated it, you nasty cheater." She winked at him.

"Madam." He bowed. "I tell you that our drinks are of the highest quality."

The girl covered her mouth and burst out laughing. She knew well that he was lying. The innkeeper also laughed, spilling some of what was in the bottle on the counter.

"Alright, enough of this noble talk, because I will stop feel like drinking," she piped and took the pot with the drink in her hands.

Mark watched him trifling with it, as if trying to warm the cold red hands.

"There's no fly."

"You are in a good mood today, I wonder why?"

"What did you do? Alright, I don't want to know. When you drink it, you will sing it yourself."

"Dodger. Forget it."

Darius watched them closely. Discreetly enough that they didn't realize it. Fortunately, the most engaging were still two sponges that didn't even thought about leaving the inn. The woman didn't disappear for long, at most three clock strokes, but returned as if changed. She was beaming, though she had looked dim and sad before. The innkeeper apparently protected her. Darius could have sworn that he schemed with the red-haired streetwalker. The previous night, he spent a long time looking closely at the sketch of the wanted girl. He looked for subtle differences in it. Drawn with the skillful hand of the draftsman, she looked almost the same as the one that chirped at the counter. He fluctuated between sending a message to the Baroness and not doing it yet. A mistake could have cost him his life. So he made a decision that he would wait. Winter was to be long. Nobody in their right mind wanders on the highroad. Even worse, that year the wolves showed unprecedented aggression towards those who inadvertently got lost in the backwood. This had several explanations, but perhaps the most accurate was hunger. Although he didn't rule out that wild magicians could have had his hands in it. He heard about them on the road and admitted that the skin went numb every time he thought about it. So the alewife wouldn't venture a sudden trip, because what for? Neither it was safe nor gave a chance to survive ... Unless ... she was a magician. Things could have gotten complicated here. That day he also received news that one of the Alchemists would come to the city soon. Lonan would probably sense what he didn't see. He hoped so, because staying in the shabby pit wasn't pleasant.

Lili drank all the wine. Not only what Mark had poured her, but also the rest of the demijohn. Fortunately, the dish was only half full with the purple drink. The woman's ears became red and began to pulsate. There was a rumble in the temples, and the eyelids were closing sleepily. She yawned a few times, hiccuped and laughed, grinning to Mark as hard as she could.

The man knew her favorite was drunk. No, no, she cut wolf loose!

"I'm not much of a heavy drinker," she giggled.

He leaned toward her. Instinct told him that in a moment the drunk girl's tongue would got loosen and she would told him a story whose content he desired.

"I will remember this day for the rest of my life," she sighed.

"Agrag is a good friend," he murmured, though she didn't notice it. "You will sing everything to me in a moment, birdie."

"You won't learn anything," she snorted and patted Mark's shoulder with a sweeping movement.

He just shook his head.

"You're too weak for such drinks," he taunted.

"Eh." She propped her head with her hand. "He's such a great man." She wandered dreamily with her eyes on the wall behind the inn owner.

"One more cup?" Mark was frantically wondering where he had hidden another bottle.

"No no. I've had enough." She waved her hand.

"Tell me."

"He is such a ... cute man. I could do it with him all the time, you know ... well ... I mean talk ... well ... yes. Talk."

Mark ostentatiously stared, clutched his head and almost screamed in terror. He didn't want to listen more, now he was sure Lilian had an affair with Morien.

"Oh no, woman! Enough! Enough! Don't tell me such things!"

"I'm in love, Mark," she sighed.

He felt sad. The thought that probably the red-haired beauty would become another magician's toy made his heart ache. He regretted that he wasn't at least ten years younger, and gray hair was rampant on his forehead, and not lush hair, as it had used to be. As a disguise, he looked worried and said:

"But you know," he began. "That you have no chance of a relationship with such a high-ranking man? Don't look at me like this! I say what I know and I'm not at all mean and bitter old bore."

He saw her grind her teeth, pierce him with the angry eyes. He saw tiny sparks jump from her one eyelash to another, or maybe it just seemed to him, after all before she came he hadn't lavished himself with a drink.

"You are from the mob, my dear, and he is from the aristocracy," he continued, leaning toward her. "It is normal that such men seek entertainment among people like us."

"It is different with us! You don't know anything! You don't know who I am!" She snarled furiously, but bit her tongue immediately. "Too much alcohol, too much," she moaned at the thought of what just fell from her mouth.

She ran out of the room with the red face. Inside, she was burning and it wasn't from alcohol, but because of fury at its own stupidity.

The fair-haired man drank a little from a mug and contorted his lips with undisguised satisfaction. His and the innkeeper's eyes met.

It was enough, he no longer had to wonder about anything, he was in the right place. Once again, instinct didn't disappoint him.

Lili slammed the door and leaned against it.

"Stupid, stupid, stupid!" She hissed to herself and felt treacherous alcohol running through her veins. "Next time, I will drink a damn infusion, not wine. I must have shouted so loudly that the whole room heard. Stupid!" She threw the coat on the bed and walked a few steps to the fire.

"You could start thinking instead of talking gibberish!"

Mark knocked.

"Is everything alright?"

"Go away, because I will say something stupid again."

He opened the door and entered. He didn't close it. Lili stood upright in the light of the fireplace and in affection. He could have sworn that her eyes were burning with a blue light, but it was probably just his imagination again.

"Lili, I know you're special. If it wasn't true, Morien wouldn't pay attention to you. I'm sorry."

"Oh, don't apologize. It is me who act so silly. I will just go to sleep. This is the best I can do now." She began to untie the straps of the dress. "Come on! Shoo! I hope you don't intend to watch me naked?"

He laughed.

"And who wouldn't?" He leaned on the door frame and crossed his arms over his chest.

"I can't stand to be around you, you know? Go now! Or I'll think you're trying to seduce me. Go!"

He pursed his lips in a half smile and waved goodbye.

"Good night. I'll take care of the guy, kick off dwarven drunkards, and you can go to sleep."

"Thanks. Good night."

She stood still for a moment, winding the straps around the fingers. The buzzing and crackling flames calmed down a bit, though not enough. Before she finally went to bed, she had scrubbed her skin neatly with a rough brush, as if trying to punish herself in this way. She squeezed a large bucket into the corner of the kitchen. She would pour it out in the morning, as always. She hid her pink and slightly burning skin under a loose robe and buried herself in a cool bed. Unfortunately, the dream didn't come. So she began to stare at the stars looming in the navy blue sky, trying to count them. The eyelids gave up after some time.

***

Morien arrived home. He slipped quietly upstairs. He knew that every step was recorded by the faithful homemaker. She never fell asleep before him, and sometimes she waited for the host to return until the early hours of the morning. Having taken off his coat, he brightened the library with the glow of oil lamps and candles. A large layer of unread correspondence piled up on the desk. Each message filled him with fear. Each of them showed what he was afraid of. Residents not only of the university, but also ordinary plebeians asked his advice on the issues regarding Alchemists, who appearing in the area, sowed anxiety, bringing the stench of death. Others rebelled against the Baroness' wickedness, which relentlessly and systematically sought to eliminate every bearer of the gift of magic. He never thought that he would become an integral part of such serious state affairs. Although he always tried to keep aloof, the vortex of events pulled him every day into the middle of the inevitable. He also thought about Lili, her smooth skin and the innocence of the child. He wanted her to stay by his side. He could then please the eye with her ethereal presence, watch her gently step on the freshly polished floor, sip tea, do her hair, smile gently ... Unfortunately, he couldn't dragoon her into what was going to happen.

For the rest of the week he met, secretly or quite explicitly, with the addressees of the correspondence. What he heard and read made his heart beat stronger. There were interventions when out of thin air quarrels arose between the guards and nervous countrymen. The fever hung in the air like a sinister omen. The Baroness would probably receive the appropriate correspondence in some time. It became increasingly clear that no one would know peace. He got frightened at the thought that Alvena would most likely go berserk and issue a decree to send Alchemists to the school grounds, although according to Aaron's laws they were not allowed to pass through the gates without the king's agreement. However, if somehow they have managed to set foot on the land of the magicians ... no, he didn't even want to debate it. These people never asked questions. Trained from an early age and sold by parents who discovered the gift in them, they carried hatred fueled by passion. Beings with faces that resemble unmoved masks, often scarred or burned. With the weapon that every mage was afraid of - rune stones and spells that changed those they touched. To make matters worse, not only mages were afraid of them, but also generals in wars. You have often heard of legions murdered by groups of Alchemists. However everything has a price, so not everyone could afford them. And this was probably the only upside.

Immersed in pessimism, he was sipping a cup of already cold tea. The maid bustled around the library, wiping off accumulated dust.

"You've been distressed lately," she said.

Morien lifted his forehead from the text he didn't even read. Recently, the appearance of work began to become second nature to him.

"What? What were you saying?"

"I'm saying you've been distressed lately."

"Yes, yes, a bit. Winter will pass, worries will pass." He forced a grimace that was supposed to be a smile.

"You can't fool me or yourself." She straightened up, holding a brush of chicken feathers like a scepter.

"I know, my dear, I know."

He stood up and left the room without a word. If his hair wasn't already shiny white, he would have probably gotten gray hair at that moment. He didn't sleep well, didn' eat enough, didn't feel like working and all the more meeting people. Thoughts were constantly revolting around rebellion, Lili and how to alleviate the situation at the lowest cost. He missed. He didn't remember how long he hadn't seen the light of his beloved's eyes. He wanted to go beyond the gates, but whenever he planned to implement the plan, there was something urgent, and he had no choice but abandon the desire to drink a pint of dwarven drink. However, the accumulation of duties at one point overwhelmed him to the ground so much that he couldn't stand it and announced that he was leaving and didn't wish any surprises that could have arisen during his short absence. He may not be able to talk to her, but at least he would enjoy the presence of his beloved. Maybe it would soothe his already frayed nerves.

***

Lili wandered around the tavern and cleaned up the remains of yesterday. She collected beer mugs, filled oil lamps, exchanged candles. She was in a bad mood.

Mark watched her, counting the takings. He was irritated by her picking at bread and sighing at every heavier activity, as if it had been to suck Lili's soul remnants.

The alewives competed with Lilian for almost everything because the regulars loved the redhead. She collected the biggest tips, and with cheerfulness, she attracted more and more prosperous citizens. She amused clients with intelligent conversation, at the same time refilling mugs. She was like a signpost for this place, but since she had bouts of apathy, the girls pulled ahead. They pushed the weakening girl into the background. Therefore Mark made sure that she ate, drank and got as many tasks as possible. So that she wouldn't sit in the corner and stare into space.

She knew from his long face that the Helper "magician", as she called him, wasn't in a good mood that day either. When repairing one of the benches, he got hurt, swearing like a trooper, which surprised almost everyone. He squeezed the bleeding and aching place and went to the kitchen, where he was looking for a scrap of material to wrap the damaged part of the body. There he found Lili, who was rooting in the oven with the poker.

"Do you have something to help it?" He reached out to her.

She gave him an absent look. The sight of purple leaking through the fingers of the skinny man slightly animated her.

"Wash it, there is a bowl." She indicated the direction.

"And some canvas? It's seeping out."

She went to the bag with which she had arrived at the inn and pulled out the ointment for wounds and a roll of linen bandage. The "mage" looked at her closely.

"Ointment? Where did you get it?" He asked with interest.

"I made it myself," she muttered under her breath and fixed her eyes on a bleeding pad.

The man raised an eyebrow. He wanted more information about what she was holding. He didn't feel like demonic tricks, let alone ointments whose composition he didn't know. He would have sooner trusted the magicians of the suburban lazaret than the maiden whose origin he knew nothing of.

She didn't mind what she did. She grabbed his wrist hard enough to produce an echo. He grimaced and hissed. She pulled the execrating man, put her hand in the water, and rinsed it not very gently. The wound didn't look deep, but it was bleeding profusely. She pressed it, dried and dressed. She did it quickly and efficiently. Before he knew it, he felt no more discomfort, only the pressure of the bandage. After ensuring that everything was in order, she turned back and returned to the place where he had found her.

"Where did you learn that?"

"Nowhere."

"Yeah, and tell me also that this skill is from the Redeemers, that they inspired you."

"If this answer satisfies you."

He snorted unsatisfied and left. She wanted to stop him and talk to him, but she decided to stay where he was and keep quiet. She was convinced that he must have been bound once. This look ... the way he moved and tone of his voice ... She realized, however, that if she dared to flood him with a wave of sentences, he would have guessed who she was. After all, an ordinary plebeian maiden has no idea about magic, rune stones, much less about binding of power. Restraint and observing from afar are the only things that could now provide answers to bothering issues.

The day was passing by. Mark ordered her to quickly visit the market. Along the way, she met a few regulars who were always eager to chat with the redhead, and if they were engaged in trade, they were more willing to give good discounts, so the innkeeper also benefited. For the evening, the cook prepared goulash with groats for those eager for hot food. The fair-haired man was still in the inn. She ignored his irritating presence.

"It's probably exciting to watch me scrape a carrot," she joked in her mind.

She knew he was following her drowsily with his eyes. Surely Morien would have been pleased to hear about his connections with the Baroness, but she didn't have the strength to cast sleep spells, so she abandoned her plan to search the room. If he is stuck here, it means he has a reason. It's not her business.

In the evening the inn was full. There was frost outside, which painted fabulous ornaments on the windows. This place seemed like a warm haven in the depths of ice darkness. The maidens were shining, distributing mulled drinks and chatting with clients sitting on the wide benches. Lili was replacing Mark, who was counting bottles in the back room and writing down again what was missing, what to order and what not. The store was quickly emptied by guests. The innkeeper had to restock more often than usual.

Lili got stuck behind the counter, forced to pour used beer and struggle with sponges, which only had to pay a few copper coins. Winter got under everyone's skin. Sharp, it only brought emptiness and a desire to hide from the deadly cold. She could no longer count those who froze. Only gravediggers enjoyed the constant wave of bodies. They cursed the ossified soil, but they knew proven ways to deal with it. The pouches buzzed with gold. That was all that mattered.

The inn door opened with a loud squeak of damp hinges and Morien's slender figure appeared. Small snowflakes danced right at his feet. However, they were immediately destroyed by the warmth of the tavern. Lili felt numb at the sight of him, but right after, blushes of happiness crept over her distressed cheeks. He sat down where he always did, but this time he didn't hide his joy at seeing his favorite face. He was looking at her with eyes vitreous from happiness. She immediately reached for a mug and filled it with a dwarven drink. In order not to carry it around the counter, she put it on the bar to take the order from the other side. Before she could get there, the magician stood up and served himself. She was surprised because Morien had never behaved this way. She smiled discreetly and returned to her seat. She wrapped one of the red curls around her finger and gave the newcomer a flirtatious look. He greedily fed on the view and soaked his mouth in his favorite alcohol. She wished she could have joined him. So, to deal with her hands trembling from emotions, she began to polish the glasses with such intensity that if they were made of thin glass, some of them would unavoidably have been broken. The alewives made a point of expressing their dissatisfaction with the Archmaster's visit. Since he began to groove on Lili, he had ceased to be a tidbit to hunt for.

Mark returned to the room. He found the kitchen cooler than that room, took a list of necessary items out of his pocket, and casually tossed it into the cash box.

"Alright." He put his hands on the hips. "I have to go out of town tomorrow. It doesn't matter whether there will be snowstorm or not. I need to stock up on wines. Many bottles were sold. Will you go with me? I have a cart and a coachman."

"Yes, if you wish it," she sighed slowly.

"But, but ..." they heard behind them. Agnes was purple with anger. "It was always me who rode to buy pisses," she said emphatically.

"This time I want Lili to see how this is done. Let her have fun. It's not good for anyone to stay long in one place and do the same thing." He looked sleepily at guests. He noticed the magician sitting in the corner and bowed to him. Like Lilian, he was quite surprised by the visit. The mage nodded back.

"This isn't right! Lili has stolen our tips and now also tasks!" Shouted the alewife.

Lili stared at the storming woman indifferently. In truth, she preferred that it was her who would have poked her nose into chill. Sitting by the stove is much nicer than ossification on the cart.

"Enough, Agnes!" Mark hissed. "I'm sick of rumors, intrigues and other behaviors! Enough! Go work! If you don't like it, you can leave even now!"

The woman gasped like a mad cat. The girl covered her mouth with her hand, hiding a sudden giggle. She controlled herself and straightened up, adopting a serious pose. Mark knew they didn't like each other, but it amused him, so he smiled slightly.

"Go to Morien, talk to him. I know you want it," he changed the subject.

"Thanks," she whispered. "If there wasn't so many people here, I would kiss your cheek."

He leaned toward her ear.

"I will remember it and dun for it someday."

"I'll hold you to your word."

Before the innkeeper said anything else, the redhead was already approaching the table at which the Master was sitting. He didn't see them radiate or their eyes meet, sparking with excitement.

"Hello, sir." She bowed gracefully. "Do you wish anything else?"

"Yes, madam," he said and pointed to the vacant seat next to him. "I wish I could talk to you."

"I will be honored."

"Keeping appearances. How boring it is," she thought.

She sat down. She folded her arms and lowered her forehead attentively.

Morien whispered:

"What's new? How are you? Is Alvena's spy still here?"

"Yes," she replied. "He leaves, sometimes he looks insistently, talks, flirts with maidens. I give him no reason to suspect. I think I'm getting used to him."

"Lili," he said even more quietly. "A revolution is coming."

She flinched.

"Revolution?"

"Yes, my brothers are starting to get angry. The Baroness oppresses each school individually. Rebellion is inevitable and I know it will happen soon. I have received reports that several mages have escaped. They probably hide somewhere in the mountains to the north. I don't want to worry you, but those who have escaped the guards will probably get involved with the savages."

"Why?"

"Because the savages usually use animals and blood magic. They benefit from their blood and vitality. They most often take advantage of wolves. After some time, when they manage to tame them enough to make them succumb unrestrictedly, they use them as a tool to threaten the mob. Villagers who have no idea about the savages' tricks get influenced by them. It doesn't end well. Tracking is out of the question, they can manipulate the surrounding environment. You can walk past the seats many times and you won't notice anything. I have no idea what conditions must be met to join them, but I suppose that sincere desire would be enough."

She stared at him with her mouth parted in surprise.

"That's why the Baroness storms so much! Hated magicians escape. Who would have thought that someone would like to take her down?"

"Yes, you're right. However, her rage reaches its zenith because she hasn't caught you yet. After all, it is you who started it all, even though your escape was prosaic. She probably thinks that you've got involved with the savages and you scheme, and what's worse, she has no control over it."

"I'm starting to think that coming home is one big mistake. I'm starting to doubt myself, Morien."

He put his hand on her cold fingers.

"Beloved, if it weren't for that, we wouldn't have met, would we? Does this mean nothing to you?"

"It means a lot, you know that. Don't play with fate, please ..."

Darius entered the tavern, rubbing his hands vigorously. He saw Lili and Morien jump away from each other, so he turned toward them. He sensed the trick they were probably planning, leaning toward each other. His face was stinging and the only thing he dreamed of now was hot mulled wine that should have let him return to normal colors. He beckoned to Agnes because she was the closest one. The woman immediately found herself next to the man and took an order. Her face took on a sly expression, as if under the thatch of curly hair, a nasty plan of harming the young magician was forming.

"Lili," Morien whispered. "Go now. We have to see each other again, but outside the tavern. I would like you to visit me at the School, on the property. By Redeemers, it's risky, but I'd like to give you books about the Magic of Whispers."

"I know these books." She got excited. "They are about ..."

"Telepathy," he finished. "We could talk, crossing our minds. I doubt that the spies have such a skill, unless they are similar to us. This ability is reserved for the stronger in the hierarchy. You were probably too inexperienced to learn it. I think that you have already grown so much that it won't cause us any major problems. What do you think?"

"I'll see what I can do." She rose from the table and bowed low.

By the time she reached the counter, Morien already went out. Only a not entirely emptied beer mug was left.

CHAPTER IV

Everything was flowing. Time, sticky snow dissolved by unexpected warming, gutter. Cool days mixed with night frosts. Adhesive slush soaked shoes and settled on the edges of garments, heavy and stinking. The growing tension, which probably everyone already felt, overwhelmed and took breaths away of the more sensitive. People fell into a strange numbness combined with anticipation. The City Guard doubled its patrols to avoid unnecessary quarrels. Inhabitants of Undercity fixed their eyes on the line of trees that in the distance loomed with a dark ribbon. They were looking for something they didn't really want to see. The chapel in the center was full of those who, praying to the Redeemers, begged for the imminent end of winter and peace of mind that was disturbed by gossip, which passed on from mouth to mouth grew stronger. Words smothered and deprived of reason.

The Archmaster of the Magician School categorically forbade leaving the university even to those who previously had had permission to move freely within Undercity. Students who had a pass at that time poisoned people against the superior and, to show their dissatisfaction, they didn't show up in class, but only sat in the corridors of the university and loudly expressed disapproval. It didn't help explaining that it was for their safety. At that time, the Supreme Council was the number one enemy of young magicians.

Morien was stuck in the mansion's walls. Lack of contact with the world caused a growing rage in him. An inexplicable, incessant anger made him thrash, causing the woman who ran the farm to sneak away every time their eyes met. She saw in his eyes a dangerous, bright glow that shimmered on the edges of the irises. She had no idea that her master had received messages from the very command center of the megacity.

Several Alchemists had appeared in the city, but after a few days only one remained. Why? Nervous agitation began, and plebeians, unfamiliar with the sight of the figure dressed in black, made various guesses. Meanwhile, the newcomer nosed. He appeared and vanished in a filthy fog. He was seen on the walls, sometimes at the gates. People told that he disappeared behind the door of the Guard headquarters, and those who opened the door reportedly stepped back in disgust. They didn't want to have the slightest contact with him.

Predictably, Lili received appropriate correspondence. Morien had written one word on the parchment, but it was enough for the magician to feel a sudden rush of blood. She knew who the one who had arrived in the city was. Since then, she came up with all sorts of excuses, including forcing herself to vomit just to not leave Ram's Head. She knew that sooner or later the innkeeper would lose his patience and throw her out of the door, but the illusion that the inn was safe was in her so strongly that she trusted that feeling. It was as if drowning, she had grabbed thin blades of grass growing over the edge, knowing that they wouldn't be able to keep her afloat.

Before Alchemist appeared on the streets, she had slipped away several times and met with Morien. The trysts took place in an abandoned house. Risk tasted delicious, whenever she drowned in the arms of his beloved, swayed with the sound of his voice. Now it was the end of the night walks along deserted alleys. Now it was the time of the numb skin and holding her breath.

Darius, bored with stagnation, often spend time at the tavern. He sipped watered wine and ate the cook's dishes. He told others that the weather kept him within the hideous walls and probably when winter finally passed, he would have happily left. Nobody, however, ever heard what reason he had to visit the city and where he came from. His mouth was stubbornly closed. Thus he mocked the curious. To be engaged in something, he seduced one of the alewives - Agnes. She seemed to him the most greedy for gold, and eager to spread gossip. She also liked intimate encounters, of course for the right coin, and although she was lacking in the beauty department, the skills in the alcove impressed even him. So what happened on the first floor became a case so famous that after a while the news from the maidens, who sometimes eavesdropped at the door, reached also Lilian. The mysterious man's behavior cooled down the vigilance for some time. It seemed that he stopped paying attention to her, which was convenient in this case. Agnes benefited much from the misalliance, shamelessly flaunting it and thinking that what was happening was the best thing she had ever experienced. However, no one thought that the dark-haired schemer, wanting to get rid of uncomfortable competition, would go as far as the deeds that would stain her hands with blood. The new lover didn't skimp on drinks and often got drunk silly. Sometimes his tongue was loosened enough for him to share some news, which she gladly kept for later, in case they were useful in the future.

Exceptionally cold evening, Darius had a few drinks, maybe not a few, but a pitcher of mulled wine spiced with cloves and honey. Sticky alcohol encouraged the younker to confide. Having invited the maiden to the warm accommodation, he suddenly became effusive and sleepy. He mumbled something about Alchemists and the highest-ranking order. Agnes listened. She picked up more interesting morsels, and when he came to the merits of the matter, he took out the portrait of the wanted and pressed the crumpled paper into the rough hands of the woman. He explained that everything was confidential, and only to him the Baroness revealed her intentions regarding the fugitive. The smart alewife immediately thought it was about Lili. Nobody had such an expression while pondering something. The characteristic furrow that formed between the magician's eyebrows pulled together, gave her an almost dignified expression. If she wasn't from the mob, she could have probably pretended to a highborn.

Since then, she kept an eye on the one for which a large prize was offered. She stubbornly waited for the girl to trip up. She smiled and asked questions which contributed nothing but were tricky, most often about Morien, the School and what could be associated with magic. Each time she was left with nothing. She quietly execrated and promised herself that one day she would go to the herbalist and poison the red trollop. In desperation, she began to tease information out of Mark and the cook, but they agreed that she was ridiculous. The landlady, irritated by her subordinate's behavior, made a point of sharing her observations with her favorite, who obviously, didn't care what Agnes was trying to discover. However, at the instigation of Erica, she approached the matter gently and diplomatically. She knew that she liked to hit the bottle, so she decided to pour a little of golden drink in her and learn the revelations that had touched her so much. Of course, she was aware that she would probably scent the trick, after all, she put her off each time. Trying wouldn't hurt, so she bided her time, which, annoyingly enough, wasn't coming.

That evening, at "Ram's Head" were few people. The maidens didn't have much work, so the opportunity finally came.

"How are you?" She said to Agnes, who was cleaning up the spilled beer. "Do you want another one?" She pointed to a piece of gray rag that no longer absorbed a drop, and only left smeared stripes.

"No," she said dryly.

She looked deeply into the interlocutor's eyes. Lili didn't blink, only her pupils narrowed like a cat's ones.

"There is no one." Lili pointed at the empty room. "Come and have a drink. Mark probably won't mind."

The maiden followed her with her eyes. Lili walked a few steps, took a pitcher from under the counter, and slowly filled two glasses.

"There's no one here but us," she continued and stretched out her hand with the glass towards the woman, pressing her lips to her own one. She withdrew it, however, a few knuckles and spoke again. "Mark is in the kitchen. She won't come out of it for a long time ... he's counting apples," she giggled and took a deep sip. "I wonder if anyone will show up today. What do you think? Will it be full?"

"Dwarves probably will move their asses. They are sponges. They will never miss the opportunity to soak their mouths in our slop," she said, but she came for the wine and, like Lilian, drank a few drops.

The magician didn't know what to talk to her about. Coming up with dialogue wasn't her favorite pastime, and Agnes wasn't stupid. It wouldn't be easy to loosen her tongue.

"I haven't tried that yet. Good. It's something new, try it." She moved the dish as if toasting.

Agnes looked into the cup and sighed:

"Indeed, and what did you want to talk about specifically? Because certainly not about errands."

There was a strange and quite uneasy silence that the redhead tried to mask. She pretended to delight in the aroma of alcohol, but she knew well that if she didn't come up with something, the attempt would fail. The situation was saved by Darius, who entered the room briskly. He looked very excited, his eyes were shining and it certainly wasn't because of the short measure. Agnes immediately blushed at his sight.

"Oh! And what are these colors?" Lilian babbled. "I think you like him, huh? Tell me what is he like?"

The girl's surprise was painted on her face. She didn't expect that from the eternally reserved girl.

"Why are you asking?"

"Eh, you know ... You don't have to talk, but then I won't tell you what Morien is like." She winked. "I know how curious you are about it. It's just such gossip between friends, isn't it?"

Agnes smiled to herself. The whole matter seemed too tall, and the tone of Lilian's voice and desire to contact completely artificial. The bodily pleasures with Darius were extremely exciting, so the whispered word could open the gates to information that would prove useful not only as a fodder for gossip, but also for the lover she liked.

"Well ..." she began. "He's talkative. I mean, you know, he likes to talk before ... We start the fun. You are adult, you know what I mean."

"Talk?" Lilian pretended not to hear the end of the sentence.

"Yeah. And you think that I only with him...? You're stupid."

"No, no," she said. "I talk to Morien a lot too," she added exhaling.

"Listen then." She leaned toward the alewife: "He serves the Baroness. He is here by her order, but shush. No one can find out about this." She put a finger to her lips like a child who is telling her friend the biggest secret. She knew that it should have interested Lilian.

Lili pretended that the news made her excited. She took a deep breath, then let it out heavily, at the same time swallowing a few big sips of the drink.

Agnes didn't see her clutching the vessel. The grip was strong enough to make her feel tingling in the fingers. She wasn't stopping.

"He looks for or rather they look, because there are several of them, the fugitive magician. His lady made sure that in each of the largest cities there is at least one spy. The hunted girl is supposedly dangerous. I know that much, but surely," she leaned forward again, this time more, "soon, this shapely lark will sing more revelations to me."

Lili gave an artificial smile. The "freshest" gossip turned out to be wood shavings, which she had long heard of. She couldn't leave the role. She continued the subject, although boredom was tearing her nerves hard.

"Why does Alvena care about her so much? She is an ordinary maiden."

"She is a mage, not only a maiden. Don't you understand? Where did you grow up?! Mage, do you understand? She pursues her because she apparently conspires against the Guard and turns people against the current School policy. So not only she opposes the Baroness, but also the king himself!"

"I find that hard to believe. One woman wouldn't be able to do such a thing," Lili snorted, and a pink blush spilled on her cheek.

"You have no clue. Recently, you don't get your nose outside the tavern. Oh, yeah, Morien. He probably already outlined the situation to you, and if not, know that apparently for several centuries people haven't seen a woman like her. As they say, 'You can't kill her'."

Lili turned purple not out of embarrassment due to the stupidity of the interlocutor, but because she had just imagined herself casting lightning with smile at the opponents while being hit by hundreds of arrows which didn't hurt her. Agnes noticed it, but she kept her mouth shut. The girl snorted, choking on laughter.

"Can't kill? It must be a joke. Everyone can be killed, but some are resurrected. It's a magician's lot, but when they are touched with a jade ..." She came to herself, driven by a wave of exuberance. "Besides, isn't that an elf?" She bit the inner part of a cheek.

She got carried away again, but she hoped Agnes wouldn't see it. The woman just shrugged.

"I don't know. I'm not familiar with those magic tricks. But enough. Now is your turn. What is this mysterious Morien like? Every time he comes here, he devours you with his eyes. So what is he like?" She sighed. "How did you turn his head? For so much time I tried to make him say at least one time something different than "thank you" after I put before him those nasty, dwarven slop. And here you are, such a disheveled maiden appears and boom. The affair like from a bard's song. Reveal this secret." She grinned in a smile which rather wasn't genuine.

"I don't know. Maybe I'm special?" Lili shrugged.

The alewife put an empty cup on the counter. She put her hands on the hips and looked at the redhead piercingly.

"Yes, there must be something to it. You look like a demon or as if fire was burning inside you."

"Like a demon?" She was surprised.

"Yeah. Your eyes ... They are so ... piercing, not very human. And this color."

"Don't be afraid," she adopted the same pose as Agnes. "These eyes won't hurt you, they just are like that. Tell me," she lowered her voice. "Does our favorite dandy have any arrest warrant?" Portrait? Anything? Since he is so outgoing, he probably hides something."

Agnes pretended to wonder.

"Oh yes. And you know what?"

This time it was her who leaned toward Lili so close that she saw a network of tiny veins crossing the whites of her eyes.

"The person in the picture is similar to you." She brought her lips to her ear. "And I think it is you. And the fact that Morien suddenly pays attention to the alewife, only confirms this. The red-haired stray looking like a hounded mongrel, which appearing, overturned the whole order of this city ..."

Lili felt cold sweat run down her back. She clenched her jaw and waited for her to finish.

"The girl with yellow eyes pretending she doesn't care. And yet stupid enough to try to play about with me. Did you want to know? You already know! This questioning was very smart, but I'm not naive. Remember that!" She straightened up and having turned on her heel, she went towards the back room.

She probably headed to the upper floor room. She left Lilian alone, drenched in cold sweat and trembling like an aspen leaf.

Shocked, she stood there for a moment, looking around the room as if she had been looking for consolation in the empty walls. The illusory sense of security burst. It left her naked and defenseless. She drank the rest of the wine, ran the back of her hand over her forehead and wiped the icy sweat from it. The blood ran straight down to her feet, making them unnaturally heavy. She wanted to go to the kitchen, but all she managed to do was walk a few steps and fall hard on the place that Mark usually occupied. She had to contact Morien! But in the morning. Now she would rest. Yes, she would calm down. She wouldn't do anything rashly, not being nervous and above all without thinking. In the morning! In the morning she would find a solution.

She turned from side to side. The bed seemed too hard, too cold, too narrow ... And everything "too" gathered into one bullet of constant anguish, which didn't allow her to sleep a wink. Maybe she fell asleep in the morning? She couldn't be certain. So she hesitated between yes and no. She waded in uncertainty as in a boggy slough. At dawn, she dropped her feet to the cold floor and buried her face in her hands. She sought to stabilize what worried her from the inside.

"Agnes can't be that stupid!" She said.

She was thinking that maybe it was different. It was just Agnes. Who would believe her stories? Everyone knew that she was a schemer and gossip girl...

"Eh," she sighed heavily.

She felt as if she had been hanging over the abyss and, although there was a hand in the distance that she could grab at any moment, she was afraid she wouldn't have made it. The darkness surrounding her thickened. She balanced between fear and certainty. Trustful like a lamb, to which only throat slitting will happen.

When the sun rose a little higher, she brought order to the surroundings and with her eyes sandy with lack of sleep, she went to the main room. She hoped that Mark, like her, had gotten up sooner and gone to the inn. She didn't find him, but at a bench there was Darius resting on his favorite seat. A bow of marvelous beauty leaned against the wall beside the seat. Darius smoked a pipe with a bone, bright mouthpiece, releasing smoke rings into the air, which waved to dissolve after a moment like clouds blown away by summer wind. There was a candle on the table in front of him. Half burned out, as if a man had been patiently waiting for someone for a long time. She thought he probably had a restless night like her, though it seemed less likely. In a moment she realized that the meeting wasn't accidental.

"Hello," he said, and inhaled bluish smoke again.

"Good morning, lord," she said.

She wanted to run away but realized that it would be better if she stayed where she stood.

"Eh." He took a deep breath and exhaled quickly.

He sat down more comfortably and stuck his light strands behind the ears.

She glanced at him, he looked confident. She would have also said that too fresh for such an early hour.

"I'm sure now." He was again carried away by the pleasure of the blue cloud of smoldering pipe. "And I'm conscious that you know it too."

Lilian froze. First, the blood hit with a powerful wave, then just as quickly drained into the deeper layers of the body. She shuddered with a sudden surge of heat and sweat that poured her from head to foot. Darius' gaze reached the deepest corners of her soul. She had the impression that he fed on fear, toying with it and chewing with pleasure no more than the one caused by the bone pipe.

"You know, my dear, what is your problem?" He asked. "Do you know?"

"I don't know what you're talking about, my lord," she choked.

"Of course you know. So, will you answer?" He turned his head in the characteristic way, as those who want you to flood them with a verbosity of confession.

Power jerked her. At first lightly, but after a while it grew stronger and, reaching the knuckles, warmed them up slightly. Lilian clenched her fists and discreetly hid them under a voluminous gray apron casually tied around her narrow waist. She couldn't get provoked. So she normalized her breathing and circled with her mind around what seemed to her to be the safest at the moment - the kitchen full of warmth, the smell of food and buzzing logs.

The fair-haired man tapped his pipe on the edge of the table. A cascade of red sparks fell on the wooden floor. He smothered the heat with a heavy boot, and then placed the object evenly beside the candle. He checked if its location pleased him. He ran his fingers through his hair and stood up, as if to stretch his stiff joints. He went around the furniture. He didn't lose eye contact with Lili and took a few steps towards her. His movements were as smooth as of a cat lurking for a sparrow. She hesitated for a moment, then discreetly kicked her heels.

"Do you think you can hide magic under the cloth? Unlikely. Your hands shine like lightning arms on a stormy night. You won't escape. I haven't stayed in that stinking pit, to now, leave with nothing." He reached into his pocket.

He rummaged in it for a moment, then took out a smooth, slightly shiny, oval object.

She narrowed her eyelids and frowned. A lion's wrinkle marked the forehead of the young magician, and now she looked identical as in the portrait which probably was crumpled at the bottom of the travel saddlebag.

"You know what this is, right?!"

She tilted her head. For a fraction of the time, she watched what lay in Darius's narrow hands. She came to herself when the thing shuddered and burned with a greenish light. The rune to bind mages! Saliva took on a dense structure and blocked her throat with sticky ointment. She wanted to swallow the accumulating lump, but the harder she tried, the more it grew and gave her the feeling of choking. The archer wasn't a magician. She couldn't be wrong about that. So ... If not him ... there must have been the Alchemist somewhere nearby! She was about to escape, when the tavern's door opened wide.

He stood in the doorway with snowflakes on his shoulders. Black separated him from the rest. Lilian had the impression that instead of the arms, he had crow wings, and his pale blue face was marked by countless scars. Deep-set eyes pierced the surroundings without stopping. The only salvation was magic ... or escape! She chose the latter.

Darius threw the stone at Lonan. It flew past Lilian's face, gently brushing her hair. She didn't have to imagine the power of this object because it touched every living cell in an instant. Sudden affect made her throat tight. Before she could take a breath, she choked, barking her knees on the floor of the tavern. The feeling passed after a while. It allowed the magician to breathe freely, but took away enough strength that she had to hold the counter firmly when getting up. Dormant vigilance brought excellent results. Darius was content. The alchemist also looked pleased. The corners of the narrow lips rose slightly as the fist clenched on his property.

It meant the end of many months of searching and an immediate return to the walls he missed so much.

Lilian was afraid, in her life she hadn't felt such overwhelming fear, which was depriving her of rational thinking in a destructive way. She was panting heavily, constantly being flooded with hot and cold sweats. She didn't want to go to the Baroness' fortress or to any other place where they held apostates.

"Hello," the Alchemist growled.

The voice of the creature clad in black meant only one thing - escape! She estimated the chances, but they seemed so miserable that tears came to her swollen eyes due to helplessness. She couldn't get caught. She no longer thought about whether she would make it or they would catch her when she tried to escape through the kitchen window. She jumped up and ran into the dim light of the corridor leading to the back room. Out of the corner of her eye, she saw a silver glow. Dodging, she miraculously escaped. A blade cut the air close to her face and drove into the hard boards of the door frame. She reached the kitchen door and opened it wide with a sweeping movement. With one leap she crossed the room, reaching the windows. She jerked the door handle. She didn't look back, she didn't waste time on trivialities. The bolt yielded easily. Big happiness fell on the troubled heart as the gates to freedom opened. In desperation, she grabbed the cane and then, as nimbly as a cat, slipped through the small window vent.

Icy air burst into the nose and throat. Freedom, if it was how freedom smelled, then she would absorb it at once. The first thought that struck her when she hid in an alley was to escape onto the route ... but in winter? No, she wouldn't have made it. The second thought was the School of Mages. She was close enough. Up, on the cobblestone. But would they open the gates for the escaped, dangerous girl and above all the traitor?! She was a magician! They must have helped! Otherwise she would have been lost! She looked around discreetly. The footsteps sounded sad. It reflected rhythmically from stone facades. She adjusted her clothing. Now, before they noticed her! She squeezed her staff so hard that her knuckles bruised. Annoyingly enough, it was snowing. Snow was stinging her in the face with particles of ice, but it also provided cover. She quickly managed to hide in its opacity. After a short run, she got tired and was panting spasmodically. This time, she turned around, looking for blurry figures looming in opaque blizzard. She slipped on the icy cobblestones, stumbled and rolled over and over again, sparing no curses.

"I'm almost there," she was repeating to herself. She counted the districts passed. "Hold on a little longer," she comforted herself, as the chase intensified with every wheezing. "Will they let me in? Oh Redeemers, look after me, because I'm poor as those who tread this stone into the soil sprinkled with the blood of the ancients!" She prayed fervently.

***

Morien didn't sleep well. He fidgeted alternately with getting up and wandering into the kitchen. Something was bothering him. Unreal, but tangible, as if alive. It crawled under the thin skin of the chest. A disgusting and slimy feeling of fear mixed with coldness and confusion. He didn't narrow his eyelids. In the morning he went to the library and poured himself a big goblet of wine. He knew that by this afternoon he would be unbearable due to a tiring and boring headache, but he consoled himself with the thought that the decoction brewers would surely alleviate his ailments. He sat down heavily behind the desk and casually looked at the papers that piled up in front of him. The desk was covered by letters. Endless wave of correspondence lay chaotically in larger or smaller piles. He didn't bother to file it, because it would have taken a lot of time, and the next day it would have looked the same. If he wanted to write back, he pushed the part aside, reached into the drawers and took out clean parchment, ink and lacker. The Baroness had sent short notes in which he read about the progress of the soldiers and the City Guard. Of course, they concerned the "dangerous magician." She was already certain that no one had seen such a fortress, so she gave up the search and although some say that the darkest place is under the candle, she gave up. However, she was reported that someone similar was seen here, so she did not wait and sent the best spy to look more closely. Morien also recently knew about the Alchemist, but he didn't come to School. He would have probably caused a sensation, especially among novices who hadn't seen many things, and certainly not this type of magician. And although law enforcers were not allowed to arrest outside the walls of Universities, they were guests of the Archmages. Most often as envoys or just to conduct thorough interviews. Fortunately, School policy forbade remaining alone with prisoners. It was not a secret that they tried to get testimonies of detainees by fair means or foul.

Bored and sleepy Morien was staring through the window. It was snowing outside, so it was brighter than usual. Dawn was coming lazily, flooding the world with the glow of a bland winter sun hidden behind a thick wall of thick snow clouds. He closed his eyes for a moment. He calmed his thoughts. Alcohol spread nicely through the arteries. He fell asleep.

***

Lili reached the gates of the Mages School. She was feverishly taking a deep breath of air, trying to say at least one word. A sudden colic attack bent her half. Overwhelmed by pain, she fell to her knees, clutching her cane and moaning something under her breath.

The guard glanced at the woman. Wrapped in snowflakes, she seemed unreal, and yet she was kneeling right in front of him.

"Let me in," she panted.

"What are you thinking, maiden?" He growled coldly.

The night watch was coming to an end, so the only thing he wanted to do right now was to go to the barracks and fill his stomach with hot food.

"Let me in, please, lord," she moaned. "I need to meet with Archmaster Morien, it is urgent!"

"Go away." He pushed her with contempt.

Such revelations always prolonged onerous protection. She fell on her butt. A heavy cane hit the ground, and the tumult betrayed the place where she was.

"Let me in," she shouted as a loud crash of pursuit came to her ears. She tried all possibilities. She sobbed. "By Redeemers! This is a state matter!"

The guard laughed out loud.

"What can you know about politics, maiden?"

Lili, having found her loss, rose painfully. She had never felt such pressure, such a chase on her back. Desperation prevailed, and the only thing that mattered was the desire to survive as a magician!

"My name is Lilian Vaal. Does that mean anything to you, bonehead?!"

His eyes widened. He had to wipe his face because the storm didn't stop, on the contrary, the snow was getting thicker and heavier.

"What are you talking about?"

To make him believe, she had to do a quick demonstration of strength. It was just a pity that she had wasted all her energy on the strenuous run. She focused, clenched her teeth tightly, and extended her hand, armed with a clenched fist. After making sure that the guard watched her efforts, she slowly opened it and moved it toward his face.

At first he saw nothing, but when he looked closer he noticed the looming faint flames that twitched to his heartbeat. The woman's eyes didn't resemble the previous ones, but two balls deprived of irides. The man jumped back terrified.

So she repeated again. She was panting, being close to collapse:

"My name is Lilian Vaal. Let me in! This is a state matter!"

A soft whistle cut the air. Pain pierced her, almost knocking her off the feet. She howled. She caught the arrow in trembling fingers, the shoulder burned and pulsed. The arrow drove deeply. She knew that if the guard did nothing at the moment, she would die on the threshold of the School as the meanest stray. She turned back. Darius stood behind the curtain of blizzard, hurrying to stretch the next portion of pain. She didn't know whether he wanted to kill her or just pin her to the ground so that, dazed and bleeding, he could give her to the Alchemist's hands. For the last time she repeated her plea for help:

"I don't want to die," she moaned.

The sentry blinked vigorously and opened his mouth. Such a turn of events wasn't expected by him. Usually boring occupation suddenly brought an unhealthy dose of adrenaline. His heart pounded hidden behind a layer of thick armor. He didn't ask questions, he didn't play with fate that treated like a dirt him and the girl staggering. He put his hand on the door handle and opened the door. The girl breathed a sigh of relief. She jumped up and squeezed between the man and the gate. She got into the free space, scrapping the wall with the nock. The arrow moved in the wound and gave the victim another spasm.

Darius, dissatisfied with the course of the situation, was seething with rage. Dumbfounded with anger, he aimed straight at the soldier. His slim fingers played on the string. The man sank to his knees. Lilian stopped midstride at the gurgling sound filling the throat of the nameless savior. Her life at the price of his life. Luckily, she was already beyond the School territory. She should have been safe here, even though a sharp-eyed archer could easily reach her body. She wanted to come to herself, drown in the arms of her lover and let him relieve her with the power of his magic. She had no idea that what had happened before a dozen or so breaths had alarmed half of the University workers, including the exalted ones. Now she was running towards the residence, in spirit begging for the end of suffering tearing apart her tissues and muscles.

Sleepy and curious residents and servants began to look from behind the frost-painted shutters. The tension mixed with strange anxiety hung in the air. The red-haired woman was traversing the square. She was stopping every now and then, at times of her greatest weakness, leaning on the cane of extraordinary beauty. The arrow protruded from her shoulder, and the blood coming out stained the cloth red. The crimson ribbon reached almost to the middle of the chest. She didn't look around, she seemed to know where she was going. Nobody tried to stop her.

Lili reached the door of the residence. The remnants of her life seemed to be coming out of her chest. She raised her fist and hit the door.

"Morien! Open up! Morien!"

The silence of the sleeping home was disturbed by the rhythmic pounding on the wood. She repeated the call several times, though the consciousness sank into the shadow of faint nothingness more and more quickly. She was surprised that nobody opened, they should have been preparing the food long ago. Or maybe she didn't realize how early she was here? She raised a fist once again and hit more weakly.

"Morien, open up!" She wailed, scratching the varnish.

Finally she heard a quiet shuffle.

Morien was woken up by a rumble in the lobby. Sleepiness, however, strongly stuck on the eyelids and couldn't be shaken for anything. Scraping and banging was repeated. He came to himself, rose using his numb hands and leaned against the edge of the desk. He waited for the moment when the brain would fully connect with the limbs. Dusk enveloped him, oil lamps had long gone out. The service was in blissful calmness, only he was plodding toward the stairs. Having reached the lower hall, he opened the gate. Before him appeared the figure of the half-sick woman, bloodied and crying. He woke up quickly. The synapses said what he was most afraid of. Lilian was staggering, and if it wasn't for her cane, she would probably measure her length. Having noticed him, she only managed to stutter out:

"Alchemist." Then she sank into the arms of confused Morien.

He took her in his arms and shouted several times. The landlady emerged from the room and lazily threw a woolen scarf over the shoulders.

"To the library!"

She nodded and ran upstairs. Morien arranged Lilian on the couch, ordered the maid to watch over the wounded, and he himself took the capot, whipped the cane off the girl's hand and ran to the courtyard. A crowd had already gathered there. In the freezing cold, there were stiffening magicians and terrified servants who crouched behind their superiors and shyly peeked from behind their backs, hungry for cheap sensation.

He squeezed through the mob and reached the gates. The guards surrounded by red was staring deadly at the cloudy sky. The majesty of death painted surprise on their faces mixed with numb specter of fear. They were not afraid of the archer, but the one who, leaning on the bone rod, was silently observing what was within his range.

Darius positioned himself comfortably behind the Alchemist and raised his weapon so that he could reach the newcomer without hindrance. Morien realized that the arrowhead was at an ideal height, that even the strong arms of the iron gate couldn't save him from the cold blade. He pushed away the thought that hit the skull like a beak of a crow. He stood a little astride, leaned against the mistress's weapon, and said calmly, amplifying the voice with mana power.

"Go away!"

He didn't know what kind of emotion was starting to tear the chest. The anger was burning, leaking from the tissues and filling the threads of veins. In a sense, he was calm, as if full of security, which the walls of the fortress gave, and in a way he wanted to go beyond them and break the neck of both. He knew, however, that he had to stay where he was, that the position he had been given was so important that thoughtlessness could end what he was fighting for.

The silence he expected was still in the air. All he could hear was rapid breathing and the coughing of those who stood behind him.

"Leave us alone!" He repeated.

Darius answered hoarsely: "You have something that belongs to the Baroness. Give it back and we will save ourselves unpleasantness ... Lord Master." The archer countered sarcastically, mispronouncing every word.

"Your power doesn't reach beyond the gates," said the magician. "You can't do anything. Go away."

There was a shuffle behind his back. Whispers and grunts got louder. He knew this slow, almost touching the ground footsteps. Toward him headed sluggishly the Archmage of the Magician School, a noble old man with a chill painted on his wrinkled face. The only thing that seemed alive in him were deep-set eyes covered with the limp skin of the eyelids, but smart and bright. Today his face expressed nothing. He hid his hands from the cold in the cavernous skirts of the robe sleeves. When he caught up with him, he raised his forehead and glanced at the Master, then said dryly:

"What's going on here, Morien? Why is the Alchemist at the gates? And why does he need a rune stone that he so vigorously turns in the pocket of his nasty cloth? Maybe you know Hmm ... Or he'll answer himself, for I was woken suddenly and I'm not sure if I'm not still half asleep. Am I, Lonan?"

Vadael, taking a thin hand from his sleeve, ran it over the head, sweeping snow from it.

Lonan winced. The old fool recognized him. Nay! He screened him better than he had expected. He didn't like pointless talk, and the Archmage loved to hold disputes for a long time, so he decided to cut the discussion quickly.

"We come for the fugitive, the magician named Lilian Vaal, who is being held here. By the Baroness' order, I demand her release."

"Master ..." Morien began, but the elder interrupted him.

"If she's here, it means she's not for you."

Anger blossomed on the foul magician's face. He frowned and hissed.

"Hand over the fugitive in the name of the law!"

"And what is this law, my dear?" Archmage scolded him gently. "I guess your law, which doesn't apply to us. So I tell you, since she was able to get to the School, I will add that I don't bother how it was possible, she is part of it and no Baroness is able to take her away. Only the king. Now excuse me, I have things to do! Having finished, he turned on his heel and signaled to Morien to follow him."

Onlookers cautiously faded in flakes of wet snow. Their presence was marked by traces trodden in white fluff, but they soon were absorbed by another layer of white.

The invaders stood a little longer. None said a word, but what hung between them resembled molasses so thick that if it wasn't for the fact that it was an illusion, they would both be stuck in it like insects in a thick soup. Lonan mumbled something for a moment, and the base of his staff glowed with a pulsing purple. Frightened, Darius put down the arrowheads and, having hung his bow over his shoulder, went to Ram's Head. Behind he heard the magician's rhythmic footsteps. What he was doing, dyeing wood, he didn't want to know. He was frozen. The plan seemed to him perfect, though so simple in construction. Now he was tempted by the glow of fire and the crackle of burning logs. The day was not over yet. Probably, when dusk laid down on the roofs, they would come to some conclusions. They would create a new, better scenario. Hopefully, because he didn't intend to excuse himself.

Mark briskly entered the tavern and threw his soaked clothes on the counter. Something from the threshold whispered that an altercation awaited him. He crossed the room and was surprised to find that nothing was prepared. No full bottles were put under the counter, the barrel in which the beer was kept stood empty in the same place where he had left it in the evening. Growing anger gathered around the larynx. He guessed that Lilian had overslept, after all, it wasn't the first time, except that she had crossed the line. He was tired of doing everything at the last minute. Stomping with the heels, he entered the kitchen, but stepped back immediately. The room cooled down completely, the fire in the furnace extinguished, and through the open window vent was coming in snow, which covered the bed of the girl with a wet coating of melting water. The girl wasn't there. He also didn't see the staff on which she liked to support herself when making trips. He put his hands on the hips and once again analyzed what he found. He couldn't believe that the alluring alewife escaped through the window. Why would have she done that when it is easier to leave through the doorway? He climbed onto the pallet, slammed the window opening, and rubbing his fists, returned to the main room.

The door opened slowly. In the brightness of the beginning of the day stood a man who began to stomp vigorously. The shaken snow settled on the threshold and turned into a grayish slime. The arrival ignored the owner, who was watching it in surprise. He crossed the room, then sat down on the bench, put down his weapon, and reached for the bone pipe he had left here a few clock strokes earlier. The unclosed door let in a blizzard. Mark wanted to say something, but when the mouth opened, the winter storm was obscured by the black silhouette of someone else. With his back to the light source, he appeared to be a tall individual with fairly broad shoulders, but when he entered, the innkeeper only managed to make a muffled moan, for he was so repugnant that even if he could, he would vanish through the kitchen window. Gnarled hands held the staff, while the robe showed signs of years of use, being frayed and soaked in the whim of the weather. The arrival closed the door and bypassed Mark. He plodded toward Darius, who already inhaled blue smoke.

"Lord?" Mark asked timidly. He wanted to make eye contact with the one he already knew. "Is there something wrong?"

"Poor owner of the lowly pit," sneered the spy. "You probably didn't know anything? Your favorite is the wanted magician."

The innkeeper raised his right eyebrow as he usually did when he didn't understand or heard a crude rumor. Nothing matched here, including the lack of Lili and the character he had seen for the first time, and which gave him strange anxiety. The skin went numb every time he turned his eyes on him. Confused, he only managed to speak vaguely:

"What are you talking about, lord?"

Darius rolled his eyes. He signaled that he was bored with pointless talk. He fiddled for a moment, reached behind his vest, and pulled out two documents that at first glance seemed heavily battered.

"Here you are, take it," he urged, shaking the papers.

Mark kicked his heels uncertainly, cleared his throat, but didn't make even a step. The presence of a stranger blocked his rational thinking, and probably if it wasn't for him, he would easily reach for parchments. However, he hesitated between wanting to read and escape. The archer saw this, stood up and shoved them into his hands.

"What the hell is it?" He blurted, but didn't unfold the evidence.

"Read. You can, right?" He mocked him again and put the pipe to the lips.

The owner of "Ram's Head" first unfolded one of them with shaking hands. A neat, even handwriting informed about a woman, who had escaped from the School of Magicians in Raghion. It was signed by the Baroness Alvena herself. The second one was nothing but a portrait of a woman with a curly mane, piercing eyes and an uncountable number of freckles on a slightly chubby face. He could have sworn it was Lili who looked from the paper, but he couldn't be sure.

"Poor man, he didn't know," he chuckled and moved his face toward his companion.

The alchemist twisted his pale mouth into what appeared to be a shadow of satisfaction, or perhaps the same malice that his guest fed him.

"So I'll tell you." Darius leaned and let out a cloud of gray smoke. "She probably besotted you with her beauty? I admit that I would have given in, I haven't had such an exotic maiden yet." He curled his lip. "You took the criminal under your roof, Mark. The dangerous magician who could sweep those walls whenever she felt like it. That's why we're here for her. Are you really so blinded? Didn't you notice anything?"

"I swear it," Mark stammered. "I had no idea. She worked well, everyone liked her, she didn't use magic."

"She used it," he heard.

In the doorway stood Erica pale and shaky, but of sober mind.

"What?!" He shouted. "You know it and you didn't say anything?"

She confirmed. She didn't seem confident now, as she usually did. She resembled a beaten mongrel which would probably begin to whine for mercy. She seemed little, as if shrunken.

Guilt consumed the interior of the old woman. She promised that she wouldn't betray her, but the situation required the truth, and she couldn't lie.

"But don't think badly, please!" She tried to excuse herself.

"How can I not think badly?!" He doubted.

"She's a good girl. If it wasn't for her, I would lose my hand. She is a healer, not a murderer. Don't let anyone convince you!"

Darius laughed even louder. The innkeeper turned purple with anger.

"Woman, you say she healed you, then show me this hand," Darius said, slightly amused at the picture of people snarling at each other.

The cook approached timidly. He didn't try to be polite, he pulled her so that she almost fell. He fastened his eyes on her wrinkled skin and stared at the furrows for a short while. Finding no wound remnants, he extended the woman's hand and showed it to the Alchemist.

"See, it's gone. No ordinary healer cures like that, there are always scars! You hear me, woman? Always!"

She broke away from him.

"Do you know where he is now? Sure you know! Behind the walls of the University. It was good thinking. Seducing Morien was a great move. Maybe you can help me get her back? If she finds out that ..."

"I won't let you hurt this poor child!" Erica gasped indignantly.

The alchemist moved slightly. In his eyes Mark saw the fire. Erica also. The man clad in black leaned on the staff and his stiff joints cracked in several places. His pale face was marked by pain. He approached.

"If it was up to me, you would both rot in the dungeons of the fortress. Since you, innkeeper, had no idea about it all, and believe me, I know when someone baffles me, you are free, I will let you live this life." He spread his arms, showing the grief of his existence. "And you will be escorted to the city prison, and from there you will be delegated to the capital for trial and sentencing."

Erica opened her mouth. Anger welled up in rotten veins, her blood was boiling and her head was buzzing.

"I'm not going anywhere!" She hissed. "You would have to kill me!" She straightened up and put the fists on her wide hips.

The alchemist became serious. Darius rested his elbows on his knees. He was waiting for what was to happen. He knew that enraged Lonan was unpredictable, so waiting for what was swirling in the mean mind somewhat excited him. So he stayed put like a hound. The magician clenched his fist. The woman clutched her throat and began to wheeze spasmodically. Fighting the lack of air, she opened her mouth like a huge carp wanting to get sated with residual oxygen. The rim, however, became more and more stuck, her bulging eyes seemed to flow out of the orbits, swollen with purple veins and backwaters of blood. The crackling of the vertebrae saturated the frozen air, Erica's hands fell limp along the body, and it itself tumbled down on the boards.

"Excellent show, Lonan," the spy approved. "One less, though she could have been useful to us." He pretended to be sad.

"She resisted," rumbled in Darius' temples. "Resistance is punishable by death!" He added, this time aloud, so that the present could hear.

The archer put a hand to his forehead. He didn't know if he thought it, or indeed Alchemist broke into his thoughts. He quickly realized that he had been plied with the Speech of Whispers.

"Cursed magicians," he growled to himself.

Mark was stunned. The dry eye sockets was burning. The throat, tightened in a tangled knot, couldn't make a single sound.

***

Meanwhile, Morien hung his head as he spoke to the Archmage. Multidimensional fear tormented him. Everything that had happened recently had consequences ... the terrible result of thoughtful and ill-considered actions. He didn't want to think about what punishment he would receive when he finally managed to free himself from his testimony. He knew the Master, and the Master knew him. He was an open book for him, a face with emotions drawn on his always distressed forehead. The Archmaster composed a series of sentences in his mind to be able to weave them into one particular string. The awareness that Lilian might have been temporarily tethered and delegated to the capital paralyzed his rational thinking. He had fought to save this amazing creature for so long, and now he would have to pay for his insolence.

The room was warm, but Morien was still shivering. He tried to hide his shaking hands, but it didn't work out.

"My dear," Vadael began. Now he was staring at snowflakes swirling outside the window. "What connects you with a Lilian? And no." He raised a hand to try to stop his verbosity. "Try to be brief. Alright?"

The magician swallowed and having put his hands on the back, he clasped his hands as tightly as he could. This gesture caused him pain, but thanks to that he could control the rising emotions.

"Master ..." he began almost in a whisper.

"Come on. Go ahead." He turned to him. "I'm human too."

Morien stared at the stuccoes. Words hardly went through his throat. Somewhere inside there was someone who wanted to shout what had been accumulating for a long time, but on the other hand he knew how stupid it would have sounded. How childish, hopeless and pathetic. He stood there for a moment. Courage, like the dust on reliefs, was unshakable.

"Master, I love her," he whispered.

He closed his eyes in relief.

"Alright. The Archmage wandered around the room. "So now another question. How long have you known about her presence in our city? Because, as you guessed, I have known for some time. Such a blow of power cannot be overlooked."

"For a long time, master," he replied contrite.

"I understand. Are you aware of what will happen?"

"Yes, master."

"So what will happen?"

"The Baroness will get mad?" He didn't realize how naive it sounded until he said it out loud.

"Exactly, my dear. The hand of the woman about whom no one wants to hear hither will hang over us! I perfectly remember the times before her Schools. I also remember that we were doing quite well, but because of the people of weak power we must now sweat. And before," He took a deep breath. "Partial binding was enough. Now, rune stones, Alchemists, and Redeemers know what else. That's not all, Morien. Rebellion. Does that mean anything to you?"

"Yes." The Archmaster curled his lip.

"Do you know why this lady has become a seedbed?"

"Because she managed to escape. Because everyone is fed up with Alvena and the king, who instead of going out with any decree, molders within the walls of the fortress?"

"Exactly. I also think that you shouldn't underestimate the elderly. Just because it's hard for us to climb the stairs and we don't show up often in class, it doesn't mean that we are blind, deaf and we ceased to feel. I perfectly understand the gusts of the young heart, passion and everything related to them. And don't," He raised his hand again. He signaled to Morien that he must have ended. He saw that he was about to interrupt him. "Don't bother yourself. You didn't foresee that such a strong magician might have a problem with controlling power. Didn't you think that enraged she could knock the city dead? Are you so in love that you do not see the obvious premises? Didn't you guess that concealing information will be revealed? It's inevitable! Morien! We are magicians, for the sake of the Redeemers!" He screamed.

"Master Vadael," Morien said. "Lilian is a smart woman, she can control the power. I vouch for her."

"You think so. I don't trust those I don't know and I haven't vetted! By the way, where is she now?"

"In my house, master. She is hurt. My maid took care of her."

Then let's go there and take our healer Aranius along the way to dress the wounds. We'll talk about the rest later. Now I'm too nervous to make any decisions.

***

Lilian was sitting huddled by the fire. The warmth of the fireplace caused that the pain pouring from the wound intensified. It brought waves of chills that crawled over the skin like swarms of ants. She shuddered and dusted herself off as if she had wanted to throw off what irritated the nerves. Magic made tissue structures boil. The covering fought the foreign body, but it didn't have enough strength to get rid of it. The arrowhead was stuck quite deeply, and any attempt to pull out the steel ended in the same - a stream of swear words.

Finally she felt no cold or fear. The twilight of the library soothed her in a magical and misunderstood way. She wasn't there alone, beside stood a swarthy woman who was trying to smile benevolently, but the sight of the red staining the glazed tile made her nauseous. However, she helpfully, as ordered, tried to wipe away the streaks and drops left by the unannounced guest. Lili told her several times to leave the blood, that she would clean it when the host came back, to not worry about the floor, but the words hit the vacuum, so she stopped.

Three men came into the room, of whom she only knew Morien. She looked up at the arrivals, wanted to bow politely, but when she tried to stand up, her knees buckled and instead of doing something that should have looked like a curtsy, she curled up, gnashing her teeth.

"Lili, this is the Archmage of the School: Vadael," the Archmaster presented the oldest of them.

The old man in black robes nodded, to which she replied, blushing with shame. Good upbringing strongly broke through impotence.

"The one here is the healer Aranius, who will help dress your wounds."

He bowed low. He was a young man wearing blue robes. The flawless face was surrounded by locks of blonde hair that gently flowed down the slim back. If she didn't know what his profession was, she would have guessed that he dealt with brewing decoctions or just healing. This group had a specific appearance, almost every of them had mild faces, nothing raw could be seen in them. She was surprised that the gift with which she was born didn't suit her appearance and feisty character. No doubt she belonged to the misfits.

"Hello," she said dryly. "I know that I come over as an ingrate, but if I could get rid of that damn thing quickly, I would ... do it myself. For now ... for now I'm helpless ..." She winced.

Talking brought fatigue. Her sore throat demanded moisturizing, but unfortunately she wasn't given any drink, which made her troubled.

Morien didn't wait for the others to do something and jumped to the girl. A moment later the fair-haired magician stood next to him. She didn't manage to object when one of them grabbed her to immobilizate her and the other unceremoniously got rid of the problem. The arrow rolled with a cling on the floor. Fortunately, the one who put his hand to the metal was Aranius, who cursed the place one breath before he put his hand to the inflamed body. In all the confusion, Lilian only managed to make a deep moan, but freed from strong arms, she felt unrestrained relief.

"Oh," she sighed, straightened and checked her skin condition.

Small fingers ran gently over the wound, she felt it was frayed and uneven. She struggled for a moment with the loose strings of her dress to free herself from the unnecessary material. The bare arm glistened in the firelight with the wetness of the blood.

Aranius leered at what he was about to do. Strangely enough, it didn't look that bad. So he beckoned to the maid to go to the kitchen for a bowl of clean water and rags, the rest he brought with him in a pouch freely dangling by the waist. The woman disappeared behind the door. Everyone heard her feverishly running down the stairs. Lilian saw that the healer wanted to take care of her immediately, so she said sluggishly:

"I can handle it. I need a moment to put my thoughts together. Please, lord, don't resent me." She looked at Aranius, who raised his eyebrows in surprise and wanted to express sharply his objection.

"Madam," he said. It turned out that this man with slightly feminine features had an amazingly low voice. "I will help, you are exhausted, I insist!"

"I can handle it. Give me a moment, lord." She didn't give up.

"So let me at least help you wash yourself more thoroughly. Of course, when the hostess comes back with what I asked for. I think she will come in a moment."

"Alright," she nodded, she wanted to end the conversation. "Let it be so."

Morien got up from his knees and walked over to Vadael. The noble personality was silent, she followed the actions of one of the students. The Archmaster wanted to say something, but he bit his tongue. The heels clicked in the corridor, the hostess entered the library. She carried a vessel with splashing water, and a large amount of linen rags was slung over her shoulder. The healer helped the girl get up from the fire, then, having took her arm, he led her towards a chaise longue located in the deeper part of the library.

Lilian didn't resist. Purple flares tired the pupils. Through them she couldn't take over the state and the place in which she was. She felt weak, defenseless and devoid of the protective bubble that magic gave. Aranius touched her skin with a soaked gray cloth. The coolness of the material stung the swollen tissues. She shuddered, but felt better with each move of the material. Her consciousness found its way. She knew that she was returning to gloomy reality. Finally, the surrounding objects began to emerge from stagnation, crests of volumes, sharp edges of furniture, a soft trimming of curtains, rugs and the floor marked by snowy shoes. She pushed the magician away, put trembling fingers on the hollow of her shoulder. She sighed. Pulsating of power began from the temple. Delicate, bright blue flares danced on the line of individual strands of hair, jumped one above the other, disappeared in the depths of the ends. Then the blood boiled, which was flowing down halters of veins tense from pain. The cascade of glittering matter filled the pads and made them resemble illusive wicks of magical candles. A cold, pulsating fire, fueled by a steady beat of the heart locked in the depths of the ribs.

The fair-haired magician moved closer. The demonstration of force of the woman, about which people never ceased to discuss, seemed even more fascinating to him than what he heard from excited lips. He raised his hand shyly and put it on Lilian's fingers. He whispered:

"Madam, forgive the boldness, but let's strengthen the magic. The process will go faster." His lips twitched to the beat of the pulsing light which filled also his bowels.

However, the color of the fire was paler, muffled, held back by uncertainty.

She knew that contradictions gnawed at him. She also knew that even if he couldn't break through the veil of power that surrounded her, he wouldn't want to be considered a schoolboy. She felt a little sorry at the very thought that she might have ridiculed him. He trembled, the tips of his hands twitched to the rhythm of fears nestling under the softness of the golden curls. She gave up. She pushed aside her obstinance and pride. Aranius' power tickling, reached the fraying and unevenness. It gently licked the bloody strands with its fires to slip into the depths consumed by suffering.

Morien went to the maid and led her out the door. The woman didn't say a word. The housewife knew that healing processes were not very complicated, but they required the concentration and presence of those who dabbled in this art. Just caring for the sick was nothing in comparison to what medical practitioners armed with magic weapons could do. She was also aware that Morien took care not only of her safety, but also of the Archmaster's himself. Just in case, she prepared a brush and a bucket. Damage that she may have found after returning to the library might have overwhelmed her a bit.

The master crossed the room. A quick reconnaissance brought immediate hiding of everything that was flammable, glass or delicate. He couldn't protect the book collection, so in spirit he asked the Redeemers for not too much escalation of power connections. Two magicians could turn the library into a mess. After making sure that he did what was necessary, he stood again next to the master and stared at those who huddled at the other end, surrounded themselves with a bubble of pulsing threads.

Small discharges first marked the dome. Cracking, they jumped from one furniture to other, to evanesce in the dim light. Over time, there were more of them swarming. It seemed to Morien that he was stuck in the heart of a storm, but one where the air stood still, stuffy and plastering everything with stinking slime of burned scraps of fabric, leather and blood. When the next flash flew past his feet, he reached out and marked the semicircle. He surrounded himself and his mentor with a protective, semi-transparent field, on the edges marked with dwarven runes that meant the shield. The one next to him apparently didn't react. He just narrowed his eyelids and analyzed.

The wounded woman felt pressure, the same tormented the healer. She wanted to release her vital forces to finally finish the process, but something whispered her to concentrate, that strengthening could have brought unexpected results. So she allowed to be led slowly.

The unbearable itching affected the skin, getting to the muscles and savaged veins. Drops of sweat flowed in the trickle and flooded the temples and forehead of the martyred.

"Just a moment," she repeated to herself. She got satiated with another wave of healing stimuli. "Just a moment," she droned, as the last tugs merged the skin into one.

She pushed the healer away firmly, the man separated from her sat on his heels. Lilian ran her knuckles along the healed skin. In the glow of the light blurred by snow, the gathered saw a pink, irregular scar winding toward the collarbone. The girl lowered her legs to the floor and wrapped her arms around her. A few sudden discharges popped around, a pale gray cloud enveloped the world around. She pulsed and writhed as if she had been a part of a living but distressed being. It lasted only a few breaths, but it impressed those present so much that Morien stopped controlling the shield. It faded and left them defenseless. The Archmage made exactly the same gesture, giving them a safe haven. After a while everything went quiet. The air hung in the room, even heavier and more stinky than before. They breathed with difficulty. The magician extinguished the magic and exhausted, she put her head on the couch headboard. She looked as she had just submerged in the river, sweat soaked through the coarse dress, created stains and damp patches on it. There wasn't even left a whitish line after the shot.

Vadael dropped the cover and walked over to the student, leaving behind the Archmaster, who still couldn't get over the stupor. Not only was the beloved only weak, but also the location in which they stayed didn't get devastated, as if she herself was careful not to overdo the force of the spells. He wanted to run up to her and catch her half-fainted, giving her a thousand brushes of lips, but the presence of two men cooled his tendencies.

"Unusual," said the Archmage admiringly. "I haven't seen such magic for a long time."

Lilian gave him a quick look, though she didn't care much for the old man's praise and admiration. She was thirsty, she dreamed of a decent glass of purple, sweet wine and a slice of bread, preferably with honey. However, she had to wait obediently. The Redeemers knew what else they would want to do, especially since she wasn't welcome there. She was quickly sobered up by the fact that she teetered. And she didn't know if she would fall into the abyss, or whether these hands, wrinkled and covered with liver spots, would protect her from the inevitable falling down.

"Aranius, great work." The archmage patted the healer on the shoulder. "I'm proud of you."

Lilian rose on trembling arms and laboriously pulled the wet cloth over her body. Suddenly she felt naked. Fortunately, the strength was returning quickly, the throbbing pain finally vanished and she could move. Unable to cope with the straps, she pleadingly looked out for her lover, who glanced longingly at her from afar.

"Morien, could you?" She whispered.

He raised his eyebrows expectantly.

"Could you help me tie the dress? I can't make it, please."

Confused and with the reddening cheeks, he came over and began to strugle with the binding. Women clothes had always been an enigmatic thing for him, which he didn't try to understand, so he every now and then grunted at her. He begged with it for any tips. Fortunately, the Lilian dress was one of those not tiring to put on.

"Well ..." began the Archmage. He hid his fingers in the wide sleeves. "Now we'll talk ... I thought that after what I had heard, you would turn out, madam, to be a demon with bleeding eye sockets, and I see the mediocre figure of the maiden who, wherever she puts her foot, leaves fear and corpses." Do you realize, madam, that our two guards died today and it's all your fault?"

Lili wanted to roll her eyes first, but then, as he continued, she felt remorse and all she could do was lower her forehead and stare at the library boards.

"Forgive me, lord. Coming here was the only salvation, I regret the death of the sentries. If you let me, lord, I will send to their families letters expressing sympathy."

The archmage interrupted her, regardless of the fact that the woman's face from breath to breath began to resemble a leaf withered from regret.

"My dear, do you know that you expose not only yourself, but also the School and all who live, study and work here? It didn't occur to you that you would have to pay for it? And, for the sake of the Redeemers, madam, but writing sad messages will not comfort anyone!"

She felt furious. She wanted to approach the old man and hit him in the face. Not because he rebuked her, but because he provoked anger that made her blood boil and fueled the body for deeds that she might be ashamed of over time. She saw no guilt in herself, but a desire to survive, and though he was right, she didn't realize that she had brought trouble not only on her head. She clenched her fists, which brightened with a whitish glow, put them in the folds of her dress and turned toward the window. Powder snow was swirling sluggishly, noiselessly falling on the windowsill. The stinging whiteness forced her to narrow her eyelids.

"Lord, I'll leave tonight," she said emphatically. She almost choked with rage.

"If I can interfere," said Aranius. "It can result in unavoidable death. The alchemist will sense your presence everywhere."

She shrugged indifferently.

"So what? I can handle it. I have done it so much time that now nothing will stand in the way of burning them along with the arrest warrants and runic stones. No worries. You won't have to worry about security." She crossed the library, and when she was at the height of the desk, Morien blocked her way.

"Let's talk, we don't have to bridle like that." In Master's eyes she saw not only begging, but also somewhere deep inside his pupils lurked embarrassment about her behavior, which cooled her temper.

"Yes, your lover is right." Archmage's voice hoarse from across the room. "Let's sit down and talk."

"Let's move to the living room." The white-haired pointed to the door. "There, we will calmly decide what to do."

Lili stood with her hands pressed under her armpits. She felt cold, but also the smell of stale skin. She didn't like to be dirty, the school taught hygiene, and sloppiness was severely punished, including drinking dirty water, after a delinquent, in front of the commission, cleaned his unclean skin. It frustrated even more than the chasing tone of the leering old man. Fortunately, not only at her. His superiority irritated her throughout.

"Come on, honey."

She grunted as he took her arm and gently brought her down the narrow stairs. The modesty of the salon immediately struck her. The center was a large table made of polished wood, with chairs placed on the side, and a vase with flowers preserved with magic, prancing in the middle. The windows let little light into the room, perhaps because instead of pane, they were constructed of differently colored glass pieces connected with silver threads. However, the multicolored twilight created such a fabulous atmosphere here that for a moment she stared at the illumination of the light dancing on the floor. A sideboard of the same color as the table was set up at one of the walls. Behind the glazed door, teapots, cups and other accessories were arranged to accommodate guests.

"The bottom probably contained plates." She ran away with her thoughts from the difficult conversation that awaited her.

The master showed her the place, so she rested obediently. Immediately after the rest joined. The noble old man leaned against the table with his chin on a hand and was silent for a moment. She had the impression that silence would burst her eardrums, but the Master fidgeted in the seat and, folding his arms over his chest, asked:

"Since we're here, let's not be at each other's throats, it's so childish. Of course, I understand what is bothering you and understand the fear of Master Morien, but the matter is so important that we need explanations, not more arguments."

The girl nodded, she knew that he kept a sharp eye on her. Maybe she got carried away too much. Now she also felt ashamed and shy. She decided to give a chance to fate, let it lead her wherever it deemed appropriate.

"Will you tell me, my dear, why did you run away?"

She sighed. She remembered when detail after detail she told the story to Morien. It didn't seem thrilling or interesting. She would have said that this was the most boring story she could have written. Already the apartment and contribution in "Ram's Head" seemed more exciting than visiting dungeons, casemates and fighting on the route for each day. Except that it was love that rushed ahead, the love of the child for his mother.

"So." She took a breath. "About a year and a half ago, worried about the lack of news from my parent, I decided to break into the archives at the School of Magic in the Capital and steal the plans of the dungeons and basements. Later…"

The gathered remained silent. All that was heard was the old man's wheezing breath, who swallowed the slightest gulp of air every now and then to let it out. Morien rested his head on his fists, and Aranius put one leg on another, folded his fingers and placed his wrists on his thigh.

"That's all," she murmured, stretching herself.

She grasped her mistake and put her hands on the table.

"Well." The old magician stared at the colorful flowers. "Did I understand correctly? The only guilt you can bear is longing for the mother? That's it? There were no other motives? Surprising, really. If you are telling the truth."

"Why would I lie to you?" She hissed, reddening again.

"To protect yourself, it's obvious. The funniest thing about it is that everyone around is convinced that the reason for leaving the school walls is nothing but rebellion and the desire to form a conspiracy against Alvena." He shook his head. "I have thought about it for some time. I look for a source of gossip. I found out that the fairy tale probably created the Baroness herself to have an excuse to pull out her favorite hounds outside the walls. And, what's obvious, she has informers at the Universities. After all, correspondence cannot always be monitored. The only question is: what have you done that it's so important for her to find and kill you, madam?"

Lilian shrugged and made a silly face. Vadael talked meaningfully. She also thought that the perpetrator of the confusion might have turned out to be Alvena, although she had never dealt with her, she hadn't even seen her, so the alleged behavior seemed unlikely to her, and gossip, as is customary, grew under the influence of animation and excitement associated with the first escape of this type.

"You see, master," Morien interjected. "I told you Lilian didn't intend to raise a dust, that she wasn't dangerous. She's rather scared."

"Boy, her presence will definitely cause a lot of speculation. I don't want to think about what will happen when the news spreads like lice around the dormitories. Novices and middle youth are burning to begin rebellion. I have tried to keep my finger on the pulse for a long time. What's worse, over these inexperienced magicians we can see an uprising, and if other schools find out, then ..."

"A war," added Aranius, most likely initiated earlier in Lili's case.

"Exactly," finished the old man. "We'll have a war. I'm sure that they have already sent a letter to the Baroness. It is good that we have several weeks or months before the armed men appear within the city walls. I will order the scribe to write the words and send a note to Aaron himself, maybe he will find an idea how to alleviate it. For now, our fugitive miss will stay here, but I don't want her to leave this apartment and talk to anyone but me and Morien," he remarked emphatically.

He stood up, arranged his robe so that it looked smooth and neat again, then he bowed his forehead, said goodbye and left. The healer followed him, also saluting them goodbye. Both men let themselves be absorbed by the whiteness of the early morning when the door slammed behind them with a soft moan.

Lilian and Morien were alone, surrounded by silent walls and equally silent equipment. Morien couldn't wait to fall at her feet. They sat for so long, she on a stool, leaning on a richly carved backrest, he with his head on her lap, embracing her around the waist.

"I was afraid that something bad happened to you. I can't describe it. It paralyzed me and took my senses away. I wanted to get rid of it, but it came back and hollowed in my head an unimaginable amount of bottomless abysses ... I was so scared!"

Lilian was breathing hard and stroking the white hair, staring at the emptiness of winter, which stuck to the thin shoots of bushes growing outside the window. She had the impression that snowfall was just what had overwhelmed her for a long time, and she was these soft branches susceptible to weight, balancing between being and final surrender.

"Don't worry," she reassured. "Somehow we will put it together ... somehow ..."

"I could do this for all eternity." He snuggled in her more tightly, she returned the gesture. "I love you too, Morien."

***

Morien caused a sheer storm. Those on the estate were put on standby. The redhead was planted by the stove, where a cup of milk was placed in her hands. She could do nothing, as soon as she raised the duff, she was immediately called to order, so she was stuck for moments that dragged on endlessly. She slurped and warmed herself at the crackling fire. So, for entertainment, she observed the feverish service, counted the bundles of garlic and onions hung here and there, and looked carefully at the tips of the shoes. Finally, when she began to lose hope, the well-known swarthy woman entered the kitchen, and with goodness that sparked in the ebony eyes, she invited her to a small room right next to the kitchen. She had no idea what it had served for, but certainly no one lived in it, except for spiders and other types of wonders she despised. Now there was placed a small, but comfortable bed, slightly dusted, but useful closet, a small table facing a large window and a chair on which she could rest. In the corner, there was a dressing table with a mirror, a bowl embedded in the back of the counter and a stool that looked more like a footstool than a seat. She knew that the lodging hastly made might have been cramped, but it was much safer than Erica's kitchen. At the thought of the good heart of the cook and delicious food, she felt emptiness, as if she had been to never meet her again. An icy stream of fear rolled through the spine. She came to herself. After all, they would probably sit down many more times and talk about a past day, as they usually did, while sipping root wine. But that when everything was alright. She trusted good coincidences - always! She looked at the lady running Morien's house, bowed gracefully, as low as she could, and the woman blushed, put her hand to her mouth and giggled. She gave Lila a gentle hint that this was her role, but Lilian really enjoyed what had been done, even if instead of living with the Master, she was stuffed into a dark corner deep inside the house. Although she shouldn't have been under the illusion that she would be treated as his partner, the School's orders clearly defined the extent of what Masters and Archmasters could do. She lamented, but fed on the hope that maybe now she would see him much more often than once a week. At that time, she missed the things she identified with boundless security, the things she had collected for some time and always had with her - a sack with which she arrived in the city, full of ointments, decoctions, and the mandrake root that had accompanied her since the beginning of her trip.

"Morien," she said as he walked through the corridor with the scroll. "Would it be possible to ..."

"Yes, my dear?"

"Look ... I have a little problem." She leaned on the door frame. "My lumber was left in Mark's home. Would it be possible to get it back? I know I shouldn't ask you for anything anymore, but ... I'm a bit attached to them."

He put the rolled scroll to his mouth, and stood there in silence for a short time, pondering what could have been done about it.

"It's a little risky," he grunted. "Surely Darius is still at the "Under Ram's Head" and is probably accompanied by the Alchemist, but I can write a letter to the house of the cook, what was her name? Erica, right?" He waited for the girl to confirm the name with a nod. "Maybe she'll be able to carry out your trivialities. What do you think?"

"Yes, I could agree to such a conspiracy."

"I'll send a letter in the morning. Don't bother, it's a matter of a few days."

"Thank you, and could I ...?" She whispered.

"Yes?"

"Could I use the library? Or would it be better if I stay in the room and don't bother anyone?"

"My dear, the house is at your disposal. Do what you fancy." He winked and disappeared into the kitchen warmth.

A broad smile of satisfaction beamed her pale and freckled cheeks. She didn't close the door, she ran upstairs, eager for literary adventures. Choosing what just caught her eye, she decided not to hang around anyone's feet, so she hid in the designated four walls and drowned in the vastness of the adventure novel.

The maid, whom she hadn't yet met, brought her food in the evening. The girl, lit by a large number of candles, noticed her hands shaking.

"Are you afraid of me?" She asked when she saw the maid's embarrassment.

The confused elf stared at the wooden floor. The directness of the new lady wasn't the type of weight she could bear.

Lili couldn't do otherwise. Confidence and lack of boundaries always caused her considerable problems when it came to making a good first impression. As a result, she was either perceived as insolent or loose, never anything in between. Only when she got here did she try to be restrained. However, it didn't always work out as planned. She went to the newcomer, tilted the head slightly and looked at her face.

"My dear," she began. She took her hands in hers. "I don't know what people say about me within these walls, but I will probably find out in a while, most likely from Morien himself, whose tongue gets too loose with a larger drop of wine." She giggled and wrinkled her nose funny. "But know that rumors are just rumors and before you start believing them, confront them with reality. I'm not bad.

Others have made me be considered such, so you have nothing to be afraid of."

The maiden paled, as if all the blood from her face had been pressed into her ears, because only they in the light of the oil lamps burned brighter than the red-hot wicks. She didn't know if she should have cried, or maybe curtsied, nodded, spoken? So she stood looking at the magician. She had a desire to return to her duties, she only managed to say:

"Thank you, madam." She curtsied and disappeared behind the door.

Lili glanced at the tray. The food here looked completely different, the hostess attached great importance to the appearance of the dishes, so the most ordinary soup was served in porcelain, and in the middle of the broth a pile of soft peas with a little cream was placed. The dish was topped with a leaf of parsley neatly stuck into the white fluff of the dairy hill. Next to it was a ruddy apple and a cup full of chamomile infusion.

"Probably to make me sleep well," she thought and grabbed the fruit.

She delved into reading again, and since the book wasn't extensive, she was halfway through the story. She wanted to finish it before going to rest.

Morien spent the evening in the library. He wanted to go downstairs and say goodnight, but he was aware that all eyes were on him. He also hoped that Lili would go to bed earlier, tired of the day, which also got under his skin. In order not to waste time on empty thinking, he wrote a message to Erica and left it in the corridor by the door, thus leaving it for the morning delivery. He didn't know, however, that the recipient was no longer given the opportunity to read its content.

***

Mark wandered around the inn on familiar trails, and only when Darius and Alchemist disappeared on the first floor, he crouched next to Erica's body and wept bitterly. He came to his senses when the first employee appeared in the doorway. He almost pushed her into a blizzard, telling her to communicate others that "Ram's Head" was closed that day and he had no idea if he would order the same next day. The maiden stretched her neck and tried to look inside, but the broad chest of the innkeeper blocked her view. He knew that if it was revealed now, the avalanche of slander would not only reach him, but also the family of the deceased, and he couldn't allow it. He slammed the door. He walked around the counter and reached into the lowest of the drawers, the one that almost never opened. He pulled a closed sign out of it and having driven a nail, he hung it on the outside of the front door.

Binding impotence slowed his every move. He did not want to look in the face of the deceased or touch her, nor could he leave her like that. So he lifted the heavy and limp body of his friend. When he was carrying it to the kitchen, he sobbed again, this time louder. He couldn't suppress what was tearing the interior. He arranged Erica on the Lilian's straw mattress, placed heavy coins on her eyes, and covered her with a leather saddlecloth. He threw the capot over his back and left the tavern. The scribe lived on the street away, had several messengers at his disposal, so he placed on their hands an unpleasant obligation to deliver breaking correspondence. He had the impression that the whole intricately arranged world suddenly collapsed, deafened him and deprived him of feeling. The most painful was the death he couldn't prevent. He was worried about the girl, but he knew that she was safely hidden in the School. After returning, he decided to review the magician's things, maybe he would find answers in them, although he didn't count on it. It crossed his mind that he shouldn't have touched anything, but braced himself and take it to the owner, but curiosity won, so he did something quite different.

The kitchen was dim. The cook's body was still invisible to the eye. He put his hand near her shoulder and sighed heavily, sat on his heels and reached for the bundle.

"Oh, Erica," he groaned, sniffing. "Why didn't you say anything to anyone? Maybe it would be different ... maybe," he whispered resignedly.

The sack seemed heavy, though it didn't look like that. He untied it carefully and spilled the contents onto the ground, looking at each object. To his surprise, a pouch landed in his hands, almost half filled with silver. She could had bought a lot of things for it. He wondered why she never spent on her needs? She probably had saved tips for her journey. He also found strange ointments and tonics with a pungent smell, as well as powders and roots, but one thing surprised him the most. He didn't know what that was. It was hidden in a soft bag with an embroidered Mages School crest. The object resembled a human figure, but twisted, as if suffering. When he picked it up, he felt that it moved, crouched with even greater intensity. Scared, he quickly put "it" back.

"It's a mandrake." Alchemist's hoarse voice heard behind him.

He flinched.

"What? Man ... what?"

The emaciated creature silently moved closer. Its clawed hand signaled him to give it what he had just stuck with fear in the pouch. Blood drained from Mark's face. He sensed the coldness and discomfort associated with the magician's proximity. Lonan urged him, as if the moments he breathed had been more valuable than anything else. The innkeeper handed him the item.

"It's a plant with magical properties," he explained. "It grows only in the fields where they hang villains. It is created from the essence of magic and the semen of the dead."

The innkeeper felt a wave of disgust, perhaps even greater than the one he felt for the magician.

"By Redeemers," he said. "And I touched it." He grimaced.

"She probably stole it. I doubt she would know where to look. Now it is rare to hang convicts on the death fields, what a pity. The mob has liked entertainment, so the executioners moved to the cities. How much I liked this silence before the final verdict. Now it is drowned out by cheers and squeals of excitement. Disgusting," he growled and having taken the peculiar object, threw it on the pile. "I don't need it. I see you are curious."

"It's weird. You, lord, would probably react similarly to the news that the best of the alewives is being hunted down, and for magic which I have been afraid of for years. Although," He pointed at the lumber. "I think she is useful."

The innkeeper nudged the intruder with his arm and left the kitchen. He sat down behind the bar, poured a big cup of wine, and drank it in one gulp. He didn't feel like discussing with this thing, if it had any human features.

***

Darius was thrashing. He was cursing under his breath, turning the arrow with his fingers.

"Damn it," he growled. "How could she?"

Lonan came back to the cubbyhole, indifferent and cool as always, as if nothing that sparkled and pulsated around him, hadn't bothered him at all, and he only had waited for fodder from suffering and tears.

"I'm going to the City Guard headquarters. I have to find out if there is a chance to get to the University by another route."

"I would go in through the gate and set those freaks on fire," the spy snorted.

"Easy," he snapped. "You are at my mercy. Keep a low profile, or the lady will get your head for consolation."

"Ha! And what would you say? Let me guess: I killed, madam, the best of your people?" He sneered.

"Don't play about, fool."

"You won't do anything to me. I'm untouchable ..."

An icy hand tightened on the larynx of the fair-haired shooter, a paroxysm of pain ran over Darius' nerves. Convulsions gripped the limbs, and foamy sputum filled the lips getting blue.

"Don't play with me!" The magician loosened his grip.

The man fell on the boards, choking with secretions mixed with blood. Having put his shaky hands to the back of his neck, he felt as if he hadn't touched the skin, but parchment dry as a bone. He coughed and vomited in the corner of the pallet.

"You will recover." The alchemist watched him pityingly. "In a few days you will look like before."

The archer ran his fingertips over his cheeks, it wasn't his face but the face of the old man. The tissue sucked out with time, became wrinkled and withered. It hid the firmness of the youthful mind under the cover of ugliness.

"Alright," he croaked.

Lonan walked around the huddled and went downstairs. Mark was just saying goodbye to the cook's family. His paleness was marked by deep furrows. He aged a good few years in one day. The innkeeper didn't look at his face, but only with disgust spat under his feet and reached for the demijohn which was on the counter. The magician let the whitened twilight of the dusk softly give him shelter.

***

The Master couldn't get back to normal, he returned to the library, settled himself in a chair and fell into a nice laziness. The body demanded respite, but the mind couldn't accept it for anything. He straightened up and put his hands on the desk, looked around carefully, and fixed his eyes on the ubiquitous mess. It clearly appeared that he had accumulated duties. Probably going to bed late would give him a hard time, but what he would manage to write now, would allow him to tame his nervousness. He deceived himself. He said that work is a cure for everything. So he reached for the pen and unfolded a parchment after parchment, marking on them symbols only known to him, thanks to which he could find himself in chaos.

Lilian got bored of reading. She yawned and rubbed her eyes, and the unread book was slammed against the table. Sleep didn't stick to the eyelids, even though somewhere inside there was a desire to bury herself in clean bedding. She knew that she would have been lying long and aimlessly looking at the ceiling. She lifted her head and thought that they should have covered it with lime, because it had gotten dirty right next to the shutters. She came to herself, after all, it was ridiculous to stand and admire the stains. She ran her fingers over her head, dressed the hair and moved towards the dressing table. Dark circles under the eyes clearly indicated that it would have been worth to go to sleep. The body unquestionably denied this condition.

She slightly opened the door, stuck out her nose and looked out curiously. The corridor was lit by several lamps. She climbed the stairs on her toes. They didn't moan under the pressure of her delicate booted foot. A bright streak of light flowed from under the library door. The hope blossomed that Morien, like her, was a night owl today.

She slipped noiselessly and leaned against wood. She winked jauntily at the magician, then almost running, she settled comfortably on his lap, throwing her arms around his neck. Startled, he dropped the document, clutching at the table. The armchair slammed under their weight and rocked so dangerously that he would have preferred to avoid falling on the boards. She giggled and having cuddled up at him, she pulled up her legs.

He embraced her gently. It was nice to feel the familiar smell. He was absorbing the transience with full chest, breathing the same air as she was. He felt that Lili didn't feel like chatting but was craving for closeness. He was silent, counting individual freckles, which marked slim forearms. He wondered how the girl would bear being locked up, after all, she wasn't humble. She was accustomed to the wind on the cheeks and emotions boiling under the skin. When would she explode? When the problems accumulated? When the Baroness got mad?

He sighed.

She pulled away from him and began to poke around with sparkling eyes. She was still mysteriously silent. She looked at small objects, lifted them and put them back, ran her finger on the spines of books, walked between the shelves. After a while, she stopped in front of the window and stared at the night grenade, drifting deep into unruly thoughts. The man watched her patiently, sitting comfortably behind the desk. He wanted to ask a lot of questions, but the language stuck to the palate and instead of conversation, there was only silence. Lilian left without a word, and after a while he heard the squeak of one of the maidens. They probably had to bump into each other. Morien rested the forehead on his hand and shook the head in resignation. What awaited him? He had no idea, but certainly this house would no longer be as quiet as it had used to be.

It thundered and vibrated. Every corner was filled with the murmur of dozens of mouths whispering in the ears countless news, not necessarily true, but so exciting that even the oldest magicians lent their ears. Morien and Lili were obviously the talk of others. The servants knew it, as they did, safely hidden behind the walls of the residence. The girl seemed to be in her world and didn't care that every appearance in the corridor frightened prying eyes that looked and waited for developments.

Now her thoughts revolved around sleepiness and the empty stomach, not prying maids, who instead of doing errands, followed with their eyes her and the master of the house. So she plodded to the kitchen, where the kitchenmaid, having noticed the intruder, dropped the milk cup, blowing it to bits.

"Madam," she moaned with tears in her eyes. "You should rest because you don't look too good."

Lili turned her head sideways and looked around the room from under half-closed eyelids.

"Good morning. I think I got hungry," she said, and yawned at once, covering her mouth with her hand.

"You could call, the maiden would have brought breakfast," she said less plaintively.

"Milk," Lili pointed at the floor. "The milk needs to be wiped and the shards collected, otherwise it will be spread over stone." She approached the woman and bent to reach for the fragments.

"Madam." The maiden almost fell to her knees next to Lili, and urgently grabbed her wrist. "Please, madam, leave it. You can't do such things. I'll clean it up soon."

"It's not a problem." Lili freed herself from the elf's trembling hands. "It's just shards. Please, give me a rag. The trouble will be solved right away," she insisted.

"Madam, I'll give you a meal shortly, please ..." Big tears danced again in the corners of the maid's eyes.

The mage managed to recover due to the strange behavior of the kitchenmaid. The fact that the elf had squatted in front of her explained a lot. She knew well how non-people are treated, but she couldn't understand why. After all, they weren't that different. She was also surprised that she had encountered this precedent in this house. She straightened and folded her arms.

"Alright. If you wish so. I would like some food. I will go to the library. Is this a problem?"

"No, madam, it's no bother. Thank you."

The room smelling of parchment and dust greeted her with deaf silence and the light chill of a wind-blown fireplace. She scooped out ash and, putting wood in it, she concentrated slightly. Small sparks flowed across the ankles, leaped one after the other, and dry logs caught fire. At this moment, the Master stood in the doorway, who didn't look impeccable. Loose hair stuck out in different directions, and sand was still accumulating under the eyelids. On the back, however, he wore a drab cloth, which without a doubt didn't belong to the night wardrobe.

"Hello," he grunted, wrapping himself more tightly. "Did you sleep well?"

"Middlingly," she replied and shifted one of the glades with her poker.

He came and bent down. He kissed Lili on top of her head.

"What are you meditating on? He asked when she didn't look away from the fire."

"I wonder how long I'll stay here."

"The Archmage will come up with something, you have nothing to fear.

"I know, but I hate to be stuck in ignorance. It's like I'm drowning."

"We need some time, I think you can understand that? It's not easy."

"Yes, I know, but ..." She inhaled with the nose and let the air out through the mouth. "I hope there are enough books ..."

"No worries." He pointed to the window, or rather what was on the other side of the square. "The University's book collection will provide "entertainment" for several long years, if not decades."

"It's not funny," she snapped and got up from her knees.

"I was kidding. What raised your hackles that you have been out of sorts since the morning?"

"Nothing specific." She folded her arms.

"Speak," he encouraged.

"Kitchenmaid," she spat.

"Kitchenmaid? And what did Mahira do to you?"

"To me? Nothing, but she looked as if she had been afraid, and I don't like mistreatment of service!"

"And who treats anyone badly here? Lili!"

"I deduced it from her behavior."

The magician moved closer, wrapped his arms around her and put his cheek to hers.

"Trust me, please, nobody hurts anyone in this house. Just like you, Mahira needs to get used to it. She is a tethered magician, she has undergone the process voluntarily, I also accepted her as a help." He pulled away from the girl. "She experienced many bad things. I think you will make friends over time."

Surprised, Lili took a step back and looked up at her lover's face. She felt foolish again.

The awkward silence was broken by the door grinding as the housewife entered the library. She carried a sealed message on a tray, but didn't put it on the desk, but walked over to Lila and handed it to her, then bowed and left the room.

"It's from the Archmage." Morien pointed out, recognizing the familiar handwriting.

"Great," she ground out. "The old man's morals, the last thing I need now."

"Oh, don't complain, read it."

"Alright." She rolled her eyes, broke the seal and looked at the content.

He wrote:

Madam!

Due to the fact that you are currently in the care of the School, I would like to meet you at my office after the last lectures. I look forward to the appointment.

Best Regards,

Archmage of the School of Mages in Archal,

Vadael

The pressure of Morien's fingers on Lili's shoulders intensified.

"Don't worry, I'll go with you anyway."

She wanted to believe that impotence would blow over. Winter turned out to be her best ally, messengers rarely traveled during snowstorms, it was easy to get lost, it was also easy to fall into an ambush. Although the Baroness' crest sewn into a jacket was a good excuse not to bother such man, who said that the corpse would start talking when the corpse was uncovered by the spring melt? Now, fortunately, she was surrounded by a shade of care, though not necessarily the one she would have liked to have. Even the safest place could be a prison. She trembled at the thought that the time would come when she would be forced to go outside the walls of the residence. What would she hear? How would they receive her? She choked on anxiety. Now also this meeting with the Archmage. It seemed not a big deal, and yet pulled the string in the heart so hard that she lost her grip.

Morien suspected that under a mask of relief there was a wounded bird in Lili, whose wing was pinioned. He had to do it well. He knew that the more he would slobber over her, the worse she would take it. Support is useful, but overprotectiveness could lead nowhere. Nay! It only would make her mad, and instead of the promised peace, it would rake over already festering internal fears.

"Alright. Come with me," she said.

"Maybe you will take a nap?" He took care of her. "You didn't sleep well. I will tell the servants not to disturb you."

"Yes. I think I will." She rested her head on the magician's shoulder. "I'm really tired."

"Then go. I need to prepare for classes."

She nodded, kissed his cheek, and walked away. In the corridor she met the elf who was carrying an oatmeal and brew. Fortunately,

Mahira had a lot of understanding and promised that as soon as Lili got up she would bring her something warm. Lilian was grateful, she curtsied and hid in the silence of the current home. Cool bedding and dusk stolen by heavy curtains slightly soothed her nerves.

The Master's classes dragged on, the students seemed distracted, and he also wasn't attentive. It came to the point that the classes were not going according to plan, and he got carried away by inquiries and curiosity of young people. He shared with them the piece of knowledge that was the safest for them, and when they began to get too curious, he chased them out of the room, explaining that he had a nasty headache attack and had to go to the herbalists.

In the afternoon a letter came. Erica's daughter reported that her mother was dead and was asking for support in the matter of burial. He guessed that the cook was the only one to support the family, so he added three dwarven coins to correspondence that would allow them to survive for some time. He felt severe discomfort in the larynx, not from grief, but rather from fear of how Lilian would react to bad news. He respected Erica, but at that time he couldn't imagine that the cook was dead. As if it hadn't hit hard enough to create an avalanche of sadness. He crumpled the parchment and went downstairs.

The magician was sitting at the table, sipping soup and staring out the window. At the sight of the friendly face, she beamed, stuck another portion in her mouth, and swallowed quickly. She quickly realized that Morien hadn't come to accompany her.

"Did something happen to you?" She asked.

"Sit next to me." He pointed to the bed.

She put down the silverware and raised one eyebrow, which was supposed to mean surprise, but sat down obediently beside him.

"I got a message," he began. "From Erica's daughter."

"From daughter? Did she have children?" Lili was surprised. "She never mentioned it. I thought we were close."

"Sometimes people keep things to themselves. She apparently didn't want to talk about her."

"Apparently," she sighed. "Well, that's a pity. She was the only one who knew who I am ..."

"What?" He jumped up abruptly. A blue vein pulsed on his forehead. "And you didn't say anything?"

"I didn't see the need." She shrugged. "She burned her hand once. If it wasn't for me, she would have suffered for a long time. I couldn't let her lose her fingers. It didn't look good. I trusted her and she promised to keep her peace."

"Do you realize what you did?"

"What do you mean?" She got worried.

Morien calmed down. Magic, however, still pulsed in his temples.

"I'm glad you wanted to do good." He took a good sip of air. "However, I think that this knowledge didn't work out well for her."

"What do you mean?"

"I'm sorry." He gave her the crumpled message. "Alchemist ... I suppose he got the things he wanted from her, then got rid of the problem and protected himself with a directive claiming she was a traitor."

Blood drained from Lili's face. She didn't know what was happening around her, she broke down, crouched and burst into tears. She felt weak. As weak as if someone had deliberately taken her breath away. The terrible pain in her ribs was spreading and taking her will to live. The Master, seeing this, put his hands on her head. A stream of refreshing power flowed down on her like a cascade of sparks. She revived, but not enough.

"But ...?" She sniffed. "She was innocent, she didn't do anything to anyone!"

"They bring death. That's why everyone is afraid of black magicians. He didn't have to have a reason. It's enough that he got what he wanted. The rest was unnecessary."

Lili buried her face in her hands. She sobbed loudly.

"It's my fault. My fault ..." she repeated and moved back and forth. Morien put his arm around her and hugged her.

"Not yours, she was just in the wrong place."

Lilian broke free and ran out of the room, slamming the door. The magician was sitting on the pallet more devastated than he looked.

That day they were to come to the department where an inevitable talk with the Archmage awaited them. All that was left after the mistress was the smell and the crumpled plaid. There were a few clock beats left until the meeting, so he stood up with his knuckles and on the way to the library, he picked up a raisin bun from the kitchen, which he put in his mouth, thus taking the appearance of a squirrel, which stuffed a large portion of nuts in its mouth. He sank in the seat, put his forehead on a cool hand and got carried away by the sweet baking pleasure.

"Still time," he thought as the last bite landed in his stomach. "We still have time!"

Dusk enveloped him too violently. Absorbed in tasks, he didn't notice that the afternoon broke through the windows. He stiffened and looked toward the corridor. Someone managed to light the oil lamps. The contributions greedily took another fraction of his life. He jumped up and ran down the stairs. He burst into Lilian's room. Luckily she came back, he didn't feel like looking for her. She didn't look prone to any contact, he considered it a good sign. Distance would do good to them.

He leaned against the door and said:

"We should go now."

She seemed absorbed in what was bothering her. As if he didn't exist. So he adopted a different strategy, more delicate. He sat down next to her and having leaned towards her ear, he whispered:

"Lili."

The familiar voice made her stiff.

"Yes, okay. We have to go, right? To the Archmage."

"Yes, right there. I'll be waiting for you in the lobby. And look." He pointed at the window. "It has finally stopped snowing, there is plenty of it. I bet that if we put on too low shoes, it will fall inside," he said cheerfully like a child who can't wait to play in the white powder.

"Yes, snow," she said.

He left. He dug through the cabinet in search of the right shoes, and when he found them, he reached for a cloth with a hood, which he threw over his back shading his face.

Lili keep sitting for a moment longer. She was winding a strand on her finger as always when she was nervous. However, the moment had come to brace herself, so she reluctantly stepped outside the threshold of safe home. It wasn't until she arrived that she realized that she hadn't taken her outer clothing. She didn't have any other footwear, so glancing at the tips of the worn boots, she sighed, because she knew that it would definitely happen what Morien had said and she would drench her shoes. She wanted to return to the quarters, but the magician stopped her in her tracks and handed her a black leather jacket, lined with a thick layer of sheepskin, which also served as a collar. This clothing was unmistakably warm, but nasty as a ghoulie's face.

"We don't have time," he urged.

"It's ugly," she moaned.

"Nasty but good. It's like a bitter absinthe, you pour it in your throat, even though it contorts your face in all directions."

"Cute." She slouched in a sad resignation.

Thus she let him clothe her with the rough crap.

Outside, white bit into the pupils. Thanks to the new thing, she didn't give in to the cold, although this one wasn't unpleasant. Gentle frost pinched only on the cheeks, pinking them slightly. In the yard, novices and servants bravely shoveled the accumulated cover. When Morien and the woman accompanying him appeared in their sight, they stopped their activities and began to intently follow them with their eyes. Lilian felt an infinite amount of painful pricks spill over her skin, as if the eyes of the gathered people had been burning the hair roots and reaching the top of the trembling nerves. It seemed to her that everything around her got silent and frozen, and she carried icy heaviness on her shoulders. She had to resist the invisible wall of human curiosity. She curled up, lifted her collar and hid in it willingly. She sought discreet consolation in the magician. Anger stirred sparks of magic that gently swirled around. Morien sensed it and stopped midstride.

"Don't be afraid," he whispered. "Nobody will hurt you here. They just ..." he paused, searching for the right word.

"I'm not afraid, I'm angry. If we keep standing here for a while, I'll teach them a lesson, because it's rude," she hissed.

The words didn't fully come out of the mouth, while the white silence was first interrupted by a single handclap, which then echoed across the ossified walls of the buildings. The sounds bounced off the stained-glass windows and simultaneously scattered along the alleys. She opened her mouth when another magician clapped his hands more rhythmically, cheering and stamping his feet.

"Lilian!" They shouted, carried in a wave of excitement. "Lilian!" They repeated.

She jerked Morien and pulled him behind her. The cheeks were burning. Popularity was treacherous. The sooner they disappeared, the better for them.

The magician also knew that she liked it, even though she pretended to be cold and irritable. A shy smile for a few breaths softened her hardened face, as if a bit reviving the image of a woman.

Vadael's headquarters and department were in the deeper part of the University. Lili didn't think it would take so long to get there, but when they finally arrived, an old, stiff elven majordomo greeted them in the doorway, looking at the newcomers from under his squinted eyelids.

"Please come in," he said nobly and with a slightly slow, respectful gesture, pointed to the library hidden deep in the hall. "The lord will join you soon. He asks for forgiveness, because he will be a few minutes late. Do you want something to drink?"

Lili put her finger up as if she had been still a student at school.

"Hot tea, please ... if that's not a problem," she added quickly.

"Immediately." The servant bowed. "Sir, do you want something too?"

"No, thanks."

Having led guests to the room, he left them alone. He closed undoubtedly the largest door Lilian had ever seen in a residential building. On it, boasted reliefs depicting genre scenes, cleverly separated by oak leaves, between which she saw tiny acorns. She stared at the unusual door leaves for a moment, then perked up her head. The Archmage's book collection was extraordinary. Several times bigger and taller than Morien's. The books were stacked evenly on the shelves, and they ascended high above their heads and some of them could only be accessed after climbing onto the high ladder.

"Amazing," she moaned in delight and spun around her axis.

"Oh yes, you would run out of life to read all this, and probably the master knows most and I bet he knows where a given volume is located."

The door opened and Vadael slipped through the gap, taking off his fur hat and saying with interest:

"I know where everything is, Morien?" They shook hands.

Lili bowed low.

"Please, forgive me for being late, but I had to extend the lectures to achieve full-time classes. We can't afford that little thing to affect the education of our gifted young people, can we? So, where everything is?"

Morien smiled at Lili.

"Volume, master. We talked about books. And yes you are right. We can't allow anything to disturb the University's harmony."

"Yes, of course. Please, sit down." He pointed to two places by the ornate desk, and he himself rested in the armchair behind it.

The servant brought Lili a cup of infusion, and to the Archmage, a glass of cherry.

"Morien, if you like, I still have a barrel of dwarven beer in the basement."

"No, thank you, master. Somehow I don't feel like today."

"Unusual," Vadael laughed and took a sip. "He doesn't feel like it. Is this your doing, madam? Anyway, to the point." He crossed his arms on the desk. "Tell me, my dear, what are you going to do?"

She got confused.

"Because, you see. We know how you got here. Let's not belabor the point, because our foreheads will hurt from it."

She lowered her head.

"I've been reported," he continued. "that the message was sent to the Baroness early in the morning, but I won't play interception. I don't get down to her level. I also learned that a certain Darius, I think, is a pet of our favorite, and the Alchemist are currently in this shabby tavern. Morien, is it called 'Under the Ram's Head'?" The magician nodded. "And that the cook, Erica nee Barth, was killed. I assure you that I will give you, madam, care and support, but only if you don't want to go outside the gates. I'm unable to do anything behind them, so you can be sure that I'm doing everything I can now, for I'm bending many directives, looking into the future with fear. I hope that our master and ruler, graciously reigning Aaron, will turn a blind eye because of our many years of friendship, and allow the matter to die and be forgotten. But believe me, it will be undoubtedly a difficult task. I also think, but I have probably already mentioned about it, that your escape, madam, was the stupidest thing in recent years that happened within the establishments."

Lili sighed.

"I would like to get my things back, which are 'Under Ram's Head'. The owner will probably want to give them back to me. At least, I hope so," she said in one breath.

"And what is so unusual about these things?"

She contorted her lips.

"Potions, ointments, herbs and ..."

"And what?" He replied curiously.

He seemed to know what answer he would receive.

"A mandrake."

"Where the hell did you get the mandrake from, my child?"

"I dug it out," she replied.

"Where?" He was surprised.

"Where the mandrake plants always grow, that is, on the fields of death."

The Archmage leaned back in his chair and sighed deeply.

"If you could find the mandrake, should I know something else?"

"But the master knows. What are you playing?" She flushed.

The old man stood up and walked around the desk.

"Madam, let's say I'm deluding myself that the power you carry is so dangerous that it is crazy to let you stay here. And yet, I want to have you under my wings, because I'm afraid that under other's, you might not grow enough, and it is about the growth of magic. About safety, which I must ensure not only for students but also for you, my dear. Returning to the subject, I will inform you about your left things, but I can't promise anything. Sending messengers to the street is not a great idea. Not now. I also think that we will have a battle. A battle that will char rotten bones. I don't hide, as young people say, that I got cold feet. By Redeemers, these sayings will make me stop thinking someday," he added.

It was supposed to relax the mood, but it sounded laconic and untrue.

Morien and Lili looked at each other.

"What are you talking about, master?"

"That the revolt was suppressed in the capital, and more are being prepared. I received mail today. The Baroness sends Alchemists and spies to even the smallest villages. Savages began to use blood to enslave animals. The more Alvena will push, the more often she will encounter resistance, and eventually she and we will not stand it. I wonder how many more spies are roaming the city. In this matter you need to be distant and alert."

"We'll try to keep our eyes and ears open," said the magician and grabbed Lilian's hand. "We promise."

"Alright." The old man went back to his seat. "It's time for you to go. Madam, finish the brew. Frederick will be unhappy if he is forced to pour out such fragrant tea."

She smiled. The visit, which she feared like fire, went without unnecessary effusion, even though it provided information that couldn't be overlooked. She knocked back her cup with the finesse as great as her shaking hand allowed and, having bowed low, she was led out into the hall, where the same stiff elf handed them the greatcoats and bid them farewell with a modest grunt.

The dark blue sky greeted the huddled people. They both dreamed about hot soup and yeast muffins with raisins. Fortunately, no one stopped them, and as they climbed the next small drifts, they giggled like children. Sparkling snow made atmosphere romantic. Lilian wanted to embrace Morien and let him do the same but reason was another matter. So they walked side by side. Halfway to the mansion, they fell silent. They enjoyed the silence. But the tension was building up ominously, hanging in the air.

***

"I want to go for a walk." She turned her face towards the light source.

"Now?" He was surprised.

"Yes. I need some fresh air."

"If you want, go, but please don't go beyond the walls. I can't accompany you. I need to recall some combat spells. They went out of my mind."

She frowned. It was hard to think that Morien might have not known or remembered something - strange, completely unlike what she imagined him to be like.

"No worries. I just want to leave the house."

"Go," he said indulgently.

She joyfully jumped up from the chaise longue and ran to the magician. Leaning across the desk, she pecked him on the cheek and ran out into the corridor. Morien turned another card, completely ignoring the act of affection.

The little room greeted her with damp darkness. And although the house was dry, here, it smelled different, as if heavier. She didn't dwell on it. The answer was very simple - it was a storeroom. Over time, the old room would take on a new scent - hers. The closet door leaf groaned, but the swollen wood didn't offer much resistance. The outerwear was hung on a simple forged hanger, and the staff was pushed deeper. A pleasant tingling marked the fingertips. The favorite object sang only to her ears a soft melody, that resembled the sound of forest bells kissed by the spring sun. She stroked the crystal. It was as much fun as brushing the cat's fur. The caress of the gleaming glass bloodied the fingerprints. The object was clearly punishing her for something. The little wound quickly disappeared, having been dressed by a blue light which hissed like a spark and died in the brown and dark blue abyss.

Frost with claws scratched her pale cheeks, adding color to them in no time. She felt the chill build up, bite her feet and attack her hands. She wrapped herself up tighter. She wanted to go ahead, go around the alleys, turn into narrow streets that led to single villas tightly huddled together, and yet so far away that they were separate entities in this seemingly dead world. The snow creaked. She leaned back on her walking stick and looked around the courtyard with her teary eyes. The emptiness was marked only by footprints stigmatizing the permafrost, and lanterns hung on slender poles. Their white light certainly didn't belong to the fire with which she could have warmed herself. They were probably magical creations, sustained by the will of the magician responsible for them. They formed something like a dome, which you only noticed when the head was raised more. She stood there for a moment, excitedly analyzing the snow flickering in their glow, which inebriated the dry air with a powdery cloud. He was like the mica that noblewomen loved so much. Thanks to it, they could shine. They often smeared their décolletages and faces with oil pomades, to which they added a little of ground mineral. She always wanted to buy herself a bag of this seemingly non-magical creation and, dancing in the morning, spread it by handful around so that the dew would shine even more in the light of the rising dawn. But the snowfall was different from the speck, each flake looked different. She enjoyed the multitude of forms. She had never experienced severe winters in the capital, the climate was rather moderate. The only thing that pleased the inhabitants at this time was wet snow and ubiquitous gray immersed in brown mud trampled by hundreds of feet. In spirit, she had long missed a landscape wrapped in the soft whiteness.

She broke away from the fascinating forms that lazily fell down to unite in the impermanent structure. The gate, lit by torches, loomed in the distance. A mesmerizing object that lasted longer than reaching out of her hand, and even if she had could grab it, it wouldn't have let her breathe free air. Although the same for everyone, yet full of demons.

The flame, stroked by the wind, balanced on the tips of the oiled rags. She felt tingling in her temples. At first she thought it was the hair, freed from under the cover, that began to spin unbearably around, but a moment later happened something completely different. The song, which grew louder with every heartbeat, made a crown over her, made up of single flashes of purple light. She clenched her fists. Something was whispering, and at the same time drinking surprise from her like the finest mead. The force surrounded Lili on all sides, full of scraps felt only by the more sensitive. It ordered her to go, pushed. Sobriety was quickly disrupted by successive tones that flooded her common sense in an avalanche. It lured towards the iron bars of the University's border. Non-being of cold gave way to hot flashes. Drops of sweat glistened like diamonds on her forehead. They inevitably got frozen into streams that stretched down like frozen waterfalls. A tug on the shoulders ended the unconscious step. She suspected that none of the magicians were behind it, that it was definitely not a novice joke. It sounded different. Stronger than ordinary discharges. She was confused when just a few paces away, in a haze like mist, a dim figure loomed. Blurred, distant, it firmly stood on the cobblestone. Secret. It was expecting something. It stood stubbornly, piercing through with unseeing eyes. Emptiness surrounded everything reached by the arms of energy. Attracted by singing, Lilian plodded to the gate. Somewhere inside, she perceived vibrations like words, and only with sufficient concentration did she understand what she was going to face. The being whispered, slowly pronouncing syllables, gave sentences a specific character. The voice sounded like the chanting of a bard humming by a fire. It wasn't an ordinary song. She knew it. The song formed into memories. Safe, but also distant, like the mumbling of warm blood flowing from the sacrificial altar - the Speech of Whispers. She remembered that Morien had wanted to teach her that art.

The phantasm extended a hand to her, delicate and thin. Its posture indicated a woman with pale, curly hair and a scarred face. Her skin sparkled, her mouth was marked by blue, and her eyes were glazed with silver fire.

Lili stepped back. Her knees snapped and forced her to stop. She wanted to escape. Scream. Run home until she had enough breath, just not to look at the one, which wrapped in transparent robe, murmured without moving her lips.

"Don't be afraid." She heard.

An icy thorn pierced the mage's forehead. She glanced at the crystal crowning the staff, hoping it would infuse itself with the power to counterattack. It was silent, however, melting with the wood like an offended lover who had been forgotten for some time. She was boiling, but that force didn't let her burn. She was surrounded by a cocoon of blockage that didn't respond to her call.

"Who are you?" She managed to stutter out, though fear marked her skin.

"You," it said lightly.

"Wh ... what?" She stumbled.

It was beyond her comprehension. This was too much, way too much!

"I alert you."

"To what the hell?" She gasped and released from the mouth a large cloud of steam.

The absurdity of the situation hit her heart.

"To you. Watch your words and deeds, otherwise everything you love will die.

Impassionate fingers clenched on her fluttering heart." Lilian began to choke. Slipping to the ground, she managed to grunt:

"Get off me, whatever and whoever you are!" The blades of crystal shards filled her eyes, and instead of tears, bloody ribbons ran down her face. "Go away! Go away!" She repeated as she fought the oncoming darkness.

"Remember," the apparition whispered, and the words echoed off the skull. "Remember ..."

The last thing Lilian saw were pupils gleaming with white and a blackness as thick as the clotting scarlet that voraciously engulfed the one who had dared to approach the University gates.

The air tasted familiar. She gasped. She was lying and breathing quickly. Something hamstrung the face, blocking the path of light. Tight and rough. She raised a hand and put it where her eyes were. The material was in her way. Fear reached deeper. She thrashed on the bedding, she wanted to get up. The body was like a rotting log, heavy and soaked in fall rain. Sweat covered her skin with huge drops filled with a foul-smelling liquid. She didn't know how long she had been stuck in the paralyzing helplessness, but she needed to get out of it as quickly as possible, tear off the shackles and find Morien as if he had been the only beacon of hope in this lousy world.

"Leave it." She heard. "Lie down and try not to move."

"Morien?" She muttered, scratching the cloth, but the magician's warm fingers stopped her from tearing the dressing apart.

"Easy, leave it, please."

"What happened? I'm at the mansion?! Morien? I can't see anything! Get it off me right now!" She pushed him aside and repeated her attempt to remove the bandages.

"Please, it won't help."

"Give me a break. I want to get out of here. What room am I in? Is it a library or a bedroom? Morien, by Redeemers!"

"Focus, Lilian." He pressed down on her wrists and pinned her to the bedding. "Listen and give in!" He growled irritated.

The girl was numb for a moment. He had never spoken to her like that, so she felt strange.

"Lie down." He touched her forehead. "Breathe with your nose and let the air out through your mouth. Oh yes, very good. Now focus, calm down. Otherwise, what I will do, won't work at all. Come on. Ready?"

"Yes." She moved her lips, but only a whistling sound came from her throat.

She couldn't see the mage uncrossed his arms with relief.

A gentle but perceptible shiver rolled through the scalp, which whirled around the temples and traveled deeper to settle there with a haze of calming discharges. Pleasant warmth marked the base of the skull and trickled down the spine. For a fraction of the blink of an eyelid, it seemed as if the magician's power had touched even the fingertips and the tips of the hairs growing on the rest of the body. She shuddered.

"Better?" He asked.

"Yes. Better. I don't know what you did, but the tension in my neck and the urge to keep clenching my jaw faded away. Thank you."

"I found you at the gate," he began. "You haven't come back for a long time and I thought that you had an idea to leave the school. It has long stopped snowing. It was so quiet that my ears were buzzing, and if it weren't for my shoes squeaking against the ground, I would have felt as if I had been lost in endless torment. By all Redeemers! Don't do this anymore or I'll go crazy!"

"I saw a woman outside the gate. She spoke but didn't move her lips. She whispered and deceived. She enveloped me in a veil of power so impenetrable that I couldn't free myself from it."

"Woman?"

"Yes, she warned, but also blocked me. She was almost unreal, transparent, and yet she stood firm on the ground as if growing into it. The fabric she was wearing rippled to the beat of the wind that wasn't there."

"Did she say something? Did you see any more details?" Morien got impatient and clenched his fists.

The face was marked by scars, distinct against the translucent backdrop. White hair ... Morien ... She said she is me!

The mage pressed his lips together so tightly that instead of full lips, a long line outlined a tense face. He stiffened and suddenly straightened.

"What happened?" She found his hand. "Is something going on?"

"I don't know. I'm wondering, but I don't think I'm going to get anything else like the fact that you've most likely formed a visualization of the future, Lili."

"What? How is that? I didn't create anything ... She herself ... I don't have the strength," she groaned in despair. "Don't say my power is acting up and I have no control over what it does?"

"What shall I say if not the truth?" He took her hand. "Magic evolves, transforms and matures. You are stronger each day, but also more helpless in the face of what you have received as a gift from the Redeemers. I don't know how to call it, how to put it into words. Maybe simply, maybe it will be easier that way. You seem to be one of those magicians who have visions. Few of them were recorded."

"What are you talking about?" She rose on her elbows.

He sighed.

"About the fact that there are those who can manipulate time, thanks to which they can summon their reflection, sometimes distorted just to protect themselves from the mistakes they are most likely to make. These are the ones hunted most often by those in power. They are more valuable than healers and even combat mages. The rulers feel safer with one of them by their side, but this magic costs money."

"You think Alvena somehow knows I can do such weird hocus-pocus? How is it called?"

"Just seeing. The seer needs a lot of vitality, because it destroys, degrades tissues, and often kills. They live short, Lilian ... too short," his voice was trembling with nervousness. "You know, at first I thought the Alchemist had somehow lured you out of the gates. Believe me, it would be much easier to accept than ..."

She touched again the place where the eyes were, carefully hidden under the thick layer of dressing.

"You think the seeing has damaged my senses?" She froze at the words as if she didn't mean it at all.

"You broke them, that's for sure. You froze them. Vadael made sure everything was back to normal. It only takes a few days."

"So I have to thank him."

"Undeniably," he added.

The first few days trailed with the strand of dark ribbon and tones that, while familiar, now seemed out of this world. The clink of a spoon against the table, footsteps on the stairway, pouring water into a cup rang in the ears like a magic cacophony. She moved, touching walls, shuffling her feet in the dark and groping for landmarks. Two steps to the left - the table. Clockwise rotation and four steps - the door. She counted, listened. The kitchenmaid used to visit her often, offering tasty treats. The clever elf put the meal in a different place each time. Forced to rely on her senses, Lilian felt an urge to shout at her on the first day, but soon she realized it had a purpose. She didn't want to feel like caged game, and yet she felt like that. She also didn't want to burden anyone, and although they assured her that she didn't, she felt alienated. Fortunately, Morien stayed at the estate in the afternoons. He gave up after-dinner teas or even trips to "Ram's Head", despite the fact that he often felt a desire for a pint of a dwarven drink. And maybe he could have bought a barrel for his own use, but it wouldn't have tasted as good as there.

In time, perhaps she would have gotten used to the darkness that swathed her from everywhere, although she longed for the day when Vadael would decide to remove the armband. The reality that enveloped her seemed sharper and sharper. Smell, taste, touch. Everything she usually took for granted was now taking shape into something that could be constructed anew, learned from a completely different side - the non-obvious one. She tasted moments. She revelled in different forms. The cake was no longer just a piece of pie, but a soft material that formed in the mouth a mixture of textures, flavor and stickiness. The smell brought back memories long forgotten. It arranged them in the shape of spectacles covered with oblivion. She realized that by longing for something, she might have unconsciously exaggerated a lot of things, and now she had much time to analyze. Was she doing the right thing, reopening long-healed wounds? She wanted to believe that this had merits, for example that thanks to being blinded, she would experience completely different realities.

One evening she said to Morien, who was working as always:

"I guess that's good. You know ... Escape from the Magician School, shelter in Ram's Head, get to know you, then this. Even loss of sight... It's like chains of events that are a way to get to know myself more, deeply, I would say. Because where would I go when the escalation of power started burning me on the raw? Where would I go, blind and helpless after I saw the one that seemed to be my projection. Do you understand?"

He looked up from the desk and put the pen back in the inkwell.

"I understand, or so I suppose."

"You sure know." She smiled, trying to scratch through the bandage. "I'm different now. I feel like I'm maturing. This characterful me is going away somewhere. I quieten down. I don't even get irritated by the novices who come here every now and then. Their insistent gaze doesn't make such an impression on me as it used to."

"That's good. You calmed down. Yesterday I was wondering how long you will hold on like this, and here you are. Instead of an angry, beautiful mage, I have a meek doe. I think I will miss that what passed. Besides, you can see without seeing. It's a good sign. Acute senses are what I have trained for a long time. You only needed a few days. I'm happy for you. Really."

"I wish you would teach me the Speech of Whispers," she said casually.

She took the conversation on a completely different path. She pleaded in spirit for his consent.

"It's a good idea." He got up from behind the desk.

"Where are you going?"

"For tea, do you want?"

"Yes, please, but don't sweeten it, I don't like sweet tea."

"Alright."

It wasn't long before the door to the library opened slightly again. Though it worked flawlessly, Lilian could hear the metal hinges rub against each other as it moved. She could feel Morien's footsteps, even though he always tried to walk softly and almost silently. Now, carrying the tableware, he tried to tread even more gently. Unfortunately, fragile objects rattled every time he shifted weight from one leg to the other. The chamomile scent spread pleasantly and mixed with the scents of the library. Leather, wood, ink and lacquer. And although the latter was used quite often, it left behind only a faint cloud of voile, which, suffocated by the smell of the oil lamps, quickly merged with the rest. Now a floral note dominated this seemingly stuffy room, enlivening it with a slightly bitter steam. Tea spluttered cheerfully in the cups, and the magician, having found his lover's hands, stuck one of them into his pale fingers marked with brown freckles.

"Here you are. Be careful, don't get burned."

Lili took the dish, wrapped her palms tightly around it and ignoring the warnings, took a long sip.

"Be careful!" he reacted.

"Don't worry. I guess you forgot that my element is fire. I'm not afraid of boiling water."

Morien shrugged.

"Yeah, I forgot. And now ... maybe something about the Speech of Whispers? What do you think?"

"Yes." She made herself more comfortable and pulled her bare feet up under her dress. "Speak, I want to learn."

Morien picked up a heavy chair from behind the desk and, before she could drink the rest, he placed it next to her, settled on it and crossed his legs.

"It's old school. Learning techniques haven't changed over the centuries, classes are always planned for the last year, and they are not dedicated to everyone. We don't try to find the more talented ones, it comes out with time. In the past, long time ago, people tried to teach novices, believing that it would be useful in their further education. It was a mistake paid for with many sad stories. Plus, imagine that it ended up in internal noise."

She laughed sonorously.

"I've imagined this. Archmage at the blackboard, and they discuss how to create a love potion." She laughed again.

"Yes exactly. Besides, well. The weak are dangerous."

"Why?"

"It's easy. These types of magicians could use Speech against others. They wouldn't even realize it, because they are unable to block the transmission. It is related to a will that is not sufficiently educated."

"Then why are the weak taught when they are unable to master some techniques?"

"The basis of education is instilling control. If they take it, they can learn, but not all learn it sufficiently. We call them the weak and observe them. If their magic gets even slightly distorted, then we decide to bind them."

"I'm beginning to understand, but I don't think it's a delicate process? Probably no one wants to have the abilities get dormient, although I suppose, that like our kitchenmaid, some are eager to indulge in the process."

"Yes, you're right. The very fact of being born a magician fills some people with such pride that, let's call a spade a spade, they freak out. On the other hand, they are subconsciously afraid. These kids are as scared as cats. Seemingly wild, wanting to scratch at once, but at the same time panically afraid of a hand that puts a bowl of milk under their mouth. There is also the worse side of being born a magician. Families. The closest ones who should give them love, support and help them get through the first contact with power. But no. They are eager to give offspring to Schools right away, deluding themselves that behind the walls and great terrifying gates we will raise them an Archmage who, for example, knows the ancient art of healing. It is not so. Every magician has talents programmed from birth that are revealed through training."

"As in my case, it was with the treatment of pets."

"Yes, but you didn't own one force, but you have many of them in your blood. Most likely, you don't know what nests under the soft tissue of your skin. You don't realize the power and importance of the spells you can resurrect by singing the appropriate formulas. That is why you awaken so much respect. Yes, I know." He held up a hand as Lilian pursed her lips to break the monologue. "You will modestly add that I'm exaggerating. We know otherwise. Me, Vadael and the rest of the Masters and Archmasters who live in this place. Don't treat it as fanning you. Rather, take it as a warning."

"You are scaring me."

"But that's the truth, you won't get away from it. Returning to the subject, because I have probably already managed to bore you to death, the bondage is under the supervision of the Archmage of the School. The royal alchemist is then called. The very thought of him terrifies me. People try to run away, take their lives, at worst they lock themselves in rooms with hostages and threaten to kill them. But there is a measure to deal with everyone. The ritual is not the most pleasant one. The mere shell of the broken runestone can lead to a short-term numbness, as if a daydream with the impossibility of moving. The worst thing is that the tied up loses the ability to feel and becomes a puppet. It doesn't happen immediately, it takes time, sometimes several or several dozen years. Such person functions normally in everyday life, but the feelings about the bound people are always the same - coldness and indifference." He rested the chin on his knuckles.

"I communed in the Capital with the silent magicians, as we called them. At the beginning they were ordinary, they stayed, because where would have they gone? They helped with cleaning, in the kitchen and in greenhouses. You understand? Common workers who were paid silver. With time they left, no one knew where, no one asked, no one felt regret. They were simply part of the University's ever-moving landscape. Gruesome. I feel fear at the thought that the Alchemist is right beside. He lurks and plots, and I can't help it. And I'm also intrigued by the thought: how will he constrain my power, assuming that he will, if a ritual is needed?"

"He's not sophisticated, Lili. He will throw the runestone."

"How's that? That's it?" She was surprised.

"As soon as the stone is in the air, it will slow down time. Slightly, you won't pay attention to it. At that moment the Alchemist will utter a spell and the runestone will shatter into countless luminous particles. These will wave, tremble and create a translucent cloud. It will gently envelop you, taking away physical strength and force. The alchemist will oversee the process, although he doesn't have to. Anyone who has experienced the touch of power in their life can do it. For example, the hired killers - the Shadows. But they seldom meddle in magical matters, preferring to slit the throats of younkers and commoners. All you need is a purse full of dwarven gold and he will appear at the right time and place. And you see, I have deviated from the subject again. Alright. Where was I? Oh yes. The essence will accumulate into a crystalline form that will methodically occupy the entire surface of your body, absorbing all that is magical. Then you will pass out and the stone will become blackened, materialize and fall next to you. There will be a wound at the site of impact, but it will disappear quickly. After a few days, there will be no trace of it, and the Alchemist will put the stone in the pouch. That's all."

Lili stared at him with her mouth wide open, sweat was beading on her forehead, and the salty taste of blood tickled her throat.

"Take it easy." Morien moved closer. "It's okay." He put his hand on her head, and the longed-for bliss took over her deeply.

"I'm better now, thank you," she whispered, though her quick breath still distorted the individual words. "Pour me some tea, please."

He handed her a cup.

"I didn't think you would be so impressed by it. I'm sorry if this knowledge bears hard on you. Only the high priests know the course of the ceremony, but I figured I would have to tell you about it in case ..."

"The Alchemist got me," she finished. "Yes I know. Don't worry. I can handle this knowledge somehow. And is it possible to regain power? Are reverse spells needed?"

"It is possible. The basic measure is this stone, without it you can't do anything, so you would have to get it back first. It's not easy, but it can be achieved. The intercession of the king ..."

"Theft," she interrupted him.

"You can try, but without magic, you have to watch the mage. The alchemist can kill without even looking into the victim's eyes. Just like that."

"But how can I become myself again?"

"Just touch him. He knows with whom he is coupled. He will recognize. However, you will be able to postpone the process. Your awareness will tell him what to do. It's so trivial and yet important."

"That's it?"

"Yes. And you know what? You have just been initiated into the arts of black magic." He laughed.

"I promise not to tell anyone" She put a finger to her lips.

"I believe you. By Redeemers, we were to talk about the Speech of Whispers, not the Alchemists and macabre rituals."

"That's alright." She shrugged. "I learned a lot, or at least I got to know. It's easier for me now. It's a relief, nothing more."

"You deserve it." He kissed her softly on the lips.

***

Mark rested his head on his hands. Business was going poorly. Nay! It was for shit! After Erica's death, the inn no longer smelled of the aromatic greasy food, but only the fumes of exhaled and digested alcohol mixed with the stench of dirty people. He didn't have the strength to tear his hair out, after all, he had so little hair left that even a bird wouldn't make a nest from it. Dissatisfaction and grumpiness floated in the thick structure of the ugly atmosphere. Guests ordered, knocked down mugs, and the door groaned good-bye as they disappeared in the damp fumes of the city. In addition, a thorn in the innkeeper's side were the uninvited compatriots who constantly nestled on the floor. At the same time, they didn't spare the innkeeper any unpleasantness or insolent words, which he chewed with contempt. He was silent, while burning inside with rage. There was something left, however, that made this disgusting habitat still attracting those who soaked their mouths in the suburban piss - the wenches and alewives who, now downcast by the owner's bad mood, invariably wandered around the hall. They smiled bitterly, collected silver coins into their belt pouches, and additionally entertained those who still had some sparkles of well-being under their skin. They wondered why the innkeeper wouldn't hire another cook to take care of the food. When asked, he only snorted and sent them back as if the question belonged to those taboo.

The only one who withdrew and avoided Mark was Agnes. She was definitely ashamed. She stared at the floorboards whenever she needed to talk to him. But luckily the man only exchanged formalities with her. He completely got away from everyone. He didn't deny that he knew perfectly well the situation of the girl and that only because of her mother he allowed her to stay. Otherwise, he would have chased her away like a mongrel, giving her a kick to the round ass. Agnes, on top of that, still hoped that Darius, who had come down quite often, was still sympathetic to her. Unfortunately, the complete indifference on the part of the fair-haired mercenary filled her already broken heart with bitterness. She became quiet and wilted. She had to bear the consequences of her actions.

That day, the cold tugged at people's skin, so tormented, they crowded by the fire, sniffed their noses vigorously, and what dripped from those noses unceremoniously rubbed in their sleeves, laughing that the extra layer wouldn't make a difference. The hinges snarled and scraped. The door slammed open, and a short figure stood in the threshold, tightly wrapped in skins. The visitor looked around the room with his teary eyes and, at the same time, frowned angrily. He grunted, spat and entered. He stamped a few times and carelessly climbed onto the seat next to the counter. Mark raised an eyebrow. He hadn't expected him at this time of year.

"Huh, landlord, why are you like that? Will you not properly greet your old comrade?" The dwarf's voice echoed roughly off the innkeeper's ears.

Mark pushed back a strand of gray hair that stubbornly fell over his wrinkled forehead, took a sip of the smuggling alcohol, and exhaustedly grunted under his breath:

"What the hell brought your hairy, dwarven bum here? Shouldn't you be warming the thighs of some mustachioed beauty now, David?"

The visitor raised his hands and his face lit up in a heartfelt smile. After a while, the bear's paws slapped on his knees, and he leaned towards his friend, grinning with his yellow teeth.

"You haven't greeted me like that before! Like some sullen maiden. You probably haven't played the field for a long time, because you are bitter. And don't." He shot at him a short but well-groomed finger. "Don't thrash, because I know you!" He straightened, pulled his shoulder blades, and stuck the fists under the leather belt, the buckle of which flashed cheekily in the light of the fire-heated oil lamps.

"Sure you know me like an old sack. But it's a pity that the long leaky one," he replied flatly.

"You should be ashamed. For almost two springs you haven't seen me, and you welcome me like that. Horror!" The dwarf raised his hands again and rolled his whites to show that he didn't like his behavior.

"You fool. Should I kiss you on the forehead? I have the problems. Don't you see?" He pointed with his chin to the rest of the room. "You don't know what's going on here! Eh." He waved. "You don't care about it."

"I don't want to hear about crises and problems, because there aren't enough of them on the highroad? I haven't yet warmed up within the walls, and they are throwing rumors from all sides as if I had liked to listen to them. Baroness, Alchemists, spies, bandits on the road, the whore's period is late! By Redeemers, let it go and prepare me some mistress. But pretty, because I haven't had anything soft under my fingers for a long time, and you know how it is with ours. Wonderful, well-groomed, with curly beards, and shining with oil pomades. Just use them, but it also comes at a price. Women are capricious and self-interested. They always want shiny pebbles, pearls and perfumes, gilded whores." He winked at Mark, rocking on the stool as if it had been adapted to this type of play.

The innkeeper wondered for a moment when he would hit the ground and thus provide entertainment for him and his regulars. Bored, he sighed and, hanging his voice, said heavily:

"Take your pick. Take whoever you want, there is no longer this ..."

"Hey, you are hedging, my lord. This, who? Who is this 'she'?" He leaned forward. "Was she pretty?"

"Unusual." Mark rested the chin on his hand.

"Uuuh ..." David wagged his finger at him amusingly. "The pitcher may go once too often to the well. How did you scare her off, unfortunate? With an over-salted stew?"

In the end, a shy but quite distinct smile appeared on the innkeeper's lips. He didn't know how the dwarf did it, but whenever he came, he could inexplicably dispel even the darkest clouds that gathered over him, the business and the place he hated now with all his heart. He chose to speak. Throw away the bitterness and fatigue that pressed him down like an anvil.

"Alchemists and the Baroness. Does that mean something to you? Of course it does. They had it in for her and she had to run away. Now I'm alone, and this brood is renting the only guest room I have, and if I wasn't a magician, I would kill him like a dog."

"Alchemist?" The dwarf got scared. "Here? What are you talking about?"

"That's right, Alchemist. Now don't tell me that you didn't know what happened to the magicians here?"

"Yeah, yeah." He scratched his chin. "I've heard this and that."

Darius, tucked into his favorite corner, shaded and safe, was listening to the conversation from the beginning. Fortunately, they were talking quite loudly, because the noise of the crowd would have completely drowned out the dialogue. He was almost certain that Mark didn't notice him or simply didn't want to see, what suited his book. So he sipped the watered-down wine, hungry for tidbits the dwarf probably had up his sleeve.

"What do you mean?" The dive owner asked.

"The magicians are supposedly fed up with this dry bat. Allegedly, she made some new unfavorable rules for them. Besides, she seemingly freaks out. Did you know?"

"I don't know anything," Mark growled. "I'm here locked up and just watch the Alchemist kill another people." He raised his tone deliberately so that the spy hidden in the corner heard it clearly. He knew that the slimy reptile leered at them and drank every word like the finest ambrosia.

The fair-haired man pretended to pick his teeth and that he wasn't interested at all, in what they were debating at the bar.

"What are you talking about? Who gave up the ghost?" David was surprised.

"Erica is gone. One of Alvena's dogs killed her."

"What? How is that? There will be no stew anymore?" The dwarf huffed and put his hands on the hips.

Mark buried his face in his hands with resignation. Maybe it sounded funny, but it couldn't be more tragical.

"Sorry, you know that I've always had relaxed approach to death."

"I feel that I'm forced to tell you from the beginning. Even though I don't want to. My head is buzzing and I must have peed for a long time."

"Yes, I think it's a good time. Just pour me, because my mouth is dry and give me this one, how is she called, I mean, this one." He pointed to the passing alewife. "On my lap, because I'm somehow sad."

He met his friend's expectations and shouted at the maid. She gave up her duties and took care of the guest in no time. The dwarf didn't hesitate to take her for a spin, pushing his paws where it wasn't appropriate to do it in public. Mark, on the other hand, got carried away by the sad story. He outlined in detail what seemed most important to him. He introduced to the mysteries, revealed the secrets of the tavern and brought closer the image of Lilian, who thanks to her irresistible charm brought a lot of warmth and uniqueness to the inn he owned. He rhapsodized over the flawlessly smooth skin, described the shade of the hair, the gestures ... and if it wasn't for David's signs of weariness at some point, he would have continued to chatter, how beautiful her voice sounded as she bent down to ask for clean glasses. He then reluctantly proceeded to the affair with Morien, or at least suspected they were close, and ended with the incident from a few days ago.

David listened and didn't interrupt. The wench on his lap began to disturb him, so having satiated himself, he sent her away to hell.

"And that's all. Now I have neither Lili, nor cook, nor anything, I'm alone." Mark curled his arms and stared at the cup.

Darius discreetly left the main room, slipped between the guests and entered the back room. Something whispered to him that the sponge wasn't of a low estate, and although the dwarves always had their pouches full of gold, they were rich to varying degrees. David didn't speak normally either, his accent was hard and throaty, indicating nobility. He wasn't a drunkard working for the state in quarries or staying in underground cities in the south of the state. He noticed something disturbingly familiar in him. He had already seen a griffin on a large belt buckle before.

David finished his beer and asked for another. He wiped his mouth with his hand and got thoughtful.

"Hmm," he grunted. "It's probably because of her those warriors are on the routes. My caravans were often stopped, horses don't like it, especially when they are thrown off stride."

"Never mind your horses."

"Don't blaspheme," he scolded him. "They are purebred animals."

"Alright, but they shit like the others."

The dwarf laughed.

"Yeah, they shit mightily."

***

"So, do you want some theory?" Morien settled comfortably on the floor and stared at Lili.

She fumbled at the bandages with her fingers.

"Yes. By Redeemers, must it itch so much?" She tried to stick her finger under the fabric.

"Stop it!" He slapped her hand. "It will itch because it is healing. You should know that." He fought with the stubbornness of his beloved, who probably didn't care for his efforts. "You are so stubborn. We will take them off in a few days, and maybe sooner."

With resignation, she leaned back and inhaled with a whistle through her nose. She clasped her hands tightly on her lap, then straightened and tensed her muscles. She fought as hard as she could, unfortunately to no avail, because after a few breaths she reached towards her face again, but this was also noticed and properly reprimanded.

"Okay, please go ahead." She pressed her lips together tightly and clenched her fists. Itching spread almost all over the body and drove her mad. She had never known such a feeling in her life, she dreamed of its end. She wanted it to go away, evanesce.

"Do you want to postpone it? I can see that you are suffering terribly." He put a soft hand on her knee.

She took it gently and moved her face towards him.

"How about you remedy this, you know ... ailment, and I'll promise I'll be the most diligent student of the Whispering Speech you've ever known? What do you think? "She smiled."

"Tempting," he whispered. "Tempting. Let's see what can be done."

Satisfied, Lilian leaned back. If Morien said it 'could be done', it meant he made a plan. She heard him lacing his fingers together, then cracking them the way he used to do when he sat down at the desk before beginning the tedious process of writing back his correspondence. He warmed up his fists. Nothing happened at first, all she heard was the shuffle of skin rubbing against itself. Then something hummed and sparkled, and a gleam reached her through the layer of bandages. It was not the blue-white glow that accompanied the healing process, but just the opposite. It glowed as red as sunset, when the horizon bursts with purple.

"What is it?" She whispered.

"Don't interrupt. I haven't done this for a long time."

"What's this magic? I don't know it. Morien, what are you doing?"

A peculiar smell of warm skin and blood swirled in the air. She quickly realized that this was probably some kind of ceremony that she hadn't heard of, or worse, that was forbidden. It was well known that the use of blood was a blasphemy against the Redeemers and an unquestionable violation of the principles of pure magic. She was silent, even though everything happened against her beliefs.

The man was breathing painfully. Single gulps of air were spluttering desperately in his throat. The discharges of the spell spread, but under the mage's tutelage they did not escape from the aura field, but balanced on the thin line connecting with his self. Morien's magic tightened around her head. It fell on it like heavy material. The grip around her eyes immediately deprived her of rational thinking, she groaned and began to scratch the affected areas with her nails. The feeling intensified, she almost taste it through the enlarged pores of the skin. She felt no pain, rather something irritating, unpleasant, and at the same time warm and sticky. She squirmed and gritted her teeth, and more waves brushed her cheeks and forehead, being warm and icy at the same time. The chill was like the touch of a dagger, and the heat burned the tissues. She no longer knew if it was happening here and now, or she was stuck between madness and reality. She couldn't find a reference point, stop at least for a moment. The biting mist beguiled, and all she could do was give up.

Morien grew tired, but despite overwhelming weakness, he continued. It didn't matter that probably he wouldn't stick his nose outside the bedroom for the next day, and he would be thundered by the council. Lilian needed to recover quickly by all possible means, even if he were to reach for the sources of ancient and forbidden magic.

Time adapted plastically to what the magician was serving him. It was flowing slowly enough for those focused on the ritual to enjoy it enough. Morien having finished, dropped his arms.

Lilian felt space slowing down. She was being freed from the cocoon. She cringed. She was trembling like he was, but not from exertion, but from fear. She hadn't noticed that the reason that had compelled the magician to do so got forgotten. Slight throbbing caressed her covered eyelids. She lifted a hand and ran her fingertips over the rough structure of the band, and stickiness deposited on her fingers and poured under her nails. The thick slime stuck to both the skin and the matter.

"What was that?" She asked with the cracked lips.

"My blood."

"But ..." She opened her mouth, but she couldn't get any more out of it.

"Don't worry," he comforted her. "Regeneration will be quick. Let's finish the tea, I need liquid. Yes, I need this goddamn bitter tea!"

She tilted her head. If she could, she would have probably stared at him with the puzzled pupils. He had never spoken like that, or cursed, or showed signs of nervousness. At least not with her. She heard him reach for the teapot and pour himself and her the rest of the brew. He stuck the handle of the cup into her fingers. She took a sip, but it wasn't good. She blindly put the dish down on the floor.

"Why did you do that?" She asked.

"And why not? I made you relieved, right?"

"What if it get revealed? What if it reach the Archmage? No, I don't want to think about it!" She wailed close to tears.

"It doesn't itch anymore. I know that, it helped. Don't scratch it. This magic is more effective than herbs, decoctions and standard healing. I can assure you that Vadael himself uses it. Nobody talks about it, and that is its charm. Everyone knows, everyone is silent."

She couldn't believe it. From the moment she entered the School of Magic, she was taught that practicing it stains mana and over time defines a magician enough to turn him into something worse than a beast forever. She didn't want to lose faith. Morien was closer to her than anyone in this lousy world, in this dirty city, stinking of a gutter and wet dogs. However, something was playing inside her, something that didn't allow her to remain calm. Morien refuted the myth of the unspotted mage who walked all his life along the path of the council. She swallowed loudly.

"Yes, maybe you're right. Maybe my knowledge of this place is as limited as that of the Speech of Whispers. Perhaps I wanted to blindly believe that the essence of foul magic would never stain those close to me and for whom I would be able to sacrifice myself.

I don't know what to think. Believe me. It doesn't itch ... so. You relieved me, but aren't the costs you incur too high? You got degenerated for me. You hit rock bottom. Is it really worth it?"

The mage rolled his eyes. Usually at such moments he breathed slowly, so as not to accidentally get carried away by buzzing emotions. One, two, three ... he counted in his mind, and the time stalled quiet, shaping it into a silence buzzing with uncertainty.

"All right," he replied. "I didn't touch any bottom even with the tip of my shoe, Lilian. I'm too, let's call it, strong. I would feel that the need for blood increases with each reaching for mana, which in this case turned out to be insufficient. Blood is the same source as the ancient power that resounds in our veins when we discover that we are special. Don't worry, I won't start running around the forest, chasing game, let alone sacrifice my students' lives. What are you afraid of? Me? Or that your idealized worldview has just been shaken?" He growled.

Lilian laced her fingers on her lap. He was right. He always was. The inner child sobbed with diamond tears. Certainty collapsed like straw constructions. She could no longer restore the old order that kept her alive so tightly. There were no ideals. Only the harsh, crunching in teeth reality remained, as dirty as the sidewalk she used to walk towards the Magicians' Houses.

"Yes. I don't want to listen anymore. I have to ... I have to cool down. Collect my thoughts. Learn everything from scratch. No, no. No worries. I'm fine. I need to wash my face and ... let's do it. Let's learn that goddamn Whispering Speech so I can feel safe."

"Sure. I'm going to get the things I need right away and we can start." He left. The door creaked, and the steps groaned under the pressure of the man's weight.Somewhere in the distance water splattered, and drawers rattled. The silence was interrupted by the sounds that clearly filled the house. The servants was sleeping, and their slow breaths were going through the walls and circling like moths. She heard everything as clearly as never before. She was immersed in the crackles of the mansion. The movement of the air sobered her as she felt Morien crouch down in front of her and place a cloth in her hand, which he had lightly soaked in water and oil. It smelled intensely of a mixture of lavender and rose. He was familiar with it. After all, tonics was his favorite hobby. From simple to so complicated that the brewers of potions envied him for the ease and intuitive combination of the proportions of natural ingredients. Unimaginable relief caressed the skin, and the cloth collected clotting blood. The unpleasant stickiness was gone and the relief came. The magician obligingly helped her reach the places she had absent-mindedly left. She felt that he ceased to be furious. He came back changed, calmer. She breathed a sigh of relief. He must have been alone for a few moments. She understood that.

"Teach me. Now." She threw the rag at the fire. "No more waiting."

"Let's get started then." The voice resounded in the room like the most beautiful melody.

"Alright." She pulled up her feet and covered them with a gown. "I'm ready."

"You must learn to control yourself. Unnecessary emotions, nervousness or haste can only disturb the course. An important step is to clear your thoughts, and balance your breathing. Even for a few moments, it will do a lot. Just let the body flow. It knows what to do, trust it. Whispering is incoherent and consistent at the same time - not obvious in its structure and completely dissimilar for everyone. It is as if you were walking a thin line. Each careless step will make you devoured by the space beyond. This is a dangerous game that can be tamed. There are techniques for moving through its phases, you just need to learn them. Then it will be the turn of the one with whom the tendrils of power will connect you. Breaking through the chains can be troublesome at first, but training will allow you to do it almost off-hand. Remember that the strong communicate this way. If it goes too easily, then you can get suspicious. This man most likely belongs to the weak group. Don't forget your might! You can manipulate with the Whisper. I know, it's tempting. In this way, you can additionally speak to creatures who don't practice magic. They won't answer, but you'll get the same result as with the Whispers with low-class mages."

She nodded. There was nothing incomprehensible in what he was saying. He had the soft voice of a teacher trying to convey something difficult in a simple and yet accessible way. He hadn't required much yet. She didn't look ahead. She wanted to experience the new skill step by step.

"We'll start by clearing your thoughts," he continued. "We don't have to work on your will. It is so powerful that you won't use much of it for such a banality as the Whispering. It's a cliche, you'll be learning more difficult things. We won't move on until you've mastered the basics, though we'll probably start soon. I will mention right away that you may feel a bit confused, but only for a moment, because the beginnings seem like a howl, scream or wheeze and are not pleasant. But no worries. Also this will become pleasing to the ear and you will definitely want more."

She put a hand to her mouth and nodded, then rested the chin on her fist. She waited for a continuation. Morien inhaled the air through the nose and continued:

"Imagine the cave. There is no exit or entrance here, no openings through which streams of light enter. You only see the form. It surrounds you on all sides and locks you over your head. Look carefully, create the smallest detail. Stalactites, stalagmites, dripping water and the echo of the drops that lazily hit the stone.

Define the color, smell and temperature. Get absorbed. Let the picture fill your thoughts and merge into coherent one. Come on. Don't be afraid."

"All right." She settled more comfortably and wrapped her arms around her knees.

Even though she mechanically closed her eyes under the bandages, now she allowed herself to close them. A few breaths later, she tried to follow the directions, trying hard to arrange the pieces of the puzzle. Instead of a rock formation, she could see only darkness and the single flashes hidden within it. The harder she tried, the more flickering lights danced and formed a veil around the glowing ribbon. So she sighed as the vision came and disappeared.

Morien watched the results patiently. Lilian's expression showed her effort mixed with frustration. It puzzled him, because most things had come easy to her! She fought, thrashed. The muscles trembled under the thin matter.

"Enough," he interrupted.

"No!" She exploded. "I can fucking make it!"

"You're weak. We will come back to this tomorrow."

"No!" She flared up. "I'll do it today!" She screamed.

"As you wish. However, please don't strain yourself."

"I have to do this! Don't you understand? It will give me no peace."

"Are you always so stubborn?"

"Always!" She folded her arms over her chest and clenched her fists so tightly her knuckles turned white.

She leaned back without changing the position of her hands, but tucked her legs closer to her, hiding the feet under her dress. She sat there for a long time, straight, with her head tilted, so the occiput touched the headboard. She decided to do it her way. She had brought her mother in thought first and the day she discovered magic, then the memory intensified smoothly. She perceived herself as a little girl who played with her peers Jerms, children of farmers and the rest of the poor. She took a specific delight in the recapture. For the first time in a long time, she returned to her roots. The relaxation enveloped her softly, and she sank into it like into a fluffy bed. The fists clenched tightly got relaxed, and the skin regained its natural, slightly pink tone. The steady rise of the chest meant the mage was on track for the purpose.

Morien breathed a sigh of relief, but he observed her closely. Toughness was clearly one of Lilian's strengths. He saw many times people who quickly let go, only to allow themselves to be helped over time. She went on like an aurochs, steadfastly, ignoring the fact that she slipped up along the way.

It was a flash, an impulse that in no time carried her to a strange but safe place. She let herself confidently to be led toward the void humming with nothingness, and now she was covered in darkness. Soft, palpable like a cat's fur. The tightness widened slightly. It seemed to have been made by a gigantic spider. Each time it was as if she had touched the texture of the walls, which bent under the pads and every now and then took unknown forms. She wanted to create something stable, something that wouldn't deform when she wanted to scratch it. Unfortunately, the tiring vacuum didn't want to freeze for anything. She gave a chance to the thoughts that circled around and formed into systems of unstable illumination. She was standing in the center, feeding on silence.She tasted stickiness. Unknowingly, her hands began to move around her body, as if she had wanted to delightfully stimulate not only the synapses, but also the scraps of nerves hidden under the tissue. She was stroking the covered parts with her fingertips. She was inhaling more and more viciously. The tension was growing.

Morien braced with his arms. The woman's behavior wasn't unusual, but the observation of the fever she was in shook him slightly and aroused a lot of conflicting emotions. Lilian was squirming and moaning. He was reading her. Now she appeared as an open book, completely stripped of her protective coat. Almost naked in pursuit of the primal instinct. On the other hand, he liked the effect of creating free space, but was concerned about the structure of the power, as if generating a separate world into which she could escape. The deeper she dipped into it, the more intensely she became absent. He decided to take a risk and speak:

"Lilian," he whispered.

He didn't want to lift up the tone too much. He was afraid of the echo. Her panic could have ruined everything.

The shaky tissue of power trembled, the voice spread around a little thunderous, and a little muffled, not obvious again. It fell in a cascade of broken formations that vibrated and fell at the feet. The name, her name tickled the smallest hairs growing on her forearms and the sides of her cheeks. She felt the most the fine fluff on the nape of her neck rise and fall, teased by the tension. She right away realized that Morien was breaking into her space like an uninvited intruder. At first she wanted to push him away, to be wrapped again in satin softness. The shape of the word stopped. She was touching it. The strange meaning of the particles wasn't desmearing, but tickling the consciousness. She softened and submitted to the padding will just before her.

Morien repeated. He hoped he would get used to it and be carried away. She reached for what was starry and dim:

"Can you hear me?" He asked.

The answer seemed unambiguous, yet too difficult to follow. She wanted to say that it was good, that she arranged the whole according to a pattern, though a bit out of the box. She was wandering. The space widened, but the walls became impenetrable. Whenever she tried to puncture the membrane, it stoned and pushed her away, creating disgusting visions. She felt so sick that a sudden spasm tugged her stomach.

Morien fiddled nervously with his fingers, looking for reflections, but they didn't exist. There was only impenetrable non-being.

Lilian was wandering. Paths that had just glistened with stellar illumination, now licked her ankles with tarry stickiness. She heard noises, calls coming from somewhere in the space. They were surrounding her above and below. They were attacking from within, as if an unreal fist had been trying to take the last breath from the lungs. The sense of security receded, paving the way for an aggressive fear that no longer existed only as an image. She hit the void, and it began to engulf her with its slimy tentacles and pull her down. She wanted to scream, but her voice was stuck in her throat. She was silent, motionless and without will. She weakened with every heartbeat, with no hope of returning to the real world.

Morien was thrashing. He knew the procedures perfectly, he knew how to act, and yet his internal uncertainty kept him from making the final move. He trusted that Lilian would handle the situation, that sooner or later she would calm down and let the magic work. Such situations always had a way out, no matter what appeared in the intrant's mind.

She stiffened. The body slumped in the chair, and Morien gripped it. She was flaccid and without spirit, so he punched her in the face. The hard blow made red stripes on the skin, but the pain didn't bring the woman back to consciousness. She still seemed a puppet. He screamed, almost making his throat sore, and coughed spasmodically. Helplessness touched the forehead of the white-haired man, and the furrow deepened incessantly. It was the first time he had watched the inability to return from the dish of whispers.

"It happens," he whispered to himself. "It happens," he repeated, and sweat was flowing down his temples in heavy drips. "There is a solution for everything, there is an opportunity! I remember, I remember, by Redeemers! Calm down! Came to yourself. You know!"

He laid her on the floor and removed the bandages. Her eyelids were swollen and tightly shut. He tried to lift them, grappling unsuccessfully with the force she put in to keep them closed.

"Providing a glow brought awareness back, as did the cold," he remembered. "Lilian!" He howled helpless as a child. "Let me act. Don't resist ... you beautiful sticker," he sobbed.

In desperation, he grabbed from the ground the cup Lili had set aside a moment ago, and splashed the chilled tea in her face. It worked. The tension drained from him, like the infusion in streams from Lilian's cheeks. The girl choked on air as if she couldn't had breathed for a long time.

She returned to normal and began to cover the eyes with her hands. Candlelight disturbed her.

"I thought I wouldn't get out of there anymore," she croaked.

"You scared me again!" He handed her a piece of matter. "I wonder how many more surprises you have prepared for me."

"Darkness surrounded me," she began shyly. "So dense and intense that I sunk in it with relish. I haven't felt so safe for a long time. I don't know if you can understand this, but the space I was creating was like a mother's womb except that instead of knots of veins, I was entwined with sparkling rivers filled with the blood of magic. Then something changed. A voice, yes... a voice that came from space. It bounced off me. I recognized it. It was whispering. I wanted to push it away, but my sobriety told me that I didn't need to be afraid, after all, it was you. Yet with each breath you became an intruder who wants to take everything away from me. Probably it was this anger and inability to push out that started to choke me. By Redeemers, how much contradiction in this. I don't know what happened, how it happened. Sorry, but I think this play isn't for me."

Morien watched her from under his white hair falling over his face. He thought that it was his fault, that he should have waited a little longer. She looked wasted. He couldn't demand that she overcome her fear and let herself be swallowed up by the vessel again, but he wanted her to return there and tame it. For a fraction of a moment his thoughts were occupied by an irresistible urge to put pressure on her. But he refrained. Probably if she could see, she would have noticed the mage's features change. Internal struggle shaped the cheek muscles into all sorts of grimaces. To hide it, most likely from himself, he covered his face with his hands.

"Maybe we could try again?" He coughed up. "If we fail, we will postpone the study or simply abandon it," he argued.

He was aware that he was doing something that she wouldn't like. But... he cared so much!

She sat more comfortably, the chair creaked under the weight. She didn't feel like it. Morien's proposal seemed silly. Just like that - the silliest he could think of. Bitterness or rather resignation probably pressed her to the seat more than fatigue and fear of what might fall on her shoulders again. Didn't he hear what she just said? Or maybe ... no, probably not...

"I'm just debating now. Maybe not today. Maybe in a while. Forgive me for pushing, I just wish you would come back there and trust me." The words choked, yet he succumbed to the better and softer side of himself.

"Maybe." She shrugged. "Maybe ..." she sighed and started to struggle with the rag. "Now, please take me to the quarters. I need solitude and sleep."

Having put his arm around her, he led her down the stairs. The cool corridor smelled of sharply polished wood. It had a completely different vibe than the library. She could feel on her skin a slight draft in the room, coming through the leaky windows and lintels. Someone had tidied her lodging. She recognized it by the smoothness of the bedding on which she rested. It probably made her a little angry. She thought that she would spend a lot of time searching for the necessary things, but the magician helped and the nightgown with the bowl and brush quickly returned to its previous places. All she wanted now was the silence broken by the howling of the wind struggling with the trees.

Morien went out, leaving the door ajar. She got up and closed it gently so as not to disturb anyone with the unnecessary clatter of the lock. The key scraped. The longed-for solitude poured into her like a spring of refreshing dawn. She fell back on the bed, brought her hands to her face and lightly brushed her eyelids with the fingertips. They were no longer pulsating, nor were they swollen. Faint pulsation spilled over the sockets, and that was all. The unbearable itching was gone, now only invaluable relief remained. She wanted to open them right now, when the evening was wrapped in a curtain of gray and navy blue. She dreamed of experiencing colors again. It was one of the simplest things she had ever done in her life. Maybe it hadn't passed enough time to disaccustom the pupils to functioning, but every move seemed to be the hardest work. The tiny spots swirled in a swarm, they seemed to be insects whirling in a heavy cloud over the heads of people who, tired of their constant biting, flee to places full of incense and aromatic oils. The spots stung and made her eyes water. She didn't want to give up, so she repeated the tests in vain hope of improvement. In the end, she lost her strength completely. The state she found herself in seemed to be a suspension of physical and spiritual forces. Dressing up in night clothes seemed to last endlessly and, although the chill of the water refreshed her a bit, she wanted to bury herself under the blanket and stop thinking. She long rolled over on the bed to find a comfortable position until she finally fell asleep. The tormented body fell into a long healing sleep.

Morien paced the house with his arms folded behind his back. His head was full of thoughts that were like herds of ever hungry, stray dogs - voracious and impossible to chase away at all costs. He didn't know whether to wait, or simply go to the Archmage to talk about Lilian and her specific problem of creating the vessel of whispers. He looked out the window, the sky was black and the strewn squares glowed white. The surroundings were lit by lamps whose flames swayed in the wind and made the impression that the world was flickering with them. With a heavy heart, he decided to continue his studies. It wouldn't hurt that he would inform Vadael about everything. It would be the best and safest thing to do. Lilian can't get hurt. She can't become a puppet without feeling, lost in constructions with no exit, the world of imaginary sensations from which there is no return.

The magician had a dream. It was clear, even tangible. She dreamed of empty space and falling. There was no fear in it, rather disappointment. She succumbed as if emotions pertained to something perfectly obvious, or familiar. She knew the place, and yet as if she hadn't. The tentacles of power devoured the remnants of life from dying creatures, leading them to decay and incineration. The space had a similar character. On the other hand, she propelled with power strongly enough to animate it and not let it disappear. She fantasized about reaching rock bottom. The feet instantly became stuck like coils of velvet matter that crawled like snakes, climbed towards the heart, and at the same time embraced her tenderly. There was no pain, rather a pleasure similar to that which entwines lovers during love ecstasies. The overwhelming pleasure was burst by a spark, which crackled just above it, and, falling apart, buried itself in a cascade of impenetrable light. When she came to herself, she realized that she had moved to a completely different place. The room, bathed in white, gnawed the skin with its icy blue glow. The light broke under the eyelids, and with its clawed paws, tried to reach the irritated pupils and bite into them greedily. A scream filled her throat. The sudden transition from a black environment made her unable to stand the light. She treated everything as an attack. She calmed down, froze in a bent position, and rested her hands on her lap. She stood so a long moment, counting single heartbeats. Blood pounded beneath the skullcap. She had to get used to it. Surrender might have been the worst thing she could do, so she kept counting: 1... 2... 3... 4...

"Stay here," she admonished herself in thoughts. "Not yet, keep your eyes closed... Now!"

The curtain of her eyelids opened a little, but she could see little through the gap. Then it went quite smoothly. There were no doors or windows there, and the vaulted ceiling resembled a dome cut through by non-parallel arteries, reminiscent of glass structures. They resembled an ornament, and at the same time a stable structure that supported the ceiling. The phenomenon flickered and beamed, with blue illuminations in between. Raising her head, she began to turn around her axis, as if making move what lived above her. The matter beneath her feet got soft and warm. She sank slightly in it, and every step she took left imprints that quickly disappeared, as if she had been treading on pressure-sensitive moss. And then she heard it... A song flowing from the area of the solar plexus in the humming voice of... her mother. She knew it well, it was one of those elven lullabies that women used to hum to their children at bedtime. The story was about love and trust, as well as a time that heals even the deepest wounds. It praised the youth of one of the Redeemers, his strength and the power to survive despite adversities. The note then disappeared, ended...

Roused from sleep, breathless Lilian sat on the edge of the mattress. She sensed someone's presence, but found no one. Nevertheless, into her consciousness was breaking the fact that someone was watching her and trying to enter the mind at all costs, using clever tricks. She realized that Speech of Whispers was essential. Therefore, she decided to learn it, drawing on various sources, even if it was necessary to cooperate with the Archmage of the School himself.

Morien returned to his office and continued the work. But then he let his eyelids drop. Activities repeated over and over again quickly tired him. Probably he didn't realize how much. Roused from the numbness, he headed towards her in his mind. The room seemed to be pulsing with the power that prevailed in the dusty corners. The girl was sitting on the bed, looking around sleepily, as if she had sensed exactly the same as he did. He wanted to get through to her, but the gates of consciousness were so isolated that he couldn't see the gap in this perfectly secured fortress. Fortunately, she quickly recovered and settled back comfortably. She also fell asleep quickly. He breathed a sigh of relief. He returned to the library and stared out the window.

Lonan crouched on the edge of the breach, from where he could clearly see part of the School walls. The sudden loss of contact took his breath away, so he leaned on his staff and mentally counted until the desired consensus was reached. He wasn't bothered by the chill and fine snow seeping through impenetrable swaths of thick clouds. He could manipulate her dreams and that was the only comforting thing. He had to direct her so that she left the safe part of the city, and this time he also would find a way ...

Dawn had come so quickly that the mage thought he hadn't slept. Lili woke up relaxed, unlike Morien, who fell asleep with his head on the desk. Fortunately, the platter of warm milk and oatmeal smelled good. Even though sleep stuck to his eyelids, eating a proper breakfast had become something he was dreaming about right now.

Lilian washed her face in a bowl of water. The cooling touch of the cold liquid worked wonders. She needed such refreshment, because that day would be the one she had been waiting for a long time. She didn't plan to put on a dressing, she wanted to slowly start getting used to the new situation. She also thought about sleep all the time. She didn't know if the strength she felt came from him, or if someone from the outside had their fingers in it. But she knew she was ready for the unknown. The speech of Whispers became a priority. She went to the office to see how Morien was doing.

She found him lazily sipping his breakfast. His hair was disheveled and his eyelids were swollen.

"Good morning," she said from the threshold.

He leered at her and went back to chewing.

"I see you're in a bad mood," she said and stepped closer.

She leaned against the desk top.

He glanced at her again. A heavy spoon landed in the bowl, he propped his chin on his fists.

"Let's say I slept badly, or rather slept here."

"Then you have to catch up. Do you want me to show you your room?"

"I've been in it for a long time, can't you see? No?" He yawned. "Then I'm running. Can you hear my heels hitting the boards...? In fact, I don't have time. I will sleep after I die, as my grandmother used to say. She was a good woman."

Lilian leaned in flirtatiously.

"And who prevents you from sleeping until noon?" She raised an eyebrow.

He shook his head. He knew she would be happy to drag him into a bed full of goose feathers and the softness of pillows. He reluctantly resumed eating, stuffing the already cooled porridge into himself. He saw that the girl was weary of the picture of the man eating, who not only looked like a misfortune, but also slurped like a subordinate sponge. When he was full, he said:

"There are many activities planned for me today. Novices will probably eat me if I'm late." He ran a hand through his hair as if to make sure it was good enough. "I think I should befriend this bloody bone contraption that will make me look at least decent." He smiled and having kissed Lili on the forehead, he left.

The girl stood in the middle of the room. Her eyelids were half closed. The time spend by Morien on reading should be used by her for something constructive, especially since the eyes had almost returned to the way they were before the accident. They still festered, but she noticed a significant improvement in visual acuity. She settled comfortably in the armchair that was by the recently lit fire. The delightful crackle of the consumed logs gave the place a unique character.

The mage came back a little while later, looking much neater. She even smelled a bit of sharp cedar water with which he moistened his freshly shaved cheeks. He kissed her and pressed a small, horribly damaged book into her hand.

"See you in the afternoon. This should interest you." He waved his hand goodbye and disappeared behind the door.

She turned the volume, searching for the title in vain. The emaciated cover didn't want to reveal the secrets of the content. She opened it slowly, savoring the moment. On the yellowed and slightly torn page was the title: "Speech of the Will, or Magic of Whispers - A Compendium for Novices and Older Mages." She smiled. He knew well what she needed.

CHAPTER V

The king was awakened by a shooting pain near the small of his back. He grunted and straightened. Involuntarily, he reached towards his back, where the throbbing obnoxiousness irritated the muscle tissue. For some time now, the pain came back every night. He didn't complain, he knew the rumor power. The ruler's ailments could echo off the walls of the castle and return with a double force that would be called the imminent leaving of the valley. And the arms of the Redeemers unquestionably were out of his way. However, the lack of sleep became so persistent that he experienced uncontrolled naps during the day. Eleanor must have thought then that this was already that age when rest is something that old and rotten bones sometimes need. However, Aaron still felt as young as years ago when he could draw his sword without fear. He hadn't looked into mirrors too often in a long time. The reflection no longer belonged to him. He had the impression that from under the wrinkled eyelids, glanced at him some stranger, wearing a drooping, flaccid and worn layer. So he relied on his sharp mind and avoided being involved in skirmishes that could disturb this sense of security.

His mouth got dry, so he poured water from the pitcher that was on the small table next to the king's bed. Nearby, Eleanor was sleeping huddled, with her hair spattered on the pillow. He liked her just like that - free and natural, with no pigment on her lips, no bone pins to hold her strands, or steel corset that painfully tightened her waist. He drank a little as he stared at the smooth face of the glass. The moon silvered the garden, and the wind stroked the tops of the garden thuyas. Shadows spread gently in the alleys. Nights like this always caused that he could have enjoyed the silence endlessly, devoid of the noise and whispers in the corridors.

His body's indisposition contorted his face. He was still massaging his back, hoping it would somehow help, and his thoughts circled around one thing - he would get up crumpled and cranky again in the morning. The views outside had tired him out, and the sand under his eyelids stung tirelessly. He sighed and huffed, squirmed, and put down the glass of the half-drunk liquid.

Eleanor opened her eyes, saw a huddled figure resting on the edge of the bed. She rose on her arms. Aaron grunted and placed the saliva in the spittoon. He wiped his mouth with the back of his hand and, turning his forehead towards his wife, said hoarsely:

"Sleep, my dear."

"What's bothering you, my king?" She leaned closer and placed a hand on his knee.

"I can't sleep," he replied.

"Maybe I'll wake the medic? He probably has herbs that will help with insomnia."

"No, my dear, it is not insomnia that bothers me."

"So, what? Alvena? Gentry? Maybe indigestion? There is also a solution for that," she mentioned what just came to her mind.

He laughed.

"My love, my Eleanor." He was still smiling. "Old age afflicts, not noble scoundrels and greedy merchants. I'm old and my bones ache, so I can't sleep."

The woman sat down next to him and put the head on her husband's shoulder.

"An aged, kind-hearted king who, instead of complaining, admires the views, sips water and beats paths in the chamber," she joked.

"A little, unbearable queen who will never grow up, and will trouble him like a little girl until he gives up his ghost," he bit back, but a delicate grimace of satisfaction appeared at the corners of his lips.

"Teaser." She nudged his shoulder.

He poked back.

They were sitting so for a long time. These were the moments when they didn't have to watch themselves and behave properly. They had fewer and fewer moments together for some time. In the stuffy afternoons, he seeked her out with his eyes as she walked through the cloisters, and she looked back, smiling gently, believing that in the evening, when night navy began to lie on the roofs, she would rest again at her husband side, and listen before going to sleep what had worried or pleased him.

The Baroness launched a crusade against the magicians. About her actions informed letters or decrees, which he sometimes didn't manage to discuss with his advisers, because soon after, a new ideas appeared. Alvena intensively doubled the size of the City Guard, encouraged the young and agile to join its ranks, and promised more pay and a wider range of amenities, such as free accommodation. There were many willing people. It was a pity, however, that to the gates came drunkards and homeless people, tempted by the promise of easy money and shelter. In a way, the king didn't mind, everyone had to undergo training, whether young or damaged by alcohol. He hoped the commandant would deal with the sea of people willing to put on leather coats. He knew that the elf would not let go and would show each of them the right path individually. It made Raghion seem safer, and while reports did show a reduction in minor offenses, he was under no illusion that things would last long - not here. At that time, he had heard little about the quarrels between the dwarven families and the rebellions of the peasantry inhabiting Undertown, or was he only spared reports? He didn't know. The richer nobles and village leaders bleated more. They were instigated by the Baroness. She insinuated that bad crops and pests were probably a conspiracy of mages that must be revealed as soon as possible, because the rebels might have acted against the poor farmers, and thus hit their masters. Funnily enough, the king didn't receive disturbing correspondence from the Mage Schools, as if they had remained completely unaffected by Alvena's behavior. Everything went on as normal there. At the court, he hosted several healers who lived in chambers located right behind the lazaret building. He could have sworn that these magicians were the most balanced and patient people he had ever known. He put himself in their hands with great delight, and after the treatments he felt great for a long time. So he spared no gold and praise. More and more he became interested in the enigmatic and mysterious being of the affected by the magic curse, as his "favorite" cousin used to say. Behind the walls of the University he had friends with whom he exchanged regular correspondence, so the unknown became delightfully tempting over time, and the desire to know, more powerful than ever.

The sense of security that the royal wife gave him made Aaron meek and docile. Relieved by the gentle tone of her voice, he fell asleep quickly, forgetting the pain in his back and the racing thoughts that untamed, gnawed at the brain tissue. The morning woke them huddled close together, tangled up in sheets and blankets. The daily bustle in the corridors was better than the crowing of roosters in the castle henhouses, mixed with the screams of peacocks in the aviaries.

The service came earlier than usual. Surprised, they lowered their feet to the stone floor, shuddering at its cold. Eleanor inconsolably rebuked the girls who dared to invade the chambers, and these humbly lowered their foreheads, but after a moment of silence they ventured to speak, bringing the news that at dawn an envoy had come to the castle walls, demanding an immediate audience. Aaron gasped inconsolably, he was in the habit of basking on chilly mornings under his thick cover and enjoying interesting reading and a hot infusion with a bit of his favorite alcohol. He started his life in the afternoons, he only went down to eat the main meal. This day, however, didn't begin lazily.

"You see, honey," he sighed. "Being a king in a small, dirty country is terribly difficult."

She swept his hair from his forehead and said knowingly:

"I know, scoundrels, they don't let you sleep. Unacceptable."

He caught the faint sarcasm flowing from her carmine lips.

"You yourself are unacceptable scoundrel."

"You might not have reminded me. I have already forgotten."

The maids were standing at the door, with the arms folded on their laps, silently waiting for any order from the couple. They knew that they were undemanding people, but adhering to old habits.

It was rare for the king to got furious, but such situations did take place, especially when the mighty and gentlemen with the village heads arrived at the castle. Angry, he was able to chase the gathered people away with invectives and hitting the floor with his stick. Fortunately, his anger didn't last long, as it evaporated as quickly as it appeared. His sense of justice prevailed, and then he sent letters with an official apology and request for another meeting. In this respect, he differed from other sovereigns, which earned him the respect and favor of small neighboring states. During his reign, there were few disputes and skirmishes, most were solved through negotiations. Of course, he knew perfectly well the political situation in a country where the nations of dwarves and elves lived in conflict. In addition, there were feuds between the vogts over a land, income from agriculture or mining of minerals, but most of the towns and villages scattered around the region had their own laws, which were the ones of the Redeemers. He thanked them in spirit that the religion they adopted was a cult of peace and integration with nature.

They ate their breakfast in the chambers - modest as always, and abundantly washed down with goat's milk. The ruler adored them, she used to say that it was healthy and stubbornly gave it to her husband, who sniffed at this drink, which stank and remained on his palate for a long time. He gave in anyway because he trusted that her overzeal was justified by concern for his health.

He donned a robe specially prepared for the audience and went down to the throne room. He braced with a richly carved staff that was part of the royal insignia. On his temples pranced a crown inlaid with gold and jewels brought all the way from the Sea of the Dreamers, which crashed with a bang against the Archal cliffs.

The envoy was already in place. He walked back and forth. The robe betrayed a strenuous journey. Dusty and dirty here and there, it tightly clung to the skinny body of the man who glanced nervously at the small door next to the throne. The room itself wasn't one of the largest. It successfully accommodated only up to a hundred people, for whom there was still little space. On one side, it was illuminated by massive windows, decorated with multi-colored stained glass, with genre scenes from the life of the ruler and his family, interspersed with traditional floral motifs. Heavy purple curtains hung in those windows, with fairy-tale vines and foliage embroidered with gold and silver threads, and tied with purple cords finished with thick braided fringes. On the other side, there was a gallery of portraits of the rulers and their families, created by the hands of the most talented painters in the country. The paintings had big frames shimmering with gold in the glow of candelabra. There was a long floor mat, the thick wool sagged beneath the feet, and anyone who visited the throne room felt as if he had been walking on soft spring grass. The room itself was bright. It also had great acoustics and a spacious, high vault giving a pleasant echo.

Aaron entered the throne room with his guards and advisers equally early woken. A small door leaf slightly opened and the stooped figure clad in navy blue and gold emerged from its gloom. After him, entered at equal intervals the noble men with black and silver on their backs that glittered in the light of the quivering fires. The delegate stopped midstride, as if unsure how to act. The king waved his hand at him to come closer without fear. The guards parted and fastened their bored eyes on the newcomer.

Aaron settled comfortably in the chair, crossed his legs and adjusted the folds of the cloth so that it ran in soft tucks onto the polished floor. It was a decent throne, though it would be more appropriate to call it solid than majestic. The armrests were crowned with lion heads with open mouths, and the legs resembled paws armed with claws. The seat was upholstered in brown leather, which had worn out over time here and there.

The man bowed low to him, and Aaron nodded back in greeting.

"Hello, my lord," he began calmly, but there was tension in the air.

"Hello," he replied calmly, stroking his tousled beard. His mind wandered around the room, in which the warmth spread pleasantly and was a comfortable bed, probably already made by the maids. He felt a little sorry that he would be forced to destroy such a nicely done job. Well... The chill of the throne room always annoyed him.

"To the point," grunted the adviser who was standing nearby, and who, like a faithful pup, followed the monarch whenever it was needed.

"Of course," replied the messenger. "Lord, I come on behalf of the vogts from the western frontiers."

"I'm listening." The crowned head narrowed his eyes and clenched his hand stronger on the armrest.

"The associated village heads are asking for a little help in the case of wild magicians."

"Magicians, you say?" Aaron leaned slightly toward him, continuing to play with his chin. "How little, youngster?"

The man kicked his heels. He didn't know whether the king joked, or he was quite serious. He frowned and continued:

"There are reports that the population is intimidated by a group of savages. Probably a wing of Illusionists or Moralists."

"So you are not sure what faction it is?"

"No, my lord. We only know that they commit theft, and if someone catches them, they put a kind of curse on the unfortunate, after which the peasant has a body covered with an itchy rash for a few days and doesn't leave the outhouse."

The king roared with laughter. And it was not a forced chuckle, it was flowing from inside the old body and carried happily around the room with a resounding echo. The secretary, as well as the adviser, put their hands to their mouths so as not to accompany him.

"Forgive." The king sat more comfortably, grunted a few times to get back to normal, though in this case it was extremely difficult. "You say rash and outhouse? And with that you come to me? What kind of help are you asking for, maybe a powder for an unpleasant ailment, or for the soldiers? Or perhaps mercenaries to kill all the wild in the woods? I guess you're not that stupid. It is impossible."

"Your Majesty, this is a real inconvenience. Due to these attacks, most people are unable to work, and supplies melt. This year we have a terrible winter, the farmyards are neglected, the peasants don't want to pay tribute to the village leaders, and those no longer have sufficient resources to resist the constant plunder."

"As is well known to me," said the adviser. "All small towns are under the protection of the Royal Guard, worse with small towns and outlying villages, there may indeed be a problem of human nature."

"The guards don't care about the requests of the peasants," added the envoy. "Bribed by the mighty, they protect only them, the rest are unattended, doomed to fend for themselves, so what should the ordinary mob do? They can't fight, and their masters have their hands tied."

Aaron leaned against the throne, clasped his hands together, and watched the irritated messenger surreptitiously. The man leered, twisting his mouth and ruffling the hair repeatedly. He was nervous. The king realized that this supposedly trivial question really enraged him, and was serious enough for the envoy, to take a closer look at it.

"I suppose the magicians starve," he said finally. "Winter is really harsh. You can get along with intruders in exchange for helping them survive a difficult period. As for the village leaders, I think a few trusted people will do the trick. We will see what have been hatched there at these ends of the border."

"Come to solution with the magicians?" The envoy moved his pale lips almost silently, distrusting what had reached his ears.

"Yes, they are people too." Aaron didn't give up.

"But, my lord! They are savages!" Saliva gushed from the lips of the newcomer.

"Savages or not, they also have families. They steal out of hunger. In a simple line of thought, as if they were eager to do harm, the farmsteads would probably be burned down, the herds would be killed, and the runts would die of entropy. I know magicians enough to know what they are capable of. Besides, you weren't trying to figure out what faction had settled in the neighborhood. If they were Magicians, you would learn a lesson. I think they are Moralists, a wing of the Magic School living in small communities that deal with hunting and foraging. They often mate with the elves and live off the produce of the earth."

The man was staring at the king now with his mouth open, he didn't know whether he was to be malicious or silent.

"How have you, lord, gained such knowledge?"

"I like to read before going to sleep." Aaron raised his arms in a gesture that meant: what's wrong with that?

The deputy debated what to do and bowed. He hid his hands behind his back and waited patiently for events to unfold. The old ruler called the secretary, whispered a few words to him, then the man in black disappeared behind the door leading to the throne room, to return in a moment with a stand, a scroll and ink. He made a note of what he heard, and gave it to the king. After reading it, the ruler passed it to the first of the guards and ordered him to bring the message to the barracks of the City Guard, from where a small unit with a messenger was to set off, only to calm the irritated village heads and try to put an end to the internal disagreements.

The visitor said goodbye and marched out of the audience briskly. He clicked his heels furiously on the soft carpet, and his gait was so heavy that his steps carried along the ceiling. When he disappeared behind the great door, Aaron breathed a sigh of relief and leaned against the throne.

"Anyone else asking to be heard?" The magnate asked sluggishly.

The adviser disaffirmed.

"Fine, then I'll go to the library, although I admit that my chamber is tempting, but ... I want a book about ... magicians."

He got up, took off the heavy crown, and solemnly placed it on the throne seat. He left the crowd, and the dampness of the castle corridors engulfed him.

The secretary, moved by the ruler's behavior, jumped up, took the heavy object gently, and having wrapped it in the sleeve of his robe, headed for the treasury. He was accompanied by armed men, the same ones who a moment ago looked wearily at the envoy. The crunch of the armor disturbed the peace of the rooms.

The king wandered the familiar recesses of the palace. On the way, he greeted the servants, wishing them a nice day. The library was located in the southern part of the castle, so by the time he got there his knees had started to ache, however, dealing with the written word always took him away from worldly problems, so he hoped that when he got there, the joints would cease to remind him of the strenuous march, or at least he wanted to lie himself like that.

The malevolent atmosphere around the mages was beginning to irritate him. He wanted to know more about them, although he had sufficient knowledge. He was well versed in factions and the ways of using magic, as well as learning the will and mana. He also knew what abilities they could possess and to what corruption the misunderstood concept of having a magical gift could lead to. Nonetheless, he naively believed that gifted people were not evil, but rather impulsive.

Early morning rays of sunlight fell into the room through huge windows, creating a picturesque ornament made of stained glass panes. As in the throne room, they were decorated with thick curtains embroidered with floral motifs. Many years ago, the floors had been laid with subtle parquet, which squeaked every time you stepped on it. The wood was most likely dried up in some places, but Aaron had such a strong fondness for it that it never occurred to him to replace it. It became part of the library, as well as the volumes it contained, arranged on wonderfully carved shelves, painted gold. They ascended almost to the ceiling, so when the need arose to reach the ones from the top places, he had to use ladders cleverly attached to narrow rails. In this, he was helped by a servant as old as he was, who devoted his life to running the royal book collection. The king saw that the man was ailing, and was likewise tormented by weariness. He tried to persuade him to rest and hire a student of his choosing who would have led the piece of the world so close to his heart. Unfortunately, the librarian didn't care about the ruler's opinion. He knew that no one could take care of dusty volumes like he did.

"Imryk!" He called from the doorway.

The king leaned on his cane and scanned the room looking for the little man. He emerged from around the corner with the volume in his hands. Thick, wire-rimmed glasses slid slightly off his humped nose.

"Good morning." The librarian's cheeks waved.

"Yeah, yeah. Good, good. Do you have anything about magicians? Something I don't know yet, of course," said the ruler.

"Let me think." He moved in place, as if checking the ground.

He scanned the edges of the books.

"Lord, I think you are familiar with everything we have." He laughed. "I will search. There are hundreds of texts here. I think that something has hidden from us, it is easy to overlook it, unfortunately."

The king returned Imryk's smile.

"I thought there are not any books in this library that you are not familiar with, or don't know where they are."

"I'm getting old, my lord, I'm forgetting this and that, but I think there should be something here that you haven't read yet." He approached the shelf, still holding the thick book inlaid with gold letters.

He ran a dry finger along the spines of the works, muttering to himself. Glancing over his shoulder, he found a place to leave the one he had brought with him. The one pulled out looked as impressive as its predecessor except that a lot of dust kittened on the wrapper.

"Lord, that should interest you."

"What is it?" he asked, watching closely as he carefully twisted it in his hands, brushing the dust off the corners.

He loved it, that honor in him, which he gave to the old manuscripts.

"History of magic and magical factions at the turn of the century. It's about creating factions, something like high schools, but they were created by seniors, gathering around them a group of intrants who were just discovering talents. Self-control was taught. It's a good book. It's a pity that such a book has hidden from me." He scratched his bald scalp. "I read it years ago, before Universities were introduced."

Aaron wrinkled up the eye area in a loving smile.

"Lovely, I'd love to know more."

The book, bound in leather dry and wrinkled in some places, fell into the hands of the old man. The librarian bowed and returned without a word to dealing with matters only known to him. The king never wondered what he did all day. For him, he was always when he needed him the most, after all, he embraced with thought and deed the whole magical world full of thick volumes and dusty books, maps, charts and pictures of the sky. He thought about this man with tenderness. He realized that soon a time would come when he would call Imryk, and only an emptiness would answer. That's why he made every effort to ensure that he didn't lack anything, especially the care of not only court medics, but also magicians associated with the hospitals. He was his weakness, as was the young wine from the vineyards on the outskirts of the city, but from reading he didn't have a headache, and from the wine, he did.

He wandered between the shelves a moment longer, and when he was satiated, he found his favorite place, which was padded with a thick mattress on which armrests and cushions were placed. He sat back comfortably and looked out the window. The snow intensified the sunlight. Penetrating, acrid brightness poured in through the clean panes. He closed one curtain, it was so much nicer. The book gripped him from the very first pages. The author skillfully used the word, thanks to which, despite the passage of time, the king was able to understand some phrases, which were no longer used, but still stayed in remote parts of the country, in places that stopped in time and didn't have a steady flow of human resources. Each of the first letters was a tiny work of art. He stared at these initials for a long moment, a little envying the artist his talent.

He didn't know how much time he had spent reading, but he did know that his stomach was clamoring for food very loudly. He stood up and painfully tucked the volume under his arm. The bulk of the book made him think of a plan to hand it to the guard which would carry it to the sleeping quarters. He would eat his meal in silence in the palace kitchen, to the big resentment of the cook, who, when she caught him, would start whining that he should have eaten in the dining room, and not like the simpletons at the stove. She always amused him, but he forgave her because she was right. It ill befits a ruler to eat unwashed apples straight from the baskets or to nibble on a cake before it has time to cool, but he loved it, and he didn't want to give up small pleasures for anything in the world. Deep down, he was a child who ventures into the pantry and steal treats when the mother or the housekeeper is busy with something utterly useless for a boy. He preferred doggeries and stables. Both ladies wrung their hands in pleading gestures, asking the Redeemers to make him at least a little similar to his father. Unsuccessfully.

"I knew I'd find you here." He heard a voice behind him.

He knew it perfectly well.

"I knew you'd know." He took a bite of a sweet cake.

"You know you shouldn't sneak in here?" She pulled up a stool and dropped onto it, sighing heavily.

He stroked his spouse's hair, now put up and decorated with shiny pins, on the tops of which wobbled blue tassels. He felt like taking them all out and letting the locks fall freely on her shoulders.

"Beloved," he said. "You shouldn't be here, either, and yet you are, and you glance at the treats with the same lust as I do."

She narrowed her eyes like a cat that has seen a sparrow. He knew her perfectly well, she had a weakness for sweetness, but she didn't admit it. After spending years together, she knew his paths, for there were two places in the palace where he enjoyed sitting. Library and kitchen.

"You could have asked one of the servants to bring you food to your chambers."

"Hunger twisted my guts. What was I to do? Reading makes my stomach rumble. The magic makes me so hungry that I'm ashamed to hang around the corridors in such a state. What would people say when they heard that the king is on short commons? Scandal, dear, scandal in the whole kingdom!" He chuckled, put a large piece of cake in his mouth, and dusted the crumbs off his hands.

"What is this book? About magicians? Have I read it?"

"I don't know. Anyway, women seem to prefer other literature." He gave her a wink.

"Old fogey." Amused, she nudged him with her shoulder. "Do you think that all women read sloppy stories and wander at night in the corridors dreaming of unfulfilled love torn straight out of the pages of books?"

"Is it not like that?"

"Sure not." She was indignant. "I don't read romances, they bore me. Let's get out of here. Will you show me what Imryk gave you this time?"

"Of course." He nodded and stood up, giving a hand to his wife. She took it gently and allowed herself to be led towards the chambers. Aaron had the chunky volume under his arm again. He wished he had disposed of it as planned.

They quickly found themselves in the palace corridors. The sun was shining through the stained glass panes, painting multi-colored mosaics on the gray floors. The ladies of the court bowed low, and they answered to their greetings with a nod. They reached their rooms in no time. They were pleased with the privacy afforded by the great carved doors. Nobody came in here except for the service that was first called. The queen looked greedily at the bulky volume that had just landed with a splat on the oak table.

"Can I?" She asked and held out her hands, though she knew she didn't have to ask.

"Take it, it is enough for me for today, although I must admit that due to this dusty contraption I felt like taking a closer look at the customs in our local school. I know Evans, he's a good man. You think they wouldn't mind if I visited them? What do you think?"

She looked at him in surprise, he had never shown such a great interest in the Universities. He created them in order to maintain a certain balance. It's just a pity that after a while the institutions began to live according to their own rules, and the mages soon started to be perceived as a threat, which made the Schools a bit like prisons. Worse still, it happened surprisingly quickly, and it couldn't have been caused by anyone other than the Baroness herself. The queen wondered what was behind her hatred? After all, magicians were, are and will remain, and not everyone is weak and cannot wield power.

"Where is this coming from?" She asked.

He shrugged and glanced out the window.

"I thought that such an escapade would refresh a bit the ossified imaginations that had built up over time. Besides, drawing knowledge only from books, we are doomed to isolate ourselves from the present facts. The written word becomes obsolete over time."

She listened intently, caressing the gilded letters of the volume cover with her finger.

"Go on."

"So I got the idea of visiting, that's all. I think they won't kick me out the door?"

"Of course not. You are their king." She flared up.

"The fact that I'm a king doesn't mean anything." He turned to her. "They have their own politics, and the hierarchy in the Schools looks completely different. I'd rather call myself an intruder."

She parted her lips in surprise.

"I don't understand," she said after a moment.

"It's easy. I rule the state, and the Archmage has authority over the School. Following the simple line of thought, he is like the mayor or even the king himself to them. I have no authority there. The law granted by the crown is respected, but it is rather a paper law, so I'm very curious about the current universities. I think Evans will be happy to show me around."

She shrugged. She knew that once Aaron made up his mind, he wouldn't give up until he achieved his dream goal.

"If you want it, write a letter. I think you will get an answer the same day. After all, the ruler can't be kept waiting."

"Great idea." He rubbed his hands together. "I'll do it right away, let me just find parchment and ink."

He shuffled papers around the writing desk for a moment. As always, it was covered with a thick layer of correspondence, mostly not very important. Even simple people wrote to him thanks to the scribes who had their small offices in the merchant district. They asked for small things. He tried to read everything. Sometimes he got one a day, sometimes there was a pile. This week, surprisingly, began quite calmly in terms of correspondence. A small pile, including the parchment from his cousin, which he hadn't touched for obvious reasons, was piled up on the desk. It lay sealed on the edge of the gleaming desktop and waited for the proverbial "better times", or for a better mood. He found a pen and ink in a drawer. He couldn't see the clean scroll, which made him extremely irritated. He looked in the direction of his wife, who was leaning against the closet and watching the search closely.

"I know what you want." She caught the glare of anger.

"I know you know."

She moved slowly to the ornate piece of furniture, bent down and opened the last drawer, taking out the vellum.

"That should be enough."

He frowned.

"I would have died without you, you know?"

"And I without you, my king. What are you going to do? Are you sure you want to correspond with Evans? When Alvena finds out, you will learn a lesson, she passed judgment."

"You know my opinion. Why does she always have to get in my way? I'm an adult, I know what to do. I don't need incessant scolding and baiting me with the Baroness."

"Then write. She shrugged. "I'll take advantage of your busy day to go to one of the ladies of the court. She's got a shameful problem, you know, women's problems."

"Of course. Such matters require delicacy. I will sit down and write a few lines. The messenger will deliver the message today."

"Agreed," she approved and left the room.

Aaron was surrounded by velvety silence, and only single flashes of fire interrupted the old man's breathing. He looked around for the unlit oil lamp, as the evening dusk was beginning to prevail outside. The writing desk was tucked into the corner of the room, in a place unfortunate as for access of daylight, and even on a bright summer's day there was dimness, which the king liked when he was younger. Now that the eyesight was lame, it made up a distressing addition. He sat down heavily in the battered chair, folded his hands behind his head and thought. An olive lamp smoked and drew shimmering patterns on the stone wall. He dipped the pen in ink and set the first words on the parchment. He wanted to fit the maximum into as little text as possible, but he knew himself well enough to know that it was unlikely that it would be a short note.

He wrote:

To Evans,

Archmage of the School of Magic

I hope you feel fully healthy, Lord, and I wish you that. As you know, I correspond with the Baroness Alvena. This is not the most pleasant form of message flow for me, but my cousin is so stubborn that it is impossible to ignore her. So I have heard that you are struggling with escapes and disobedience on the part of adepts. Personally, I regret this fact and would like to handle the matter as soon as possible. Of course, I have the idea that the system of supervision of students in schools is quite different than in houses of study. I would like to visit you in the coming days to discuss the above-mentioned issues.

I hope for a quick response.

Best regards,
Aaron Orthen II

He yawned and wrinkled his nose. Probably it was decent. He hadn't managed to write such a short and factual message for a long time, he was famous for long, even tiring letters. He also didn't like to sign with the nickname given by the priest of the Redeemers, which every crowned head received at enthronement, but he respected traditions and the older he got, the more consistently he succumbed, and even worse he began to blindly believe that they were needed.

He rose, and folded the letter into a neat envelope, which he closed with a royal seal. The smell of lacquer wafted in the air.

There was a knock.

"Just in time," he thought.

He allowed to enter the servant which stood on the threshold with tomorrow's dress for the royal wife.

"It's good that you're here." He looked the man in the eyes. "I was just about to send for you."

The minion nodded his forehead, passed the master, and as if nothing had happened, he went towards the closet and placed the garment inside, groaning, closing the heavy leaf door of the furniture. He stood opposite Aaron, holding out his hand for the mail. He was a man of few words, but when he speak up, he always confused others.

"Here you are, Ungrik. Take it to the gates, I'm sure some messenger is still available. If not, they'll deliver it in the early morning. I'm in no rush. I have time. It's nothing urgent."

"Yes, my lord." The servant disappeared behind the door.

The senior went to the window, the snow swirled in the air again. The winter wind carried tiny scraps of white powder, creating an impenetrable curtain.

CHAPTER VI

The lecture hall was deserted. The shuffling of the chairs in the student benches had died down, and the footsteps of the novices heading for their afternoon meal echoed through the halls of the largest Magic School in the country. It was a typical winter afternoon for this area. The frosted windows let in a pale light that drew dull ornaments on the gleaming floors, stained here and there with slush. Evans rested his chin on his wrist and mused. He had to deal with internal disputes between the magicians and the City Guard, which not only grew considerably and gained popularity, but also scrutinized life at the University even more closely. He dared say that this silent behavior only aroused the discontent and disputes that occasionally broke out between students and teachers. He wanted to believe that this situation would somehow find its place, and that the dense and unbearable atmosphere would one day burst like a soap bubble and all that would be left was a memory and a greasy stain on the floor, if not bloody, of course. He wore purple robes for the profession. In a way, he was one of the combat mages who used hand-to-hand combat and elemental magic. Trained as a fire mage, he was fluent in this art. He bettered many in will. It was feared by those who were aware of the damage he could inflict. He was one of the youngest Archmages in history, only a fifty-four-year-old man with a focused face and a keen eye. Evans, in addition to the classic pyromancer strategy, was fond of one-on-one skirmishes, so he worked on his physical condition as hard as other acolytes, which over time developed his flexibility and incredible endurance. He might even be considered handsome, and most women would probably be glancing at him were it not for a small fact. He wasn't interested in women.

The royal messenger entered the hall, a pale man looking shiftily, as if he had expected an attack from nowhere. The magician folded his arms and waited, the envoy looked at the Archmage with his green bulging eyes and, having taken the sealed message out of his bag, handed it to him with trembling fingers.

"Lord, on behalf of the mercifully reigning King Aaron Orthene II, I come with important correspondence."

Evans straightened up and reached for the envelope without a word. He wasn't used to talking to ablegates, so he just nodded at him and told him to leave. The visitor took it with undisguised relief, and in spirit, he wished he had been treated with a small coin.

The mage turned the vellum in his hands a few times, then went to the window and broke the seals. Aaron wrote dryly, as if the words had been drawn by a complete stranger, which made Evans suspicious, though he admitted that he hadn't exchanged letters with the king for a long time. Maybe something had changed? The monarch was eager to make an unofficial visit and hoped that he would agree. In truth, he had nothing against, after all, they knew each other for a long time and in most cases got along. He supposed that Aaron wanted to discuss the tense situation, including Lilian's escape, of which he had probably been made aware long ago. It irritated him, the wretched news that escaped like rats through suburban sewers and then grew enormous and attacked with absurdity those who were, by Redeemers, innocent!

He had to write back, but he was in no mood for it. He diced the message, tucked it in his coin purse, and went to do the afternoon inspection of the senior mages' dormitories. Such a schedule was set for that day, so the message from the king couldn't thwart his plan of action.

Dormitories were located in the northern part of the school, pressed against the wall surrounding the facility. They were divided. The novices slept in the biggest ones. They were not co-ed, but separated by a wide corridor. As the law dictated: girls occupied their bedrooms, boys theirs. The higher it was, the size of the alcoves decreased. At first, ten magicians lived in each room, and as they grew older the room capacity was limited to two people. They lived on the top floors and were mostly lecturers who came here to train new magic techniques, as well as guests of the Schools. The university, surprisingly, didn't have guest rooms, but it was built twice as large and housed many educators. Evans was aware that the more young people in one place, the more likely it was they would do something extremely stupid. This was what the unannounced visits were for. This post wasn't derogatory to him. He got along perfectly with this community. After Lilian's escape, the rigor was tightened, and checking the order became something completely natural. The intrants tacitly approved it, although they probably had discussions among themselves, in which they cursed the Archmage for the afternoon raids on the trunks in which they concealed treasures.

In one of the corridors he saw a small figure cursing something in the corner. The young magician held out a hand glowing in the gloom of the corridor towards that "something". Minor discharges that can be observed in a storm jumped from one finger to another.

Evans watched it from a short distance, the boy didn't hear him come in, he only cursed and tried to hit that 'something' with a chain of lightning.

"What are you doing?" Evans asked, cocking his head in hopes of finding what was causing the boy's irritation.

The novice jumped out of his skin, and a chain of lightning flashed past the Archmage's ear and struck the wall next to him.

"I... I... I..." he stuttered. "I'm trying to catch a rat, master." He bowed slightly, but kept looking at the place where he was cursing so intensely.

"That rogue ate two of my robes. Please take a look." He pointed to the gnawed part of the bottom of the blue cloth.

Evans curled his lips indulgently.

"And because of the stupid rat so much fuss?"

"I can't hit it," the student snorted. "It runs under the cupboard."

"You think epithets and lightning will help? Iten, when will you learn that rats should be burned? Stand back, I'll find that obnoxious rodent before it eats my robe too."

He frowned and passed the young magician. The animal cuddled up to the corner and glared at the executioner with its black eyes. He saw their glow in the twilight that the furniture gave. It didn't surprise him that the student was having trouble getting to it. This year many young students came to the school and some closets with clothes, due to the lack of places for beds, were placed in the corridors. He crouched down and looked at the rodent again. There was a hiss and crackle, and a red glow illuminated the gray. After a while, he smelled the burned animal fur. He repeated it. He lit his hand and hurled a small formation of fire at the hypothetically dead pest. The fire bounced off the floor and hit the target precisely. This time it only sizzled, and after the unwanted guest there was only left a pile of ash. Iten was looking at the headmaster with his mouth slightly parted.

"That's how it's done, young man." Evans stood up and dusted off the bottom of his robe.

It crossed his mind that he should have called the servant to sort it out.

"Nice trick," the delighted kid squealed. "I have to tell the boys about this! You are the best master." He was joyful.

The magician raised his right eyebrow slightly:

"It's not your job, take care of the storm and lightning, you'll be better than me at this." He stroked his pale, stiff hair and went back to inspecting the dormitories.

The rookie acknowledged and looked towards the place where the incinerated carcass lay.

The Archmage didn't find anything suspicious this time, neither in the cabinets, nor shoved between mattresses. Winter didn't favor the young and clever, the herbs didn't grow wild, and the greenhouses were closely watched by gardeners and botanists. Partly contented, partly restless, he left the dormitories and plunged into the twilight of the ending day. Snow creaked slightly underfoot. He could hardly see anyone outside, they all hid in their houses. They were running away from the approaching frost, which was supposed to strike that night with redoubled force, and only the chimneys released smoke, which indicated that living creatures were in small houses. The windows shone against the winter landscape, warming with the light the most weary. Indeed, Evans looked and felt sleepy. The urge for hot soup reminded him that he hadn't eaten since breakfast. The reply to the royal correspondence would also not take care of itself, so he quickened his pace, hoping that the hostess had left the food on the stove.

He resided in an estate that was tucked in the most corner of the School. Right behind the University there was a small house, a quiet haven now plastered with snow, with windows topped with richly ornamented arches, and green straight doors with painted golden leaves at the edges. An element made by one of the servants. Crossbreed of elf and human - typical Jerm. Sensitive, delicate, perfectly organized and extremely submissive. He adored her. He was impressed by her steadfastness and the fact that he was unable to upset her. She had received that job recently, but after such a short time he could deduce that she was one of the special people he could trust. Her predecessor died last spring. He took it badly, he used to get along with those who gave him a sense of security. One of them was the service, which he selected very carefully.

She greeted him in the hall as always joyful and with slightly pink cheeks. Her pale and thin hair was pinned up high, creating a braid that framed a tiny face like a crown. Big blue eyes smiled kindly at him.

"How was your day, my lord?" She stretched out her hands to his outer garments.

"Thank you, my dear, great."

"I'm very happy. Right away, I will serve a hot meal in the dining room." She curtsied and placed the old and slightly worn coat on a hanger, hiding it in the cavernous closet.

Evans entered the private quarters, lit the lanterns and a fire in a small fireplace with the movement of his hand. The air smelled of fresh wood and burning resin, and faint wisps of smoke glided towards the room. He glanced at them and they obediently returned to the chimney.

"That's better," he sighed and changed into more comfortable clothes.

Meanwhile, the hostess called from downstairs that everything was ready. The cook wasn't a master at her job, but he endured it bravely. He salted what she served him, because the old lady believed that salt was evil and should be avoided for all the treasures of the world. He didn't share this enthusiasm, and she was terribly irritated when he reached for a salt shaker. He ate slowly. He wished to spend the rest of the evening preparing another lecture on fire magic and writing back to the king.

The office faded into the gloom, only the hearth sparkled the room slightly. The fire crackled cheerfully and devoured the next logs, and the bookshelves were visible in its glow. He liked this place. It had a specific atmosphere. He lit the largest oil lamp on the desk and sat behind it in an armchair padded with soft fabric. He was fed up with the light. He let down his long black hair, already interwoven with silver gray at the temples. Parchments lay in a neat row in the corner of the desktop, and next to them were several inkwells with colored inks. There was also a lacquer box and a seal. On the other side was an unopened internal correspondence. He glanced at it, it was unlikely to find anything urgent, so he started writing a message to Aaron:

Sire!

Thank you for your message. I also hope that Your Majesty is doing as well as I am. Your visit, sire, is as surprising as the correspondence that was delivered this morning. Of course, I'm very happy and I will welcome You, Lord, to our place with great pleasure. I would also like to mention that nothing remarkable has happened in the facility since the escape of a certain Lilian Vaal. If such situation happened again, I would notify you immediately. I will make all possible efforts to make Your Majesty feel at home here.

I bow my head.

Archmage of the School of Magic in Raghion,

Evans

He glanced at the drawn words. They seemed too stiff and official, but this is the tenor a letter to the ruler should have, even if the man is a long-time ally. They had known each other long enough to be able to be on a first-name basis. But he tried to avoid it, at least in the presence of others. He folded a message and sealed it, leaving the mark of the University's coat of arms. He went to the hall and looked for someone he could distract from the constant household errands. Amhara appeared in sight, as always with a slight smile, as if she had known she needed something.

"My dear, I have an urgent shipment to the palace, be kind and take it to the gate. It's urgent, the king can't be kept waiting. In the meantime, I will pay a visit to the masters. Probably tomorrow or the day after tomorrow we will have a visit of the gracious ruler."

She looked at him with eyes, in which he saw pupils dilated with excitement. She ran towards the servants' rooms and returned in no time, wrapped in a not very thick coat trimmed with foxskin. Before he could get a good look at her, the green door leaf slammed hard. He felt sorry for her, the frost was starting to bother. He himself thought about a winter hat and a thick scarf, and she out of spite to the world probably wanted to get her ears frostbitten.

Most of the Archmasters resided in the same building, and only those with the degrees of Master and Doctor had seats like him, although they could be counted on the fingers of one hand. The rest took care of the novices - a bunch of crude or fearful beings. Magic, especially at the beginning of training, could be painful. After classes, beginners left in charred robes, with small wounds on their hands or deafened by the roar of minor spells. That is why constant care and counseling of an experienced and calm person became so important.

Wrapped in a thick cloak, he passed from quarters to quarters. His nose reddened and his eyes watered, and it was not the fault of the frost, but of the liquors he was given. He never refused good alcohol. After all, the royal visit is, how can I put it, an important event. It would be a real treat for beginners and older students. He only hoped they would behave with dignity.

Morning greeted him huddled in the middle of the bed, tightly wrapped in a fleshy duvet. The night storm extinguished the fire and chilled the room. Dissatisfied, he cursed the cold, chattering his teeth, but he had to dig himself out of the warm harbor and consistently take care of the preparations. Such a small thing as a soft, woven rug laid right at the legs of the bed made him more happy than a decent glass of strong drink. He crawled out of bed, rubbing his eyelids with his numb fingers. The water from the pitcher placed next to the toilet bowl pierced the nerves with paroxysm. He shuddered. How much he hated winters. The chill of autumn mornings, saturated with the scent of falling and rotting leaves and the fog lazily floating above the ground, yes, but the last season of the year was definitely not a favorite. He dipped his hand in the liquid and once again a grimace of dissatisfaction ran over his sleepy face. He lifted his fingertips over the vessel. It began to react and warmed the skin with pleasant licks of steam.

"That's better," he sighed.

The morning bustle behind the door put him in a good mood. He had a feeling that something exciting was going to happen that day, after all, the nightmarish awakening didn't doom to failure the rest of the day! There was a delicious smell in the air of baked milk rolls, heated preserves, and chamomile infusion. Though he dreamed of an egg and bacon sandwich, this alternative was also delicious. After all, how can you live without candy? He didn't understand people who didn't like confectionery, he could eat it all the time. He ate intently, celebrating every bite, and relished the warmth of the stove that warmed his back. The girls who helped run the house arrived at first light. They didn't live in the residence, but enjoyed the privilege of moving freely between the city and the University. Now they greeted him refreshed and willing to serve. When he looked at them he often wondered what real life was like outside the walls. In the evenings, stayed only the housekeeper and the old gardener who looked after a small greenhouse right behind the house. In the long evenings they often played cards as well as other party games.

Outside the window, the snow beaded up and sparkled in the bright sun. Evans saw a clear sign in this that there most likely wouldn't be any snowfall that day. He breathed a sigh of relief. He walked towards the window to contemplate the peace for a moment. However, he didn't stand for a long time, because there was a loud thud in the hall. He budged and went to open the door. On the threshold stood the guard, happy and pink-faced.

"Yes?" Evans demanded.

"I'm greeting you, Archmage Evans." He bowed deeply, placing his hand on the hilt of the sword that dangled freely at his belt.

"Hello, Patrick. Do you have any news?"

"Yes, my lord. I'm to convey that His Majesty will arrive at noon, along with his wife and bodyguards."

"Great." He smiled. "How much time do we have?" He turned his head to look at the hall clock. He was surprised when it turned out that it was already ten o'clock. Fortunately, they had a day off from studying. According to the law of the Redeemers, everyone was entitled to divine rest, so there were four working days, and the fifth was considered holy. Evans had such an adjusted internal schedule that he didn't need calendars to know when he could sleep longer.

"Perfect. We still have a little bit to use."

"Yes, sir," he replied.

"Please check if everything is alright at the gate. I will inform the rest and we will go out to welcome the king. Go to the school kitchens and take a look. Maybe the service needs something."

"Yes, of course." He marched off, bowing first as befits a well-trained security guard.

A cloak was blowing behind him, creating a light cloud of frost-dry snow.

Evans didn't have to worry about anything, the school was working like clockwork and everything was sewed up. The unexpected visit didn't destroy the schedule, but only aroused curiosity. The students, glued to the windows, watched the noise accompanying the inspection of the entrance to the facility or the presentation of weapons. Time slipped through the fingers, though at times it might have seemed that beyond the walls, it dragged endlessly.

The king was famous for his punctuality, so at an afternoon o'clock his winter cart pulled up just outside the University gates. The solid, painted sleigh stopped smoothly in front of the noses of the guards reddening from the frost. The black-colored horses shook their heads nervously, and from their nostrils rose fuzzy puffs of exhaled air. This breed was the property of only patricians. The blood of these animals was mixed with due care, and the weak specimens were killed and the meat was given to the hounds. They were also famous for restiveness which was tempered by the coaches. The profession of a horse trainer, passed from father to son, so some families were permanently associated with the royal stables, and the creatures coming from their hand belonged to the elite among the bucephaluses. The experts took care of their condition, and were able to assess individual skills from the foal, as well as flawlessly sense their disposition. The stallions were used in many ways, but most often they accompanied on hunts, in wars, and in these mundane activities, such as now - as a cart horses.

Aaron was impatient, or rather looking forward, to see his foot touching the step of the carriage. With a scolding gaze he followed the minion who feverishly struggled with the steps. His spouse only raised the corner of her mouth, she knew that this childlike joy was justified. When it finally happened, despite the throbbing pain that had spread through his back again, Aaron poked his head out from behind the door. He looked for a familiar face in the crowd, and he brightened when he saw Evans. The mage lowered his forehead and placed his right hand on the chest.

The gates of the School hadn't been opened wide for a long time. Usually there were two gates, which were located on both sides of the wings, therefore the passing townspeople stopped and looked with interest. After a short while, a large diverse crowd gathered - from aristocracy to dwarves and servant elves. Distressed, they observed the movement around the built-up sleigh, which looked more like an ornate carriage than a means of winter transport. Aaron adjusted his robe and, having turned, gave his wife a hand. There was a buzz at the sight of her, for the royal wife was rarely admired up close, and when the opportunity arose, the judgments were endless. Literally everything was commented on: from the color of the dress to the shade of pomade applied to the lips. Today their silhouettes were wrapped in sable coats, and on their heads were white fox hats with single fringes freely dangling over the forehead. The woman, a bit embarrassed by the vivid interest, felt ashamed and, led by her husband, lowered her head. She hoped they would be inside quickly. Fortunately, the arrival ceremonies went smoothly, greetings and quick exchanges moved to the main square, and the mob disappeared behind the wrought gates, still cheering for Aaron. The ruler glanced at the Archmage with evident relief. The magician knew perfectly well that the old monarch dreams of a cup of hot honey and relaxing for the moment in empty talk, into which they would work these more important matters. However, they had to wait some time for this, the school council decided that it was worth showing the ruler around the University, paying special attention to the greenhouse and the library, where probably all the available books on magical arts were collected. They also boasted a rich collection of historical volumes, maps and astrological charts. The king listened to the lectures with undisguised interest. He didn't seem overcome by weariness at all. The papers seemed out of this world - enigmatic and fascinating at the same time. Every now and then he asked and entered into short conversations, and the Archmage continued the content, discovering fascinating flavors. Eleanor was carried away by the word, the magicians told so beautifully about a world she knew only from the writing and the rumors she had heard in the cloisters. She was interested in literally everything, even the colors of the robes and the fabrics from which they were sewn, because she noticed with a penetrating female eye that they differ significantly. So Evans explained ranks and classes, including the insignia they were entitled to, and added a handful of information about the fraternities. The difference is that the brotherhoods wear the same symbol around their necks, and only the garments differ in color.

For example, purple clothes and tunics are worn by magicians who practice the art of pyromancy. The more intense the robe color, the higher the grade. They start with bright red and end with deep purple. Magicians who deal with healing wear white robes, and Archmages gray ones. The mages taming element of water were clad in a blue color, which with time turned navy blue. Botanists and mages of the earth, as well as the forces of nature, who can summon wild beasts and have power over vegetation, wear light brown clothes, which with time turns into brown. Those who use lightning and create thunderstorms wear blue garments from the beginning, which over time turns into a deep blue combined with silver. And those who engage in filthy magic, that is bloody magic, derive vitality from living creatures, or tether will, that is Alchemists, from the very beginning clad in black. However, if any magician discovers in himself a different talent, he can write a letter asking to be allowed to wear a black robe as a sign of multi talent. However, this is an exception, which doesn't change the fact that Lords Masters, Archmasters and Masters of the first order may wear them as a symbol of their rank. In this case, they are girdled with a leather belt, at the side of which there is a bag with the emblem of the school embroidered on it. The Council of Archmages of the School of Magicians and First Degree Masters decides to grant a special medallion and a staff to support a talented magician. It is also rare for a chosen Archmage to stick to his robe color. They choose velvet black and the appropriate insignia just to stand out and emphasize their status. It has long been considered a good idea, because it was easier to distinguish rectors from students. But if a given magician left the University, thus completing his studies, the color was appropriate to the talent. He wasn't allowed to wear black. Alchemists and wild mages, instead of a belt, gird up with a thick rope with a decorative tassel. The colors of these strings also show the advantage of talent. For example: if a wild mage wields fire, and it is a guiding gift, the rope is red. Alchemists only have black belts and medallions with the symbol of the brotherhood.

Fascinated, Eleanor burned with excitement, and it flashed through her mind that it was a pity that it was impossible to emphasize families in such a way or the degree of service in the castle. It would make life much easier for those who have no idea who performs which function. After a while, however, she came to the conclusion that it should have remained as it was. Why destroy the already existing harmony, especially if the idea came from behind the gates of the Schools? It could have aroused an unhealthy interest that she might have dealt with, worse if Alvena started to suspect something. Then everyone would have learned a lesson.

There was still a speech awaiting them in the auditorium of the School, in which crowded students and senior intrants, stretching their necks over each other only to see the top of Aaron's head for a fraction of a breath. He was as exotic to them as the unknown flowers in the school greenhouses. Isolated from non-magical creatures, they absorbed every news from behind the wall like a sponge. Unfortunately, the misfits, during the annual passes, often got into fights with the locals or got drunk with the dwarves in the merchant's guild. The girls acted more prudently, but they didn't avoid flings and shedding tears after such a day off. It is widely known that what is forbidden tastes better.

The auditorium looked great, although it no longer impressed those who used often. The details got overfamiliar so much that they remained invisible. Aaron, on the other hand, cocked his head, immodestly opening his mouth. Eleanor stopped and scanned the details, wanting to ask questions, but intimidated, all she could do was breathe deeply, overwhelmed by the sheer beauty. No mortal without will was involved in the formation of this place. It was built from scratch by mages - brick by brick, board by board. It rose inscrutable. The vault gave the impression of a starry sky, the shimmering mother-of-pearl imitated stars, and deep navy blue obtained from lapis lazuli completed the rest. The room was clad with wood shaped so as not to use nails. The floors were decorated with shimmering and smooth as a mirror black marble, exported in galleys all the way from across the Sea of the Dreamers. It might seem that the room is overwhelming, but nothing could be more wrong. Surprising heat radiated from the ebony elements, the velvety matter of power gently moved through the air, warming it with particles when the cold set in, and lowered the temperature when the aura disturbed even the most resistant to heat. In the middle there is also a rostrum made of marble, but of a slightly different, lighter shade, which smoothly turned into impenetrable navy blue. The smoothly polished pedestal grew into the floor with iridescent roots, which surrounded it with a crown, climbing its branches upwards. They created a support on which a mighty book rested. This place was surrounded by benches on each side. Carved furniture in a semicircle, in perfect synchronization, climbed higher and higher. This arrangement provided excellent acoustics. Aaron was here many springs back. He had already forgotten. Now he could delight it again.

Evans spoke slowly and solemnly, celebrating and savoring the moment. The words shaped an atmosphere that rumbled only in the tone of his voice. The natural sounds of those in the room faded into the same ribbon of magic filling the place. The archmage wanted to run away, lock himself behind the safe gate, and have a few shots with his friend. Nevertheless, he proclaimed passionately what an honor this visit was and how glad he was to be able to host such a noble person after many years. Aaron was smiling with only his eyes and was sipping a cup of sweet cider from his goblet. After the event, he left the lecture hall before the students, he was accompanied by his entourage and the most important masters. The queen was invited to afternoon tea by associated botanists, who grew a delicious plant under the cloaks of the greenhouse, which after drying became so aromatic that it is difficult to put it into words. They excitedly explained that it tastes like a bouquet of raspberries mixed with the aroma of juicy strawberries, delicately vibrating on the palate with vanilla and blueberries. After hearing paeans and admiration, Eleanor couldn't refuse. She moved away with delight, mentally rejoicing at the fact that she would rest from the noise and the eyes staring at her with unbearable insistence. The king stayed in the square with Evans, who wanted to show him around the University and the senior mages' dormitories, but Aaron wasn't enthusiastic. The fatigue that was visible on the guest's face convinced the Archmage that it was the perfect time to rest, drink something refreshing and have a snack. They could finally talk. Aaron needed no protection here, the University was one of the safest places. He chased away the protesting guards from sight, expressing approval for their presence nearby.

At the door of Evans' mansion, they were greeted by a startled, Jerm hostess. If the eyes could get as big as saucers, it probably would. From the impression, she swallowed a few large gulps of air, almost choking on the frost. She bowed very low and pulled back, making way for the newcomers. The unfortunate woman couldn't get the slightest word out of her throat, even though she was aware that she would see the king today, but not from such a distance. This didn't escape the attention of the old man, who as he passed her patted her shoulder and thus made her understand that she shouldn't have worried.

"Beautiful house. It is still as I remember it: warm, set in a slight twilight and smelling of sweet cake. I guess you'll never change, huh?" He turned to the man in purple.

"You see, old friend, I overstayed like a hen and I don't intend to give up old habits."

"Good old habits, and who would like to give up on them?"

"Probably not me, undeniably not me." He raised his eyebrows. "Let us drink something stronger, let us not stand in the middle, because there are still servants ready to bring us honey into the hall."

"No, my lord, I think they'd bring a stool sooner," Evans joked.

They laughed. The magician indicated the way to the living room with his hand, and in the meantime he soliloquized about the unchanged appearance of the School and the new upholstery of the armchairs in the room. Evans remembered Aaron from a time when his uncertainty with magicians made him stiffen and distance himself. He wasn't surprised, people are afraid of the unknown, but the king was a knowledge-consuming person, even though he had been fed from childhood with nonsense theories about power-wielding beings. Fortunately, he gained a healthy reserve with age. The same was true of the exercise of power. Maturity resulted in a warming relationship between the ruler and the nobility, but in a way it became a source of minor quarrels between ministers and advisers on, for example, relations with dwarves and elves, not to mention contacts with neighboring countries. The people loved him, and he loved his subjects. He didn't give rise to a dispute between nations. The only thorn in his side was the Baroness about whose actions he was going to discuss with Evans.

"Tell me, my lord, about the fact that gives sleepless nights to my beloved cousin," he began, sipping a cup of steaming infusion.

"Well," Evans sighed and leaned back against the chair. "You heard about Lilian. She's one of the brightest students we've ever had. No, not such with the highest marks in class, walking with books under her arm, and prancing - he laughed nervously. But such that was almost bursting with magic boiling under her skin. We don't know why she chose to run away. We read from the correspondence with her mother that the girl wanted to find out who her father was. She asked several times, unfortunately the parent never answered, so she gave up hope. Then contact suddenly broke off and we assume the woman has died. This didn't prevent the intrant from sending a few scrolls a month. After a while she stopped, but quite a long time must have passed. But that's not what I want to talk about. I don't know if I mentioned it, but also one of the staffs secured in the basement is missing. The ancient seals had been broken, they crumbled as if someone had hit them on the ground, only scraps remained. I couldn't do that. What power must have this someone had? After all, the repository is isolated with an impenetrable wall! Fortunately, this tool won't be of use to anyone, because it is necessary to be able to relate to it, which is not an easy art. I have reliable inside men among the fences, so I'm waiting to hear from them. It would be a pity if it was wasted. It is a powerful subject, but we are not talking about it, ah, these my digressions. He folded his hands on his lap. - What was I talking about? Yes, Alvena, who secretly got the appropriate note about the loss. Unfortunately, we cannot figure out who the spy is. Returning to the question of a certain Lilian, she dissolved into thin air. I will say more, the hounds couldn't pick up her scent. I don't know if the Alchemists managed to follow her. I don't have their tricks, which are disgusting, and I detest them, although I suppose the Baroness has taken the appropriate steps. Of course, I had informed her beforehand about what had happened, just like about any such incident. Worse, the runaway is becoming a silent heroine among novices, leading to escapes and fanciful information about the Schools. Among other things, there are rumors that she is one of the expected liberator mages, wielding all possible magical arts. However, I dare to doubt that after a few hundred years such would have appeared. She is of the people, it is impossible."

"So what's Alvena afraid of?" Aaron cocked his head curiously.

"The baroness is afraid of revolution. As you know, it was under her pressure that you created the Schools."

"Well, that was over thirty years ago." Aaron took another sip of tea.

"In the past, factions and brotherhoods that took young magicians under their wings were enough, now the walls of the Schools are becoming something like a prison. Have you noticed it?"

"Yes, it's true. Alvena keeps them tall. The schools are also guarded by armed men, perhaps too many warriors."

"You can see for yourself that this course of events can inevitably lead to rebellions. A man subjected to captivity will sooner or later want to break away, and by fair means or foul."

The king got up and walked around the room several times, folding his hands behind his back and thinking hard. The archmage was right, the more pressure he put on, the more he would feel discomfort, and not only he, but also the rest. People, prompted by instigations and bad propaganda, would want to wind up hate gears targeting the innocent. He also couldn't issue a radical decree to ease the law regarding magicians without first consulting the Baroness. The situation tightened around his neck like a noose made of hemp rope. He felt cornered.

Outside the window it was already gray, and the clouds were beginning to cover the sky with a thick quilt. A harbinger of damp rains hung in the air. This winter was irritating. He wanted to stamp his foot, telling it to let go and let him live. Evans watched as the king stared out the window with face drawn.

"What will happen to the fugitive when Alvena catches her?" The monarch asked unexpectedly.

The archmage got up and stood beside him.

"They will probably tether her will at first thanks to the Alchemist, then they will subject her to a long and arduous interrogation, and finally the executioner will take care of her, although I don't think the Baroness will go so far as, after all, Lilian is a citizen of the School, though she didn't graduate from it. She wasn't assigned a robe, staff, or medallion, so the killing would involve a trial aimed at the Baroness herself and would cause a wave of riots. It would be different, if our fugitive had completed her education and mastered power control, then she would have become a citizen of the state, so the Baroness would have the right to subject her to the same coercive measures as a common urchin, and all this in accordance with the law of the crown."

"I think I understand," the king sighed. "One thing puzzles me. Why does she care so much about her? Who is she?"

"I have no idea." Evans spread his hands helplessly.

The door in the hall squeaked and the interlocutors heard the rhythmic thumping of tiny heels. The queen returned. Beamed, she entered the living room, attracting the attention of the men there.

"Have I interrupted something important?" She asked.

"No, honey, we were just finishing. I think we can say goodbye and thank for the wonderful hospitality."

"It's my pleasure." The mage bowed low.

Aaron put his arm around his wife's waist and led her to the hall, where the housekeeper handed them coats.

"Delicious drink, my lady." She praised the maid, who burned again with a blood red blush. Also this time, no word came out of her mouth, she just curtsied slightly as a sign of respect.

The archmage accompanied them to the gates where the entourage and the royal guard waited. Students stood by the windows, waving vigorously goodbye, while the teachers went out onto the lawns and shone with the staffs glowing at their tops. It was very spectacular. The queen was burning with delight. No one had escorted her in this way before.

As Aaron disappeared outside the gates, Evans felt a strange melancholy. The storm gathered in a swirl of drab clouds, thick snowflakes were falling heavily to the ground. After the bitter frost, there was an echo. The first thaw was about to come, which in fact was only the beginning of something new. The mage didn't know what the king was going to do. He trusted that the decisions he made would be good enough that both sides wouldn't suffer too much. He wandered home. He dreamed of loneliness and an alcohol strong as hell. He wouldn't fall asleep that night.

CHAPTER VII

"I have something for you." She heard Morien.

She was just in the middle of the room, following the snowflakes that clung to the world already tired of the incessant snowfall. After just a few days of bitter frost, a sticky thaw came. It made her shivers run down her spine at the thought of soaking wet shoes, the dirty bottom of her robes, and the runny nose. She turned to his newcomer, narrowing the cat's eyes.

"What is that?"

"A gift from the Archmage, delivered today. I wanted to swing this in the morning, but you were so engrossed in reading that I had no heart to interrupt you." He tossed the package several times.

She held out her hand, so he gave her the package. He didn't hide that he was very impatient, curiosity won everything against such behavior. The package was wrapped in gray fabric, which was tightly tied with a packing rope. Lilian had the impression that there was cloth inside. She sat down in front of the fireplace, crossed her legs, and untied the tape. The fingers neatly got to the content. She felt the softness and delicacy of velvet under the pads, and for a moment she was terrified.

Morien was almost freaking out with anticipation.

"Show me it now!"

She turned her face and looked up. He was standing there, rubbing his hands together. He was looking hilarious. She had to react to it somehow.

"Maybe you want to do it yourself?"

"No, no," He separated himself. "You do it, and I'll stand and wait. By Redeemers, Lilian! Show what's in there or I'll go crazy!"

She laughed aloud, and the magician rolled his eyes, making a face like 'big deal'.

"Alright, alright!" She giggled incessantly, wrinkling her nose in a funny way.

The gray fabric fell to the wooden floor, revealing the black robes of the highest-ranking magicians.

"Do I see well?" She took a deep breath and held it for a moment to let it out with a whistle.

Her heart was pounding like with a hammer, and almost foamed blood was buzzing in her ears. She turned red to the tips of her ears.

"I suppose so," he replied.

The blood drained from his face.

"But, it's impossible, I'm not ..."

"Decent? Enough educated? Is that what you wanted to say?" He was blinking vigorously, as if his eyeballs had suddenly gotten sandy and dry.

"No, Morien. I wanted to say that I'm not ready for such an honor."

"This is the perfect time to find out." He tried to smile sincerely, and while he felt it was the right decision, it still didn't reach the surprised self.

"Go change your clothes," he suggested. "Let's see if it fits. I probably have a belt somewhere, just in case the robe is too big." He left the room, going to private quarters.

On the way, he tried to calm down, but it was with no little difficulty.

Lilian allowed one of the servant girls to help. She, like her, was more confused than she showed. The clothes fit properly, although it wrinkled slightly. It didn't cause any major problems, because the defect could be covered or processed. She remembered how interested she was when the first time she saw the master girded with a wide leather belt, to which was attached a pouch that bounced as he walked. She wondered for a long time what treasures were in it. But when she discovered the secret, she was disappointed. Practical magicians carried in it... colored chalk, small coins and linen nose rags.

Morien went downstairs. Clear satisfaction lit his face. In the depths of the trunk, he managed to find a new belt, which he didn't wear because it was too short. He didn't remember who he had received it from, but was now glad he hadn't passed it on. The length should perfectly fit the delicate figure of the girl.

The elven maid clapped her hands. The gesture looked rather timid, but Lilian figured she couldn't afford anything else, not right now. After a while she whispered:

"You look, miss, so dignified."

And she fled the room, chased by the duties of which she had been broken.

Lilian didn't know whether to be happy or worried. Embarrassment was confusing her. Somewhere in her heart she felt that she wasn't yet ready to wear the robes that symbolized magical status. On the other hand, she wanted to run out into the cold of the day and show everyone the gift.

"Great." The mage leaned against the doorframe. "You look amazing."

Velvety black contrasted with the white, freckled skin of the young magician and hair red as fire. Her eyes seem to be burning. Maybe it was from excitement she couldn't hide?

"The Baroness should see you now. She would burn with rage." He laughed.

"Oh yes." She got sad.

The image of the mother who would never see her again in moments of small triumphs stuck in her head. She won't taste happiness or enjoy the achievements of her only child. Pain with its claws cut the tissue of mourning. She didn't contain her tears.

"Did I say something wrong?"

"I thought about mom," she sighed, sniffling and wiping her eyes on her sleeve. "She would be proud to see me now."

He walked over and put his arm around her.

"I can assure you that she would be proud of her daughter." He kissed her forehead, brushing back the wisps of tangled hair.

"Probably you are right. Although my head is troubled by thoughts, or rather questions that I cannot answer ..."

"Speak. Maybe it will bring you relief."

"What would have happened to us? What would have happened to my eternally ailing mother if I hadn't gone to the School? I would probably secretly learn the art of healing just too..."

"Extend her agony," he interrupted her.

"How can you say that?!" She broke free from his embrace. "How dare you? Only she loved me! She was the only person that wasn't afraid of me!"

Morien watched her get angry and foam. He tried to understand the woman's sudden outburst. He understood the bitterness, especially to the authorities who did not deign to inform her of the mother's death, but how were they to know what facility she was in and if she was still alive? For years, she was convinced that the only close person still lived outside the city, and that the house hidden in a thicket of fruit trees would again become a safe haven without fear of power shackling or eternal observation. He decided to leave her alone. In moments of escalating emotions, she was able to stun him. A little loneliness usually helped. Lilian was one of those people who preferred it to the tiring presence of another person.

"I'll read in the usual place. I'll send you a teapot. What do you think?"

"Yes. It's for the best. I need to… I need to cool down."

***

David gasped at the sight of his leather overcoat soiled with snow. The drab slush attached so effectively that he couldn't get rid of it. He felt dirty and sandy. To make matters worse, his "almost" new item didn't look "almost" new.

He entered the Ram's Head, as always, with his forehead held high and the pride painted on the dwarven face. The interior of the tavern was empty. Suddenly, somewhere inside him, he longed for the buzz filling the main room. He was no longer greeted by the clink of glasses, the laughter of the wine girls. Now the place was more like a gloomy pit with no soul. Only remained the peculiar smell of dwarven beer and fire, still illuminating the interior. He noticed a few regulars, sponges with faces plump from an alcohol. In the corner of the room was sitting a fair-haired younker, furiously picking his nails with a small knife.

Mark rested his hands on the counter and looked at the newcomer. The dwarf pursed his lips in a pleasant smile, though he didn't like what he found. He spent the last days digging through papers. Not because the bills didn't add up, but because he was worried by the fact that the innkeeper's guest had with him an item that looked very much like a bow his father had ordered from the elves. He knew sketches were always kept in chests with weapon diagrams that were handed-down ... and he found. Now everything was clear. Darius was definitely the son of Kirsten - a noble who thought he could allowed himself too much. David remembered that he had partly contributed to his falling into debt and disfavor. You don't play with the dwarves, especially when smuggling an alcohol from overseas is at stake. They're too smart for that, and people, as David himself used to say, are stupid, long-legged creatures. He assumed that some water would pass before the man companied him, or rather his parent, whom he didn't contact frequently anyway. David wasn't one of the dwarves who sit in one place, warming their asses and getting fat. The tract was calling him. The minion needed the wilderness and life on the road, so when he grew older enough not to hold on to his maternal apron and to be able to leave without any obstacles, he left the house and let himself be absorbed by the vast expanses of the world. A troupe of mobile actors took him in. It quickly turned out that he had a keen eye for business, and he was great at negotiating and brokering business. Now he owned a caravan and moved freely from place to place, not only within the kingdom. He often visited neighboring countries, which made him recognizable in every major city. He spoke several languages and was second to none in bargaining. He was loved by wenches and innkeepers, hated by merchants and younkers who wanted to line their own pockets.

He put his arms on his hips and leered at Mark again. He was wiping the counter so passionately that he didn't notice that his friend was silent expectantly. There was a deep resignation on the innkeeper's face, and the line across his forehead seemed deeper than it had been before. David quickly realized that the business was rather slow. Nay! Hopeless.

"Hey, old friend!" He probably shouted too loudly, because those present stared at him in the space of breath. "Don't stare, dog sons, or I will put pokers in your asses!" They turned, although they leered every now and then.

Mark smiled with the corner of his mouth, wielding a gray rag in his hand as if it had been the highest quality weapon.

"Oh, hello, old fogey." He forced himself to joke. "Are you still here? What's keeping you here?"

"The mud is keeping me, damn it! It is so boggy that if I left now, I would be stuck in this mess right outside the walls."

"But your cart is right outside the walls." Mark picked holes in what he said.

"But I can't move. The only good thing is the dry stable and the fact that my purebred horses don't get wet in this damn woods. The stable man is a great guy, but also a drunk. He always wants a lot of gold, but I'm eager to give it, because he cares for the mares properly. I think that the beasts will gain weight thanks to the oats and hay, which he so often put under their muzzles."

"Yeah," the innkeeper sighed slowly, sitting down behind the bar. "He's a good man. Your priceless horses will be safe. I like Sorley, he wouldn't hurt a fly. When are you going to leave?"

"And why are you in such a hurry to throw me out of town? Does my gold stink to you?" He laughed.

"What stinks are your dwarf feet in the summer."

They laughed loudly. A large mug of beer landed in front of the dwarf, with a thick foam dripping down the sides. David's face lit up at the sight of the drink. That was what he needed. He had a little trouble with one of his women, and there is nothing more enjoyable than getting drunk with a friend. Mark complained about the guests, especially about Darius. He lamented the loss of most of the maidens who had left out of fear, asking for payment in advance. He blamed bloody Lonan for it. He himself had a problem with being in the same room with this individual. A dark aura was emanating from him. The piercing chill stung the skin. Darius, on the other hand, didn't part with the bow, stubbornly carried it with him, even when he went to the toilet. He walked the alleys every day, hoping Lilian would get the idea of sneaking out of the School. He noticed a change in the younker as well. And it wasn't clear, but big enough. After one of the mage's visits, he didn't stick his nose out the door for several days. He ordered to bring food and water, not wine - water, to the door. He went out uneasy, with his face as gray as if he hadn't slept at all. Deep furrows marked the forehead and the lines of a smile. The Baroness' dog didn't come at that time, but he felt it was lurking in the shadows in the corners. Now it was probably following the archer, prepared for a strike.

The dwarf was slurping, drinking hoppy ambrosia. Thick foam stuck to his upper lip, so he licked it, closing his eyes lovingly. Darius wasn't discreet. The narrowed eyes pierced the newcomer, making the tension thick and unbearable. The innkeeper wanted to hit the counter with his fist and chase them both away, but the voice in his head whispered that if they were to fight, they'd better do it here. At least there would be an opportunity to smash the spy's head, even if he were to use the most expensive bottle he owned. It would be worth it! But David was ruled by a different bouquet of emotions. He was totally indifferent to him, even made him laugh, so he started to finish the mug, carefully keeping an eye on his rump.

"Why don't you have any girls for me today?" He asked, and put the empty vessel down, sweepingly wiping his mouth on his sleeve.

"Don't you have enough trouble with the women?" Mark snapped.

"There is never any trouble with the girls. He slapped his large hand on the bar. - There is this luxury with girls, that you pay them and get what you want. As for the women, you have to live with them. And when it's that time of the month, it is better to run away from the cart, because she is ready to hit you on your head with an old pot."

Mark rested the chin on his hand.

"There's only Agnes. I don't think there is a stupider person in the city. I thought that she had all her marbles, but now I know that it isn't true. After Erica's death and after this baroness' spawn had settled here, they left. I struggle alone. But you know." He winked at the dwarf. "If you are eager, this can be arranged too. Just be warned that there is no cozy playroom. There is a kitchen. Lots of space. For example, a comfy table." He laughed out loud, slurping with his nose.

David waved with resignation.

"Oh, come on. I have the nice girl in the car. I have to go to the market and buy a nice scarf. Maybe she will cease to be in a pet. I think someone had fingers in my good married life. As soon as I know who, I'll break his neck. And how is your, what is her name...? Do you have any news?"

"No news. I'm not worried, all I have to do is pack the bags and take them to the gates. I've already missed Morien. It sounds ridiculous, but the silence and the lack of activities annoy me. People stay at home like rats and only go to the market for food. You see for yourself that when the Alchemists show up, it's not business. The whole city suffers from it. And they warm their buttocks and don't intend to move." He raised his voice deliberately. "Stocks are running low, because, by a strange twist of fate, the winemakers are reluctant, and I cannot go alone. They argue that there are some savages outside the walls. If this shack doesn't collapse until spring, you can come, and if it does, I will sell it and I will move out of here to the backwoods to raise poultry," he flared up.

"I won't let you go broke, old fool. Where will I eat and pour an alcohol into my throat, when you will move out to raise those stupid hens? You're not fit for dung, and you probably can't sprinkle grain either. I bet the most expensive barrel that you would fuck it up too. Don't worry, I'll take care of the business and you'll be behind the bar until your bones rotten. And now fill it up, because my throat dries up." He tossed a gold coin on the table.

"Take your dwarven change." Mark pushed the money away from himself. "Promise me that if I need it, you will really support me in this mess. I have bad feelings."

The dwarf leaned back against his chair and folded his arms over his chest, staring at the innkeeper like at a statue dedicated to the Redeemers.

"What are you talking about? Nothing will happen. Catch this payment, and don't worry about safety. When David is in town, it's quiet."

Behind himself he heard a laugh muffled by a hand. The stocky individual turned in his seat, stood up, and slowly came over to the man's table. He carefully pulled the sword from the scabbard and put it quietly on the table where Darius rested, then leaned the back of his hand on the edge of the piece of furniture. The archer glanced again at the buckle on the dwarf's belt, then at the blade decorated with runes. Thought circled the pattern incessantly, whispering that he wasn't seeing it for the first time. In addition, the individual had something familiar in his face.

"Watch yourself," David rumbled low. "Today I'm gracious because I'm in a good mood. If I was in a bad mood, I would put you on that pretty gladiolus like a pig. Be warned, don't mock. You saw too little, you know too little."

"Go drink," Darius muttered, hoping that he would go away.

"Don't talk back, little shit. I know who you are. Your father, Kirsten, is he well?"

The archer felt a strange shiver. He turned pale. He took a few gulps of air and stared at David with sparkling irises. Guesses were dispelled, he received an answer. In his eyes, he was no one like his father loser. A paroxysm of cold rolled over his body, making the hair on his arms and legs bristle. David also had this sensation, as did the feasters. Lonan was approaching the inn. He stood in the doorway in a black coat soaked with rain and snow. David ostentatiously took his sword and put it into the scabbard. The mage entered the room, stopping in the middle.

"Upstairs, dog," he hissed.

The archer wanted to say something, but the words stuck in his throat, so he only uttered a strange grunt, then reached for his bow and disappeared in the back, mumbling hideous curses. The alchemist walked past the dwarf, poking him with his shoulder. David pulled the 'almost new' coat on his back and disappeared without a word.

"The insult must be paid with blood!" He seethed.

Mark buried his face in his hands. Such a mess was the last thing he needed. Angry David was ... whole guilds against Alchemists. It wouldn't end with an apology. The streets would run purple, hopefully not now, hopefully not in this city, hopefully he wouldn't have to see it at all ... He was cooled by the clink of copper coins rhythmically hitting the counter. The room was deserted, only the sound of crackling wicks and the sizzling of the fire prevailing in the sooty fireplace.

***

It took some time for Lilian to get used to the new clothes. At first she felt very awkward and poked her nose out of the property occasionally. At one point, Morien had to resort to trickery to make her go for a walk. The dress was not only dignified, comfortable and fit well, but it also gave a silent acceptance, silent because some lecturers didn't agree with the Archmage's decision. The students took it better, but there were murmurs among them too. The only ones who crowed over were Morien and a handful of early school students admiring the mage. She was a symbol of freedom for them, however they could explain it in their own way. The rebellion hung, thickened, and spread across the corridors as secret correspondence written in a code, the key of which only a few had, gestures that didn't look unusual at first glance, rubbing a nose or putting a pen behind an ear. Those who mastered the Speech of Whispers communicated this way, although it was one of the most dangerous. The life of the School was cooked in its own, tasteful sauce.

She listened persistently to Morien's advice and teachings. He introduced her to the secrets of unknown magic and communicated information that she would never have learned from classrooms. She spent days reading the volumes that hung in piles around the legs of the chair. She tormented her eyes with charts and calculations, and if she didn't find something in her beloved books collection, she put on a shabby coat and tramp to the Archmage's library. It happened that she didn't find the necessary information there, and then she was consumed by the dimness of the university library. There, she edged herself with knowledge and was occupied for hours, often forgetting about meals. Many have sneaked between the shelves to experience the blows of Lilian power with their own eyes. What's more, bets were made about who would come closer, as it happened that the daredevils either fainted or vomited, being burdened by the essence emanating around them. Within a few weeks, she mastered the skill of starting a fire, forming windstorms and snow blizzards, creating storms so strong that horses fell under their weight, which the Archmage didn't like and categorically forbade her to practice. Morien, on the other hand, was boiled with pride, not only because of the progressive education, but also because of the fact that his feelings for her grew stronger and stronger. Every day he woke up with the thought that he was a woman for whom he could give his life. The romantic visions of uninhibited freedom and thriving affection, however, were shattered by the fact that Darius and the Alchemist were still in the city.

Spring was approaching inexorably. It hovered in the air mixed with the stench of the city. It rumbled, masked by the gray of muddy streets and gutter. It floated lazily in the breeze brushing the tops of garden thujas. It irritated the nostrils of students digging through the sticky soil of the square in front of the library.

There was a busy period ahead that the botanists had eagerly awaited. Dormant seeds waited for a soothing touch of moisture. Seedlings turned green in oblong clay pots. The birds, agitated by the first warmth, timidly trilled, still hiding among the tangle of branches. A lazy, buzzing fly flew here and there. Everyone, from teachers, through students and servants, awaited a radical change of aura. Lilian looked forward to continuation of learning of the Speech of Whispers and an opportunity to retrieve the things that still rested in the inn. She supposed that little detail had escaped somewhere in the fervor of education. Now she felt stronger than ever. The power was burning and raging under the skin. A risky thought formed in her head to use the secret passage to the Morien's house, and from there at night sneak into Mark's kitchen. The window had no strong hinges, and she could always melt them. However, there was a fear that if caught, they might have treated her like a thief, so she gave up for a while. Besides, she wanted to find her mother's grave. She dreamed of it many times as if the grave had been calling her. The mother's voice thundered in her ears for a long time after waking up and she couldn't cope with it, which made her have trouble concentrating. Maybe the deceased needed relief, intentional prayers or the discovery of the burial place? But how to identify a body in a mass grave, hidden somewhere in the woods outside the city, in a place where nobody goes, and the only visitors are vermin and game? Probably the mayor has notes with burial places from many years on them, but how on earth could she get to him without arousing suspicion?

The day was exceptionally warm. Tongues of dirty snow receded from under the feet. Trickles leaking from it steamed hastily, attacked by the spring sun. The soil breathed again. Lilian opened the bedroom window and the fresh air burst into the room, dissipating the stench. She closed her eyes and for a moment plunged shamelessly in the gusts of cool wind. Bare arms, covered with goose bumps, yielded to the chill through which barely perceptible tones of heat went through. A delightful feeling for which it is worth to stand still for a moment, forgetting about the surrounding world.

Morien entered soundlessly. He regarded her silently.

"Hello," he whispered, fearing he might have scared her away.

She blushed and playfully pulled the scarf over her shoulders in such a way that the heat flooded his face. How attractive, how fresh she was, only his.

"Good morning darling." She turned flirtatiously and threw herself on his neck.

The delightful scent of the female body touched him from everywhere. He sighed deeply and pressed his face into the fiery curls.

"To what do I owe this outburst of joy?" He whispered.

"It's a good day. I think so. I wrote a letter to the mayor. Oh, don't look at me like that, I didn't sign. I made up a colorful story about my cousin. I want to find my mother's grave. I don't want to, I have to."

Morien frowned. She didn't mention about vellum, although everyone has a right to a little secret, and this one didn't seem dangerous, but the fact that the shipment would be delivered by a messenger from the Magician School could prove disturbing.

"Why didn't you tell me earlier? I would try..."

"I didn't want to cause any trouble," she interrupted, tucking a strand behind her ear. "You had so many classes. You prepare students for spring exams, you spend time with me until late. You are always busy. Recently you have eaten little, you haven't slept much. You wilted and you lost weight. Probably if you had hair of a different color, you'd go gray," she blurted out in one breath, stroking his rough unshaven cheek.

"I would always have had time for that. You know how much I want you to be happy."

"Forgive me for not telling you. I will calm you down. I sent the letter thanks to a courier from the city. I asked the guard at the gate to pass the correspondence to the appropriate man. He agreed without hesitation. The letter will come to private quarters. I'm grateful to him, he is an extremely nice man, it is strange that he serves. Such people should live with their families, and not sacrifice themselves for the cause."

"Some of the guards have families and some don't. It's their choice. Don't worry. Do you think the mayor will write back? How long has it been since the message was sent?"

She rested her chin and closed her eyes, counting the days since the correspondence had been sent.

"Two weeks, I guess."

"And there is no answer yet?" He was surprised.

"There isn't. Apparently he has a lot of work to do. You know how it is with officials. Before they read something, it must gain strength, collect a layer of dust." She laughed. "In addition transfer of messages to the appropriate institution. Bureaucracy is doing its job, after all, it is a huge habitat."

Her forbearance surprised him. In her place, after two days, he would have stormed, and if that didn't help, he would have paid a visit himself, which wouldn't look as friendly as the correspondence itself.

"As who did you sign in the message?"

"Lothera. Just like my mother's friend's name. But I wrote that she is a cousin."

"All right," the mage sighed. "We'll sort it out today. I will go to the mayor, I'm having a day off, and you get ready for the news, though I don't know if they will be good."

"Are you crazy? They will find out and it will be disaster. Morien! Behind the gate there is the Alchemist and his dog. They are ready to arrest you to force the School to hand me over."

"About it, flower, don't bother. I know ways of jamming Alchemists. And Darius can't reach me. Trust me sometimes."

Suddenly the pleasant day got filled with hail clouds. The very thought of the magician leaving the School made her tremble.

"And what about the Archmage? Will he not mind? I'm afraid! Maybe you better not go and we will wait? Oh, stupid, why have I said that!" Her eyes filled with tears.

"Oh, you and your oversensitivity. I always go out on my days off. Where? He doesn't care. I'll swing it on the way, and you could go to the greenhouse classes. Apparently, one of the older botanists today conducts entertaining lessons on the use of mandrake and wolfberry."

"Sounds interesting." She sniffed. Concerns about Morien remained just as strong.

He turned and left. She heard footsteps pounding on the stone floor in the hall, then the rustle of a coat being put on, and the slam of a door. She felt helpless and stupid. The fault fell on her shoulders like a heavy curtain. She sat on the edge of the bed and listened to the wind rustling in the twigs awakened by spring. The prospect of spending the day between people seemed a nice change from the dusty bookshelves. Although she liked them very much, today she would get a bit messy.

Morien visited the stables and, having chosen an old mare, left the thresholds of the Magician School. He didn't bother himself with the Alchemist and the spy, he knew that the veil of power with which he wrapped himself like with a blanket on a winter evening would drown out the vibrations of magic and let him move freely in the districts. He didn't think he would meet them. The cool aura that the Baroness' helper spread around didn't penetrate the walls of his essence, didn't mix with it, which made him invisible. Step by step the horse tapped its hooves on the pavement. Regular hoofbeat bounced off the walls of the narrowly lined houses, mingling with the throbbing of the city. He hoped to find the Mayor, he didn't know his office hours, but the morning hour augured the success of the expedition. In order not to forget the name Lilian had written at the end of the message, he repeated it, inserting it into short rhymes. He cursed himself for having terrible ability to remember such things. After some time, something like a melody was formed that was hard to forget. The sun was starting to warm. The bustle of the market pleasantly caressed his ear. The townspeople and vendors in the stalls greeted him with a nod. Due to the amount of scents mixing with each other, he felt hungry. Despite the hearty breakfast, he dreamed of deep-fried pancakes stuffed with pieces of smoked cheese. He promised himself that if he didn't forget, he would call by the baker on the way back.

The town hall was gray against the whitewashed poorer quarters. It was unfortunate that the fallible creator of the conurbation had placed it in the trade circuit. He hoped that it would be on the inhabitants' way, but the truth was quite different. The agglomeration was ruled by the upper classes, placed on a pedestal of wealth. The effect? The mayor was reduced to the role of a servant of the elite who didn't care about royal decrees and freely acted according to their own rules. The king was informed about the situation by appropriate networks of spies, keeping their fingers on the pulse, so Aaron, hidden behind the thick walls of the capital, constantly verified those who could have harmed him in some way. Contrary to unfavorable predictions, the system functioned quite efficiently. The skirmishes and disagreements were settled in their own circles, somewhat relieving the higher institutions. In short, the city was a small state within a state.

Plaster was falling off the town hall building. The damp walls scared with mildew spots that rose upwards. There was a stench of urine and vomit all around. Morien didn't want to know what was lurking in the corners to which the next lodgings adjoined. The fragments of the polished plaster undamaged by the fungus were used by children to sprinkle it with paintings. Several beggars sat on the steps, holding out dirty hands for alms. A multicolored mob swirled around the square. It was a part of the city that anyone could easily reach. No one cared about class, background or race. Also young pickpockets lay in wait there, and in the alleys lurked assassins and mercenaries. Rarely did any outsider venture into dark alleys, unless they felt the need to find a "soul mate" who would agree to make a small or big grunt work. The world absolutely alien to visitors and the nobility. Those who lived in it were on the verge of poverty. These alleys didn't bear fruit that wouldn't be soaked with rot from conception. The building, like most households, grew into solid rock that formed the main support. It was topped with a sloping, semicircular roof with red tiles on it. And it was they who made it stand out among other objects. The soaring windows, patched here and there with plain, undyed glass, shone in the glare of the awakening sun. All window vents had blue painted shutters. Thanks to them, officials gave a signal that tightly located offices were inviting potential applicants. This custom had been going on for many generations, so no one thought about where it came from. A squat wooden door, too ornate for Morien, invited inside. There was too much of the lush vegetation, intertwining with genre scenes illustrating the life of suburban winemakers. He had been wondering for a long time what the artist had in mind when he created the bas-relief that nobody paid attention to anyway, and which, over time, started to frighten with peeling paint?

The hall was surrounded by a circular colonnade. On both sides there was a marble staircase leading straight to the rooms in which nested people saturated to the marrow with bureaucracy. There was a registration on the first floor. Behind a large mahogany top rested an equally monstrous lady with a hairstyle too fanciful for hair thinning with age. Before the mage could approach, she stopped him with her hand, signaling that he had come close enough. She looked at him from beneath her fleshy lids with eyes as pale as water.

"What do you want, younker?" She asked singingly.

Morien was surprised by the timbre of the clerk's voice. It seemed completely out of place for her exaggerated stature. He would have said that she sounded girly and quite pleasant.

"I'm looking for the Mayor. Will I find him today?"

The woman adjusted the strand of gray hair falling over her forehead and lazily glanced at him again.

"Honey," she began. "First you have to make an appointment with the mayor, unless you have an urgent matter. Then you will be received. So you have an appointment today?" She turned a pen in her fat fingers as if it had been more eloquent than necessary.

The magician twisted his lips in displeasure, which didn't escape the attention of the lady behind the desk.

"So no. So you have to make an appointment. You're lucky, there should be an open slot in about a week's time. Ekhem," she cleared her throat.

Morien folded his arms over his chest. The eyes sparkled with white, and a tiny spark ran through the white hair.

"I request a meeting with the mayor NOW!"

The clerk leaned against the edge of the desk, looking at him closely.

"A mage, right?"

"I'm looking for someone, so be so kind as to announce me to the supervisor. If not, I'll go upstairs. I know the way."

"So I won't stop you ...?"

"By Redeemers!" He screamed. "We are not on a first-name basis!"

She paled dazed, and the guard swinging on the heel of his boot straightened and peered cautiously from behind the column, keenly interested in the tumult from inside the hall.

Morien rested his hands on the desk.

"I have an urgent matter for the Mayor," he repeated. "I want to meet him TODAY! I'm going upstairs now, unless you want to announce me, then go ahead." He straightened up. "My name is Morien and I'm the Archmaster of the School of Mages," he said loudly.

The woman paled even more, and her pink lips turned bluish.

"I'm really sorry," she stuttered. "I'll check if the Mayor is free. Please wait a moment."

She began to clump upstairs. The breaths dragged on endlessly. Morien kicked his heels. He didn't deny that he felt irritated, but not with the waiting time, but with the woman's behavior. The guard, an elderly man in light armor consisting of a mass of straps and buckles, kept glancing at the steps, then at the visitor. He had to be careful not only about this, but also about the entrance, because every now and then beggars entered the building seeking shelter from rain or scorching heat. He was forced to direct the unfortunate to the lazarets and shelters run by the priestesses of the Redeemers, which were in one of those dark, vile streets which he preferred not to visit.

A stocky lady appeared in the gray of the corridor. On her face was an unreadable grimace that irritated the magician even more. She descended unhurriedly, clinging to the railing. He assumed the stairs were slippery.

"The mayor is expecting you," she gasped as she came downstairs.

He passed her by. A mane of white hair fell over his face, he pushed it back and began to climb the polished marble. He heard a snort behind him. She muttered under her breath that she hated magicians. He ignored her. It wasn't worth wasting his breath.

The mayor was sitting behind his desk, leafing through piles of yellowed papers. There was a line of concentration on his forehead. Morien walked in vigorously, closing the old wooden door that hadn't been restored for centuries, and was as frightening as the front door. Fortunately, they were stripped of fancy ornaments. The man glanced at him and casually pointed to an ordinary stool on the lion's feet, classic in this region. The washed-out material on the edges revealed the yellowed interior of the furniture, which could have appeared as the insides of the former glory. He sat up, and the stool groaned under his weight. The state dignitary, as faded as the office, stared at the visitor with his calm, dreamy eyes the color of green grass mixed with brown reflections. The rest drowned in monotony, wrinkled and dry. The magician noticed that the dominant element of the decor was dust. It kittened almost everywhere, gathering into formations of all structures. He wondered if he could have worked in such conditions. The answer was unequivocal, however, supposedly great minds need chaos, although here he had slight reservations about the word 'great'.

"Hello, sir." The mayor bared a row of yellowed teeth. "I heard you have a pressing case for me. So I'm glad that I can help, although I'm not sure if I will be up to the challenge." Again, there was an unforced grimace of sympathy on his face.

The mage's skin stiffened from the tone of his voice, and he decided to ignore this inconvenience. He squirmed on the seat for a moment, then got to the point.

"My name is Morien and I'm the Lord Master of the School of Magic in our city. I've come about a letter you received two weeks ago because no reply has yet been received. I must admit that this is a pressing matter, because the person who sent it cannot stay here any longer and I would like any information," he lied.

"A letter, you say? I get a lot of correspondence, especially from those who live far from here. You know, sometimes it's better to wait and get it done here. I'm drowning in it. In complaints, grievances, requests, as well as what lies here." With a sweeping movement he pointed to the desk and a dresser with notes closed in leather briefcases. "I had a helper, but he resigned and I was left alone with this stuff, and Rose, the lady in the hall, won't take any extra work within her own hours. I'm really sorry." He sighed heavily, folding his hands on the desk. "So you see, it is probably stuck somewhere. And please tell me what it was about and from whom was this message?"

"Lothera wrote it. She is looking for the grave of her cousin who died several years ago. She lived in Undercity. She didn't receive information about her death, and she would like to pay tribute to the deceased just before leaving for the capital, where she comes from. It is sad that the authorities don't care about informing their relatives about the deaths of family and friends, and they only had each other."

The mayor twisted his bushy mustache and thought. It only lasted a moment, then his eyes lit up and he sprang up from his chair. He went to the small dresser and searched several drawers, finding, surprisingly, an open and read correspondence from Lilian. Morien recognized the delicate and ornate handwriting from a distance. He read the short note again, cleared his throat a few times, then turned to the visitor.

"Yes, I remember, it's thanks to this writing. I left it on the top while debating how to get out of it. You see, the gravedigger who worked in those years is no longer alive, and the books were burned five years ago in a fire in the archives. I don't know if you remember, but it happened during the rebellion that took place in the dwarven district." Morien nodded. "It spread to half of the poorer districts, including our archives. Damned dwarves," he growled.

"So," Morien added. "What now? Is there any chance that we will find out where these mass graves are?"

"I think it would be good to ask the current gravediggers. They should have any news, but be warned, it is not easy, even if you and Mrs. Lothera lavishly pay them with dwarven gold. The graves have long been overgrown by forest and wild shrubs. In those days, people from Undercity died like flies. They said it was the plague that was digesting them, maybe a bloody cough. Then it suddenly stopped. Now we burn those who were homeless or too poor to be buried in the municipal graveyard. You probably know where it is. Only the richest build comfortable tombs and catacombs, just like you magicians."

Morien nodded. He had the impression that the gentleman in the oversized frock coat was talking too much, but he conveyed in verbosity the most important information.

"So I have to go to the suburban gravediggers? I hope that at least one of them remembers where the bodies were buried." He feigned resentment.

"I have a question." The mayor leaned towards him. He was still holding the letter, rumpling it in his plump fingers. "Why does Mrs. Lothera look for her after so many years? It didn't seem suspicious that her cousin didn't contact her...? They were so close."

Morien was bewildered. It immediately occurred to him that the mayor wasn't such an ordinary jack-in-office, because he revealed elements of logical thinking, so rarely seen recently outside the walls, which was not overshadowed by what was in the room, in his desk and on it.

"I don't know. I didn't ask." He shrugged. "I'm not used to meddling in not my affairs."

"But you meddled by coming here," the Mayor said. "Why didn't Mrs. Lothera herself come here?"

Morien was composing an answer that was convenient for him.

"She's not well, she's older," he lied. "They parted years ago in not the best terms, now it is probably time to settle accounts with the past." He swallowed, hoping it would be enough.

"Oh, that explains a lot, and she has a powerful friend, so it's all the more." Satisfied, the clerk sat back comfortably, staring at the vellum.

"Well, that's about it," the mage said, stretching out his hand. "I think it will be solved somehow and thank you for the information."

The mayor stood up and returned the gesture.

"You're welcome. I'm glad that I could help."

Morien was relieved to leave the claustrophobic office. The corridor suddenly felt stuffy and saturated with the scent of cedar floor-cleaning polish, teasing his nose. He went downstairs. The woman was sitting behind the desk. She stared him out. He bowed and left, making her quite confused.

The temperature outside had risen a bit, so he unbuttoned his coat. For a moment he wanted to toss it over the saddle, but his confidence faded away. He wasn't used to show up outside the walls only in his robe. He regretted a little that he hadn't dressed in ordinary bourgeois clothes. He untied the horse. A few children gathered around the animal, stroking it and offering it crinkled apples. He put copper coins in their hands and trotted to his destination - the suburban cemetery. He knew that the farther from the University, the more faces would turn towards him. Not because he belonged to the magic tribe, but because no one had trusted a man like him since the arrival of the Alchemist. He passed by 'Under Ram's Head'. Something urged him to dismount and be swallowed by the dimness of the tavern, but he would be a fool to do so. And yet it was one of the few places he liked to come back to. The innkeeper never attempted forced courtesies, he could express opinions without fear and he wasn't judged for his words. He missed it in a way. Another place which he visited quite often was the brothel tucked between tall tenement houses in the merchant district. There, noblemen as well as well-groomed middle-aged women bored with fat, lazy husbands enjoyed pleasures. However, the door of the brothel remained closed to those who didn't have enough gold in their sacks. There were days when he returned with his thoughts to the sensual times with his favorite courtesan. Only she satisfied the exuberant fantasies of the young, promising magician, the rest trembled at the thought of what he wore under his skin. Now he no longer bothered with paid passion and whores in the service of overdressed pimps. Feelings re-created him. He had matured. Now he valued deed, learning, experiencing and drawing from what fate had offered. Even though existence had left its mark on him, he waded through it, awaiting each day.

He didn't realize when the horse led him outside the walls. Now the space in front of Morien hit him in the face. The City Guards raised their visors. The horse danced, the mage pulled the reins to calm the animal. Perhaps in their exhausted minds appeared the thought that he was trying to run away.

"Which way to the necropolis?" He asked.

A finger pointed at the course, but not a word escaped from his mouth.

"Thank you," he said, and moved slowly away.

The municipal cemetery was at the western road. The outlines of tall tombs could be seen from a distance, but he was so far away that he was forced to bypass a large part of the residential buildings, so-called Undercity. He stopped right on the edge of the vile houses. Tiny huts separated by parcels of equal size stretched sadly, drowned in the darkness of the slush. The stench of sewage and animal dung vibrated from everywhere. The people didn't look good, they differed significantly from those who lived in the bowels of the city. The elves blended with the humans, and the dwarves couldn't be seen, he suspected they would have rather thrown themselves on the blade than rot here. But he could see Jerms, dressed in light blue robes with embroidered sleeves. Most tended to be superior to others, although it was not a rule. Some residents of Undercity wandered along the alleys, others bustled about in the farmyards, still others drank their own homemade moonshine. He wanted to feel sorry for them, and he probably did, but weakly enough to blame himself for it. He stood for a long time, the wind blew his eardrums. He felt it with all of himself. Involuntarily, he missed the route and the dense forests stretching along it. He loved to travel alone, only him and the cart drawn by one stallion. He had gone to Archal many times only to attend Evans' lectures. It was a pity that such an opportunity wouldn't appear soon again.

He spurred his horse and galloped towards the cemetery. Lumps of earth still wet rose from under the hooves. He raced on, hoping to get an answer today. He slowed as he passed the first graves. The place had an unusual aura, it hovered like a colorless fog, discernible to those who can feel. Despondency wrapped him, heaviness fell on his chest. He scanned the area. The graves concealed someone who had a family and dreams, led a more or less extraordinary life that ended in a more or less unpredictable way. Places for urns with ashes had been carved in the wall, so they stood proudly there, contrasting with the stone. Under each of them were placed plaques with a multitude of names and surnames, if anyone had them, an innumerable amount of unsaid stories locked in the dust of the last breath.

Silhouettes loomed in the distance. He furrowed. The workers, clearly consoled by moonshine, struggled with the local soil, stony and full of roots. He could hear the juicy invectives from afar. He didn't feel the need for immediate confrontation, he was making a plan that could speed up the dialogue. He wandered around, pretending to look for the grave. They spotted him from a distance and called him with the sweeping gestures of their dirty arms.

The mage looked around, dismounted, and, adjusting his bridle, said outwardly timidly.

"Gentlemen," he began. "Is there a governor here?"

They looked at each other.

"There is. And who's asking?" Muttered the shorter one, with a balding head, on which already little hair was left.

"Lord Master of the School of Magic, my lord. I'm looking for someone who can clear up a personal problem."

"And don't you magicians have catacombs?" Interjected the other, with stilt-like legs and tousled pants.

"Yes, my lord."

He glanced at each other every time he used the word 'lord'. They were undoubtedly amused by courtesy. Morien continued on. He remembered the Mayor's words. Gold likes to loosen tongues, but if they don't ask for it, they won't get it. He could see greed in the drunks' eyes. They knew mentors smelled of what they liked best. They smiled at each other eloquently.

"Lord, we could do something, but you know, nothing here in this valley is for free. If you're looking for news, chances are one might have it. And the word 'chance' is probably a good incentive to dig deeper into the pouch, isn't it?" The lower of them twisted his purple mouth, revealing defects in the dentition.

The mage folded his arms over his chest. He wanted to roll his eyes like a schoolboy who had been scolded for something he didn't think was important, but he kept a stiff upper lip. Without getting into a scuffle, he explained the purpose and would be glad if they showed him the way to the board or someone who dealt with the inventories. They remembered the times when graves were dug outside the borders: in forests, far from the seats. However, at that time they hadn't worked as gravediggers. So the minions didn't care too much about the dead when other, more fascinating things happened around. Morien pressed into their hands gold dwarven coins as an encouragement. They ate them with their wide pupils, squeezing them in their hands full of blisters and abrasions. The dwarven golden coin bore the mark of more valuable than a normal coin. Despite the fact that the coin itself looked less impressive than its cousin, with which merchants settled up. They looked as if the Redeemers themselves had blessed their wretched lives by sending the lord to ease their woe. They eagerly pointed to a grove away from the cemetery, where the cottage hid, in which lived the graveyard manager. They warned that the resident was "specific". Apparently, he couldn't cast spells. They sprinkled it with a very ornate vocabulary, thereby making the debater amused. He expressed his will to move away and, having bowed, thanked for help. Before they could say anything, he was trotting towards the goal.

It took a little longer than expected to reach the cabin. From the moment he left the cemetery, he had the impression that someone was with him all the time, as if that person had been sitting next to him and whispering in the horse's ear, setting the rhythm of the march. He walked for a long time between the mounds covered with grass. The dismal, often crooked and lichen-covered stone tablets protruded and formed a specific labyrinth. He could feel the bushes blocking his way, and their twisted arms transform into an impenetrable entity that prevents access to the nucleus.

On the spot he was surrounded by a crown of old beech trees. A silver bark on them, fell off here and there. One of the logs had deep furrows, as if an animal had sharpened its claws. In the center was a stone house with a red brick roof, copiously covered with green moss. It was the only one here in the spring color, the rest were overwhelming. Morien's head rumbled with scraps of magic crowding around the cabin. Every nerve twitched. It was impossible that he was dealing with an old mage! He would have known that someone was residing in the backwoods! He got off the horse and tied it to one of the trees. Dry twigs crackled underfoot, and last year's leaves bent softly. There was light in the windows, and a thin trickle of smoke was rising from the chimney. Before he knocked, the door opened slightly. The ambiguities disappeared. A man with gray hair and an unusually long beard loomed in the shadows. At first glance, he appeared to be a dwarf, but he wasn't. To Morien's surprise, he greeted him warmly, extending his old hands. Morien took them, they pierced through with cold, stabbed with the boniness so contrasting to the firmness of the magician's body.

"Lord, welcome!" The old man's lips were twisted by the toothless smile.

Morien reciprocated. The man looked neither dangerous, nor the more like the men who dug graves portrayed him. Perhaps he might have appeared more off-putting, but not dangerous. He invited him in, pointing to a large armchair next to a small fireplace. The mage took advantage of the courtesy and made himself comfortable. Surprisingly, the piece of furniture pleasantly wrapped the body worn by the long horse ride. He leaned towards the governor which also sat comfortably in the equally cavernous seat.

"I came here for a specific purpose. I hope you will be able to help me. All attempts to find out anything were burned in a flash pan, which is starting to annoy me, frankly."

"Do you want tea?" The landlord pointed to the cast-iron teapot hanging just above the fire. "I've just made a fresh one. The cups are at the top." He showed multi-colored vessels, placed on hooks attached to a wooden board. Each shone in the light of the flames.

"Why not? Tea hasn't hurt anyone yet." He poured it and sat comfortably.

"Who do I owe the visit to? I'm not used to visits. And if someone comes here, it is these two clumsy gravediggers without a hint of brain. I hope they didn't bore you to death, they can be annoying. They come once a week to hand over the burial documents. I have always wondered why together, as if they had grown into one body over the years. Well, maybe they love each other?"

Morien's lip twitched in a smile.

"No, they were not annoying, rather humble as servant dogs."

"Yes, it's true. Well paid plebs sings more beautifully. But to the point, we don't want the night to find us here. What trouble are you having, Lord Master?"

The magician was frozen. He didn't introduce himself.

"How do you know, my lord?"

"Oh, my dear, you can see it with the naked eye. You don't belong to the mob that venture into haunted lands."

"Haunted?" Morien raised an eyebrow.

"Yes, sir mage, it is better not to go outside at night. No one has been buried here for years, and the ground has not been blessed. No priest of the Redeemers has prayed here or sprinkled with sacrificial oil. People were buried hastily, because there were a lot of dead bodies, and the vermin quickly used the rest of the coverings as a food. When this modest office was built." He showed the interior with a gesture, as if he had been proud of the order and cleanliness of the room, which existed as one, but independent room. "It hasn't been said that the remains of those who died of a bloody cough rest under feet. It is known that those who are not blessed are reborn as restless spirits wailing mournfully and pleading for redemption and mercy."

Morien listened with obvious interest. He got what he came for. He didn't have to ask, though there were a few things on his lips.

"It was said that the last of the rulers is long dead, and the information about the burials in those sad times was burned along with the archives," the magician said.

"It's true, but the Mayor doesn't know much. He's a busy man, things like this don't concern him. He watches over those who are still breathing. The fire consumed a lot of documentation. It's sad. We won't get those lists back. I took up this position a few years after the tragedy of Undercity. As I got old, I wanted a quiet place away from the hustle and bustle, but close enough to be reached without major obstacles. Since then, I have been keeping chronicles and collecting death certificates. Name of anyone who gave up the ghost within the city walls, I have in my files, even yours, honorable mages. He demonstrated with his finger several files stacked one over the other, bound in red leather bearing the school's crest. Once a year, I send a report by courier to the municipal archives. In this way, I make room for another one."

"Sad job," Morien replied as he finished his tea.

"Yes, but for a dwarf who has no family, this is a perfect position. I have peace and quiet here, only at night the damned, not blessed specters sing outside the window. Now no priest in their right mind will come here, they are cowards who hide themselves under the power of the highest. The phantoms are not dangerous, you get used to it. Sometimes you can see them hover above the ground, reaching out to the stars."

The mage's skin stiffened. He had never seen these souls, although he had read about them. He got what he came for. Here, somewhere under his feet, lay the buried body of Lilian's mother. He hoped the mage wouldn't come here.

"Do you need anything, old man?" He asked, getting ready to leave.

Through the little pane, he saw the horse nibbling at the young blades of luscious grass barely growing from under the leaves.

"No, I don't need anything. I'm glad someone came. I could talk, I do it so rarely that I wonder if my vocabulary is getting impoverished. Sometimes reading is not enough, and contact with the two is focused only on exchanging the same information. And I get the impression that they don't like me." He laughed, got up, and escorted the visitor to the door.

"Thank you for the valuable information. I got what I came for, and I didn't even have to ask."

"I knew what you came for, but she's not here. They burned the body and put the ashes together with others in a collective urn, then scattered them under the city walls. She was one of the lucky ones - she received a blessing. The name plate is hanging right next to the entrance to the cemetery. Go soothe the troubled heart of your loved one and don't let her worry. The mother rests in the arms of the Redeemers."

Morien looked at the old man with his mouth parted wide:

"How do you ...?"

"They told me. They whisper, they are always here. I've known for a long time you were coming here. Go, it is already late, it will darkle soon."

Morien walked away with mixed feelings, surprised and full of fear. The feeling rumbled icily and bitterly pierced through. As soon as the door closed behind him, the image of the gray dwarf faded from memory and he couldn't remember his face for anything. Only the taste of the tea remained on his tongue, clear and almost irritating. He came back to town at a gallop, he didn't want to dwell on the past. Indeed, in front of the gate was a well-worn engraving commemorating the victims of a bloody cough.

However, time had wiped out the letters, leaving only the indentations that once appeared as symbols. Weird. He hadn't noticed it before, as if the tile itself had materialized solely for the purpose of the search. He stood for a long moment, stubbornly staring at the signs. Then he galloped to the Magician School. People were getting out of his way. He wasn't looking at them, all that mattered was getting home as quickly as possible.

CHAPTER VIII

"You better leave him alone!" The innkeeper yelled at Darius, tugging at the messenger's frock coat.

The small man glared at his opponent with cornflower blue eyes.

"Not your business, you stinker!" He snorted in response.

"Mine, you Baroness' dog! My inn, my rules! If you don't let him go, you'll get hit in the head!"

"Dare, farmhand, and I will beat you up so that you will remember me!"

The tugged unfortunate man no longer defended himself, but waited calmly for the development of events. The excruciating exhaustion drained the last of his strength, and his stomach twisted with hunger. He was riding for a good few weeks with a message from his lady, but on the road he faced a lot of adversity and it took much longer than planned to reach his destination. The highroad was exceptionally not peaceful. There were swarming all kinds of highwaymen. He also met several groups of wild mages, to whom he gave a wide berth, thus making his way longer. To make matters worse, some of his messages got wet, and at the end of his journey he was robbed and beaten. Were it not for the mercy of a merchant who fortunately passed through those regions, he would probably have ended up in the stomach of a hungry animal. As a result, his passivity was most desirable for him, and the only thing he thought about now was a bowl of warm soup.

Mark didn't give up. The deputy showed a strenuous journey. His swollen eyes and smashed nose were telling the sad story of the route. He took a step closer to Darius and sweepingly punched him in the jaw. He instinctively got off the delivery man and jumped to the innkeeper. Freed from his hands, the messenger sat down on the ground, smoothing his clothes. He lost two decorative buttons in the scuffle, which saddened him more acutely than the taint on his honor. He knew that the damage to the garment equaled the baroness's harsh rebuke, so he began to look for the lost, ignoring the two men struggling with each other. Darius turned out to be stronger than the owner of "Ram's Head". He quickly knocked him to the ground. They were fighting for a moment, knocking over stools and tables, and thus making an unimaginable tumult. The fair-haired man was surprised by Mark's strength and agility. They both had torn eyebrows, and from their noses blood oozed profusely. None of them was giving up. The innkeeper was boiling inside, he was heartily fed up with uninvited guests, lack of profit and disagreements, and he couldn't get over the death of the cook, which accumulated into one large ball of energy boiling with anger. He hit the void, spewing out curses, but every time he reached his opponent, one could hear the hiss and fury of Darius blocking the attack. They lavished blows, and was it not for Lonan's return, they would have kept pummeling each other until one of them fell, either from exhaustion or with a broken skull. Mark hovered in the air, his eyes pop out as the magician raised him by the collar with one hand like a puppy is lifted by the skin on the nape of its neck. Darius wiped off with his sleeve the gore oozing from his split lip. A large blue stain began to appear under his eye, and it swelled more and more intensely with each passing moment.

"About time." He spat foamy red saliva straight onto the boards. "Where have you been? I almost got killed here." He sniffed.

He felt a more intense metallic taste in his throat.

"Don't be interested, younker, where I go. What happened here?" He pointed to the battlefield with his free hand.

Broken stools were scattered around, and the pleased envoy was sitting in the corner, tossing two golden buttons from hand to hand. Probably he was the only one who wasn't interested in what had happened. Worse, he also didn't care that the innkeeper stood up for him. He raised himself on his hands and approached, hiding the lost items in a small pocket on his chest.

"Gentlemen," he began. "I brought a message from our lady. I would be glad if one of you wrote back. In other words, I'm in a bit of a hurry. If I find the way back in the same state it was in a few days ago, I dare to assume that it will take just as long to reach my destination." Then he bowed nicely and stared with his little eyes at those present.

"Message?" The Alchemist growled. "There's a message and I don't know anything?"

"There is." He pointed to the scroll on the counter.

Unsealed and read in part, as half of the vellum was blurred by moisture.

Lonan released Mark who landed with a crash on the floor, bruising his back. He got even more furious. He felt as humiliated as possible.

"What is this?!" Lonan waved his hand with the correspondence in front of the envoy's face. "What the hell is this, I'm asking?!" He thundered.

"Forgive me, my lord, but such situation occured and not other, and unfortunately, while escaping from the gang prowling the highway, I got the letter wet. However, if you look closely, you will probably be able to read the rest. I'm sorry. I was supposed to deliver it at any cost, so I did. Now excuse me, I'll go to the market to try to get some food. I suppose that in this inn." He looked around meaningfully. "I won't be hosted with warm food."

"Cheeky reptile," Mark growled. "I protect you and you insult me."

"Will you be silent?" The alchemist hit Mark with the back of his hand.

The innkeeper collapsed to the floor, losing consciousness.

The alchemist unfolded the letter again and read the contents, focusing on the water-stained part. The delivery man was right, approaching the fireplace, he could read the blurred letters. A murmur of discontent carried over the room. He didn't like small things disturbing him in carrying out his tasks. The baroness wrote:

Dear Darius and you, Lonan,

I'm very glad that you managed to find the fugitive in such a short time. The message may not have reached me as quickly as possible, but it was satisfactory, which is rare. I took the liberty of calling off the rest of the Alchemists I had sent to the lesser towns. It doesn't change the fact that I'm dissatisfied that it wasn't possible to capture her. Unfortunately, my power ends right at the gates of the Magician Schools. I hope that you will be able to lure her out of her safe hiding place. You absolutely cannot count on Aaron. Correspondence is silent. But remember: SHE MUST BE LIVE! Don't try any necromancy tricks, I would know about it from a distance! Good luck.

P.S. I managed to get support. Two prison carts are already heading towards you, along with a detachment of the best trained mercenaries in the country. I believe, Lonan, you will be pleased with the surprise I have prepared.

Best regards,

the lowly maid of the king,

Baroness Alvena

"What are we going to do?" Darius ran a hand through his matted hair.

"We'll get her out of there, even if I have to go in there through a hole in the wall," Lonan snorted.

"Yeah, right. Even a mouse wouldn't slip there."

"Mages are smart, but Alchemists are smarter. We have been hunting them for centuries. We have tricks about which you, your lady's dog, have no idea."

"Watch your mouth!" The man snapped.

"I think I should beat you too." He gestured at Mark. "Maybe you would learn a lesson, you spoiled younker. Now go get some water, this man needs to be revived." He glared at the messenger standing nearby, still waiting for an answer. He reached into the pouch that was dangling near his belt and took out a silver coin, then said to the man, "Go eat something, and when you come back, your lady will have a letter."

The man caught the coin in the air, bowed and disappeared through the doorway, leaving them alone.

***

Morien rode to the gates of the School. He was feverish and distrustful of what he had heard just a few clock strikes earlier. He had a sincere desire to learn more about restless souls, but not now, because he had far more important things to do. He dismounted and led the horse through the small wicket gate. The mare was taken by the groom, who was glad to see it. He patted its side and with the other hand he stroked the back of its neck. The animal took the caress with great joy, snorting and pricking up its ears. The air smelled of horse sweat and something else, a fear coming from Morien. Maybe he had satisfactory news for Lilian, but he didn't find the one thing she wanted most - the grave. The very thought of the ashes trampled and blown by the wind seemed unpleasant, and worse still hopeless.

He improved his overall appearance, thanked the farmhand, and went directly to the greenhouse. He guessed she was still there, her power thundered like a throbbing heart. Wherever she moved, he could hear it and he followed it. He found her bent over the newly dug bed. She was accompanied by a young botanist. Clearly fascinated Lilian was absorbing every word, watching as she sowed tiny plants with the finesse only given to her. It seemed to Morien that it wasn't her first time.

She heard footsteps behind her. She turned beaming, and a storm of red hair rippled happily.

"You're already back," she said, greeting him with outstretched arms.

He resisted attempts to show tenderness in public, so she quickly came to herself and wiped the mud-stained hands on a scrap of her robe.

"I'm back." He took a deep breath.

"And how was it? Did you learn anything specific?" She asked feverishly, as if her whole future life had depended on this news.

"Yes. I have learned a lot, but I don't think this is the right place to talk about it."

"Yes, you are right." She looked around.

Several other magicians in the greenhouse looked at them. Like the young botanist, they were now taking classes in planting rare seedlings, and Lilian was only a helper in their studies.

"Let's go home. Let's have a cup of tea with rum, you have no idea how much I feel like this drink. My mother liked it, especially on cool autumn evenings, when tired we came home from work. I think this is a great occasion to celebrate something. - She beamed."

The mage pursed his lips.

"Yes, there is something to drink to, although I don't know if so abundantly."

She tilted her head and looked at him closely, now it dawned on her that he might have had news, but not such she wanted to hear. Lifting her dress a little, she walked through the greenhouse and along a path dotted with tiny flowers, she headed towards the mansion. He plodded behind her. The house greeted them with the afternoon sun flooding the hall, where an already slightly worried maid was waiting.

"You've been gone a long time. I already thought that I would be forced to send someone. The city is so restless now," she wailed, taking their coats.

"You have nothing to worry about, my dear, I'm fine," he replied, smiling shyly.

As always, she sensed something was up. She stopped bothering herself with irrational worrying.

"The meal is still warm, if you'd like, my lord ..."

"Yes, I'd love to eat something. Lili, will you join me?"

"No, no, thank you. Just a tea to my quarters, please."

The maid bowed and disappeared into the hall. Morien followed her, she would eat with the others. Strangely, he wanted a homely atmosphere rather than the polished countertop in the dining room and those horrible, preserved with magic flowers he sincerely hated. Whenever he looked at them, he felt he was looking at something artificial and unreal. They didn't even smell.

There was a nice and friendly atmosphere in the kitchen. The noise and the large number of people relaxed him. He immediately got food and a seat at the communal table. The servants behaved naturally towards him, you might say that they were as thick as thieves. There were no secrets in this house, and mysteries remained within its walls. The man in his position cared for the employees, and they paid in kind.

One of the girls brought tea to the mage. She found her huddled on the floor not of her room but of the office upstairs, and staring out the window. Lili didn't notice her coming in, so she set the teapot on the ground next to the fire and left. The young magician used to feel melancholy, especially when something fell on her and when she was burdened with some news. Sometimes these were good things, but her innate gift for worry made her susceptible to numbness.

Morien thanked and left the kitchen. The cheerful atmosphere and the stew with groats he liked so much made him feel better. Breaking the news seemed easier now, but it was only appearances. Lilian was huddled and silent, didn't react when he sat down next to her, and only when he spoke did she revive and lay her head on his shoulder. He returned the gesture. It was nice to sit like that without unnecessary chatter, enjoying the silence, the aroma of freshly brewed tea and watching the dust particles floating in the air and being illuminated by the sun.

"You seem worried," she began in a whisper, not taking her eyes off the crumbs dancing in the air.

"I'm a little bit."

"So you have bad news?"

"Not entirely bad, they are partly good if you are deeply religious. They're partly not the nicest, and partly, well, I don't even know where to start. A lot happened today, and I have a feeling that even more will happen."

She sat more comfortably and rested her head on the mage's shoulder again, entwining her fingers with his.

"Nothing you say will worry me. You can satisfy my curiosity. The pain seemed to ease. It melted, entered me, and with time it will turn into sentimental memories that I will start to fuel during long winter nights." She didn't think so. She didn't believe that she would live to better times.

She wanted to cheer him up somehow. He seemed overwhelmed by what he was carrying inside him.

"Don't cheer me up, this story is mine now as well. I spent the day traversing the city from one side to the other, and when I got to my destination, the news came from a dwarf who knew who I was, what I was looking for, and on top of that said more than I asked."

She looked at him in surprise.

"I don't understand."

"How to put it ..." he sighed. "Your mother was burned. The city authorities decided to incinerate some of the bodies, and some were buried in the unblessed ground. Her ashes along with the others were placed in a collective urn," he blurted out. "The names of the deceased, whose families gave for the census, are engraved on the memorial plaque of the bloody cough on the city walls. It is right at the entrance to the cemetery."

She reached his face hopefully with her eyes, so he continued, even though the glistening pupils indicated that she was close to crying.

"It's not everything. The last piece of good news is that she was one of the few who received the last blessing. Now she sleeps in the arms of the Redeemers and is safe. The priests didn't manage to reach a large number of the sick which got buried a long way from the main road. The man who told me about this called them restless souls. To this day, at night, they beg for prayers to the Creators."

"What does this have to do with my mother?"

"It concerns her, my dear, because these souls are whispering to the steward, communicating with him. I don't understand it myself, because it is rather unexplored, and I have never read anything like this, even though I know about the phenomenon of specters."

Lilian started to blink vigorously.

"What did they tell him?"

"The office, or maybe a cottage would sound better, was built on this unblessed land."

"It's terrible." She covered her mouth with her hand.

"He learned to live with them. Surprising, isn't it? They whisper and he listens and sympathizes. There is one more thing you need to know."

"Urn, Morien, where's the urn?"

"There is no urn. That's what I wanted to say."

"What do you mean, there is no urn? Someone destroyed it?"

"No. After the plague, the remains were scattered in front of the gate, so that the ashes returned to the bosom of the earth. The aforementioned plaque and the fading memory of the victims remain a remembrance. Forgive me for not having better news." He got sad.

Tears filled the rims of her eyelids, but she didn't cry. Finally, after a long time she felt calm, her thirst for knowledge was satisfied. Relief but filled with pain appeared on her face. It worried her that she wouldn't experience any tangible place where she could put a wreath of even wild flowers. Maybe under the plaque? Would it make any sense?

Morien watched the tiny muscles under her skin tighten and relax. Lost in thought, she barely noticed him. She was struggling with the inner self. Thanks to the outpouring of truth, he learned that demons don't have to bring anger with them, they can bring relief. He was worried needlessly. All that bothered the mind at the time was how the dwarf spoke to the damned. And how do restless souls know who Lilian is? And how did they know that he would come to get the information about her dead mother's fate? The feeling irritated unbearably.

"You know," she said suddenly, resting her head on his chest. "I'm finally calm because I know she will be safe, and she will wait for me alongside the Redeemers. I will gladly run to her when someone crosses my life line."

"You talk nonsense, you know?" He took her face and kissed the tip of her nose." Nobody's gonna kill you, get it in that pretty little head.

"You don't even know how many would like to. Mostly the Alchemist. I can already see his lips twitch as he tethers my power, and then when no one watches, he will humiliate me like an ordinary girl, except that he will cut my throat at the end."

Morien pushed her away.

"What are you talking about?! Nothing like that will happen! I won't allow it!"

"May you be right. I'm starting to freak out. I've been locked up too long."

He hugged her. From that day on, he kept his eyes on her, considering that spring had come incredibly fast, and the young mage would often leave the property only to enjoy its benefits.

The surroundings blossomed, burst with green. Spring composed reality anew. Bud by bud, flower by flower, saturating the space with the buzzing of insects and the chirping of birds, which happily hovered overhead as excited as people. The inhabitants lingered in the delusion of the most beautiful awakening that had softly fallen on heaviness in the chests. They breathed calmly, even though the darkness clothed in the garments of the bloody magician lurked somewhere behind the curtain of a juicy delusion. They finally got rid of clumpy boots and thick, woven coats. Although they delighted with the craftsmanship, and probably more than one magician regretted having to say goodbye to the beautiful clothes, they were relieved to do so. Now light robes were put on and silk scarves were thrown around the neck. It served fashion more than warming the owners, but intrants, tired of the monotony of costumes, tried various ways to diversify the image. The same was done with hairstyles. The lion's share of the girls wore long or semi-long hair, usually tied into loose buns. Sometimes they stuck feathers into them, or a new invention that was allocated to the dwarves: a carved piece of charcoal covered on both sides with birch bark wrapper. Innovative, suitable for quick notes. The magicians were crazy about the pioneering writing article. Boys who decided to wear long hairs usually didn't pin them up. There were individual cases of ponytails or braids, and Morien liked the latter very much. Lilian braided his hair every day after breakfast, which later became their morning ritual, like eating oatmeal or greeting in the hall with a kiss on the cheek. She, in turn, combed tightly the unruly curls on top with bone combs. She had to admit over time that the efforts were pointless, because despite the pains she was unable to tame them. One of the maidservants proposed a beeswax-based pomade, which resulted in the creation of something like a sleek helmet. She thanked for the offer, but didn't use the remedy any more.

Lilian became unruly and difficult to contain over time.

"Her head was always full of the wind," Morien used to say.

He tried to practice hand-to-hand combat with her, which was usually complemented by cursing and leaving of the girl. The explanation that strength and endurance are as important as will hit the void. She insisted. She thought that magic was enough and that he shouldn't have wasted his breath. She knew better. After a while, he gave up. There were also days when she was unable to concentrate, her mind wandered outside his self, locked in a vessel of whispers like in a glass fortress. At that time, she wandered around the courtyard completely inaccessible and icy. He watched her from hiding, trying at all costs to break the border. He knew that she had already read the book about the Speech of Whispers. She had lied in the same place next to the bed for a long time. In the evenings, she reached for the book to refresh individual paragraphs, but never once did she find it in her heart to try again to reconnect with Morien's essence. He knew her fears. She wore them like outerwear.

Lilian was afraid. She isolated herself and ran away from her beloved into the deepest layers of herself. The fear of knowing her plans paralyzed the urge to get closer. She experimented with her speech in great secrecy, and the service fell victim at first. This was somewhat of the intended effect, but it scared the girls more often than she talked to them. Suddenly, it began to amuse her to such an extent that she refrained from hurting them. He mentioned that Morien had warned about it, but it was so... After much thought, she gave up trying, focusing on something completely different - a trip to the city.

She had been devising a plan to retrieve the stuff for a long time. Despite the fact that she was aware of the seriousness of the deed and the fact that the Alchemist and the spy constantly resided within the city walls, the temptation to get out of the school's prison was felt more and more strongly. She was concerned by the thought of whether she would still find this place unchanged, whether the old stuff was still there, or maybe Mark simply got rid of it and appropriated the purse with the silver earned? Now she could use the money, there were many opportunities to spend it. Of course, she hadn't planned to announce anything to Morien, he would have gone mad and ready to lock her up. Her thoughts circled around the secret passage to the old tenement house, which had once been the site of their secret trysts. At that time, despite her best efforts, she couldn't locate the place. She knew she was inside the University and probably in the house where she had lived, but the secret was well disguised. She wished she had listened then and hadn't had her thoughts focused on a completely different, nicer path. At present, she would give a lot to snatch that knowledge from Morien. In part, she sought to see Mark.

Dreamy, she was resting on the wall right in front of the university building. She put her face up to the sun, which painted her cheeks slightly pink, thus also making the amount of freckles on her nose drastically increase. She had aroused quite a stir among intrants, but the biggest one among adolescent boys. The girls envied her freedom and lack of prudishness. Shyness wasn't part of her temper. She emanated with something that attracted the opposite sex. The older she got, the more visible it was. She didn't realize it. She believed that everything about her was natural, so she was blissfully unaware of the spreading of alluring fluids. Only Morien mattered, no one else could break the fetters of affection she had for him. On that day, she decided to use a trick to obtain information about the secret passage to the old tenement house. She knew her man's habits very well and knew how to loosen his tongue. Meanwhile, he gave lectures. With persistence worthy of himself, he instilled in young minds the secrets of the art of using the elements, fortunately today only in theory. They listened, but as the lessons progressed, the falling petals of cherry blossoms, which were planted at regular intervals in the alley, became more intriguing. He struggled with growing irritation. Maybe he was not one of the most exalted speakers, but he didn't bore! Unfortunately, spring was a distraction. He hit the desk with a thick book and sat down, crossing his legs. Now all faces looked at him, with eyelids slightly drooping with weariness.

"Go." He waved at them, wishing they would go to the dormitories.

There was a slight hum in the room, as if the acolytes hadn't believed it. It was unlike him, because he used to hold them until the last minute, without any exception. They watched him prop his head on a hand and look out the window at the same picture they had just seen a moment ago. And indeed, the landscape of pink, tiny petals of cherry blossoms waving in the light breeze turned out to be extremely pleasing to the eye and ... lulling.

"Is it for real, professor?" Said a young boy with albescent hair from the middle bench.

"Yes, yes. Go and admire these petals, but outside. Today I won't teach you anything anyway." He waved his hand again, signaling that he was serious.

He heard the hum and the shuffling of chairs. One by one, they shyly packed and left the room. Out of the corner of his eye he noticed the spring joy painted on their faces. An extra hour for gossiping and doing so-called nothing was rare, so they enjoyed their privileges whenever the opportunity arose. He was most pleased with the secretly forming couples of juvenile magicians. Even though they knew they would be severely punished when caught, there was nothing to prevent them from arranging meetings in the broom closets. After all, the school was full of nooks and crannies that were eagerly discovered by new students or passed on by older students to younger ones. As the last of the intrants left the room, Morien stretched his legs on the desk and yawned several times. He also needed a moment of rest. It was so nice.

Lilian saw the youngsters leaving the building. Surprised, she raised an eyebrow and watched them scatter in all directions. Those who passed her by, politely bowed and greeted her, some were too kind, of course for obvious reasons. She couldn't stand it and accosted one of the girls who was just passing her, unhappily grabbing her sleeve. She snorted, showing a lack of sympathy.

"Don't snort," she admonished. "When someone politely accosts you, stop and find out what that person wants."

She looked from under the bushy mane of night-black hair.

"If someone wants to know something, doesn't tug at the robe," she growled, tearing the sleeve from the surprised Lili's hand.

"Alright," she sighed to calm a little the nerves, which began to play under the skin. "Why are you leaving so early today? Shouldn't the lessons last one more hour, approximately, of course."

She tried to be nice, but wanted to set the student's fringe on fire. She was asking for it.

"The dear Lord Master finished the classes, madam," she stressed 'madam' so strongly that a few students leaving the school cautiously stopped.

"Thank you very much. That's what I wanted to know." She stood up and dusted off the robe.

The girl, however, didn't let go and was ready to throw herself at the magician.

"You think you're important?" She hissed. "You come here as if nothing had happened, you turn the School upside down and think that everyone will start falling at your feet?"

Lili raised an eyebrow.

"I don't understand."

The girl continued: "Yes, you do! Do you think that when you sleep with the Lord Master, you are allowed to do everything? You cause us troubles, it would be the best if you ..." She fell to the ground, holding the head.

If she had longer fingernails, she would probably have plowed the skin to the bone. Lilian stood above her. The redhead's pupils were blazing with living fire. The assembled onlookers moved away terrified.

It was the first time she had used the Speech of Whispers on a magician. It worked. Still weak will of the student couldn't withstand the pressure of Lilian's power and her skull was torn with a powerful attack of pain. The girl was squirming, ripping the skin of her face and scalp. The mage continued to torment her until Morien broke the chain of power. Lilian came to herself, unclenched her fists and let her breathing return to normal. From somewhere outside, a gentle cloud settled on the troubled heart and, hugging it with a wreath of arms, swayed to the beat of her breathing. She let go. She realized that she had been accumulating anger since entering the School on that ill-fated winter morning. She realized how dangerous she was and how quickly she had to get out of here! Morien helped the student to stand up. Flooded with tears, she was shaking and sweating. Fortunately, the harm she had done to herself could be repaired with a short visit to the healers.

"I'm sorry," she sobbed. "I shouldn't have upset Mrs. Lilian, I'm sorry," she wailed as she tried to control her trembling.

"You knew how powerful she is. I have asked for tact many times. Lilian bored into Morien with her glazed eyes. He said things that he hadn't mentioned at home. "A mage of this class can't be irritated, especially if the mana is unstable. Don't blame her for being here and leave your self-serving to those interested. We are lucky that she is here. Thanks to us, she will learn to control, and you may use this knowledge in the future. Trust me, none of the professors here intends to hurt anyone. Now excuse me. In the lazaret, they will help you come to recover. Lilian, let's go." He took her hand and led her forward.

The students stayed behind. Several students jumped to the tortured to help her get into the office. They seemed to be heading towards the property, but she had a feeling that he wouldn't lead her there. She also didn't believe the words that were said. He warned them, he warned them against her! As if she had appeared to be a human who is not quite so, that somewhere under the covering she carries an enraged beast that must not be woken up. They turned left in front of the mansion.

"Where are we going?" She asked.

"You will see. We need to talk seriously!" He hissed, squeezing her hand even tighter.

His irritation stung. She probably exaggerated. She didn't behave well. That girl was a teenager, she used to be one herself. By Redeemers!

They walked for a long time, avoiding the University buildings and greenhouses, and losing themselves in the meanders of narrow streets. She didn't come here often, but she knew the area. These were places where young magicians used to go, tempted by their intimacy. He led her to a gray alley. Out of the corner of her eye, she saw that it belonged to part of the dormitories. Behind the thicket of slow-growing, lush green shoots, subtle outlines loomed, as if someone had casually roughed out with a sharp tool, the shape of a narrow door, which was absolutely unremarkable in color from the rest. She had to take a good look to understand its uniqueness. It didn't have a handle, but only a diamond-shaped opening. Morien searched the pouch and took out a brass knob with a tip that matched the opening in the door. The door creaked and swung open. No magic, no incantation, no glare, no runes… just the knob! And in front of them appeared a dark cavity of a secret corridor that reeked of damp wood and rock.

"Come on in!" He ordered and looked around, wanting to check if no one really followed them, although he knew perfectly well that they were alone.

She obeyed and allow herself to be absorbed by the sticky blackness. The only light she distinguished, and only for a moment, was the sun breaking through the still open door. Morien took a step behind her. She tasted silence interspersed with the dripping of water somewhere in the abyss, which echoed through the air, giving the impression of an unusual depth of the room. They stood there a moment longer. The mage struggled with the purse. As he pocketed the knob, she heard a hiss and a trembling brightness enveloped them. Every few meters, oil lamps were swinging on metal hooks, and their flickering light was illuminating the passage. It didn't look high or wide. A tall man could easily fit there, but you had to walk single file. Morien overtook her and glowed a purple fire flower on the back of his hand. It pulsed and shimmered, giving even more light than tallow vessels. The mage seemed more formidable now than ever before. The red of the fire marked the irises with purple tongues, and the hair was burning from the glare. Scared, she clenched her fists. She wouldn't have liked to fight him.

"Follow me," he said flatly, and started walking.

She was walking behind him, carefully watching where she was stepping. The stones, damaged by erosion, frightened with unevenness, and in some places looked damp and slippery. She had to hold on to the wall several times to prevent a fall. Rodents scuttled in front of them, and the spiders hid in the crevices, sensing the approaching fire. She reacted with goose bumps to every of them. They didn't get far when a small room appeared in front of them, on both sides of which there was a door, and in the middle was attached a huge closet full of volumes, documents and gathered scrolls, damp and probably already rotten. It smelled of musty old leather. She assumed that this wasn't the end of wandering through the underground corridors. Morien was silent. A few more galleries right, left, then right twice, and they found themselves under a hatch. A ladder lay at their feet.

"Would you mind?" He gave her the fire.

She didn't protest. The flames leapt to fingers, glowing and flickering blue. He glared at her, so she pulled herself together and they flashed yellow and red again. He set up the ladder, climbed it, and pushed the hatch. It opened without the slightest resistance. She immediately guessed where they were, she no longer had to use tricks to find the place of descending to the underground. She smiled with the corner of her mouth, narrowing her eyes in satisfaction.

"Come on." He gave her a hand.

She put out the flame and allowed herself to be helped. The little room looked like it had before, nothing had changed, but to her relief it was dry and cozy. Morien had just lit the candles as he stood at the wall. She closed the hatch gently and, folding her hands on the lap, assumed the position of a schoolgirl who would be reprimanded. There was no nice chat for her.

"Can you tell me what that was?" He spread his hands in a gesture strange for her.

"I don't understand."

"You know perfectly well what I'm talking about. Why didn't you say you are secretly learning the Whisper Speech? Why do you throw yourself, by Redeemers, at the novices? I thought you were sensible enough not to get provoked. And here you are!" He put his hands on the hips.

She cringed and felt as that novice who had been beaten like a dog.

"You gave me the book, so I read it. I thought I would learn a bit before we start practicing together. It came naturally, as if the consciousness itself had been opening up to whispers. Then she. I won't let others to offend me just because I live with you under one roof, and there are all kinds of speculations at the school."

"Lili, this is not speculation, but reality. Everyone knows what the truth is. It's hard to hide anything here. The Archmage only agreed to my relationship with you because ..."

"Because what? Because I'm valuable to the country, because it's a matter of great importance, because what? Because I can do more and I can put a torch to your school? You all deserve each other!" She snorted and sat down on the bed, leaning against the wall.

Morien sighed and walked over to her. The anger eased a bit, but it didn't disappear completely. Lilian's hair was crackling with accumulated emotions.

"You know I don't think so." He was looking at her. "But you must, by gods, be careful. Do you know what's going to happen now? We already hoped they calmed down, and here we are, such an incident. In addition, with the intrant, who no one likes, and who makes younger students scared. This mouthy little girl from an aristocratic home can only do us harm. Fortunately, I didn't allow her to correspond with the tutor because it was too frequent. Only I keep her mother informed of the progress. It's an influential family. May her anger pass."

"I'll solve it," she finally said. "I will go to her dormitory and talk to her in private. I hope she will be understanding."

"If not, we'll restrain her power," he said emphatically.

"This move would be too radical, wouldn't be?" She got alarmed.

"Radical, not radical. I want to avoid disagreements in the future, and this way I can show others that they are not above the law."

"Aren't you too ruthless? I'll talk to her, leave it to me, and don't think about tethering her power. I won't let you hurt her!" She stood up for her, but Morien thought otherwise.

"Do you know what will happen when this news reaches the Headmaster? We can still invent some ridiculous fairy tale and get rid of her. Also some of her memories will be removed during binding."

"No! There are also witnesses, remember that!" She screamed.

"They will be silent."

"No! And the end of the topic. First me, then you."

"Alright. So be it. But remember that I have my eyes and ears open."

She nodded and fell silent, staring at the glow of the candle flickering at the wall and smearing it with tarry smoke.

"How long have you been whispering?"

"Not long."

"How long?!"

"All right." She sat more comfortably on the pallet. She folded her arms over her chest, but she still didn't look at him, and he was standing in the same place, waiting for a response. "First I was scared. After the first try I had a dream. I don't know if it was a nightmare or maybe a vision? It allowed me to break a certain barrier and taught me what I couldn't comprehend. Then, when we were sitting in the library, you gave me the textbook. It was lying on the cupboard for a while and it was dusting, and I got absorbed in the science of fire. I broke down and started reading, at first it went slow, but over time it started to absorb, so I delved into the reading to such an extent that consciousness itself began to create a niche, like a whispering vessel. I wasn't scared anymore. It started to go my way. The sticky blackness was replaced with something friendly and warm, like a soft and throbbing mother's womb, safe and silent, and the only break in this silence was the rhythmic beats of the heart. Then it became tangible. I started to whisper. It took a lot of effort until now, when I can easily find cracks and can pour visions and sounds into them," she spoke softly, he could barely hear her.

He was preparing to be struck by the force that was sneaking under his skull. He anticipated it. He had much to hide, and the sinful past was no longer safe. Building trust on such a foundation was not a sensible move. He wanted to leave her in sweet unawareness. He adored her so much that to inflict such wounds would have amounted to falling.

"Did you practice on someone?"

She nodded. She felt ashamed, but she didn't hurt anyone, didn't succumb to temptation. "On whom?"

"Mostly on the servants, but it was nothing serious. For example pouring water in the middle of the kitchen or watering the same plant several times. Sometimes I asked for a cake and the girls baked it for me. Oh, Morien, just innocent pranks." She hid her face in her hands.

She didn't want him to notice her searing shame.

"And you've never been tempted to hurt someone with the Whispers?"

"I was tempted," she moaned, still holding her hands on her face. "It was fucking tempting. I felt something like the pleasure of just thinking about it. Am I that bad?"

She glanced at him through her fingers.

"No, but with your power you could confuse someone."

"So I'm glad I didn't give in. Will you forgive me sometime?"

"Of course." He sat down next to her, putting his arm around her.

She nestled her head against his soft hair. The anger suddenly disappeared, and she felt again as at the time when she had first come here with him, innocent and dazed by the charm.

"Let's get out of here before anyone realizes we're gone. We've spent too much time here anyway."

"Yes, I've lost count."

"Alright," she nodded.

They didn't speak to each other on the way back. Only perfunctory glances revealed that the storm had ended. Lili was stubbornly counting every turn, trying to remember this place. And although she guessed that Morien could see through the prism of her behavior, what she had done, he didn't betray himself. She devised a sophisticated plan to sneak up to Ram's Head undetected and get her things back. She got sobered by the light of the afternoon sun that gently cast long shadows across the square.

"Not yet," she thought. "Soon."

Morien closed the door and hid the doorknob. Lilian straightened her dress, which was damp at the bottom. She placed her hand on the wet piece and in a moment the water evaporated with a gentle hiss.

"That's better."

"Definitely," he nodded.

"Let's eat something or I'll starve to death."

"Great idea." She rested her hand on her chin. "I want, let me think ..."

"A cake." As always, he forestalled her words.

"I hate you, you know?"

"Why?" He raised his arms.

"Because you know me better than I know myself. And yes, I feel like an apple pie."

They laughed and headed towards the common mages' dining room. The aromatic smells of the afternoon meal wafted from the kitchen.

Most of the masters and intrants already had eaten dinner, the persons who were there were latecomers or bookworms, slurping their soup lazily, not taking their eyes off the books. Morien and Lilian were also sitting, eating their meal as if it had been their last.

They caused quite a stir as always, though they were rarely seen together. The fat cook only smiled with the corner of her mouth when they asked for more. Morien had his servants and housewives, but he sometimes came here to diversify his diet with a common meal.

Evening mists quickly obscured the school, it got bitterly chilly, and in the distance they could see lightning bolts cutting the sky in half. Immediately after them there were loud thunders that heralded a downpour. Morien looked forward to the storm, it would clear the gutters and the atmosphere. The air, crisp with rain and ozone would soothe. He needed the breath and sound of the wind tearing at the still young leaves on the flowering trees.

Lili followed the unfolding of the weather with her nose stuck to the glass just like when she was a little girl and she tried at all costs to count the drops on the glass. At that time, she organized particle races, sitting with her mother at the window. Whose drop earlier, joining on the way with others, reached the edge of the glass pane, this one won. Memories overtook her from everywhere. They didn't hurt anymore, she wanted to experience them without reproach. Morien fulfilled the need to regain his former self. The weather wouldn't give up for the whole week.

The seemingly salutary storm hung over the city like a bad omen. It was pouring constantly, and people snorted with dissatisfaction every time they had to go out into the rain. Drenched robes and shoes took revenge with pouring noses. Now instead of rejoicing, people cursed and sneezed. But the soil got the best of the rain. The once juicy green took on a more intense color, and the trees flowering a week ago got rid of the white and pink cover, and in its place fruit micropyles appeared. Botanists foretold harvest, and only the fat cook and her assistants winced at the thought of spending an innumerable amount of time making preserves. Nothing was ever wasted at school, no one threw out food, swill was given to pigs, and bread and unserved portions went to the poorest.

The magician was stuck in the house, devouring the titles one of the servants had suggested to her. She had had nothing but textbooks in her hands for a long time. Now she decided to rest and take a look at the readings that differ significantly from their predecessors. A not very thick book described the funny adventures of a young fox who decided to live on its own. She smiled, because in some fragments the playful animal went through adventures very similar to those that had happened to her on her trip home. She devoured the yellowed pages with an appetite worthy of a fantasy literature lover, and at the same time wondered how to get through to the young magician. She didn't intend to burst into the room immediately after the incident, ask her roommates out and start conversations with the usual: Well, hello. She would probably have been bounced. She wasn't liked there anyway, and even worse, the presence of Lilian on the upper floors of the dormitories was inadvisable.

In the evening, the rain drummed, hitting window sills with the rhythmic pitter-patter. The music of the stream echoed through the house. The inmates settled down comfortably in the library, sipping herbal tea. Everyone sniffed resoundingly. Even magic didn't help with the persistent ailment. To relieve themselves of their 'suffering', they smeared the skin above their upper lip with a mint ointment, which provided relief for a while. The cook was wandering around the house, constantly smelling an onion cut in half. Morien was writing back, and Lilian delved into the reading about the smart furball. In the corner of the library, the housekeeper and the gardener were standing, bent over the unfolded game table. The rest of the service finished the job and returned to the town.

The girl got bored with reading and watched the writing man. Concentrated on his notes, he ignored his surroundings. She had the idea to speak to him in the Speech of Whispers. Since the discussion in the tenement's room, she hadn't braced herself to overcome her internal resistance to this art. She still trembled at the thought that she could have done some harm. She gathered her thoughts and let them drain into the vessel formed in the subconscious. She didn't want to make him angry, much less scare him. She completed the words into resonant structures that flowed into his inner ear.

"Morien," she whispered. Unfortunately, she hit the barrier that he preventively created while working. "Morien," she repeated, hoping that increasing her power would help. This time again, she found resistance turning to dust what was on her mind. "What am I doing wrong?" she thought.

She rose from the chair and walked down the stairs without a word. In the quarters next to the bed was the familiar textbook. She leafed through it for a moment in order to find an unambiguous answer. Irritated, she concluded that she had come there in vain. She only discovered a pattern of a state of mind. She gasped and sank heavily on the stool. She found with her eyes the light source. The candle was on the windowsill half burned and flecked with dripping wax on one side. She reached for it to light the book. It is not known which time already she flipped pages, analyzed notes and fixed in her mind incantation formations. After many long breaths, she put the book back in its place. She probably found a problem that was blocking the transmission. She climbed upstairs and sat comfortably in her favorite piece of furniture. She pulled up her feet and tucked them under the folds of her dress. She put her hands under her bottom, squirmed for a moment, and closed her eyes. After steadying her breathing, she concentrated first on the skin, then on the component parts of the tissues, and at the end on the sparks leaping between the synapses. It was quite difficult. It didn't go as easily as it was with weak selves. It took a long time to identify the vulnerability. Morien isolated himself, following the flow of his activities, and most likely didn't notice when she left the room and when she returned to it.

Sweat beaded on her freckled forehead, heavy breaths marked the tiny chest. The players hidden in the corner were happily discussing the game they had played. Another line proclaiming victory landed on the parchment and belonged to the old steward. The housekeeper shrugged and after a moment she said that she would outplay him anyway. Then Lilian felt the slight vibrations of the aura. An imperceptible spark rolled down her cheek. At first it was insensible, then it hissed, vibrated and, led by the woman's will, broke into the yellow irises only to reach the black pupils. Lili found out that this light illuminated the way to the divisions of the Archmage's mind. The space used for whispering made wider and wider circles just under the skull, to slowly fall down to the heart area. She was breathing calmly, and her sweaty forehead stopped shining from the drops. She heard only rhythmic heartbeats and couldn't decipher whether they belonged to her or to Morien. The lightness accompanying the phenomenon made the ritual a pleasant blanket, which she carefully covered herself with. The vessel was constructing reality. She isolated herself from the formed space and poured into it what made the essence.

"Honey," she said shyly. The word traveled across the room in the blink of an eyelid, and after stabbing Morien, it stopped exactly where she wanted it to be. The man put down his pen but didn't look up. He placed his hands flatly on the smooth top of the desk, as if he had been looking for a comfortable support. "Morien, can you hear me?" She repeated.

The mage frowned.

"I hear all too clearly, don't scream."

"Great." Joy marked her face, and sparks of excitement rolled over the hands glowing in the twilight, now clenching on the armrests.

"You don't idle, baby. I struggle with correspondence here, and you attack me mentally. You crouch like a cat that saw a pigeon and then jumps." He still didn't look at her.

His voice was reaching Lilian distorted, it seemed to be rising from under the water and bouncing off the walls of her vessel.

"Do you hear me that weird too?" She asked confused.

"No, on the contrary, I can hear clearly. I think it's only a matter of time. You need to exercise. Did I tell you that you gave me the nice surprise? No? So I'm telling you, and it is the truest truth. I'm proud of you, you know?"

"You are not angry at me?"

"I've told you that I'm proud!" Only now did he look at her with his honey irises. They didn't present a natural image, they had neither irises nor pupils. They were reminiscent of the eyes of a blind man. There was an internal fire behind their curtain, making Morien ghastly. It didn't cross Lilian's mind that she looked the same. "Over time, my dear," he continued, "you will stop to spend so much time constructing. When you feel like Whispering, it will fill you to the brim. However, remember to take advantage of the twilight. This is what upper-class magicians appear to be, monstrous, I would say." He pointed at his face. "You can control it. Today I didn't do it, I'm showing you the first stage. The glow will soften over time, and no man standing next to you will guess what you are doing. In fact ..."

"Tempting," she sighed. "Why didn't I notice it before?"

"Because you grow. The essence of the magic you carry under your covering matures. It forms the final image of who you will become. Well ... All that's left for me to do is to congratulate you on your first successful Whisper Speech. Not the one that scares or hurts, but the one that serves. Since we have a nice chat, it's time to put out the fires. In one go." He pointed to her eyes. "Get rid of them."

"How am I supposed to do this?" She rubbed the area of the eye sockets with her wrists in vain hope of success.

Morien laughed, quickly extinguishing the fire in his eyes.

"Just like that."

"Very funny," she snorted.

"Put out the fire, the candle that illuminates the vessel. Imagine it is there and then put out the flame. Come on, tighten your fingers on it."

"That sounds easy."

"Because it is."

Lilian traveled deeper into consciousness. She wandered for a moment, and having found her destination, she carried her thoughts as Morien commanded. A candle appeared on a stone catafalque, and a chill surrounded it. Lili was under the impression that the candle had been held by a creature resting on it, dead and cold as a stone pedestal. In the blurry forms, she found the figure of a woman clinging to the flame as if it had been the only reason for her existence. She hesitated. The closer she got, the anxiety more strongly overtook the bodily covering with sharp talons.

"Do it." She heard in the distance. "Don't be afraid."

She tightened her lips and eyes. It took a lot of effort to make this gesture, she didn't want to peer into the abyss of dead eye sockets of the one that didn't allow her to move closer. Air whistled in her nostrils, and she stretched out trembling fingers and touched the flame. It was cold, as was the spot pulsating and rumbling with the echo of beats of the strongest artery. The glow was gone. Lilian was covered in sticky darkness, but she felt the soothing presence of the one who supported her, led her by the hand and whispered soothing blessings. It didn't take long for her to get used to it, and what began to emerge from the bleaching blackness was nothing but the library she was just in.

"I've made it!" She was glad.

"Yes." A flush of satisfaction bloomed on the pale face. The breakthroughs happened so quickly. Maybe she just discovered a way to survive?

"Now, my dear, it's time to sleep. Tomorrow you have to use your intelligence. We will end the case of the magician. I think you can handle it."

"And I think that the bratty lady will eat me alive, or possibly send a pack of enraged cockroaches," she said casually.

Morien chuckled, covering his face with his hands. Sometimes she made him despair with funny phrases, although a trained pack of cockroaches would be something.

The man rose from his chair, the occupants of the house did the same. Lili stayed where she was. Outside the windows, the rain stopped pounding on the panes, only droplets flowing lazily remained. A painful melancholy overtook her. The swing of moods ruled the fleetingness of moments. Once on a wave of euphoria, only to in a moment roll down into the abyss of despair. Freedom was a road and a prison at the same time. Sometimes in desperation she wondered what it would have been like to be born an ordinary woman? Probably now she would have had her own place and maybe even a family, such a modest one: a garden by the house, a dog next to the kennel, and a cat basking on the stove on cool evenings. She would have worn a coarse gown on her back, and the wind would have raved in her hair. She would have placed a loom in the corner of the room and weaved fabric for clothes for her husband and children, knowing that this was how life was about to go. Nobody would have despised her or called her a witch. Oh, how much she wanted to exist as a woman from a house by an old apple tree.

"Are you coming?" She heard overhead.

She didn't realize that the servants had left the room, and most of the oil lamps had stopped burning. The depths of the library were dark.

"What?"

"You were thinking. Go to sleep, it's late. You are supposed to help with alchemy lessons in the morning, don't you remember?"

"Yes, I remember that. Me and glass vials. Do you know, Morien, that if I break something, you will pay?"

"Nobody's gonna pay for anything. Now go to bed. I won't go from here until you disappear from the armchair."

Lilian snapped her fingers, wanting to joke that if she made such a gesture, she would have vanished from the seat, materializing in the quarters, fresh, washed and in comfortable underwear.

The magician laughed.

"No, you can't do that."

"It's a pity. Life would be so simple. Look. A snap, and I appear in front of the Baroness with a bucket of cold water. A snap, and the bucket lands on her raddled head. A snap, and she remembers nothing, standing wet, furious and perplexed." She giggled.

"Oh, you sly fox. I wouldn't suspect you of such atrocity."

"I'm a sinner. Oh, punish me, my lord," she chirped and ran out of the room.

Morien retired in an excellent mood.

The day greeted them, surprisingly, without rain. Puddles spread over the tracts of unevenness, and the slushy mud eagerly stuck to the soles. Lilian threw a warmer scarf over her shoulders, the chill was still irritating her delicate skin. She tied the sack with essentials to her belt and trailed sleepily behind Morien, who was bursting with geysers of energy. She rarely appeared in general classes, but this time she got persuaded. The magician hated teaching alchemy, but acolytes probably hated hearing about it more. He didn't mention the guest's visit to the lectures, he didn't have to. He thought the girl would bring a breath of freshness to the cool walls. He was just debating whether the last year students would sniff at it. From experience, he had a feeling that the demanding group liked to arrange scenes of dissatisfaction, but the lovely assistant could warm up the difficult moments before the exams, which were held at the end of the spring semester. Lili, from nervousness, couldn't think of anything else. She knew herself. She knew that the glass in her hands was an immediate, total disaster, injured fingers and a shame before all students. So she avoided activities where the specifics were brewed in vials or glass vats.

"Needs must when the devil drives," she repeated when, having found no alternatives, she went to the laboratory.

The auditorium thundered with talks. Morien handed her the list of items she needed, just before entering the room. She looked at the amount of glass needed and froze.

"You can do it. It's time to get started."

She rolled her eyes, squeezed the note, and slipped behind the magician. The students fell silent as soon as they entered the doorway. Lilian curtsied, turning red, and disappeared behind the curtain leading to the little storage adjacent to the classroom.

Morien took his place behind the desk and started to prepare the attendance list. From the back room, they heard the clink of moving objects. The helper got nervous every time the glass rang louder than she wanted. The master ignored the tumult and conducted his lessons, patiently introducing acolytes to the arcana of alchemical knowledge. They listened, although the newcomer, who emerged from time to time from the square, effectively distracted them from the importance of the topic. There was no breakage or confusion of ingredients. Even though she did her best, the thought was constantly drifting towards the topic she decided to solve that day. Morien noticed that she was distrait.

"It's enough for today. You prepared everything we needed. You can go now. We'll be fine," he whispered.

Lilian gave him a knowing look and disappeared behind the matter to take the shawl from there. The Speech of Whispers now seemed an invaluable ally. She was so happy that she had already gotten over the gamut of the fears related to it behind her. He followed the girl with his eyes, as she having bowed, left the room. Only when she was behind the heavy door did he return to current affairs. The students looked at each other. He knew that they wished him no harm. They were just curious. After all, she was beautiful, but also dangerous. Dormitories and corridors had been buzzing since the last incident. And she belonged to Morien. The mystery surrounding their misalliance hung in a cloud over the heads of the dreamy girls. After all, forbidden things taste best like a box of chocolates carefully stolen from parents.

Lilian sat down on the stone wall and sighed heavily, as if the simple activities she had just been doing had been the most strenuous things she had ever done. The weather was slowly but steadily returning to the state everyone longed for. The heat poured lazily through the clusters of clouds still saturated with rain, and slowly moving across the sky. They drew on the gray sidewalks of the School darker streaks of shadows from the trees growing on the sides of the alley and broodily rustling in the light breeze. The birds, hidden among the branches, was chirping, excited by the changing aura. Late spring smelled of earth and grass, but from time to time the breath of heaven brought the smells of a big city. Fortunately, the turbulence of the wayward wind didn't harm the magicians that severely. She closed her eyes and allowed herself to rest.

"Hello." It came to her.

After lifting the curtain of eyelashes, she saw the noble Master of Botany. They had already gotten to know each other, one might say, even befriended when Lilian had fought the power surges following the incident at the gate. Both bore similar stories on their shoulders, and though they were separated by a nearly thirty-year age difference, they got along well. She also belonged to the small group of magicians who remained faithful to their colors, so she didn't wear a black robe, but a brown dress with a large hood trimmed with delicate leafy fabric. She attached a sachet to her belt, in which she carried the most necessary medications. As she had been ailing recently, the healers had supplied her with a few spare bottles of tonics and drugs strengthening a body.

"Oh, hello. It's unclouding, isn't it?" Lilian asked, trying to hide her surprise.

The older mage looked around.

"I dare to assume that in about two days we will have an unbearable heat."

"Oh no! Don't say that, lady. You can cook yourself alive in these robes!" She complained.

"Get used to it, young lady, or wear what I do. The linen cloth is perfect. It is neither too hot nor too cold in it."

"That's right. I used to wear it and I wouldn't have exchanged it for anything else then. It's a pity that it gets rumpled because it makes you unprepared."

"And you see. Though ..." She thought for a moment. "Yes, the damn should be mixed up with something, maybe then the fabric would behave differently? I'll think about that. Anyway, does something bother you, sweetheart?" She sat down next to her, folding her hands on the lap.

They were slim and wrinkled, like an old woman's. Under some of the fingernails damaged by work there was dirt.

"Many things trouble me, so much is happening. Probably too much." She leaned her hands on the edge of the wall, watching the clouds drift across the sky.

"Nothing's gonna hide here, my dear. I got bad news, did someone tell you that you are extremely unlucky?"

"And do you know that you are right? I even debated it once. Wherever I appear, I destroy order and introduce chaos."

"Don't get paranoid, sweetheart." The older mage puffed up his cheeks.

"I don't intend. I was just thinking."

"What are you going to do next?"

"I don't know, I have to find it in my heart to visit someone, then time will tell." Mentally, she followed the dark tunnels straight to Morien's secret room, and from there to freedom.

"Good for starters, but my advice would be to use the new skill to make your way." The older magician tapped on her forehead, smiling with one corner of her mouth.

The girl raised an eyebrow.

"What new skill?"

"Speech Whispers, my child."

"How do you know that, lady?" She was surprised.

"These are the things you know. Now take advantage of the gift you have and talk to this person. Remember, now you can manipulate the will of the weak, so you can gain a lot from it."

Lilian was staring at her a little incredulously. The elderly botanist was telling the truth. A tempting thought swirled under the skull, but Lili knew her conscience, so she was not sure if she would be able to get out of the awkward situation in such a cunning way.

"That sounds pretty sensible, I suppose I will."

"Then I'm going back to my duties. This year we will collect fantastic strawberries, I can't wait. I have to run and help weeding the garden. Greenhouses in the morning, patches in the afternoon, I don't think I'll ever get bored of it." She winked at her.

"How can you like to dig in the soil full of earthworms? Ugh!"

"Well, I like it, and earthworms are cute."

The young woman twisted her mouth in disgust, and the botanist laughed cheerfully.

"See you, sweetheart." She moved away, waddling heavily.

She was sitting alone again. Now she could think, but she completely didn't felt like it. So she was swinging her legs, watching birds pecking at a stone sidewalk. She gathered herself together and returned to the University to read the list of today's classes. The young magician she was interested in finished her lectures at noon, so she decided to wait for her in the bedrooms. Confrontation in front of the group was absolutely out of the question.

Dormitories were by the wall of the school. The multi-story building glowed in the sun, and huge swathes of the walls were slowly drying up. Lilian stared at the stains of light and dark plaster and thought came to her of a docile and heavy cow, grazing peacefully on a pasture full of daisies and dandelions. She chased away the thoughts and let the pleasant interior of the building absorb her. Behind a small, slightly ajar door sat an older gentleman with a pointed beard and a bushy mustache, slurping his tea dispassionately.

A slurp.

"What do you want, young lady?" A slurp.

"I came for a visit? May I?"

"Of course. Do you know the way?"

"I think I will get there, thank you very much."

"Go ahead." A slurp.

Solid stone stairs made of perfectly fitting blocks, polished and clean, led to the top. There was a slight smell of dust in the air, mixed with the scent of oil lamps, freshly washed underwear, shoes and spicy fragrances that young schoolgirls enjoyed using. Few of the intrants passed her. Most of the time she went unnoticed, but those who recognized her bowed low and moved quickly out of her way. It should have annoyed her a bit, but it only made her smile. Rumors liked to grow to a size that was difficult to comprehend, so it was absolutely not the magician's nature to belabor them.

The second floor where Falera lived overwhelmed with stuffiness and dimness. At the higher floors the rooms were smaller, and the number of people inhabiting them decreased to two magicians. In such a cramped place, a daring teenager lived a life. Lili was nervous.

She put her hand on the handle, wondering if she was doing the right thing, coming here, and not organizing a meeting, for example, at the estate. It would have been simpler, more intimate that way ... She cast aside her doubts and pressed the handle. It yielded slightly. None of the doors had locks, only professors and masters had entrances with bolts. Of course, the ones who didn't have their own residences. Some, however, preferred the top floors of the dormitories, which were as comfortable as the apartments. However, over time, as a magician's health deteriorated, he was taken under the roof of one of the highest-ranking Archmasters. He then received the lifelong care of the best medics and healers, and his place in a comfortable mansion.

The little room was, one might say, just right. Speckled with a mass of childish elements like rag toys and colorful cards stuck to the flowery wallpaper that pranced, yellowing on the walls. There were curtains in the windows, structured like cobwebs already torn by the wind and as shabby as the walls. There were two beds one above the other, giving more living space for the girls. Under each window was an ornate, massive desk with rows of drawers and piles of papers. Next to them were chairs covered with velor cladding, stained here and there. On the side of the door were two modest dressing tables for each of the girls, as well as spacious closets located in the corners. Everything, bathed in the rays of the lazy sun, looked dull and sleepy. She walked around the room several times, examining with the curious eyes, small equipment and woman's stuff on the countertops. It was a little while until noon, so she decided to read. On one of the desks she found a book on the magic of healing. She was going to refresh her memory.

The girl climbed the steps quietly. Her soft leather slippers didn't make the slightest noise. She wasn't expecting a guest, because who would have come to her? The roommate was only the person with whom she shared the space. The only thing they had in common was that they attended healing classes together, otherwise they probably wouldn't have exchanged words. She was one of those who nobody liked because of the social status. It was well known that the children of the aristocracy always had a better start, and that truth was as old as civilization itself. She herself didn't make it easier for anyone to get closer and after a while she was pushed to the margins of the community of young novices, which resulted in extremely big outbursts of resentment. So, whether she wanted it or not, she was forced to stay in her own company or commune with plants in the charming greenhouses. Relationships with others remained cold and sporadic, so she was stuck in indolence and anger at everything. After the incident with Lilian, irritation was boiling in her, no one felt sorry for her despite the help of the older girls, but she was worried about herself for the first time in her life.

She noticed the slightly ajar door. She hesitated. She reached out to the brass handle in the shape of a vine leaf, pushed the door hard, and it responded with a silent opening. By the window a huddled figure was sitting on a stool, intensely analyzing a book. She recognized the visitor by hair and black robes. The guest was so absorbed in reading that didn't notice her. The lips moved in time of lines being browsed. If it weren't for the sunshine, she would have noticed that her skin was glowing from the blue light and the accumulation of healing powers. Falera wanted to turn on her heel and run away, although something held her back, as if an inner hand had been commanding her to remain there. She heard noises in her head. They were buzzing in her ears like a flock of intrusive mosquitoes.

Lilian noticed her as she stood in the center of the entrance. She couldn't let her go. She knew what she was just thinking. Escaping would be the biggest failure, so at the instigation of the botanist, she used the Speech of Whispers. The girl didn't expect an attack. Lilian's head was filled with visions of what the young intrant thought about and these were smooth stairs leading down the dormitories, then paths, and finally the ubiquitous green veil like a mysterious hiding place in which no one would find her. She looked up with her eyes burning with white. Falera stifled a scream. And if it wasn't for the mage's will, a dozen inquisitive eyes would probably have gathered immediately. She put down the textbook and moved closer. And the closer she was, the glow in her pupils got smaller. The inner flame was extinguished, but the Whispering continued. The apprentice's chest rose in time of her rapid breathing. Lilian closed the door and pointed to the stool by the window. Farela sat on it without the slightest objection, clasping her hands.

"Let's talk."

"Maybe we can talk normally, ma'am?" She stammered out with her lips pale with fear.

"Alright," she rumbled again, but this time the sound felt more dull and distant, as if it had been sinking into the depths of a dark well.

Lilian returned to her pre-Speech of Whispers state. Her forehead was slightly sweaty, as it still took some effort, but the thick mane of red hair masked the strenuous activity.

"Thank you," Farela said, eyeing up the black-clad girl.

Lilian knew that look well. The young mage regretted nothing.

"You know what I'm here for, don't you?" She began, silently hoping that the troublesome conversation would soon reach the longed-for finale.

"Of course," she snorted.

"You have to always be so biting?"

"And why does it bother you? You don't know me anyway."

"Maybe I'd like to know you? Haven't you thought that by such behavior you will not attract friends, but only enemies?"

"Someone asked you for a sermon?"

"Actually, no." Lilian propped her chin with her hand.

The view outside the window was very promising. The youngest magicians had a great time playing ball in the alleys.

"So what did you come for?"

"Well, I just wanted to apologize, but I see that it was pointless."

Falera's eyes widened. She didn't believe Lilian.

"Excuse me?" She said, somehow too hurriedly, because the words were more like gibberish than specific information.

"Yes, I came to apologize for the inappropriate behavior and I hope you will forgive me. I guess that's all, she said in one breath."

"You made the effort to come here to falsely prostrate yourself, hoping that I wouldn't go to the Headmaster?"

Lilian pursed her lips. She wanted to say something on parting, but ... she dreamed of a rhubarb pie. It was out of the way for her to engage in empty talk. She did what she had planned, she dared to climb into this pit called the living room. Now it was time to reward herself.

"Goodbye," she said, and turned to the door.

Farela overtook her and squeezed between the gap in the door frame and Lilian herself.

"How dare you" she hissed, "to treat me like that?!"

Lilian raised an eyebrow. The student looked as if her senses had been mixed up. Sparks were coming from her eyes, and her hands were glowing alternately with fire and ice.

"Calm down, or you will hurt yourself!" She ordered firmly, though she hadn't used that tone for a long time and she didn't know what it sounded like.

The intrant was getting more and more furious.

"Falera, goddamn it, buck up!" She slapped her face.

It worked, but only for a moment. The magician quickly realized that the girl fueled with anger a power that she couldn't control in any way. She noticed that the suffering girl's eyes got the expression of pleading for help. She tugged at her robe and pulled her to the center of the interior, barring the door with the same stool on which she had rested recently. Dazed, Felera was in the vortex of escalation. Lilian remembered seeing something like this before. At the Capital Mages School, one of the apprentices set himself on fire in the small town square just in front of Evans' house. Sometimes the power just killed, she had to accept it or try to save her. She chose the path to a consciousness fighting heat and ice. The speech of Whispers seemed to be the most appropriate method again. Breaking into the novice's skull was not a problem, but there she saw... the way to the worst nightmares. The intrant was in the center of the terrifying scenery. Lilian could see the blood and the belt that hung over her, curled up in the center of the oval room. A scream cut through the thought. She didn't recognize the man who had abused her. Falera kept her out of this memory zone. She fueled fear mixed with anger, and drove it in the wheel of constant torment. Lilian didn't know what to do. She wanted to cry. She couldn't, not now, when cringed, she needed support. So she spoke gently to her as she stroked a mop of her smoldering hair. She assured her that she was safe and that no one would hurt her anymore. It took many breaths for the words to successfully settle in the mind of the hurt child. She supposed the incident had triggered the opening of old, scarred memories. These caused a wave of destructive power. She surrounded her and herself with a soothing and reassuring aura. She created a glyph on the ground and settled into its center. The treatments brought the expected results, the young magician became sleepy, thanks to which the outbursts softened, then disappeared completely. When the girl fell asleep, Lilian healed her wounds, and she herself rested nearby and waited until she woke up. She hadn't expected this, rather the opposite. She realized that she didn't let her imagination run away with her, and that young magicians weren't so defenseless. Youthful arrogance results in an increase in the wave of power. She was puzzled by what she showed her. Was it a cry for help or a deliberate creation just to win sympathy? The pain Felera felt was real through and through.

She couldn't remember how many clock strikes had passed. She must have taken a nap, because she was roused from stupor by a vigorous tug on the sleeve. She opened her heavy from sleep eyelids and saw a girl squatting down and watching her closely. The tousled hair stuck out in different directions, but she looked conscious.

"I see you're better now." She yawned.

Felera nodded and sat down beside, leaning her back against the dressing table.

"Are you okay?" Lilian consciously prepared for the scolding.

"Yes," she whispered.

"That's good."

"What did you see? You know, when you spoke to me in a way unfamiliar to me."

"Enough." She leaned her head against the wall and closed her eyelids, on which still was sticky sleep.

"What?" Felera repeated with more emphasis.

"Torment, is that what you wanted to hear? I saw a poor, frightened child being beaten to blood by someone he once trusted. Will you tell me who he is?"

"Does it matter?"

Out of the corner of her eye Lilian noticed that Falera's pupils were vitreous.

"It always matters, since you can't get over the nightmare that has probably caused what you are like to others."

"You're too smart, you know?"

"No, I'm not, but I can listen and see more."

There was a strange atmosphere in the air, so conducive to confession. No one is ever sure when it happens, it suddenly falls on people and opens their souls. The aura was also favorable, the sun was going towards the horizon, dancing for a moment more along with the shadows of garden trees. The birds fell silent, and the only sounds they heard were the music of the wind and the single words torn from the mouths of mages walking down the corridor.

The student took a deep breath, as if giving herself courage, but she knew it was a vain effort, and boldness in this case was nothing.

"This is my father ..."

Lilian opened her mouth slightly. The young mage continued.

"He always dreamed of a son. Oh, you have no idea how many times I heard he wanted an heir. And he had daughters. Four girls year after year, each time more delicate and sickly. He cursed every time the midwife took the bundle from the obstetrician. He didn't look at the children. I was the second. The oldest sister died less than a year before I discovered my magic talent. First, he beat and offended her for not being a boy. There was even a time when he made his handmaids dress her like an adolescent just so that he could fantasize about having son. He cut her hair one night with a horse mane cutter. I'll never forget her crying all day. Then she died. Nobody knew why. She faded out as the stars in the early morning sky. Quietly. The funeral was fast, without major ceremonies, as if the father had been getting rid of a punk. After her death, all the hate fell on me. The mother tried to protect the youngest daughters, she even slept with them to prevent the tyrant from reaching them. Many times she herself bore traces of his impulsiveness. One evening he hit me so hard he cut the skin just above the collarbone. The wound started to bleed a lot, and he was furious that I was dirtying the floor. That night I felt the power pouring into my hands. It started at heart level and climbed higher and higher to the shoulders, then flowed down to the fingertips. I sat huddled in a corner bleeding and praying to the Redeemers for his death. It happened so fast. He got closer waving a leather belt studded at the sides, and I closed my eyes and in my mind I saw him burning. Fire was consuming his disgusting, fat body. For a fraction of a breath, I heard the whistle of air as it was cut by the belt, inexorably approaching. I put my hands over my face and focused on the fire again. I don't know how it happened. First, tiny flames jumped from one fingertip to other, then the fire was all over the hands. I was surprised to see it, and he stood over me with the pain tool raised. I didn't hesitate. For the first time in my life, I was sure. I only heard him screaming that the last thing he needed was a magician at home and that I wouldn't see dawn anymore. He took fire. I was watching him. Not once did I look away. He stumbled and howled, trying to smother the flames. But they came out of him and wrapped around him like a shroud. My mother ran into the room, followed by several awakened servants. Neither of them helped him. They waited for him to evanesce. The smell of the burning flesh was in the air. It settled in a cloud on everything it touched. He sizzled for a longer moment, as if the process itself hadn't been to end. I relished the sight of the corpse resting at my feet. He shrunken and curled up, baring his teeth from his lipless mouth. A strange mist appeared on my mother's face. I couldn't guess what she felt, but subconsciously I knew she was grateful. The next day she packed my things and kissed me affectionately on the forehead right outside the gates of the Magician School. I didn't get there in a carriage, but on foot. I was glad that it was the end, and that awaited me a life in a place that was not marked with the blood of my sister and mine. I was wrong. They quickly found out what status my family had. They hated me for my father's money. And here I am, mad at the world. I don't allow anyone to get closer to me, and I discouraged those who wanted to be friends with me. I think that's it. Now you can report to the principal.

She got up and went to the window. She folded her arms over her chest and watched the lanterns twinkle in the light evening breeze.

Lilian was speechless. Usually she had a lot to say, but this time the voice was stuck in her throat. She had never experienced anything like this, although she had quarrels with thugs on the route. In the Capital School of Magicians no one destroyed or brought anyone down, just because of being a member of the aristocracy.

"I don't know what to say." She finally managed to speak.

"You don't have to say anything."

"I wish I had wise words, but I don't. Forgive me the earlier judgments. I was unfair, not trying to get to know you."

"It's okay," she sighed. "This is normal. I am myself like that. I don't want to see these good qualities in others." She turned to Lilian. "I learned to defend, and the best defense is a good offense. This is what my father taught me. It's a bad teaching, I know it, but other magician would have left me in this room and wait for me to die. Sometimes I wonder why it didn't happen sooner and I didn't burn in my anger? You had to show up and make me realize that sometimes it's worth being yourself. Thank you. Just like that. And I don't." She held up a hand. "I don't want anything else."

"I won't tell the principal." Lilian stood up and smoothed her robe.

In response, she received a nod of relief.

"I'll go now. Probably Morien is wondering where I've been all day."

"Go. I got something to do."

She walked over to the deliverer and stretched out her cool, small hand. The magician returned the gesture and left the room. She ran down the stairs, and in her head circled a million thoughts that she couldn't control. They were mixed with pain and suffering. The feeling was fueled by sadness and a desire to shed a sea of tears. Falera's tragedy opened her eyes and Lilian swore that she would never judge anyone again on the basis of guesswork and understatement. Meeting her became a breakthrough.

CHAPTER IX

David wandered the drab streets of the city muttering to himself. He was still in it, but it wasn't a forced stop. He had established a lucrative business with traders of precious stones, and tended to it with a delight befitting a real dwarf. The days passed one by one so imperceptibly that he didn't notice that he had settled down for good. As the weeks passed, his relations with the woman with whom he had shared his life for some time warmed as well. Now he didn't think about the tracks and mud forcing the caravan to make longer stops. He warmed himself at his home, setting his heart on a villa in the dwarves' quarter, abandoned but exquisite.

The spring sun warmed his skull, and the ancestral blade accompanied him wherever he appeared. He often visited "Ram's Head" and although Mark had turned into a grumpy old woman, he still liked to hang out there. Darius couldn't stand him, which David enjoyed immensely, because he quickly escaped from his favorite place whenever the dwarf appeared at the counter. He didn't meet the Alchemist, as if he had dissolved into thin air. Sometimes someone mentioned in a game of cards that he had seen a strange person on the walls, with glowing eyes and a ball of white energy in a hand, with which had illuminated a path through the darkness. It's hard to say what darkness he lit up: whether that of evening sky or of his own soul, which was as black as the grave ground. Everyone who experienced this presence retreated, and his skin went numb not only from the cold. The heyday was over. It melted imperceptibly with the gold of summer, which spread like a ribbon to the horizon. The city rumbled from the hustle and bustle, the warmth eagerly attracted behind the doorsteps people who tilted their heads with delight towards the sun's disc. The air smelled of yellowing grass, fruit and herbs brought from beyond the walls. David liked those city scents. They reminded him of his hometown, once the power of dwarven technical thought, a subtly interconnected world of humans, elves and dwarves, who after all appeared as beings created from stone and gold. Once a great gate led to it, intricately forged for several centuries in solid rock by the greatest stonemasons of the era. Only a complicated mechanism and a hundred short-legged creatures with the help of huge oxen with curled horns and long, curly hair could tear it open. Now only one leaf remained, and anyone could enter the Garhendarhm abyss. You no longer experienced the guards or the front entrance stalls where lucrative businesses were conducted. It crumbled to dust, and the survivors, who had even a modicum of dignity, scattered around the world. Only the underground megacity was left, whose cavernous chambers are still illuminated by a cascade of lights once left by mages. It is said that this fire is a gift for creatures who like darkness, creatures who saved thousands from the plague, but the legends took on a completely different tenor over time. David was as proud as that city. Unyielding and tough, like the symbol of the creature worn on his belt buckle. Griffins nested on the ridges and acted as guards. Over the centuries, the dwarves learned to cooperate with them, and the more relentless ones had the honor of being moved on their wings. They loved gold as much as the dwarves.

The day was spent on pleasures. A game of cards in the merchants' guild, then small business, a visit to the stables, and now a stroll. Nothing special. The simple life he liked so much, though he knew it would become disgusting over time, and he would probably go to look for a trouble only to beat someone up. Tempted by the wind from the side of the main gate, he climbed the walls. Most of the time, the Guard didn't raise an alarm until there was a brawl, so the privilege was exercised, though surprisingly rarely, as if the view from there hadn't been all that great. However, attention was paid to drunks and Styg addicts. Dazed in their last stages, they often took on their shabby lives.

The stocky dwarf grotesquely, but with a grace that was only given to him, climbed the steps of one of the turrets. Before him, he could see the tiny houses crouched just outside the walls. Small plots, green gardens, small game, children playing when the adults bent their necks. And the road leading straight to the city. It was crowned with a gate open like arms inviting tired travelers and all the scum of this world into the interior. Dust was rising in the distance. The clouds wrapped the vehicles in a thick slurry so impermeable that, despite straining his eyes, he couldn't decipher the characteristics of the carts. So he stood and waited for them to come closer.

Hidden on the wall, Lonan also was waiting. In his coarse hands, he was rumpling vellum, which had only been delivered to the barracks of the City Guard a few days earlier. The long-awaited caravan of the Baroness was approaching the city, informed the general himself. Alvena was not a stupid woman, she predicted and controlled every move to inflict the most painful blows. The group wasn't consisted of armed men hired for royal service, but mercenaries - a ruthless band whose god was gold and blood. They were paid, endowed with the best iron enriched with runes, and unwilling to negotiate. Outlawed, so as to break the law without problems, all in the name of "the good of the kingdom." The alchemist knew that the one he was waiting for was traveling among them. The cavalcade was getting closer, clouds were rising from under the wheels. The wagons left behind a braid of agitated sand. The closer they got, the more clearly they stood out on the yellow-gray road. The carts were pulled by four black horses with shiny coats. One was an ordinary vehicle in which food supplies, water and weapons were transported. The other one without shutters, with a sign of a black eagle on the roof, belonged to the elite prison wagons dedicated to criminals sentenced to death. The man smiled with the corner of his pale lips and ran silently down the stairs. He went before the gate to greet the new arrivals.

David saw a figure flash just one turret away. He realized who the man was and just as quickly understood what the cavalcade approaching the gates was.

***

Lilian was getting used to the sadness that had nestled at the bottom of her heart, and though she hadn't mentioned the incident in the dormitory to Morien, she still carried it, and it got stuck and didn't want to go away. She fell silent. She devoted herself to lonely meditations more often and wandered sadly in the vicinity of the School. She analyzed what she had heard. She was bidding with thoughts that whispered all kinds of solutions. She couldn't come to order. She wanted to put herself in Farela's place, but images of suffering obscured the rational analysis of the problem. She suffered in silence, scratching her visions again and again. Relations with the young magician remained neutral. The lecturers noticed that the girl changed, she spoke more often, and her relations with her peers warmed up as well. After a while she gained a friend, but secretly kept an eye on the fiery hair magician. She was someone important to her, a person who not only saved her from bad fate, but also a confidant of a secret. Lilian didn't betray herself, she also felt that her feelings for Morien were fading away, as if the routine had been burning passion. She blamed herself for it. Morien, in turn, was puzzled. The redhead didn't sleep much, ate little and disappeared from the quarters for hours. Attempts to get into the self burned on a flash pan. With time, the mysterious behavior began to give sleepless nights also to him.

The magicians continued to write letters to the Archmage, even though the mood at the University had thinned a bit, or so it seemed. They controlled the situation of the megacity from behind the walls. The servants turned out to be the perfect informers, the mob who loved whispers and gossip. Quickly caught up in a web of intrigue, they became the tools of magicians. Fear mixed with curiosity and readiness to fight emerged from every darkest crack. Lilian didn't want to participate in it for anything. She was accosted many times in the courtyard, with a roll of parchment hastily stuck into her fingers. She usually read novelties and then burned it, hidden between the bookshelves in the library or shielded by the green curtain of the greenhouse. She never wrote back. With time, she was excluded from the correspondence list, as if the conspirators simply had quitted and plunged themselves into a thick conspiratorial soup. She started to suffocate. The alleys seemed too narrow, the shadows of the trees too long, and the dining rooms and lecture halls were oppressive and overwhelming. The abandoned plan to go beyond the walls returned intensified by an intense longing for the breath of the city.

"I'll just take the lumber," she thought. "I'll take it and come back. Nobody will even know I left. I'll just take a walk. It's just a clock strike, maybe two," she sighed.

She didn't delude herself that it would happen. The open gate would have not only woken up the desire to lay up in the dark alleys, but probably, when she got what she wanted, she would have left the gates of the cluster with a broken heart and the wind tearing the red hair. Maybe somewhere in the backwoods she would look for wild magicians and live with them? It was becoming all too tempting, more thrilling than the love she had for Morien, though... maybe she never loved him? Or maybe she just needed him to satisfy her need for security? The thought frightened, tearing her heart to shreds. However, he would stay here, would be safe, continue to teach and keep order, he would forget about her, he would forget for sure! And she would return to where the space is, without restrictions and rules. Happy and, moreover, free. The only obstacle she noticed was the lock on the door to the basement, and whether she remembered her way through the maze of corridors. Her head was filled with swarms of solutions.

Today she was sitting in the library with a book on her lap, staring out the window. Her mind traveled to the places she dreamed of. Morien glanced at her surreptitiously. He wanted to have hours of dialogues like when they first met. Talking about important matters, but also trivialities, such as over-salted soup or wet shoes. Debate about the situation at the University, discuss the dangers and solve pressing problems, but for some time she had only replied briefly: "what?" So he quit, but was still worried. Pale was marking her distressed face. He also noticed that the robe sadly hung from her bony shoulders. He concluded that she must have lost a lot of weight.

"Lilian," he began.

He couldn't withstand the tension that grew inside him and was becoming a glass through which he couldn't reach her.

She turned her head. From under her lowered eyelids she asked indifferently:

"Did you want something?"

"Yes. I wanted a nice chat over afternoon tea. You know, such gossip, that is, who burned uppers to whom or poured soup in the canteen."

"Aah," she snorted casually.

"Are you okay? You look haggard. Maybe a hot cake will improve your mood? I will say ..."

"No, no, it's not necessary. I was pondering." She waved her hand in front of her nose as if shooing away an insect.

"So what are you thinking about? It must be fascinating since you are always worried about it?" He tried to get a little bit out of her.

She settled back in the armchair, sitting on her hands.

"About nothing special. I think about the forest and the birds, the sound of the water in the streams, the cold wind on a face and a wet hair from the rain." She sighed heavily.

Morien understood her longing. He realized she had entered the state he feared most. He also knew that he couldn't let her go beyond the gates.

"You know you're safe here. You know I couldn't bear it if you get hurt. You know, right?"

"Yes. Don't worry, these are just such minor matters. Let me dream at least. Dreams won't open the wings, no worries."

"Promise me you won't do anything stupid." He got up from behind the desk and walked over to her.

He looked down at the girl. He cast a long shadow that absorbed her entire body, and her long white hair, like a crown, glowed under the afternoon sun.

"Dummy." She held out a pale hand. "And where would I go? To Mark? They would find me sooner than you could pronounce the protection spell." She smiled slightly at the words, but it was more a smile of bitterness than amusement.

"I know you, my feisty mage," he addressed her affectionately, taking her slender fingers in his hands. "I know you well enough to know you won't last long here. By Redeemers, you've endured more than six months, even more. I should have guessed you are bad. Forgive me." He lowered his head.

"I'm fine," she contradicted his words. She knew the truth in spirit. "Don't worry anymore." She rested her head in his hands. "I miss, but it will pass. Same as when I came to the Magic School in the Capital. It's a matter of time. The alchemists will get bored and will go, the Baroness will let go, everything will return to the state it was before my appearance here," she whispered.

"You know perfectly well that it will not happen."

"Then let me think about it that way."

"I won't harass you anymore. Drink a little tea. Why don't you go for a walk?" He kissed her forehead.

"I think that ..." The school principal entered the room. They jumped apart as if someone had poured a bucket of boiling water over them. The old man sized up each of them individually, but his eyelids didn't even twitch. His mouth, on the other hand, was pursed in a grimace that only expressed irritation.

"Am I bothering you?" he began.

The hostess with flashed face, ran after him.

"Tea is enough, my lady, don't worry."

She curtsied and disappeared from view, all they could hear was the rhythmic click of her boots.

Lilian sprang to her feet, mechanically straightening the folds of her robe. The headmaster's presence must have been caused by something, and she had the impression that the news he brought wouldn't please anyone.

"You are not disturbing, master, we just talked."

"I noticed."

"What brings you, my lord?" The Archmage estimated his superior.

Extraordinary energy radiated from him, taking Lilian's breath in a way.

"Let's start from the beginning." He walked around the library several times and finally found a comfortable place to rest, behind Morien's desk. "I got a message today." He waved the scroll in the air. "A certain David wrote to me. Do you know him?"

Morien shook his head. So he took a second piece of news from the bag, this time with the seal of the city guard.

"Or maybe you, my dear, know who David is?"

"No, my lord, I don't know," she replied softly.

"Imagine he knows you. To make matters worse, he is a dwarf and quite influential in the city recently, I asked here and there. I didn't have much time for this, but I found out that he is a sales broker and a globetrotter. He travels in caravans with other members of the community, and it is a jumble of all kinds. He only stops in the winter in major cities. This year he stayed here exceptionally."

"What does this have to do with me?" She asked.

"I don't know. I got this roll. Now watch out. Earlier, the one from the Municipal Police was delivered. Incredible. My dear, you probably don't know how many friends you have outside the gate."

"I still don't understand."

"I'm already explaining. The mercenaries of the Baroness arrived in the city less than two clock strikes ago. Two messages were brought in almost at the same time, one from David being the first. I was finishing to read the first letter when the messenger, gasped and concerned, burst into my chambers with this one." He waved the paper again.

The landlady appeared in the doorway, with a teapot jangling on a tray. She placed it carefully in front of the visitor and waited for the Archmage to allow her to pour the brew. The guest, without interrupting the conversation, expressed his approval and let her go.

"Where was I? Oh yes. The Baroness' mercenaries. They have just made themselves comfortable in the barracks. Together with them is the Alchemist and another individual that I didn't expect here. But this is the work of the Baroness, so I should have known. Nay! It's a certainty, after all." He shook his head and propped it up on a wiry arm.

Morien and Lilian looked at each other. They slowly opened their mouths in undisguised surprise.

"Who, master, are you talking about?" Morien asked, though probably he didn't want to hear the answer.

"You know the renegade Seneh?"

A shiver ran down the mage's spine, and a cold sweat covered him.

Lilian looked at him even more confused.

"Who is it?" She asked.

Morien ran a hand over his chest.

"Remember when you asked about the scar?"

"I remember."

"He and Lonan are unstoppable evil."

"Exactly," answered the Archmage. "And if she has a Baroness's decree signed by the king, she can enter the School. However, there is a plus." He took a sip of his tea. "She won't get in with the Alchemist."

"Nice plus." The woman was irritated.

"We have an advantage. He only has daggers and paper. Remember, young lady, magicians don't give up easily."

"Yeah, right, they will fight on behalf of someone who put them in trouble. It's ridiculous! Old man, can you hear what you are saying? The only right solution is to put yourself in their hands without shedding blood. Or I'll find him myself and kill him."

"Enough!" The principal hit the table top with his hand. "You can't do it alone. He is cunning and extremely intelligent. Can predict any false move. Morien dealt with him, he's not just a mercenary, he's an elven shadow! Hired killer! There are few of them, but they are damn effective. Mages are their favorite targets. They kill them with jade before they can take their last breath. Seneh is Alvena's right hand man. Nobody knows how he found himself at the court of the woman who despises other nations. She gave him an education, but also a bad name. People say that he is her lover, but I dare to suspect that these are just fanciful theories, you know, flavors created by jealous maidservants. Lonan must be rubbing his hands at the thought of being able to work with him again."

"So what are we going to do?" She spread her hands in a gesture of helplessness.

"We will wait."

"That's it?"

"Yes."

"He's crazy," she sighed. "You're crazy, right?"

She only received a nod in response. The archmage drank up and as if nothing had happened, bowed and left, leaving them where they stood.

***

Mark put another polished glass back into place. There were still clay mugs soaking in the tub in the back room. As soon as David burst into the tavern, he ran out of it, with the parchment and pen in his hand, which he had drawn from under the counter, without even asking if he was allowed. He only managed to tell him that all hell would break loose soon, because more dogs of the Baroness appeared at the gates of the city. The innkeeper stood frozen for a few breaths. The door behind David was closing extremely slow, as if time had begun to pass more slowly than usual. When the Ram's Head door leaf finally made contact with the doorframe, he yelled at the regulars to go to hell. In response, he got huffs, curses and a scuff of seats. Several mugs glided towards him, but he dodged and urged the marauders, shaking his fist at them. The only maid also escaped from the tavern, furious that the sack was empty again and that she would most likely not come there again. He snaped his fingers also at her. The innkeeper's bitterness tormented him himself, and everything was senseless for him.

Darius was packing a bag in the back room. He was leaving the inn for good. He was sick and tired of it. The cold treatment disgusted him so much that he only slept there. Going out for many hours during a favorable weather had a great influence on his mood. He walked down the bustling and colorful streets, chewing a straw piece. No wonder the Alchemist called him a dog. Probably if he walked with his nose to the ground, it wouldn't have made a difference.

It was already graying a little outside the window, but it was still bright. The bird's trills continued to vibrate in the air, saturating it with tremors. Stuffiness flooded the streets, a storm hung in the air. They waited for it, because the heat had been tormenting the community for several weeks, and although the farmers were rubbing their hands because this would make the grain ripen perfectly and the vineyards would flow with wonderful, sweet as honey young wine, they still wanted to dance in the rain. The spy was afraid of meeting Lonan's old companion. A cold chill ran down the back of his neck at the mere sound of the name Seneh. He had heard too much of him to ignore it. Despite this, he had to go to the barracks to prepare a plan of action against the escaped mage. He thought that without Shadow, they would have been fine. Sometimes he wished he could bind magicians. He would have been on a par with the Alchemists and no hired killers would have been necessary.

He walked down the steps, with the bag slung over his shoulder and a quiver and bow in his hand. Candlelight spilled through the open kitchen door. He peered inside. The innkeeper was resting on a stool next to the tub and soaking his hands in soapy water. On the bench, freshly washed mugs were set in neat rows.

"You're getting rid of me finally," he said.

"About time," Mark muttered, taking the foam off the scrubbed vessel.

Water splashed across the wooden floor.

"I can see your enthusiasm, you are burning with joy."

"Oh yeah, I'm gonna dance with a broomstick. What a delight, after all, alone, alone for so long," he sighed. "I have to celebrate. Yes! I will get drunk with a smuggling Styg. Oh, and when you leave, pay me. You owe me six gold coins."

Darius' lips twitched in satisfaction. It was hard for him to admit it, but he was used to the innkeeper and even liked him. And although the last argument ended with a bruise on the face, he still trusted that the peasant was a decent man.

"Yeah, yeah. An old miser only with gold on his mind rotten from wine. You rip off like dwarves, you wangler."

"I included your honorable annoyance, my lord." He made what was supposed to be a bow.

It looked like a wobbly gesture of a drunk.

"Great joke."

"At your service."

He counted out the coins and tossed them on the table. The innkeeper thanked with a nod and went back to scrubbing the mugs.

"Goodbye."

"Good ... riddance," Mark replied, looking at his face.

The archer picked up his lumber and left. Mark followed him, on the way he wiped his hands on his apron, which he tied around the hips. He locked the main entrance. Silence surrounded him, broken by the crackling of burning logs and conversations from outside. He realized how much he missed it. He made the decision to stay overnight and enjoy the benefits of the inn. The plan was to cut wolf loose.

The archer walked slowly around the city. Even though the bag was heavy, he wanted to do his daily round. Outside the gates of the Guard barracks, the guards scowled at him. The reluctance wasn't difficult to decipher. As most people, they didn't like the Baroness' cavalcade. He also knew that no one would speak to him.

"Open up!" He screamed.

They stepped back and opened the door, which creaked, and yielded to the pressure of the muscle. The paved courtyard appeared in the crack, and in the background he could see fragments of carts standing close to each other. Between them were the Alchemist and Seneh. They were discussing something. Broken lines of sentences echoed off the stone walls. He didn't feel they were arguing, though lively gestures might have indicated it. They talked about rather trivial things, horror of horrors, they reminisced. He slipped inside, and the heavy gate closed behind him. The clatter of the latch tore the debaters apart, two pairs of eyes turned to him. A strange paroxysm of cold swept through his body. He swallowed, straightened and adjusted the bag. He crossed the courtyard, intensively clicking his heels. Inside, he trembled like an aspen tree. A condotierre sized him up contemptuously.

"You are finally here," Lonan muttered.

The runestone loomed in his bony hands. The mage looked at it with delight, and from time to time tossed it up very pleased with himself.

"Mark stopped me." He indicated the entrance to the barracks. He wanted to absolve himself this way, but quickly realized that he looked like a schoolboy now. "The fool asked for an extra fee."

"I would have paid him back with steel." Seneh's voice vibrated in Darius' ears.

The depth of color penetrated the brain. He wanted to look at the mercenary, but he shaded his face with the large hood of his leather coat, covered with the dust of the road he had walked not so long ago. Only individual wisps interspersed with gray had freed themselves outside.

"It's a pity to dirty good steel," he tried to handle the situation.

Seneh squinted and turned to the newcomer. Darius could see the narrow slits of his eyes, almost drilling into the tissue. Shadow reached to the hood and took the cover off with a sweeping motion. What the spy noticed bore the hallmarks of many years of blood service. The Alchemist's friend was an elf, but not the one he had seen on the route or in the city. A piercing terror emanated from him. He fed his surroundings with it, pouring it inside like the nectar of poison. A wreath of hair gleaming like a sheet, tightly tied at the nape of his neck, framed his terribly emaciated face. Now tousled thanks to the strenuous way. A long scar with ragged edges stretched all the way to the brow bone. An eye seemed unharmed. Shadow was looking at him from under the curtains of surprisingly long lashes. He was twisting his mouth in an unreadable grimace. This face endured a lot. A face scarred with wrinkles and affects deeply seated beneath the structure of the skin contained the image of an angry mask.

"You can always break his neck," the elf thundered.

"Yeah. That's right," added Darius.

The alchemist moved closer to the spy to finish the pleasantries.

"This is my friend Seneh." He pointed to his companion.

The fair-haired man bowed low.

"Your fame is ahead of you, my lord."

"It's a good thing not the head." Lonan laughed. "Find the quarters, the commander of this lousy place should have already prepared something. You will find him in the office, in the barracks." He defined in which direction he should have gone.

Darius looked at the indicated place. At the end of the square was a narrow passage, a sort of gorge leading to the deeper part of the barracks. There were also the most important administrative buildings, training rooms, canteens, latrines and everything necessary for existence. The square was only a place which was crammed with the stables and smaller tenement houses for the grooms and service. The place was constructed so cleverly that during the riots, the enraged crowd, even if it broke through the gates, would have been stopped in a narrow passage with turrets on both sides, at the top of which were guardhouses. However, Darius thought the place was a trap. Nothing could be more wrong, as he was about to find out soon. The air without natural circulation stood still. Stuffiness was penetrating the nostrils along with the stench of sweating bodies, latrines, and steel. The only ornament against the gray and dilapidated walls was the ivy laboriously clinging to the irregularities in the wall with its claws. One realized how hard it was to exist there. The blackened leaves dried in the twilight of the barracks buildings, still clinging to the plant as if they had wanted to remain there as a reminder of their former glory. He felt a depressing aura. He began to understand why people disliked the Guard so much. The king used to issue a decree once a year, in which he announced that there were recruitment to the ranks of this noble institution, so those who balanced on the margin appeared within the borders. They received nourishment and basic education - the law required future guards to be taught writing and counting, yet they suffocated. A drill, swordsmanship and harsh living conditions toughened the body, although they appeared to be magicians locked up behind the walls of the Schools. Frustrated, oppressed and fused with stone, deprived of decency and good manners, but obeying orders. A mob worthy of Seneh and Lonan. Now the mercenaries joined them. Darius knew he would find gems from noble families among scum, proudly bearing family crests on their belt buckles.

He traversed the narrow passage between the turrets and found himself on a large square where the stationed people could move freely. He was invisible to them. They lived in a familiar and seemingly safe place. From duty to duty, from patrol to patrol, from guard to guard. They spent their free days on getting drunk and having fun with whores who were willing to take their pay, and often also dignity. Many suffered from embarrassing diseases and were often hosted by barber surgeons or healers' guilds financed by the city treasury.

Finding the commander's quarters was no problem for Darius. A low, stone building, slightly protruding from the others, with a large wooden sign with the words "Command" on it. He turned his steps there, but couldn't even get halfway, when he heard a loud voice:

"Hey you, blondie? Yeah, you."

He turned his head to make sure that he was called, though this was the first time someone had referred to him like that.

"Finally, come on." The dark-skinned stranger made a summoning gesture.

He furrowed. The short gentleman in a leather vest was still waving his wide hand to him, not carrying about the newcomer's cloudy forehead.

"Are you talking to me, farmhand?" He exclaimed.

"Do you see other blondie here?"

"Call me that again," he hissed, "and I will ..."

"Don't get so tense, younker, or you will burst a blood vessel."

"What did you call me?" Darius was foaming.

"What a dude." The stranger got irritated. "I've been preparing a nice quarters for you since the morning, to place your lord asshole well, and you insult me?" He put his hands on the hips, wrinkling his little nose.

"What did you say, peck?" Saliva spurted from the spy's mouth. He threw the bag on the ground. He placed an arrow, tautened the bowstring, and aimed it at the opponent's chest: "Take it back!"

"I'm not going to. There are too many such people here." He ignored him. "Come on, don't make a scene."

Darius was ruled by anger, and if he had the gift of magic, the man would have been burning with a living fire.

"Alright, that's enough." He heard.

The alchemist walked slowly.

"Let him take back what he said, otherwise he will die." He hold his position.

"Enough, I said!" He jerked the man and snatched the gun from him. The spy didn't manage to retrieve his property. Lonan possessed the agility of a lynx and he deflected all of Darius' charges with a power shield or blocked them by intercepting his hands.

The short guy watched the scene with great amusement.

"Like children, like children," he repeated under his breath.

Darius gave up. He was boiling and shaking, red in the face and almost humiliated.

"Give it back, dog!"

"Enough, I said! Calm down!"

He picked up the bag and passed Lonan. When he was delving into the gray of the previously prepared room, he significantly nudged the servant standing in the aisle with his shoulder. The alchemist threw a bow to the dwarf.

"Give it to him, because he's ready to cry."

"Yes sir."

Lonan nested in the room that had been raised on the upper floor of the command building. He deliberately asked for other place for Darius, he was fed up with the spoiled, wealthy duke. They might both be under the Baroness's orders, but he had no need to endure him. His love of comfort and the conviction of infallibility got on his nerves. He would have broken his neck with pleasure.

Darius yanked the property from the host's hands and sweepingly closed the door behind him. The room turned out to be a bit bigger than the one at "Ram's Head". Simple furnishings betrayed the military character of the place, but it had what was needed for existence, including a lame table leaning against the wall. There were rows of oil lamps on the walls. The stuffiness rose from everywhere, and the musty smell vibrated in the air, but it was quiet and bearable there. He stuffed the lumber without taking it out of the sack, in a trunk located at the legs of the bed. The furniture didn't match the style there, so it had to have been brought specifically for the needs of the apartment.

Gray twilight lay on the walls of the barracks, making this place even gloomier and unfriendlier. The last rays of the sun flashed over the walls, kissing the gray stone for the last time that day, which a moment later burned with the bloody glow of the sunset. The birds fell silent in the stone partitions. The guards ate a supper and cleaned themselves up. They knew that they wouldn't get a good sleep for a long time. The presence of the dogs of war and the Alchemist caused anxiety. They feared more than when Lonan came to the command building to discuss matters known only to him.

It was going to be a long and tiring night. Seneh and Lonan debated locked behind command doors. Shadow, tired from the strenuous journey, allowed himself to settle in the wide furniture, sipping a mug of Styg. He grimaced at the stimulant drug as if it had been bad wine. Probably if he wasn't exhausted, he would have reached for mead, but he knew he wouldn't have been able to take part in the deliberations. Darius was strolling around the room with his hands folded behind his back, and the Alchemist was tirelessly arguing with Kedom, who was a commandant. The large, squat, bear-like man sat on an equally bulky seat, smoking a bone pipe. The room was saturated with smoke. They didn't complain, even though the younker coughed every now and then, because the quality of the pipe vapor left much to be desired. The blond-haired man stopped by the window and struggled with the brass handle, which yielded after a while. Some night air got into the room, the drowsiness faded for a moment, then fell on the lids again like two heavy coins.

"Can't we sort it out in the morning?" He complained.

"We can," Kedom replied.

He settled back and inhaled a blue cloud, which swirled, created several vortices and enveloped the smoker.

"So what are we still doing here?" He spread his hands in disapproval.

"We are discussing," the mercenary cleared his throat. "Don't disturb, younker."

Darius wanted to counter it, but the inner voice honestly advised against polemics with the elf.

"Damn you!" He drawled.

"Don't curse, sit down and don't bust our balls." The commander indicated the bench by the wall.

Meanwhile, Lonan bent over the city map, analyzing passages unknown to the mortals who inhabited the walls. Old sketches of underground corridors dated back to the beginning of the city's existence. Some corridors were probably collapsed, others were used by thieves and smugglers, and still others were dug just outside the Magician's School, and they were the ones of particular interest to those gathered in Kedom's stuffy office.

Darkness fell on the city. The sun soothed shaky bodies during the day, and in the evenings the air became sticky and saturated with fear. The more religious ones brought sacrifices to the temple. They strove to appease the Redeemers, so that they would take the loathsome obnoxiousness off their shoulders. Candles were often lit in the shutters to illuminate a pall. Faces glued to the windows shone in the depths of night with whites. Insomnia spread around the townspeople like a scratchy woolen blanket.

Only two weeks had passed since the appearance of the carts. Mercenaries prevailed on the streets. Not only with appearance, but also with behavior, they drove the townspeople to their homes at earlier times than usual. Not only that, the whores preferred to be like mice under a broom at that time. The more courageous ones paid for the lack of fear with battered faces and crotches that ached for long nights. And the mercenaries didn't give up, didn't pay, much less did they prostrate themselves before anyone. The guards didn't intervene. Seneh - commander, constructed a plan completely indifferent to the actions of his people. This news reached the School of Magicians. The servants asked the headmaster to reduce the hours of their obligations, so those who lived outside the walls disappeared even before the grayness settled on the streets. Those living at the University area also benefited from the concession and devoted themselves to pleasant activities. It was not easy for the magicians, the increased rigor irritated the acolytes, they didn't like the earlier calling in at the dormitories, checks as well as talks about the alleged safety, alleged, because what was to threaten them? The most recalcitrant of them were sent to the principal. He drew the proper consequences. The unrest grew.

Lilian and the rest were scared. The only thing that bothered her at that time was whether the Alchemist would somehow get a map of the passage to the University! The security that Morien had talked about so often seemed fragile. And who, by Redeemers, was the one who arrived with the cavalcade? The one about whom such horrors were whispered? After all, no one is able to do such evil? She wasted her time, traveling in her mind to "Ram's Head". The awareness that she would do wrong was not that strong, on the contrary, it strengthened her belief that it was a good decision. She wanted so badly to get out of the trap. She longed for the scent of the underbrush. Her ears demanded the sounds of wild birds floating in the free and uninhibited wind of the wild forest.

She observed Morien as he woke up in the morning, ate and went to class. Like a shadow, she followed him, analyzed his gestures, wrote down the schedule for the day.

"One more day," she thought. "One lousy day. I will take what I have to take and I will leave. They won't find me, and he'll be safe," she said as she paced nervously around the library. "One more day!"

She rumpled a vellum in her fingers.

Dawn poured into the study bright and frighteningly loud. She was awakened by the scream of pigeons in the square. They pecked at grass seeds, cooing and crowding. A tangle of gray bodies interspersed with different shades of bird feathers. It was stuffy. Another day with the forecast of a storm, and although jagged fragments of clouds were floating in the sky, she noticed the moisture bursting into the room. She sweated. She felt in her chest the weight of her shaking heart. Hair stuck to her temples tickled pleasantly, and her eyelids waved faster than usual. The breath came out of the lungs in quicker, shallow bursts. She looked around the room. She made sure what she needed was still where she had left it. Morien lived in blissful ignorance. She learned to manipulate him, though it wasn't easy. Deep down she still loved him, but constantly believed that she was doing the right thing. It's for the best. She would sacrifice herself for the good of the School! No blood, except her own or those who would have threatened her. Outside the walls, out of reach. Morien would certainly understand. He would forgive her in time. She would forgive herself! Intrants and staff would pardon her! She calculated patterns, anticipated every move.

She stretched on the bedding and fixed her eyes on the staff, which had covered with a thin layer of dust. She wanted to tighten her hand on it and experience the rough texture of the wood. It always radiated with warmth. Its internal illumination caressed skin with pulses of power. She had never thought that she would be tied to something so strongly. The irregular crystal flashed, fueled by her will. Inside, a blue light flickered, circling around the irregular shape like a small fish in a spherical aquarium. She knew that feeling of bondage well.

Morien was just munching bits of bread toasted on a tray. He greeted the girl standing in the doorway and pretending to be immensely tired.

"Good morning darling."

"Hello, my dear." She yawned slowly. "I'm so sleepy."

"Why don't you stay home tonight?" He put a piece of toast in his mouth.

"I'll take a walk. The stuffiness is unbearable, but I want to go outside. Will you need me today?" Her eyes gleamed with excitement.

"Today I have long and boring classes, then a meeting with one of the masters about weak students. May it not drag on endlessly, I don't like such meetings. Can you handle it? Maybe the hostess can do something for you? I know how you like candy. I've heard she has cinnamon buns planned," he soliloquized.

He didn't realize that only a few words reached her.

"Yes, that's a great idea. Hot rolls will cheer me up. And now I dream of a decent breakfast. You didn't eat everything, did you?"

"I left the crumbs."

"There can be crumbs, as long as there is milk with butter."

"It can be arranged." She caught shuffle with her ear.

One of the maidservants entered the hall. She was carrying a basket of freshly picked early apples.

"Let the lady look how beautiful they are." She handed her one. It had a light green skin, and the flesh yielded under the fingers. "Wonderful, right? They are perfect for cakes and buns, because they are sour. They will fall apart during baking."

She remembered those apples, one such tree was growing at the neighbor's yard. As a child, she sometimes had stolen apples lying on the ground. She had already forgotten what they tasted like. She dipped her teeth into the flesh, and the juice aromatically irritated the taste buds and ran down her chin.

"Mmm, it's so good," she said with her mouth full.

"If you mix them, sweetheart, with milk, they can make your stomach ache."

"Don't worry." She swallowed. "A stomach may ache from hunger, never from good food. She took another bite." Morien laughed and ate the last piece of toast.

"All right. I'll see you in the late afternoon. I will miss you!" He kissed her forehead and disappeared into the gray of the hallway.

"I will miss you too," she sighed, moving her lips silently as if the farewell had scratched the bottom of her heart. "I will miss you too ..." she repeated.

"Are you alright, miss?" The maid realized that her mistress must have been ailing.

"Yes, yes. Don't worry about me, I'm in a melancholy mood today."

"I'll improve it with a cake. I'll make it for dessert!" She declared.

"Great, I can't wait."

"Your milk, miss!" She heard.

She went to the kitchen and received a cup, having tossed the core into the heat of the stove. She thanked and plunged into the dimness of the house. She walked around the rooms as if she had been feeding on the pictures she would take with her. She wanted to stuff every detail into the meanders of memory, as if they had been the most precious trophies.

She hid silently in her current place. A few days earlier, she had asked for the hinges to be lubricated for no reason, as they were working well. She had made up a fairy tale, so the gardener smeared the joints with a large layer of grease. Now she wasn't afraid of its groans, which might have attracted curious eyes. She hadn't had time to air out the quarters, so now the night stuff was getting into the nostrils. She sighed. She leaned against the door and let her nervous breathing level out. She would miss the dust kittening in the corners, the clink of glass, the crackle of fire in the kitchen stove, the rustle of pages being flipped, Morien ... A single tear ran down her pale, covered with million freckles cheek, and another one hung on her lashes. She rubbed off the moisture with the sleeve of her robe. Heaviness sat down right at the ankles, she wanted to walk around the room, but her leaden legs held her in place. She sniffed several times. And it was supposed to be so easy, so usual ... She took the staff in her hand, the spark inside the crystal danced. She smiled at the object as if it had appeared to be a living creature. Blood red marked the stone, then seeped into the wood which quivered. The pads sensed imperceptible pricks, blood rolled over the grooves and merged into one. The little gate behind which the treasure was hidden was full of magic. She couldn't remain indifferent to it. She remembered debating with herself because the repository was sealed by ancient magic. She was wandering at the gate. The inner voice was rumbling. She surrendered to the will of the place. She felt the grooves in the gate. They were hidden between runes that burned tissue. They glowed and blackened under pressure. She smothered the heat. They yielded. The room was carved in rock. Its esthetics hadn't been important to the builders. It created an isthmus between the cracks. The oblong crate lay at the feet, old and half bitten by time and dampness. Inside, an unfamiliar heart was rumbling, attracting her and whispering insistently. It took Lilian a moment to break the signs ... She recalled her memories fondly. The moment when she touched the structure of the cane - perfect, shining with reflections which, under the influence of contact, crept into the clenched fist. At first she reacted with pain, and as her breaths went on, she felt pleasure. The staff chose, and although it allowed itself to be led by another mage, it made it clear each time that it belonged only to her and that only she could use its full powers. She had never wondered why it had been blocked by the gates that separated with seals from those who wanted to reach for it. Why were the ancient signs so strong, and why does it act the way it does? She felt confident knowing it was there. Over time, just looking at it helped to gather her thoughts and let the mind rest from important and less important matters. Morien couldn't understand the admiration for the object, but he forgave the ridiculous, in his opinion, behavior of the beloved, who protected the staff as the most precious treasure. After all, he himself had a nice collection of sentimental little things, which at first glance seemed worthless, but for him contained much of his life locked in a small wooden box.

She peeked out from behind the door, made sure there were no mistresses or elven servants running around every time she appeared within their sight. Besides, the stick wasn't small, its length equaled the height of the magician, and only the dancing crown of the boughs with the crystal trapped inside it protruded beyond the cloud of her red hair.

***

"Lonan! Lonan, damn it!" Darius run behind the Alchemist from the City Guard library.

They had returned from their reconnaissance this afternoon, but this time they were walking through the narrow tunnels underneath the city. They assumed that they would find the one who opened the inner door to the Magician School.

The man stopped and turned in the direction of the call.

"What do you want again, dog?" He hissed.

Darius kicked his heels and looked around with the wandering eyes as if to make sure no one was there. He renewed his call. The alchemist had no intention of approaching.

"What?" He repeated. "I'm not your minion."

"Let it go and come on. I want to talk."

"About what?"

"Not here. Too many eyes are watching."

"I have a minute, but be brief, you bastard. I'm already sick and tired of your presence."

"Just a few questions. I'll buy you a mead."

"May this mead be worth this lamentation," he gasped.

He wondered what the Baroness saw in him. Maybe really just his pretty face.

He returned to the dimness of the room, a place where no one had gone in a long time. The dusty volumes were moldy due to moisture. They were crammed one next to the other. The room reeked of musty skin and dampness, and in the corners were gray hideous cobwebs. Their inhabitants with ugly and long legs looked at the guests, hidden in the funnels of nests. Lonan stood in the middle and looked for a suitable place to rest. There was an old seat by the bookcase, over which someone had thrown a perforated wool blanket. The legs of the furniture were bent. The furniture groaned, then quivered under the weight. The mage snorted. He didn't want to land with his backside on the flooded floor. He supposed that the younker wouldn't have let him forget it for a long time.

"To the point. We have a few entrances to analyze. We'll explore again tomorrow, but the maps await."

The spy leaned against the shelf. His face got so serious that the Alchemist realized that it was going to be one of those talks about bees and flowers.

"Tell me about him," Darius began.

"About who, idiot?"

"About Seneh."

"What for?" He was amazed.

"I wasn't expecting an elf."

"And what about it? Do elves disgust you?"

"Come on, Lonan, don't bullshit me, just answer. This is not an ordinary elf. I haven't seen one like that." He spread his hands, taking a step closer.

"Better stay where you are." He made a finger gesture in the air, ordering the interlocutor to return to the place. "Because he's not an ordinary elf, you moron." He leaned back, but somehow not very steadily.

He dreamed of decent support for his aching back. Half a day in the tunnels with the neck bent resulted in its numbness.

"So tell me," he continued, adamant to learn the truth about the mercenary.

"What should I tell you?"

"I want to meet him. You know what I mean. I haven't seen him fight, how do I know if empty fame doesn't follow him?"

The alchemist moved on the wobbly stool as if he had been unable to find a comfortable position. "Uh," he sighed and crossed his legs.

Darius expectantly pressed his back against the bookcase.

"Where should I start?" He thought aloud. "Once upon a time ..."

"Really?" He bridled. "I don't want a fairy tale. I think I made myself clear?"

"Shut your mouth and don't interrupt, or I won't say anything. Where were I? Oh yes. A long time ago, a very long time ago when the country was torn by wars, mages fraternized with dwarves, and elves possessed sovereignty. There were seven clans of elves when the skirmishes of the separated wild fighters broke out over the tracts. They had culture, history and traditions. They didn't feel the need to fraternize with anyone. They remained as one body connected by threads of magic."

Darius folded his arms over his chest.

"Scattered across the territories of the then empire, they had the ability to move by will. In families, children were born with a power so huge that human mages didn't enter the lists against elven mages. It made no sense, since they destroyed armies. It was enough to initiate a conflict with at least one group, and the countrymen immediately appeared. They emerged out of nowhere, decimated the torturers and melted away in an equally enigmatic way."

"Does this lead to anything?" Darius cut him off.

"Weigh in one more time and you won't learn anything more," he hissed, and his eyes sparkled with a cascade of silver.

So he fell silent. It sounded like a load of bedtime nonsense told to children. Lonan sighed and began speaking again in a flat, dull voice:

"After some time, the people wanted to overtake the lands where the elves lived. They gave up the tactics of lightning raids, but they united and watched. The areas inhabited by the sharp-eared beings gave an excellent harvest. They didn't associate it with magic, but with the fertility of the soil. In the cold winters, the tribe didn't suffer from hunger or get sick, and the mortality was extremely low. The elves lived to a ripe old age, and family seniors passed on the secret of longevity by writing it down in books kept in secret libraries. There was a rumor among the mob about an alleged body strengthening elixir potions drawn from the blood of the ancestors. It was all just guesswork. And the elves were long-lived, but they died of old age just as humans and dwarves. The myth, however, grew from year to year, from decade to decade. People in a blind rush to the body refinement and the promise of a long life couldn't bear the well-being of the enigmatic beings who resided in the wilderness. The desire grew so strong that the united lands turned against the elves. The country was in chaos. There were casualties on both sides. Inhabitants dropped like flies, due to curses and diseases. They died of wounds and ulcers, and their bodies were ravaged by voracious, carnivorous vermin. Neither side gave up. The nightmare took its toll, broke will, caused bleeding to death. And when the humans began to believe that they had taken everything from the elves, there was one clan left, wedged between the peaks, in a place so inaccessible that it was almost a miracle to get there. There was only a narrow gorge separating them from the outside world - a pass like a light in a tunnel. There the survivors gathered. The crown of the mountains with its arms protected the remnants of the lives that were tightly packed in the middle of the valley. It was there that the last sovereign clan was based, and the care of the people was exercised by an ancient elven mage, stubborn as the rest. And when the refugees healed their wounds, he decided to issue a decree. The last from the independent lands, saying that the elves of this family would never bow their necks to humans and would always defend themselves to the last drop of blood. And so it was. Soon after that, the settlement was discovered and the inhabitants were killed. In an act of revenge, the bodies were left to rot and be torn apart by wild animals. The dying weren't killed, but left to die in torment. The area swarmed with wolves, which attracted by the scent of blood, plunged into screams of the torning apart. The torturers, how to put this, miscalculated. The sharp-eared beings showed a great will to fight. A handful of them managed to escape into the high mountains. Under the cover of the moonless night, they fled between the peaks. The ancient forest and inaccessible ridge engulfed them. They have vowed to rebuild the community, not to allow generations to forget who they had been and who they become. Memories were recorded in the "Great Book of Wrath", and everyone born in the rebuilding group, from childhood was introduced to the secrets of assassination, magic, agriculture and hunting. All this to protect what is most valuable - the family. However, time verified these aspirations. The land rose from ruins, new rulers sat on the throne, some better, some worse. Some were tyrants, others ruled carefully but reasonably, just like now. The purges were forgotten. The memories faded like bone dust, and daisies and poppies grew on their bodies. The forest took what was due to it. That's how the trough hidden between the peaks was forgotten. There are rumors that someone built a settlement there, which became a jumble of outlaws, people who don't fit the imposed standards. Apparently they live in a small group, safe and unaware of the history of this land. However, returning to the family, it has survived to this day. It raised extremely formidable warriors in its bosom. Hardened by the harsh climate, they were able to survive mountain winters, hunger and droughts. Skilled artisans, builders, or hunters, and all born of hatred. Sometimes those who, driven by the wind of separateness, want to live on their own, break away from this group. They are tough warriors with ice hearts. They emerge from the shadows and you don't even manage to squeal when the blade cuts your throat. Sturdy, emotionless mercenaries, as well as paid killers. The clink of coins attracts them, and death makes them happy. Some are called Shadows. They appear, carry out a command, and then vaporize like a drop hitting hot stones. Seneh is like that. He is one of the few dissenters of this breed, a purebred killer with an animal instinct. All of them walk according to their destinies straight into the arms of death, which appears as the mother's womb. As long as they breathe, they will kill. If you mutilate one of them and he thinks that the wound inflicted on him deprives the hunter's abilities, he will throw himself on the blade as a sign of honor. The price of freedom is premature death. Clan seniors make sure that in a sacred ritual memories of renegades are bound so that they don't remember the way back to the mountains, to the place where they were born ... that they forget the past, and only know the present, and that the future constructs their character. Sometimes, however, memories are released under the influence of strong emotions, and then the family rushes to eliminate such person. Seneh remembers, so he is pursued. Therefore keep your mouth shut, younker. What you heard is only for your ears, although I missed a lot of details anyway, because what do you need them for? You probably wouldn't understand anyway."

Darius listened to the story with a slight consternation. He had wanted to ask who the mercenary was and he got the answer. However, he hadn't counted on a history lesson from Lonan. He tried for several breaths to decipher the purpose of the Alchemist's story, so he stood leaning against the bookshelf, and the silence hung between them as heavy as the stuffiness that surrounded them from everywhere.

The alchemist stood up and straightened, his gaze pierced the archer.

"Satisfied?"

The man moved his lips to show that he had gotten what he expected. The mage walked past him and disappeared behind the door. Clouds gathered in Darius' head. He wanted to meet the elf, he wanted to learn about an assassination. He knew it would have been a vain effort. He would have only gotten a twist and would have been sent to hell. So he planned to keep a close eye on him and learn in secret. After all, she would spend all the way back with him.

***

Lilian pressed her face against the wall, putting her hands on it. The sheath containing the staff comfortably rested on her back. How grateful she was for the piece of leather that held the cane in place so that it didn't interfere with her walk. Now she was waiting. Single footsteps got closer, then receded, forcing her to retreat into the shadows. She tilted her head around the corner. One of the servants inadvertently had left the door open. Maybe she wanted the afternoon heat to flow into the house, or maybe she actually forgot? A shy smirk appeared in the corners of her mouth. The soft slippers carried her noiselessly toward the exit. On the threshold, she cast a last farewell glance over her shoulder at the place that had saved her from death, and which became the essence of knowledge and the quintessence of love hidden in Morien's warm hands. The stuffy air reminded her that she had left the walls. Sweat was beading on her skin. Was it from the warmth, or out of emotions? She glanced at the deserted square. During the classes, hardly anyone wandered the alleys, so she passed unnoticed. Several lecturers loomed in the distance, followed by a group of novices. They were moving slowly along the paved sidewalk. The elderly people equipped with canes was explaining passionately something that probably belonged to the hated fields. From the acolytes' expressions, she knew that they would have rather played cards. As they passed Lilian they exchanged greetings. She trembled at the thought that one of them could have come up with the idea of asking why she walked armed within the University, but fortunately they themselves had combat equipment in their hands. The Archmage had to have issued a decree she hadn't had time to learn about. The relief relaxed her breathing. She wandered around the square, then sat down and counted the clouds that marked the blue of the sky. As the group disappeared behind the college door, she almost started running. She wasted many breaths. She cursed that she hadn't stolen the knob from Morien that would have helped her get inside the basement, but he and the bag were inseparable form of existence and it would have been foolish to reach out to it. Apparently he didn't carry anything exciting in it, just a pen or chalk or that unfortunate brass door handle, but the feeling that she would have invaded his privacy worried. Nay! It terrified through and through!

The buildings grew and thickened as when she first had discovered this place. The green took on a more intense color, she no longer saw the half-transparent leaves climbing proudly on the hidden door, but the dignified, heavy foliage full of gray buds at the ends of the twigs. An ear caught a few hasty footsteps and scraps of broken sentences. She squeezed into the crack between the buildings. The footsteps receded as quickly as voices. Once in front of the hidden entrance, she stuck her hands in the thicket of vines. A vision of spiderlings and earwigs running across the skin flashed through her mind. She shuddered. The gates were there, she experienced the rough texture of the outline of the door, and beneath, of a cold latch. She tried to push, maybe somehow Morien forgot to lock it? His distraction was no match for hers, he didn't forget. She focused, her fingers pressed against the metal clamp. The heat marked the lines of the skin, and the hot metal flowed between the delicate pads. She squeezed into the crack, slamming behind the last chance to return. Freedom was at hand, literally. A ball of red flared on the back of the hand. She sealed the access and melted the hinges, lock, small metal ornaments and links. Now there was a thick, impenetrable darkness. She didn't want to light the oil lamps, she knew exactly what it would end up with. In the distance, water splashed and crashed against the floor, somewhere a gray rodent ran underfoot.

"Let's do it and get it over with!" She sighed.

With her hands spread wide, she walked down step by step, carefully examining the ground. When she reached the foot of the stairs, she lit the fire again, which this time she transferred to the crystal of the staff. She had a lantern fueled by its own magic. The illuminated walls showed ugliness and degeneration. She paused in the middle and recreated the map of the passages. She lost her way a few times and made a full circle, returning to the closet filled to the brim with scrolls and volumes. She hissed and, dissatisfied, took yet another path.

The ladder was still there. It emerged from the darkness like the most beautiful picture. It was enough to climb. The room was enveloped in silence hidden in the gray web of swirling dust. She dropped the ladder and slammed the entrance. She had to wait until dusk, just a few clock strikes. She curled up on the bedding, a void filled her from everywhere. She debated for a moment whether Morien would stop her, for she left a string made of power threads behind her that, like a hound, he could have read without hindrance. Would he let her go? And if he stoped her, would she be sentenced to watch the world from behind the bars of the school prison for the rest of her life?

Her eyelids drooped soon. She fell asleep, hugging her beloved stick. The sleep was light. Nothing danced on the fringes of the delusions, as if the heart had become a heartless stone. A murmur woke her. She sat up and started to listen. Her nails plowed the head of the bed. Heavy boots moved from one edge of the room above to the other. Muffled male voices were magnified by the echo of old and abandoned walls. Maybe it would have been better to go back to the corridors and wait? She was standing motionless when they were daddling. They had no right to thwart her plans! But it happened! Fire again seemed the perfect solution, but she restrained her temper. She might have inadvertently incinerated the entire quarter.

"How exhausting idleness can be!" She wailed in spirit.

She sat down heavily on the pallet and looked for the end. As velvety and soothing silence wrapped her again, she gathered courage and emerged from the room. The sour and nauseating smell of unwashed bodies hit her nostrils, then the pipe smoke still rising above her head. She tiptoed around the scattered objects and got out of the tenement house. How happy she was, and how much she thanked the Redeemers for the graying sky, for the gust of evening wind, and the stench of gutter. The narrow streets were almost empty. The few vendor girls bare their firm breasts, encouraging to have fun. She tied her hair at the nape of her neck and tucked the rest behind her collar. She kicked herself for not taking her coat. Maybe she would buy one along the way, if her savings had survived. Now it was time to visit "Under Ram's Head".

***

Morien felt strange. He was missing something, but he couldn't learn what. The meeting dragged on endlessly. Among the novices admitted at the beginning of spring, there were a few who were unable to cope with the power. The only solution turned out to be tethering. He hated it, because it involved a visit from a lower level Alchemist. He was still a filthy magician who, in a way, disgusted not only acolytes but also professors. In light of current events, he could have aroused even greater anxiety. With his back to the wall, Morien helped write a letter to the guild in the Capital asking for an enforcer. In the morning the messenger would set off on a long journey. The meeting thundered incessantly. The sky turned subdued blue. Morien was in limbo between the professors and the sunset red world. He drank the wine from the goblet and nodded to voices debating inside the stuffy office. The meeting was over and the teachers began to disperse to their seats. They paused for a moment, as if midstride, to end the threads, drawing Morien into a discussion that didn't interest him at all. Released from unpleasant duty, he turned to the estate and thought about the unfortunates. He tried to convince himself that it was for the best, and despite they probably didn't deserve, at least they would live and wouldn't end up as twisted pieces. Something, however, bothered him, something he couldn't decipher.

***

Lonan and Darius were walking wearily. Forced into company, they didn't chatter in vain. The fair-haired man was making circles in the air with an arrow just to keep his hands busy. The townspeople they encountered either spit at their feet or closed the windows. Uninvited guests aroused hostility, and if it weren't for a deep-seated fear, they probably wouldn't have reacted that way.

Seneh disappeared in the afternoon and so far they hadn't seen him. The assassin walked his own paths. He nosed. Sometimes he emerged next to Darius, taking his breath away. Darius could see the gleam of his yellow eyes in the shadow of the hood, and the sly smile that faded the moment the archer looked away. They glimpsed him as he sat on the threshold of Kedom's quarters, tenderly stroking the green jade blades. Darius didn't understand the love for this material, after all, it was not a permanent one. It was enough to drop it and it shattered into small ones. But the power of the weapon fascinated him, and he promised himself that as soon as he returned to the castle, he would search the bookcase for detailed records on the subject, or consult the magician. Lonan made sure that his companion didn't drill the elf too often. Shadow hated onlookers, he could kill people only because someone had the nerve to get too close. Darius obeyed the Alchemist, although the role of a doormat started to be worse than the disgusting woman. In the coolness of the moldy library walls, the magician explained what Seneh needed the jade for. He was also given a detailed plan to capture the mage.

If Lilian was dangerous, Seneh would kill her, as well as those who wanted to help the woman. Jade had another wonderful quality that killers loved so much, namely that a person fatally stabbed couldn't be resurrected. Destroy a mage with steel - they said - and another one will come and put him on his feet with a wave of a finger, and then the wrath of the mortally wounded will take away your mind and strength. That is why these blades were so expensive and so rare, and the only ones who possessed them and knew the location of jade deposits were the Shadows.

The evening was going to be deadly boring, maybe they would have fun with some girl. Darius thought of Agnes, which gave him a pleasant feeling in the groin area.

***

Lilian was looking around nervously. A fat rat crossed a path and disappeared between the stones, jumping straight into the gutter. She emerged more boldly from her hiding place and ran through the well-known intersections, tiny squares, and quiet alleys overgrown with perennials. The green respite of gray rose skyward, now nudged with a gentle breeze. She was invisible to passers-by. She became part of the mob that followed the beaten paths. She blended with the shadow, stopped at the thresholds, waited. Lighthouse keepers lit the first lanterns. Walking in familiar territory amazed her. The longing for ordinaryness stung to the blood. If she could, she would have choked on air, which despite stinking, was the air of lost freedom.

"I'm almost there," she gasped.

A few drunken dwarves staggered out into the avenue. Having noticed the wench lurking in the corner of the street, they took her for an extremely beautiful harlot. The accosted mage spat at them, saying that she would have preferred have sex with a boar rather than with them. They stepped back dissatisfied. She knew that the fools had gotten drunk at Mark's inn, as there were no other such places nearby. She turned. The dead end looked at her with the familiar window. She took a chance. The wall was overgrown with well-established ivy. There was a dim light in the window. She climbed slightly on her toes and peeked inside. Mark was sitting on a small stool. The huddled silhouette against the background of the dying fire appeared to be a misfortune that balances on the brink of imminent collapse. The decayed man hold a chunk of raw meat up to his face. With his other hand he was waving in a bowl full of suds. Only when he put the scrap on the table did she understand everything. The innkeeper apparently had gotten into a fight. As he was no longer young, the outcome of the skirmish usually became obvious. She was touched. The former employer, a bean counter and creep, was healing his wounds now, and deprived of the cook's support, he was soaking mugs in the tub himself. She pushed the door with her finger. Surprisingly, it didn't groan as it had used to. She looked towards the hinges. A thick layer of fat was sticking to the metal parts. She smiled to herself. She didn't intend to scare him, so she knocked.

Mark turned his face to the humming glass and saw the familiar face staring at him. Lilian was smiling shyly at him.

"Lili?" He whispered, as if he had been afraid that someone would come in and catch him at a shameful act.

"Can I go in?" She asked so softly he could barely hear.

"You can, just be careful, the windowsill is high." He stood up abruptly. First he glanced at the kitchen door, then jumped to the window vent to help her enter.

"I know this windowsill all too well," she chirped.

Mark's non-swollen eye gleamed with excitement.

"What the hell are you doing here?"

"And what do you think?"

"I don't know. Have you missed me?" He looked at the door again.

"I've missed my mandrake. Do you still have it?"

"Man... what? Ah, I've got it. That swine which the lousy Alchemist threw in the corner of the kitchen. Sure I do. I have everything you left."

"Then why didn't you send it to me?"

"Somehow it happened ..."

In the corridor they heard the small footsteps of one of the girls.

"Shit, get in." He pushed the mage into the pantry.

He closed the gates with a staple. Thus, Lili landed among the hanging hams, meats and vegetables in crates. Tucked in between potatoes and sausages.

"Delicious," she groaned, pleased.

She felt a growing hunger. Agnes entered the room. The magician was watching her through the crack enter the kitchen and leer at the host, who was standing midstride like a statue, between the pantry and the tub.

"Are you snacking again?" She muttered casually.

"Uh, um, yeah. You caught me." He sat on a stool and pulled up his sleeves.

"How's the eye?"

"I'll be alive."

"Comforting. Why is this window open? Insects will fly in." She closed it.

"I felt stuffy," he lied.

"That's news to me. You complain all the time, that your feet are cold, that your circulation is poor, and now suddenly it's too warm. Maybe you will say you have hot flashes?"

"I'm hot today. Why are you picking at me?"

"There's no one left. When mercenaries hang around the city, even the dwarven sponges don't care about spirits and stay in the guild. I brought the takings." She tossed a handful of coins on the table.

"Why didn't you leave it under the counter?"

"Calculate so that you don't say that it is not enough. I did my job and I'm going home. My mother is sick, and there are mouths to feed."

"Take the silver coin." He pointed to the table.

"Why are you so generous?" She put her hands on the hips.

"Take it and get out. My head aches from your screeching."

"Did you hear yourself?" She huffed, although on her lips appeared a delicate grimace betraying satisfaction.

"Go now." He urged her a little, already irritated.

The maid took the coin and left. Mark reached the hiding place in one bound, finding Lilian eating a sausage in full swing.

"I was struggling to chase this harlot out of the inn, and you've been eating here."

"You do it yourself, so don't complain."

"Alright, you've been forgiven."

He allowed her to finish. After all, he couldn't let her be hungry. Out of the corner of his eye, he watched the staff whose crystal glow shone, then darkened. The object's inner life pulsed.

"It didn't do that when you worked here." He pointed at the cane.

"No, it didn't," she replied with her mouth full.

"Then why is it flickering now? Let it stop. It's getting on my nerves."

"Oh, come on, it won't hurt you."

The innkeeper was still leering and kept moving away from the annoying object until he returned to the stool. "Your stuff is there." He pointed with a wet hand to a large closet pressed into the corner of the kitchen. "At the bottom, behind the blankets. I hid it so that this reptile wouldn't get to it."

She pulled out the bundle, and immediately her eyes lit with happiness. There she found what she hadn't taken with her, plus... a full purse.

"I didn't take out even a copper coin," he muttered. "You can count it."

"I don't have to. I don't know how much was collected." She laughed. "I didn't count, I just put coins in it. They were supposed to be for the further journey. Your honesty amazes me!" She ran up to the man and gratefully kissed the top of his head.

"Stop it, little witch, because you will scramble my brains."

She giggled in amusement and placed her hand on his cheek.

"We can do something about it. We can't leave you like that. What will people say?"

"What? They'll say that I was beaten, that's all. Don't worry about it!" Mark's voice trembled with fear of what was swirling under the red thatch.

"Don't be afraid, I'll correct this and that," she announced happily.

"No way, I won't let you touch me with magic, you could turn me into a toad. Shoo, woman." He was jokingly trying to push her away.

He knew she wouldn't give up, but in spirit he hungered for her warm skin to touch his rough, unshaven cheek. He had dreamed of closeness for a long time.

"Oh, come on, it's not a problem. You were a good employer, so kind, so honest, you forgave mistakes, you allowed a lot," she buttered him up. "Now it's time for a little good deed, let me do this. It doesn't hurt!" She brought her face close to his, peering into the depths of his irises.

"If you turn me into a toad, I swear to Redeemers that I will jump behind you and croak until the end of your days."

"An annoying frog. Sounds tempting, so don't provoke."

"Little red-haired witch," he retorted.

The girl crouched down.

"Now don't be afraid, okay?"

He nodded, appalled. Nobody had treated his bruised face with magic before.

She focused and surrounded him with a sphere of pure healing essence. Minor discharges skipped from one strand to another, making fragments of them begin to smolder slightly. Mark felt a warmth where she was brushing him. Unknown, penetrating heat coming through the skull. Lilian's eyes changed expression, they no longer looked gentle and warm, the color of the irises blended with the white of the whites as if she hadn't had any at all, and the skin became transparent and pulsed in time with the heartbeat. The energy ball consumed him as well. The air became stuffy and unbearably heavy, but he wasn't afraid. Somewhere in the depths of his shaky heart there was a being of peace, he didn't recognize himself under this sparkling dome. The wounds ceased to burn, and the swelling decreased with the flutter of the blood in the healer's arteries. The blind eye regained its joy of seeing. Lilian sighed and pulled down the curtains of her eyelids. When she opened them, the eyes turned yellow like cat's again, piercing and sharp.

"It's over. You're cute again."

He ran his hand over his face to make sure it wasn't a dream, but the events of yesterday had faded away with the flickering glow of her power.

"Unusual." He peered into the bowl of water, taking advantage of the fact that the suds floating on top had already disappeared. "Unbelievable and how fast."

"The simplest healing spell. Nothing special, believe me."

"Maybe for you, for me it's miracles." He gasped at the view. "And maybe would it be possible to make this furrow here," he pointed at his forehead, "smooth somehow?"

"Don't overdo it, okay?" She was laughing again.

***

Lonan stopped. He grabbed Darius by the forearm with one hand, and drew a good gulp of air into his narrow nostrils. He stood there for a while, like a hound that picked up its trail. The spy frowned and regarded him with undisguised interest. The alchemist froze, the threads of magic irritated the senses, broke into the pores of the skin, twitched under the tunic's skirts. His eyes began to turn white, at first slightly, then covered his pupils with a curtain of impenetrable barrier. The quivering flames of street lamps painted on the ground chaotic and frightening ornaments of night phantoms emerging from the bowels of the city.

"What's going on?" Darius seemed to be a ghost.

Lonan was changing, the covering he had worn became a translucent border through which the knots of black veins showed. They were pulsing, fueled by the blood as thick as pitch.

"She's here," he panted. "Not far. I can feel her, she used magic. What a stupid and mindless whore." A trickle of bloody sweat rolled down his temple.

Darius snapped his hand away from the sparrowhawk's grip that almost shattered his tissue.

"What are you talking about?" He gasped and rubbed the sore spot.

Lonan was panting excitedly. The essence of the magician's power was swirling in the air. He was tasting the purity and creation of the healing spell. He was nosing to find the direction it was coming from.

"She's near. I know that," he croaked. "Somehow she went outside the gates. I don't know which way, I don't know when. Most likely, she had created a shield to protect herself from detecting vibrations, and now she betrayed herself. She had to drop it to turn on the incantation. I know where she is!"

"We have to find Seneh." Darius gasped with excitement.

"Screw Seneh. He will find her himself, sense her just like me. He has the essence of mages in his blood. He knows where they are."

The spy raised an eyebrow.

"What essence? Secrets again?"

"Have you seen his hands?"

"No."

"Then take a good look at him next time."

"What for?"

"You will see."

He spun around a few times, tasting the air. The shadow of the black cloak followed him like the wings of a giant night bird. The archer saw the Alchemist in a frenzy for the first time. The mage drew a runestone from his purse. The object was pulsing and sparkling in his hand, and the rune carved in the center was glowing red. Lonan brought it closer to his face. The red gave way to blue. The hideous blackened lips twitched in growing ecstasy:

"There she is. I know where she went. Move your ass."

He ran down the narrow alley, followed by Darius gripping his bow tightly and ready to attack.

***

Morien was plodding to the estate, feeling a strange state of mind. Anxiety sat on his shoulders. He felt as if someone had taken something valuable from him. Unnatural fatigue was pulling him to the ground. He was breathing heavily. Painful inhalations and exhalations disrupted the rhythm of his steps. His neck was being bent by the weight of an invisible horse collar. And then he felt it ... The essence of magic, like a shawl woven from the thinnest threads, touched him casually, wrapped around him and allowed him for a subtle and elusive caress. He stopped. He knew who had weaved this essence. He felt that it hadn't come from the university. Too big dispersion of the essence of magic was caressing the tissues. The power swirled for several breaths, then let itself be led by the evening breeze.

"Lilian," he whispered. "Where are you? What did you do, darling?"

He ran home. The road felt like a wave of anguish, the cobbled avenues resembled an endless maze. He reached the door and ran into the hall. The lady of the house showed up immediately. From her expression he knew that nothing nice awaited him.

"Miss is out," she sighed sadly.

"Since when?" He panted.

"I don't know, my lord."

The blood boiled in him. He passed the woman and burst into Lili's quarters. Necessary items, clothes and books were in their places, nothing but the black robe and ... the staff disappeared.

He burst into the kitchen, looking for the kitchenmaid which he found bent over reading. "When was the last time you saw her?!" he seethed.

"Who, Lord Master?"

"Lilian!"

"During breakfast, sir." She got sad.

The servant girl who had served the magician an apple in the morning entered the room.

"The lady left right after you. I don't know exactly when, sir, because we didn't hear anything. I haven't seen her since then and I'm starting to worry. Please, Lord Master, bring her back."

"I will, don't worry." He put a shaking hand on the girl's shoulder. "I will, I promise!"

He left the house quickly. The night enveloped the city in deep black, the starry sky was quivering from thousands of sighs going to sleep. He stood for a while on the main alley, tasting the air, and analyzing the essence of magic accumulated in the walls. It was still here, but separate from the rest, fuzzy, though the pulsation constantly rumbled. She didn't get far, she certainly didn't make it to the route. She was stuck inside the megacity, alone and defenseless.

"Where can you be?" He thought. "Which way did you get out? Where did you go? I know you are close. But where?" He whispered. He sensed the worst-case scenario. The option of leaving the school through the tenement house flashed through his mind. "No, that's not it." He touched the sack and found the knob. "What are you gonna do, girl?" He debated.

He ran to the gate hidden behind the foliage. Storm clouds gathered over his head. He reached the spot, ran his fist over the texture of the wall. The entry remained unshakable, so it wasn't it! Did the guards, without consulting the staff, just let her leave? No! Impossible. He found the lock with his fingertips. An irregular lump of metal disfigured it. Morien's heart leapt into his throat, he felt that it was about to get stuck in it, and he would evanesce at this gate, where the only witness to the death would be this majestic green plant.

"You're a smart little fox," he sighed. "You found a way."

He wouldn't have been able to figure out the elements quickly, it would have taken too many precious clock strikes. The only way out was through the main gate. He was tempted to notify the Archmage, but his heart whispered something else. He would find her and bring her back, and in the morning the sun would rise over the horizon in the same way, and a new hot day would arise.

***

The mage stretched out delightfully on the bench. Mark gave her the evening meal, therefore the girl didn't eat enough. He enjoyed the visit, but it was mixed with a strange movement. He had a feeling that it probably wouldn't end well. He nagged her to leave the walls in no time, saying it was not safe there! Lilian answered with a charming puff of her cheeks, which made her look like a funny squirrel and moved the innkeeper.

The taste of freedom lazily warmed the magician's members. She calmed their senses and allowed them to rest, the muscles no longer resembled taut ropes. The skin didn't go numb, and the sweat cascading down the spine was gone. She was safe! That night she would leave the border, go to the track, and then out into the backwoods as planned.

"Mark," she said, savoring the sweet wine.

"Yes?" He broke away from the boring job of cleaning knives.

"Would you have a cover? You know, such a large one. I will pay. I didn't take mine, it is too thick, it would cause unnecessary stir in the summer."

"I think I have something." He rested his chin. "Yes, I do! Once a visitor forgot to take it, well done, too bad it is too small for me. It should be in the storeroom."

He left, with his tired feet scraping the boards. In truth, he didn't feel like lifting his legs, he had walked too much that day.

She looked into the glass, half of the drink flashed in the light of the lamps. She drank it down, a few drops ran down her chin, staining it with carmine. She rubbed the skin with her sleeve and leaned against the back of the stool. The fire was crackling pleasantly. Red tongues were leaping from one twig to another like joyful fireflies hovering over the meadow. Mark struggled with the lumber from the storeroom. She was shuffling and moving objects in search of the coat she had asked for. Alcohol played in the veins.

***

The Baroness' helpers ran to "Ram's Head". The Alchemist's blood was boiling beneath his skin. The bluish covering was emanating a power so dark that the spy was choking on the air that was forming around him a cocoon full of vile sparkles. The archer understood the fear he had heard about many times. The chill of Lonan's aura broke through the flaps of his coat, gathered at the tips of his fingers, and creaked when he moved them. Darius felt like he was in the middle of a completely unreal cold winter. The magician took the handle, in his other hand he clutched the runestone, the luminescence of which pierced the hunter's skin.

The vein bundles were swollen and hungry. The mage was thinking only about Lilian. He was tasting the breath, which in a thin envelope was vibrating around the inn. He was analyzing and arranging a convenient plan of binding. He was feeding on the artery heat, debating the construction of mana and concentrating on the task ... Only she existed.

"Are we going in?" Darius croaked in the dark.

Lonan took his hand off the doorknob.

"No."

"How is that?"

"She's in the back. She is not alone. It's probably a kitchen, there is only one way to escape from there. Stay here and don't play the daredevil. I'm gonna go to the back ... and ... don't fuck this up."

Darius rolled his eyes. He wanted to yell at him to shut up and do his job, but he merely nodded and, having taken his bow off, prepared an arrow. Now he was hiding in the shadow of the junction of two dingy buildings. Seneh was missing here! Where the hell is this elf? Well, these creatures love ambushes, and maybe...

***

Morien reached the gate. The sentries looked at the mage a bit wearily, he could see the tiredness on their faces. It was the hour that heralded the change and they were waiting. Getting rid of heavy leather armor from the backs, putting away the swords and cooling the body with cold water, like prose, and yet a long-awaited ritual. The air, heavy with heat, took away the will to live, even though the gray had already flooded the streets and took its hat off to the thick night that still choked the breath with the heat of day.

"Open up!"

"And where you, Lord Master, are running so out of breath?" The lower guard leaned on a sword.

The smell of sweaty body mixed with the scent of a leather mantle hit the mage's nostrils. He straightened up, brushed the hair from his face with the trembling hands and, having wrapped it around his finger, let it go. He wanted to appear composed, but unfortunately keeping up appearances was often pointless. However, he decided to continue playing this role, because now, with the restrictions issued by the Archmage, trips outside the walls of the University were, in a way, forbidden.

"I felt like eating dwarven beer, I haven't had it in a long time. I know it's prohibited. The same decree is also on my desk ... But, gentlemen, the tavern "Under Ram's Head" has been closed earlier recently. Maybe I will manage to get the glass before closing." He was boring the blue of the eyes of the man who held the way outside in his hands.

"Aaah." He laughed. "A little trouble with the woman, I know. You don't have to explain yourself, Lord Master. A beer at Mark's tavern always heals wounds."

Morien raised an eyebrow, then lowered it. He had the idea that men often, well, always flooded their throats when women stung them too much. So he continued the thread:

"You can put it that way." He made a sour expression. "Will you let me in, gentlemen?"

"She's fiery, huh?" The other man sighed, now leaning against the doorframe. "She's so wild. She has fire not only on her head, I can already imagine ..." he said knowingly. "And come back soon, she's probably, you know, waiting to make amends for being rude. What are these women doing to us ... go, sir, but be careful there. At this time of the day, wanders people sent by Baroness," he sighed.

"Do I have it painted on my face?" He held up his hands.

They looked at each other.

"We've seen many different thing in our lives ..."

The clank of a key opened the gate. The mage squeezed through the gap and plunged into the darkness of the city. The crunch of the guards' armor disturbed the almost velvety silence for a moment. It seemed to him that the city had died out, as if the people nesting in it had stopped breathing. All he could hear was the hiss of oil lanterns, around which the nocturnal insects whirled, completely unaware of death, lurking in the delightful golden glow. He ran down the alley. The block where the tenement house was situated was shrouded in darkness. He knew the lanterns had been put out by the lighthouse keeper leaving the quarter. The door groaned sadly, the interior was drowned in a gray twilight torn apart by the only burning tallow candle with a wick made of the remnants of hemp rope. Totally drunk wild residents were sleeping on the floor. To his nostrils came the smell of urine, unwashed bodies, exhaled digested wine, and tobacco, so foul that the dinner that had been to left the stomach, returned to his throat. He bypassed the sleeping people and found a way to the hidden room. She had been there! The crumpled bedding showed the outline of the silhouette. Delicate bursts of power nested in the folds of the bedspreads, still strong and biting the skin. He gathered them up and let them die between the partitions of his fingers. She also had left a smell, a delicate scent of rose and lavender water, which she liked to wash her face with. For a moment she beguiled with an imperceptible presence. Nerve strings torn by Lilian magic captivated. Now he was sure. He already knew what he would do when he found her and brought her to the School. He would send an official letter to the Archmage himself in Archal and to the king ... asking for permission to get married. And if they didn't agree, he would run away and, with the help of the priest of the Redeemers, promise her love until the last breath, the last word, the last blink of the eyelid ... He couldn't exist without her anymore, she allowed him to mature as a man. A small, red-haired girl with the power to rule the whole hermetic, full of secrets life.

He left the tenement house. The arms of the night spread out on the walls. He picked up the remnants of the traces she had left.

"Where did you go?" He turned around his axis. "Or maybe ... Yes, definitely there! Your stuff is still there, you wouldn't have moved without it, it's so obvious! Why haven't I thought about it before?"

He ran down the alley. Lights glowed in the windows here and there, accompanying the reflections of street lamps. The silence hummed, unnaturally dense, sticking like matter. The clatter of heels faded away. He felt as if he had been walking on a soft oriental carpet. The reality seemed to be in a strange sleep. He stopped. It was magic, but it wasn't from the Alchemist or any man he knew. A murmur scratched the silence, a shiver ran down Morien's spine. He increased vigilance. Confidence vanished with the exhaled air. Clenched fists, stimulated by the red glare, were trembling like lights trapped in menorahs. Only a short path separated him from "Ram's Head". The feeling that he wasn't alone arose again. The agitated hairs on his forearms rose and fell. Morien ignited heat inside himself. He was looking for a source, sensing. A shadow flashed past. The mage knew who it was.

"Seneh!" He growled furiously, and the honey glow of his gentle pupils got flooded by the purple fire.

A pair of yellow eyes flashed in the shadows. Like a fat cat, the killer was lurking out of reach.

The assassin drew the jade. He moved his fingers on the hilt for a moment. There was one occasion, only one. He let himself be absorbed by the crack in the wall. He disappeared from sight again, and Morien could have reached him, but no. No, he didn't risk burning down the city for one enemy. He was an altruist! Ultimately, it was to happen faster than a blink. He climbed onto the roof of the warehouse and flashed across it silently. The arrangement of tenement houses was favorable to Shadow. He knew the mage well, all too well, it seemed.

Morien stretched out an arm, along which a tongue of fire was crawling. He was concentrated and alert. Fighting this type of enemy was always difficult. Contrary to appearances, the Shadows were not very muscular, so they had an advantage because of their speed and the ability to change their position noiselessly. Even though he had experienced him for a moment in partitions of houses, he knew that he was now probably lurking at a completely different place.

"Come out," he hissed.

No answer came. The heart melody was rumbling with a rhythmic clatter. He was panting. There was an overwhelming tension on his shoulders.

Seneh knew him, he was looking, covered with a thicket of plants. The stone windowsill was trembling uncertainly under his feet. The lack of footwear, and the feet adapted to climbing made a decent balance, but a single sliding crumb could have revealed his location. He changed the place. He reached the ledge gracefully and sank down on the cobblestones. The mage was nearby, the assassin could reach him, but Shadow wanted confrontation. He hoped to get close enough to reach soft places with the jade. Places where arteries are shallowly placed under the skin.

Luring Morien out of the University wasn't a problem, as in the case of the wanted. Now, unaware, she was chatting with the graying inn owner. He knew their secrets, the paths hidden in labyrinths of damp corridors. And it was enough to put the blade to the appropriate dwarven throat. Visit a mother who misses her daughter. Feed the longing. Create an avalanche of doubts. Outshine the emotions. He loved the game. These subtle traces that everyone leaves behind. The analytical brain created situations so obvious that the victim never realized that someone was pulling the strings. The girl didn't realize that she hadn't been alone since she left the tenement house. He wanted her purple. Blood. He wanted to taste the scream trapped in the cords of the larynx. The pleasure of the body that took away the senses with its firmness. He smiled. Later that night, the walls of the cart would experience the degradation of the soul. He got back with his mind to the man who had moved away a little. Not so much to make Shadow struggle. A puzzle he had been composing for a long time, formed into a neat structure of matching pieces, and it was now complete. Two birds, two at almost the same time.

Morien didn't manage to spot the elf. He wandered between the shadows, looking for the gleam of jade inadvertently reflected by streaks of fire. He probably wasn't afraid, at least not for himself. If the elven assassin reached Lilian first, then he wouldn't be saved. If the blade rested on him first, he would be relieved. He was trying to reach the vessel of Lilian whispers. Disturbed rhythm of vibrations ruined the pursuit, a protective barrier surrounded the inn. Whether she was transforming the field unconsciously or trying to create a luminescence dome - he didn't know. However, he sensed that the moment of death would unleash what assassins usually couldn't stop - an escalation of magic that destroys whatever stands in its way. Sacrifice. Thundered in his ears. Yes, a sacrifice for her good...

Seneh silently approached within an arm's length, the mage was standing with his back to him, and he was safely balancing on the edge of darkness. The corner of her lips twitched. The jade glowed in the reflection of the heat. The air groaned painfully. A piece of strands sprinkled with white spun and fell like goose down. Morien involuntarily pressed his fading hand to the cut spot, the red blended with the white of the skin. Despite applying pressure, the effusion of purple with a cascade of foaming waterfalls tinted the robe. The killer walked around the victim. He moved with slightly bent knees like a cat lurking for a sparrow. Pain was fragmenting the threads of Morien's will. The sparks went out one by one. Shadow knew which arteries to strangle. The archmage dropped to his knees, his mouth was sinking in the water. The assassin moved closer, his dying pupils didn't notice any movement. Seneh caught the dying man by the hair:

"We're meeting again," he rumbled. Morien was about to answer, but the cut had gone so deep that he only could make a gurgling sound. "You remember! Of course! I haven't forgotten how badly you treated me last time. I've waited. I've waited a long time," he murmured. "And here the surprise, Alvena feverishly looking me in the kingdom. You don't know how eager she can be, how impatient." This time he hissed. "She brings the news of the mage protecting someone. He thinks no one knows it, but she guesses. She reads between the words. She needs that someone, Morien. So she will get what she wants. I will make sure she is brought in almost one piece. I'll nip off a little for myself, she must be sweet, right? Is she? Yes! She is sweet. Will you share with me my friend?" He grunted next to the mage's ear.

Morien was weakening. The elf with words reconciled him more than with jade. He tried to collect his thoughts. The speech of Whispers could have spurred Lili into action. Maybe there was still time to get out. The power left him with each rapid breath. Spots were swirling around the edges of the irises. Shadow was supporting his head. If it weren't for him, he would have probably been lying in a pool of gore. The chill touched his fingertips lightly at first, but after another breaths, it climbed up his arms and thighs. The Whispering Vessel was empty.

"It's time to say hello to the Redeemers, Lord Master."

Seneh plunged the silver blade straight into the mage's heart. The heavy essence of blood slowly poured over Shadow's fingers. The body slumped breathlessly. The elf crouched down and laid his daggers on the ground. He wiped his soiled hands on a white embroidered handkerchief, cleaned the knives carefully with the corpse's robe, then stuffed them into the inside skirts of the black cloak. He stepped back into the darkness. He was there for a while, watching the body around which the rest of what drove the gears of existence was pouring out. Satisfied, he departed to finish what he was entrusted with.

***

"Oh, I have found it!" Mark yanked out the richly decorated cloak. "It took a while before someone put it on again, but it's worth it. You just need to clean it!" He exclaimed.

"Oh, come on." She came over happily.

The alcohol drunk was merrily playing under the skull.

"Well, look, the spiders have managed to make a nest in it during this time." He pointed to a cluster of cobwebs.

Lilian put a hand to her mouth as if she had wanted to laugh, but something was wrong. The painful sting in her heart took her breath away. She opened her mouth like a large carp and tried to swallow a gulp of air. She crouched down and hit the boards with her knees. A few blurry spots blocked her vision for a moment. At that time, the neck was marked with pinching jerks, as if someone had put an invisible noose on it and quickly tugged it, rubbing the epidermis with the roughness of the hemp. She brushed the stinging spot, the chill of her little fingers muted the sensation. She was boring the room with her wide eyes.

Mark threw off his clothes and in a few bounds got beside her.

"By Redeemers, are you okay?"

"I don't know. I felt strange." She touched the stinging skin on the back of her neck.

"Oh, shit!" The innkeeper groaned.

"What?" He was shocked.

"It looks as if someone tried to slit your throat." He reached out a finger and pointed to the wound. "Oh, it's the deepest here."

She rubbed the place and felt stickiness. When she looked at the pads, they did show what she felt. They looked at each other.

"What the hell?!" She jumped to her feet.

The innkeeper shrugged, unable to answer.

"It doesn't add up!" She grunted.

She was in consternation. She analyzed the incident, but couldn't find the source. The man saw blue light coming through the thin skin, merging the broken tissue with a cascade. It was different than when she was treating him. Probably magicians dealt with their wounds in a simpler and less spectacular way.

***

Darius listened for a fraction of the breath. Snuggled against the rough planks of the door, he picked up words and bits of sentences, but nothing else. The alchemist came silently from the other side. There was an unreadable silence in the dead end. So he raised his forehead and started to nose. Faint specks of once-powerful essence bounced off him and broke like glass goblets. Seneh was satisfying his thirst for blood. The magician twisted his lips in an ugly grimace, leaned over and glanced at what was going on in the kitchen. Well shielded by a mirror of power, he became invisible to the eyes of people chatting inside. Mark got up and pointed to something that was out of sight of the Alchemist. The woman wiped her mouth, smiled, and followed the clue, and the innkeeper waddled behind her. With a bony finger armed with a cracked black nail, Lonan pushed the window vent. The glass rattled, but the entrance didn't yield. Lonan frowned and touched the surface where he should have found the bolt. It hissed and melted like hot wax. The alchemist slipped inside, pulling up the large hood of his cloak. He glanced at the rune pulsing in the fingers resembling the claws of a bird of prey. The change needed for the restraint come about. He supposed that the mage wouldn't recognize in him the man who had pursued her. He licked his lips excitedly. The shuffling in the shadow of the corridor continued. He inhaled the scent of the room. He distinguished soap suds, wax, oils and food, as well as a specific aroma that stopped his fiery lust. There are scents that evoke a trip to the most beloved places: the smell of sweet cake, wood burning in the fireplace, soup or perfume. He inhaled the fragrances through the narrow slits of his nostrils. It would have seemed that this monstrous, humanoid creature destroyed by magic felt something and carried scraps of reminiscences at the bottom of his soul, which the growing darkness couldn't stick to. The alchemist had memories. He came to himself. He found himself right next to the kitchen door. He examined the view through the gap left.

The archer touched the handle. The chill left behind by Lonan had partially broken away from the stuffiness of the surroundings. The door handle was still damp and cold, as if it had been touched by death itself. The door yielded. The maid leaving last, hadn't closed the inn. She had relied on Mark, who at that time had been serving as a washer. Darius stepped inside, the floor creaked slightly. He cursed soundlessly. The ornate bow with a prepared arrow was at the ready. Darius was trembling with excitement. Trismus marked the line of the lower jaw. It was happening now. There was no turning back, and no chance of failure.

The mage, wrapped in twilight, tried on her coat. She masked the head surrounded by a halo of red with the depths of her hood.

"Perfect," she whispered, touching the embroidered edges, which now was deep emerald green. "Mark, you are my savior. I promise, therefore, that I will reward you with a goodness hundred times bigger!" She chattered. "You owe me nothing, it would be rotted with moisture. If it comes in handy, take it. I don't need it. I wanted to give it to the cook one day ..." He thought. Lilian put her hand on his shoulder. "But I didn't make it." He pulled away her caring fingers, delicately but firmly.

Erica's death still niggled him.

"I understand. I really understand ..." She sighed heavily as he passed her by. He stopped midstride. He wanted to hear what she had to say. "I loved her too, although I knew her too shortly. It's unfair. Only the best die, only ..."

His face tightened. The grimace was nothing like a bitter smile or an expression of sadness, the straight line of pressed lips showed enough.

"Here." He pointed to the broom closet. "There's a pair of pretty neat shoes. And you know what?" He put the fists on his hips. "If it weren't for you, it would be different, but I don't know if better." The voice trembled from Mark's slender neck.

She stood gently on her toes and kissed him on the rough cheek, wrapping her arms around him. He received the gesture gratefully.

"Let's go to the kitchen, you can try the shoes on later. Why did I bring you here ..."

And then they saw him. He was standing silent, leaning against the doorframe. The whites of his eyes blended with the irises as if he hadn't had them at all. The fire of power was sparkling deep within them, as if embedded in the back of the skull. The woman pushed the innkeeper so hard that he fell. At that moment she heard footsteps pounding rhythmically right behind her. Darius aimed at her chest. She jumped as Lonan took the first step beyond the edge of the kitchen. The runestone was singing sweetly and pulsing intensely, reflecting in the victim's yellow eyes. She couldn't resist the melody, but she remembered Morien's advice to close the space of magic's light. She evened her breath and painted a glyph on the ground that protected against the influence of the rune and the Alchemist's look.

The mage boiled with anger. The will of the fugitive constructed a neat dome that almost completely reflected the echoes of the stone's song.

"Darius!" He hissed. "Your turn."

The fair-haired man frowned. The silver-headed arrow flew through the air electrified with magic. She managed to dodge one more time, but cornered, she got a slim chance. She struck Darius with a chain of lightning, the stunned man fell on his back and rode a few steps on it. He cursed. He leapt to his feet and drew his dagger. Lonan chanted a string of binding spells. Lilian tried to bypass the spy. The small space between him and the counter opened an escape route. The man, however, sensed the plan and, jumping to the redhead, touched with his dagger the white of her thin skin on the back of the neck. She stopped. The chill of the steel made her dazed. His sturdy hand pulled her. She felt his heart pound in his chest. She was boring the room. Every opportunity was good, she just had to look for it in hopelessness. She thought about the kitchen. She could have offered the Alchemist's helper Whispering Speech.

"It's over," the archer whispered, brushing her earlobe with his hot breath. "You're not going any farther."

"It remains to be seen!" She screamed and, pushing herself away from Darius, made the maneuver unexpected for him.

She slipped out from under the blade with the finesse of trained assassins. Dazed, Mark got up and found next to the younker. Two bodies swirled for a few more moments to fall deafly on the boards. The girl moved between the rows of chairs. She couldn't set a target course. Puzzled and confused, she stopped for a flash. Lonan was finishing the ritual. She saw the rune rise from the magician's hand and break into countless luminous particles. With the rest of her will, she burst into the magician's mind and crushed him with a curse of suffering. A moment of distraction opened another chance for rescue. The executor howled, and the stone reassembled but was still suspended in space. She pushed the Alchemist. Chained by a curse, he hit the wall with his back. She ran into the kitchen. The cane was standing in the corner where she had placed it.

"Two steps and you're mine," she groaned, but before she could grab him, he was already in other fingers.

She froze. A tall, black-clad figure rose in front of her. His yellow eyes were looking from behind the shadowed face. She could read absolutely nothing in them.

"Elf?" She debated in her mind. "Shadow? Shadow of the Baroness!" She swallowed. She realized that it was all over. Seneh grabbed his jade blade and placed it ostentatiously on his chest. The hand clenched on the hilt bore traces of silver tattoos. Lines of knuckles glowed in the firelight.

"Don't even think about it." The alchemist croaked with the effort.

"It's over, mage." The elf's voice sounded dull.

She struggled to use the last surge of magic to reflect the singing. Unfortunately. The chill gathered around. She felt the ice blades penetrate the tissue. She covered her face. The broken formula of bonding again reverberated in space. The stone formed into a sparkling ball. Directed by the force of spinning particles, it was incantated. The last spurt, the last desire to break away from the piercing pain was in vain. The harder they touched her, the more the power was destroyed, carried away by the storm saturated with black magic. The breaths merged into one, causing beats of blood in the temples. Bloody streaks adorned the cheeks. Darkness came, velvety and fluffy as a quilt. She allowed herself to be covered. Lonan grunted hoarsely, finally sat down and waited for it to complete itself. The rune accumulated particles, a multitude of sparkles hidden in the recesses of the crumb, as unusual as the hunted. Thanks to it, she became the one she once had thought about - ordinary knocked under the thatch of self. Convulsions jerked her emaciated body, the skin turned white, and the veins blackened like Lonan's. Seneh was on the alert. The cane in Shadow's hand faded as steadily as the magic in Lilian faded out.

In the main hall of the inn, Darius was polishing Mark off. The man tried to extract the blade from his chest for a moment longer, but it was too deep. The archer was standing over him, with an arrow aimed at the center of his forehead.

"What are you waiting for?" Mark gasped out. "Let's get it over with."

He choked on bloody spit, crepitant breaths were filling the tavern space. The fair-haired man frowned, adjusted his grip, and released the arrow. Mark stiffened, and Darius lowered his gun. Tired of the fight, he dragged himself into the kitchen, where Lonan and... Seneh were waiting. On the floor, curled in a fetal position, was lying the chased magician, whose body was being jerked by a twitch, and from whose mouth was coming foam.

"Will it take long?" He asked.

"No," the elf replied.

He was right. Before Darius could settle down on the seat, the show was over. The mist that enveloped the lying turned black. Not right away. Gradually, breath after breath, the vortex shaped the cannonade of colors. Shades of silver turned charcoal to finally shone with navy black. The area around Lilian's heart glowed with a bloody circle in the candlelight. She was no longer convulsed, and her pale lips were not marred by the foamy saliva. There was only a stain on the boards. The rune was spinning. It refilled and re-formed into what Darius had seen until recently, but it was not like a moonstone, it resembled a queen of the night full of illumination whose uniqueness can only be revealed by the sharp glow of the afternoon sun. Lonan held out his hand, the mineral slowly settled into its hollow. He stared at the prey for a moment, and when he saturated his eyes, he hid the stone in a pouch that he fastened to his belt. Now the archer realized that he became the same mage he had known before.

"It's over," he ground out. "This bitch has to be brought to the Baroness."

"Are we carry to her?" Darius wiped a trickle of blood from under his nose.

"I'll take her," Seneh said.

"How? She is lying." The spy didn't give up.

"I have remedies for relentless wenches. Go. I have a surprise for you. You'll find it on the way."

Lonan knew what the elf was talking about, but the archer didn't. They left without a word, satisfied with the hunt.

CHAPTER X

The thick wings of night still hung over the city, and the wind prevailed on the deserted streets. Maybe its gusts didn't bend the twigs much, but they stubbornly clung to the hair of the two men. Lost in their own thoughts, they didn't feel like an empty talk. Lonan kept touching his pouch, fearing that the valuable object might have evaporated. He wondered about the future. After all, there was a long way ahead of them. The mage calculated the time they would spend on the road. He hoped they would come to the fortress in mid-autumn, and now the prospect of sleeping on a coach-box deformed his face with discontent. Maybe he would lie down in a supply wagon, on sacks, anywhere, but not sitting and behind the horse's rump? He was content. Time in the city dragged on for him. It was as tiring as Darius' company. He missed the gray, rough-hewn walls. He fantasized about the shadows crawling across the courtyard that stretched out in the afternoon sun. And also about the recruits. Shrunken, with frenzy painted on their faces. How much he wanted to hear again the screams when the weak had been taking their own lives, tearing their wrists with their teeth, and blood from the torn arteries had been profusely flooding the smooth polished marble floors of the cells.

He was roused from the bliss of flashbacks by Darius. He was constantly wiping his nose as blood was oozing from the damaged vessel. The spy was spluttering and blowing his nose. The alchemist slowed his pace, turned, and unceremoniously placed a finger where the man's eyebrows met.

"What are you doing, fool?" Darius reacted sharply.

"Don't fidget. That puppy whimper drives me crazy."

Darius stiffened. An icy chill seeped into the sinuses. He felt his eyes turn into round balls of ice. The bleeding stopped, and without a word Lonan overtook him and walked on.

He caught up with the mage and blocked his way.

"What did you do this for?"

"Just for you to ask stupid questions," he gasped out and walked past him.

"Lonan the benefactor!" The archer joked.

The alchemist hit him backhand in the face. The spy staggered and put his hand to the stinging spot.

"You talk to me like that again and I'll cut your throat, or better still, Seneh will do it and I'll watch," he growled.

"As for Seneh, what are we to see along the way?"

"A corpse."

"Whose?"

"And what do you think, fool?"

"I'm a fool, I don't think," Darius added sarcastically.

"Morien's. But there is nothing to watch. Go. The wagon must be prepared before Seneh brings this exile."

"Morien's?" Darius caught up with him. "And he let himself be deceived?"

"Let's say they had scores to settle, now they're even. Don't bust my balls."

A trickle of blood ran from the spy's nose, he glanced at his smeared fingers and looked expectantly towards the mage. Lonan ignored him.

"Lovely, here we go again."

He trailed behind him, muttering curses so that he wouldn't hear.

***

The elf settled on the pallet by the window and waited with his hands resting on the cane shaft. Bored with immobility, he began to analyze the object. He quickly understood what he was dealing with. He admitted that he had seen them only in books. Five items carefully hidden in distant places. Artifacts with power so terrifying that the only right thing to do had been to seal them. So... if the masters put barriers on them, how had she broken them? It was not a replica, he was sure. The dragon bone gave off a specific wave of vibrations. Sensitive to particles, he felt them penetrate his skin and reach the hard structure of his bone. He had just wished he were a magician, he might have become even the master of the lands behind the sea. He stroked the shaft with due reverence and enjoyed the view. It crossed his mind that the unaffiliated brotherhood of savages would be interested in the toy, of course for a sufficiently large sum. He didn't need it, the redhead neither. The Baroness, as far as he remembered, was not interested in magical artifacts, unless he missed something. Thanks to gold, he could have disappeared somewhere between the peaks proudly rising on the borders. He wanted to die alone, at that time what kept him alive was ... The thought of the woman he loved and who didn't care about him hurt. He returned to the room where he was stuck. The woman huddled at his feet was resting on the dirty floor, with her hair spilled around. Faint chest movements indicated she was breathing. He was waiting. It was going to be a while before she would recover. Accustomed to stillness, he didn't bother with the fact that he was wasting time. Regeneration after tethering took many forms. The mages, or rather empty shells, reacted in many ways. And while most of them stood on their feet after less than one strike of the clock, some still needed a few dozen. He was rarely involved in this type of practice, but stillness often accompanied surveillance. It was at these moments that he found a job. He examined what he found around. He envisioned a fly's flight only to catch it and end its miserable life. The highest-paid assassin on earth. He asked no questions. He performed the indicated task after getting acquainted with the details. There were times he refused, but it was rare. He never took the payment directly, he sent a messenger. Another one of his kind, Leto, was moving around the country. Equally trained and effective but he could also do what Seneh couldn't - he gained the trust of employers. Infiltration Master. The one who deceived him didn't survive. Seneh hesitated, he didn't. He remembered that once the white-haired elf had begun to disturb a certain merchant, so the trader demanded his head. Shadow didn't kill Shadow, except in a fratricidal clash. Seneh stuck to the codes. So it ended with a sharp exchange of views and mysterious disappearance of said client. The mercenary also found out that his rival had gone missing about a year ago and that no one had ever seen him. Had someone gotten his comeuppance? When he left the clan, Leto was an adolescent. Now he was becoming more than just a competition.

The woman on the floor moved. Shadow frowned, looking closely. First she stretched her fingers, then raised her head. She checked where she was with her shifting eyes. Lilian could see white points stuck to the pupils. Dryness was bitting her throat, and the mouth dry as a bone, was crying for liquid. The wound on the chest closed, leaving only an irregular circle with jagged edges. She predicted it would never be the same again. The overwhelming sensation of vulnerability stripped her of the last scraps of confidence. She knew she was not alone. The lurking in the shadows could have done with her what he wanted. She leaned on her arms and sat down, wrapping her arms around her legs. He was still there. Leaning against the staff, he followed her every move. The penetration of his yellow pupils made the hair on her forearms bristle. They looked so much like her eyes. She seemed to be beginning to understand the fear that settled on those who watched her. She swallowed, or at least tried. The elf was silent. She wanted to go out, leave this place, experience the night wind. Long breaths hung between them. Lilian tempered every move.

Seneh memorized the details. Refractions of light softly laying down on the curls, the arrangement of freckles, the glare reflected in the glassy eyes or the ways in which she intertwined her hands or moved. She was not to be a mystery to him. He read the twitching of muscles, considered the wrinkles in the skin caused by facial expressions. She was definitely not a common girl. She had many features that were interesting, but also irritated ... So similar to ... him. Those frowns, scowls, and hiding a thumb under her fingers when she got nervous. He wanted her blood on the blade. She teased him with the tilt of her neck and the deep sighs that cut the air every now and then.

He tilted his forehead towards her. Lilian automatically stepped back to the wall. A few strands of dark hair spilled over the assassin's face tightened with concentration.

"You're alive. That's good. I have waited," he whispered, but the hum was not the one expressing concern, but rather contempt.

She nodded. She managed to sober up enough to be able to reason logically, and hence, began to look for a way out. The Magician School wasn't far away. Maybe she would have managed to escape like the first time? After quick analysis, she concluded that she couldn't have done it. Her skinned wrists and knees stung cruelly, and at more violent movement she experienced great dizziness.

"I'm alive," she said slowly.

The elf got up and took her by the arm, lifted her up as if she had been weighing nothing. He held her so for a moment, until her feet found support. Her joints, however, buckled as she tried to stiffen them. Seneh waited patiently for her to get her balance. After a while he pulled her behind himself. She protested, which ended up in hitting her cheek, which knocked the tied over to the floor. Blood oozed from her split lip. A metallic taste spilled over her tongue. She shielded herself with her arms.

"Get up!" He pulled her up and put against the wall, pinning the woman.

Lack of breath triggered red blotches that flickered under the eyelids. A quick lesson taught Lilian to obey, but not to submit. He loosened his grip and brought his face closer to her.

"Don't get any ideas," he hissed.

The smell of warm skin and linden flowers hit her. An imperceptible scent that remained only to the one who wore it. She nodded and allowed herself to be led to the main hall. On the floor, between the scattered and broken stools, she saw Mark surrounded by a pool of clotted blood. She groaned. Dull eyes stared at the ceiling as empty as those of the executioner who dragged her behind himself. She wanted to say goodbye. She jerked her arm to free herself from the elf's grip, but Shadow cooled the spurt. It was the last time she escorted the innkeeper with her eyes glazed with tears. She knew she would never speak to him again.

"I have a gift for you." She heard right to her ear as they stepped outside.

A shiver ran down her spine with claws.

The mercenary led Lilian into the arms of the night. The damp chill of the night breeze laid down on her cheek stinging from the struck. She shivered, not from the cold, but from the fear that was coming from the thick and silent structure of the darkness. He bypassed her, clenched his fists on her clothes and pulled her to himself. He was so close that the warmth enveloped her again like a fearful cocoon.

"I have an eye on you. Don't forget."

He nodded at the alley uphill. She was surprised, it led in a direction completely opposite to the one in which they were supposed to go. After all, the Guard barracks were located in the lower part of the city.

"Go. I'm right behind you." That voice again.

More velvety this time, as if the tormentor had been enjoying something. She moved unsteadily with trembling legs, mentally praying that what she was about to discover, wasn't a horror, but only a shadow of madness. She wanted to wake up in the morning and be relieved to find it a dream. She wanted someone to pinch her.

"It's a nightmare," she said. "Hallucinations."

Instinctively she touched her chest. There was still a nasty circular indentation there. Maybe she wasn't dreaming? It might have been an illusion, but the attempt to start a fire hit nothingness. All she gained was sweat and exhaustion.

She traveled the way, almost suffocating from the effort. Seneh's breath was wheezing in the back of her neck, even though she didn't sense his physical presence. The bifurcation of the alleys shone with wobbling oil lamps. Some of them had time to dim, so the picture blended into a dull blur, cut here and there by gleams. Footsteps echoed along the sleeping walls. She saw something in the distance. A heavy hand fell on her shoulder, and she felt warmth through the soft cloth.

"Today I'm merciful. Take advantage of it." She shivered. The eyes, somewhat already accustomed to the night, caught small elements that didn't fit into the well-known puzzle of streets. A dozen or so steps away something was resting on the cobblestones. She came closer. What had appeared to be a pile of rags one breath earlier, now looked like a man lying on his back with the arms spread wide. A black spot had formed around his head. She came over.

"Who was the one he called 'the gift'?" She thought.

It was getting colder. She turned back to see if Seneh was still there. He was standing a short distance away, his hood fell off his face, and his hair was fluttering in the night blasts. Her staff rested on his back in a leather sheath. When did he take it? She didn't remember. He held a bare green dagger in one hand, as if the clue of a riddle she was about to unravel. The weapon gleamed against the lanterns, and the blade's shadow stretched out like a cat after a long afternoon nap. She understood what he wanted to show. She fell to her knees and hid her face in her hands. The sobs escaped in long, spasmodic spurts. On her knees she walked the rest of the way. She put her arms around the corpse.

"Morien," she whispered. "Morien."

The lover's hand didn't tighten on hers, she didn't hear her beloved's heart pounding in the rib cage. There were only left dead eyes, gore and curls dipped in it, no longer white but black as the very bottom of the soul. She was touching his knuckles with trembling fingers, trying to stroke her cheek with them as he used to do when she was nearby. She ran her fingertips over his face and the outline of the white lips. She nestled her face in his hair. She was torn by emotions she had never experienced. Despair that could be compared to tearing from the guts the last remnants of a vile existence. She plunged into the mourning. She inhaled the scent of his skin for the last time. Why wasn't this nightmare over? She wanted to share his fate, never to wake up, to put herself into the arms of the lords of death. She realized that the mistakes she had made and the decisions taken were fatal. She hadn't thought anything through, naively believing that it would be good to save those she loved ...

Seneh waited. He gave her time she probably wouldn't have gotten from the Alchemist. It wasn't due to mercy roaring in him, after all, he had cut the mage's throat, but because it was a right thing to do. It also had some kind of benefit. Bringing the victim down to the lowlands of despair deprived her of the urge to continue the struggle. He moved a step closer. The woman was wailing. He grabbed her by the hair and pulled her away from the body. He led her to the barracks. The verbals he heard made him satisfied with the botch well done. When at some point she broke away and ran towards the alley, he lavished blows. He didn't do it with passion, but cooled down the aspirations for further tricks. Despite knowing that she wouldn't achieve anything, she fought to the end. She enraged the mercenary. He trailed the bruised to the gates of the barracks. Lilian kept saying over and over:

"Morien, why?"

"Open up!" He screamed.

The guards, bathed in the gray of the morning waking, opened the door slightly. They pierced her with their eyes through and through. Once they hadn't believed that the mercenaries of the Baroness would succeed, and yet they did. They glanced at each other in unequivocal approval of Seneh's efforts.

The Alchemist was standing beside the carts prepared for the road, along with Darius, who was leaning on the bow. Both tired, with blue circles around their eyes and gray complexions. In the stables, a group of paid thugs who had arrived with Shadow was dozing. The elf handed Lilian to Lonan and disappeared into the darkness of the stable. Stimulated by kicks, they went out to the square. The alcohol drunk in the evening didn't manage to evaporate yet, the blurry image took real forms with each passing moment.

The stable man, leaning against the wall, was watching the scene. At the same time he was smoking weed, which with puffs obscured his furrowed, aged face. Kedom rolled inside through the gullet of the barracks. He also was content. The uninvited guests would finally mark their presence in the muddy track. The city would rest.

Lilian was pushed into the wagon. The smelly, windowless place closed over her like a tomb. As her eyes got accustomed to the dark, she could see a cluster of rags and a bucket covered with a cloth. In the twilight, the scratches on the walls assumed ghostly forms. She didn't know why she suffered such fate. Because she was a magician? Or because someone hated her so much that he had decided not to rest until he reached her? After all, escaping was punished with imprisonment, but in the School prisons, and not in Alvena's dungeons. Something smelled wrong there, and she didn't involve the planks of the wagon in it. She huddled in the corner and waited.

Seneh walked around the cart. He checked fasteners and locks, wanted to make sure it was prepared. The mercenaries dragged their buttocks onto the saddles. The heavily laden animals neighed every now and then. Probably the prospect of a journey in the heat was not to their liking. However, great moods surrounded people. They left the walls, which had already begun to disgust everyone with their hostile aura. Only the Alchemist and the fair-haired man yawned.

Before leaving, the commandant offered them a cup of Styg which brightened their minds for a moment. The small dose contributed to a short-term activity.

"Perfect." Lonan laughed, dragging a travel bag.

"Yes, excellent." Darius turned his face to the morning blasts. A delightful moment of rest. He was already in the castle in his mind, drinking honey and frolicking with the maids in freshly starched sheets. "Where's Seneh?" The archer asked, roused from his pleasant meditations. "The rest are on standby, and he's gone again."

The alchemist scanned the square with his sleepy eyes. He put his hand to his mouth automatically to hide a quick yawn.

"He was standing here a moment ago." He looked around. He noticed the open padlock of the wagon. "Oh, he is visiting our good traveling companion." There was sarcasm in his voice.

"Visiting?" Darius snapped.

"He likes games before a long way." Lonan smiled meaningly.

"Okay, I don't want to know. He just spoiled my plans for the evening."

Lonan laughed hoarsely and hit the younker in the shoulder.

"I like you sometimes, but only sometimes."

Darius waved at him and went to the other wagon in order to throw a bundle of old things into it.

The elf entered the cart noiselessly and closed the door. In the impenetrable darkness he saw the former magician sitting on the ground. She was playing with the hem of the dress. She ignored the newcomer, and he couldn't get enough. She teased him. That state had been growing from the moment he had seen her engulfed in casual conversation. The mage seemed natural. The fluidity of gestures and honesty came from her glassy eyes. The full, slightly pink lips seemed to be of familiar and close shape. For nothing he could remember the one who had similar ... the captive differed from the raddled wenches. He wanted to touch her, no matter how. Just brush a scrap of skin. The mind was going crazy. He felt like a hound. He was only a few steps away, a few fucking steps in the cart reeking of sweat and blood.

"Look at me," he hissed.

She turned her face away from what she was doing and fixed her eyes on the planks of the side wall. The presence was enough, she didn't have to look, even though he expected it. She wouldn't approve anything he wanted to present, he had hurt her enough. He would get discouraged over time. Now to be silent was the best she could do.

"Look!" He shouted.

Seneh's breathing quickened in unrestrained anger. It pulsed under the skin, ready to crawl through the pores and dominate common sense.

She succumbed to the pressure and slowly stared at him with her irises. The glow broke through the depths of the cell. Maybe passivity was not what she wanted? Maybe she should have faced what had happened? The one who now was panting, with an insatiable desire for pursuit? The elf never imagined anyone could look that way. This was not the look of the person who had just been degraded. She was proud. Conscious of what he could do to her. Unyielding and still confident despite her wounds. He was getting ready to break her will. In the dark he heard a murmur. She got up, straightened and, having folded her arms over her chest, she whispered:

"Why did you come here, elf? Haven't you had enough?"

He was about to say something, he was already opening his mouth to speak, but he couldn't. For the first time he felt that he was stripped of the power to dominate the inmate and it was done by the prisoner herself - the beautiful prisoner. He walked through the wagon. He came face to face with her. She didn't succumb to the pressure, and yet she should have been afraid. Whined and begged for mercy. She should have, damn it! He drew his dagger and held it to her cheek. The cold metal was biting her skin, and yet she wasn't cursing or yelling. She was waiting. Sooner or later the Baroness would do her job. There was no salvation anymore, only waiting for death, which was worse than death itself.

"If I could, I would have killed you long ago," he whispered. "If I could ..."

He withdrew the silver blade and carefully hid it inside his capot. His emotions were painted on his face. She watched the man balancing between what was commanded and what he wanted to do. It wasn't her who had been deprived of the will, but it was him. They were both victims, surrounded by fear and the stench of blood. Victims of one and the same person. She wanted him to go away. To leave her in the dark. She felt him grab her hair. Was she wrong? Did she too soon judge him by appearances? She groaned. She tried to push the attacker away. He was quick, and probably it wasn't the first time he did it. Now she was standing with her back to him, her face pressed against the stinking wood, her arm on her back and her wrist twisted.

"Die," she growled.

Seneh held tight. Contentment crawled across the body tense with emotion. He waited for Lili to calm down. He enjoyed limiting her room. He relaxed when the redhead stopped protesting. He took a deep breath, but it was not a sigh of relief. Rather something thoroughly different.

"Finally. I was beginning to think that you would keep leading me by the nose for a long time."

"Do what you gotta do, and evanesce."

"I would like to."

He brought his face closer and plunged it into her hair. She moved. The unexpected act of affection terrified her. He released her wrist and put his hands on the woman's shoulders. He stood so for a few breaths. Gradually, he moved his hands along her body. The touch didn't hurt, it wasn't violent. Slowly, his pads ran along the sides until resting on her hips. He pushed back the locks of red and brushed her neck with his lips, as if casually. But there was something in the gesture that terrified the killer himself... it awoke memories. He stepped back abruptly. Lilian remained paralyzed, with her cheek glued to the wall. She was waiting for the blows, knockdown. For him to finish what he had started. The blood was rumbling in her temples so loudly that she could hear neither her own thoughts nor the prayers she was carrying to the Redeemers. She closed her eyes. Seneh left. On the way, he shaded his face. She heard the squeak of the lock, followed by a hoofbeat. There was only one rider.

Something died in Shadow. He was moving away from the city. Bits of earth torn from under the hooves were swirling in the air. The morning dew was sticking to the ground, and the air was filling his lungs briskly. He hoped that peace would come with another breath. The fire was consuming him inside. He was moving away not only with his body but also with his mind from where she was. It was time to collect his payment. He hoped he didn't have to look at her again.

Two men settled themselves in the coach-boxes. Surprise painted mysterious expressions on their faces. Darius wished he had shared the travel time with the killer. He was counting on some combat tips. The alchemist pulled the reins and led the horses towards the gates. An escort formed behind him. They rolled out of town in the early morning, when sleep still lingered on the lids of the people who had been sleeping in the walls. They left behind blood and a cloud of dust along with wheel marks on the road.

***

Morien's body was discovered by a burgher who was on his way to work. He alerted the School Guard. It was the first time the city saw so many magicians going outside the gates. There was a ghastly silence all around. The archmage, surrounded by armed men, approached the protégé, and a moment later they got tightly surrounded by a group of others dressed in multi-colored robes. The magician touched the face of the dead man. The wide open eyes got sealed by the spell, and the wound in the neck and the heart area became scarred. There was a deep sadness in the eyes of those gathered, and although a part of the mob didn't know the hierarchies of the University, they realized that the magician lying in front of them was important enough to move the tribe.

He was moved to the crypt. A narrow path led to it, with sides thickly overgrown with manicured thujas. The magicians were not a group that used to pray earnestly, but it seemed as if the building had been singing mourning songs, and the wind had been wailing mournfully in the alley shrubs. The maidservants and the mistress of the house broke the silence with pitiful sobbing.

In the place where Morien was killed, the townspeople found no blood, only a half-dried puddle, as if only there had been the unexpected rainfall. It disappeared soon. It obliterated any signs of the incident that had happened that night.

***

Several weeks passed. Autumn began to paint the leaves gold, and the cold silvered the yellowing grass with the freeze. The birds no longer carried such long songs, and the earth didn't smell sweet. The heavy scent of mycelium and mold vibrated in the air, the same that he had experienced a year earlier. He looked for the gifts of the forest, he searched for mushrooms and late fruit that were lifted by tenuous branches. Leto liked the highroad. Despite rumors of the dangerous backwoods, he didn't meet anyone who would have liked to get its hands on his belongings. He sang from time to time, but fell silent as soon as he realized that the voice echoed, resonant and too joyful for the person he passed for. He was convinced something had changed, as if an element of his soul had been ripped out and crushed with a blacksmith's hammer. He longed for a lack of emotions. Fortunately, the lost harmony returned with each day. After the experiences in the village situated between the peaks, one might have said that his eyes shone with some unknown glow ... and he would have probably not been mistaken. Simple, idyllic life left its mark on him. He became more accessible, more willingly oriented towards the needs of those who had somehow stayed in his heart.

The day was going to be tolerable. Nay! He supposed that by noon the sun would warm the bones tired from the strenuous march. Bored, he fixed his eyes on fallen trees, stared at the colors of the underbrush and foliage, which almost closed over his head in a tight crown. He thought about the place he was going to. He had to winter and the city would give him what the way couldn't: money, shelter and namelessness.

He heard the pounding of hooves behind. A horseman was riding towards him and, what's worse, rapidly. He got out of the way and hid his face, and the hands stuffed in the pockets. Prudently he plunged into the shadows that were creeping along the way. The rider passed him. Risen dust burst into the elf's nose and eyes. He had to stop to catch his breath. He pulled off his hood and rubbed the face with his hands. The man passing him suddenly stopped. The animal reared, almost throwing the horseman off its back. He turned and approached trotting. Leto saw a pair of shimmering yellow eyes hidden under a broad cover, and on his hands distinctive tattoos. He understood who he was. Leto's fists clenched on the handles of the daggers hidden in the pockets. Seneh was silent. A characteristic sound rose from the horse's snores, and the animal danced several times. The mercenary grabbed the reins and rode away. The elf sensed the tension growing between them. Two Shadows on one road, two pairs of eyes staring at each other, and between them a wailing silence. He slipped the hood back on and headed towards the fortress. There was still a long way to go. He should have arrived before winter.

Seneh smiled and urged the horse.

"You are alive," he said to himself. "May we never have to meet again."

He vanished behind a veil of dust and trees growing on the sides of the road. The winding path obliterated his traces.

To be continued...

www.ingramcontent.com/pod-product-compliance
Lightning Source LLC
Chambersburg PA
CBHW060211030726
47499CB00004B/1002